Requiem

Also by Ken McClure

Pestilence

Requiem

Ken McClure

SIMON & SCHUSTER

LONDON·SYDNEY·NEW YORK·TOKYO·SINGAPORE·TORONTO

First published in Great Britain by
Simon & Schuster Ltd in 1992
A Paramount Communications Company

Copyright © Ken Begg, 1992

Simon & Schuster Ltd
West Garden Place
Kendal Street
London W2 2AQ

Simon & Schuster of Australia Pty Ltd
Sydney

A CIP catalogue record for this book is
available from the British Library

ISBN 0-671-71761-8

Printed and bound
by
Billing & Sons Ltd, Worcester

'The first requirement of any hospital is that it do the sick no harm.'

Florence Nightingale
(1820–1910)

PROLOGUE

A crowded gallery watched Sir Martin Freeman enter through the swing doors and bid good morning to the assembled team. Surgical theatre number two at College Hospital, now one of the most modern hospitals in England, was ready to begin the business of the day. As usual when Freeman was operating, the observation gallery was packed. Today he was scheduled to perform a rather special operation involving the almost complete reconstruction of a human face.

Freeman had announced a new technique for the repair of severe facial deformity and this had excited widespread interest. The predominantly medical staff in the gallery had been joined by correspondents for several national newspapers. A number of other journalists, who did not have the stomach to witness such an operation in person, were waiting for the post-operative press conference that Freeman had promised. Cameras mounted above the table were in position to record details of the operation on video tape for future teaching reference.

Freeman, anonymous in green like the others, looked about him and up at the gallery before announcing through a microphone pinned to his smock that his patient was a thirty-three-year-old woman.

'Miss Marsh has been deformed since birth,' said the clipped, business-like voice. 'Her appearance has dictated that she spend most of her life in an institution. Although normal in terms of intelligence, her jaw defect has decreed that she never articulate well enough to be understood by anyone other than those who know her intimately. The bizarre nature of her appearance has precluded her from any kind of social life. In short, Miss Marsh has been a recluse from the time she became old enough to realise that she was different from other people.'

Freeman nodded to the anaesthetist, who removed the mask from his patient's face and positioned her so that she could be seen from the gallery. Despite the professional nature of the audience, more than a few involuntary gasps could be heard.

'As you see, the patient has a severely protruding jaw-bone, but very little in the way of a forehead. It is my intention to rectify both problems.' Freeman paused to let the hubbub die down a little. He was not displeased with the reaction to his statement. Like most surgeons, he was extrovert and enjoyed attention. Being a member of nearly every influential medical committee in existence had done nothing to encourage humility in him. His confidence was reflected in the way he stood with one hand on his hip, and in the tilt of his head while he spoke.

'Working from inside the mouth,' announced Freeman, 'I will cut through the mandible on both sides and remove an identical section of bone from left and right. This will effectively cause the patient's chin to recede by approximately two inches, giving her a more normal jaw line. Next comes the difficult bit.' Freeman paused and his eyes sparkled appreciatively at the murmur of amazement he had caused. 'To give Miss Marsh a forehead, we must in effect detach her face temporarily from her skull. It will be peeled forward to permit the implanting of a prosthetic forehead, which will then be fixed to the underlying bone before the reattachment of her face. All being well, Miss Marsh will wake up a new woman without any visible scars to show for her experience.'

Another murmur filled the gallery. The woman was about to be made to look normal for the first time in her life. Onlookers tried to imagine what this would mean to her, but baulked at the enormity of it. Up till now her life must have been a living hell: she was a circus freak, a human mutant, who could have inspired only revulsion in all who saw her. Now, in a matter of a few hours, that would change. When she left the hospital she would be able to go shopping, walk in the park, feed the ducks – and all quite anonymously.

'How is she?' Freeman inquired of the anaesthetist.

'Steady as a rock,' replied the green-clad figure sitting at the head of the patient. As if to illustrate the point, the man inclined his head towards a bank of monitors where an unobtrusive bleeping sound followed each regular green spike on the screen.

'I'll begin.' said Freeman, reaching out his hand.

The theatre sister slapped the first instrument into his palm.

There was silence among the others as Freeman issued a string of monosyllabic requests and the sister complied quickly and impassively.

'Swab her, will you?' said Freeman, taking a step back from the table and glancing up at the gallery. His assistant, a woman surgeon, mopped the blood away from the operating site while Freeman said, 'Just a routine access procedure. Now I'll cut through the bone at an angle of forty-five degrees.'

Someone in the gallery asked about the angle, and Freeman snapped out the answer with more than a hint of suggestion that the questioner should have known it in the first place.

The theatre sister handed Freeman an instrument connected by cable to a grey box that sat on a trolley by the side of the operating table. Freeman pressed the trigger on it and a whirring noise filled the air. His assistant moved in to reposition the clamps and retractors so that access to the inside of the patient's mouth might be effected.

'Left a bit,' snapped Freeman.

The assistant nervously moved the clamps again.

The whirring started again and the gallery knew that the air down in the theatre would be filling with the smell of burning bone as the cutting disc bit into the patient's jaw. The glass screen stopped it reaching them.

The electric motor suddenly changed note as the bone was cut clean through. The procedure was repeated and then Freeman extracted a chunk of bone and dropped it with a clunk into the metal dish a junior nurse proffered. Freeman and his assistant changed places and a piece of bone was removed from the other side of the patient's jaw and dropped into the same dish.

People leaned forward in their seats as they saw Freeman manipulate the patient's jaw backwards. As if by magic her chin receded to form a normal, firm line below her mouth.

'And now I will pin it.'

The gallery looked on in tense silence.

'And now the forehead,' announced Freeman. He turned to the anaesthetist, 'Still all right?'

The man nodded.

'I will cut round the hairline and continue on down past the temples on both sides until I can pull the facial tissue away from the bone. We'll then insert the implant, secure it and reposition the patient's face over it. Quite straightforward, really, although we'll have to be careful that we don't damage the eyes. We don't want to pull on them too much, do we?' Freeman's eyes caught those of his team.

The gallery held its breath as the confident sweep of Freeman's scalpel traced a line around the patient's hairline, the blade keeping in front of the blood that welled up behind it to be dabbed away by the nurses.

'Now I'm going to start pulling the flesh back.'

Mouths in the gallery went dry as they saw the woman's face become detached from her head. Freeman folded it over to reveal the bone behind it; glistening, moist, white.

'The implant, please.'

The theatre sister held out the prosthesis, but Freeman appeared to have some difficulty in inserting it at the correct angle. His assistant leaned over to help, but Freeman damaged a glove. He held up his right hand to show the tear and said, 'New glove, Sister.' The theatre sister removed his damaged glove and replaced it with a fresh one. Freeman started to position the implant on the front of the patient's skull again, but still found it too large for the opening he had prepared. He asked for another scalpel. 'Just a little more room,' he murmured, cutting away more tissue. Suddenly he seemed to go absolutely rigid.

'Sir Martin, are you all . . .' began his assistant.

Freeman reared up from the table, his scalpel hand swinging

10

round to catch his assistant across the face, opening up a livid cut. She cried out as Freeman fell to the floor, clutching his chest. A nightmare scene unfolded, leaving the gallery aghast with horror.

'My God, I think he's dead!' someone shouted.

Freeman's assistant, now revealed to the gallery as a woman in her early thirties with the removal of her mask, stood away from the table with a gloved hand holding a swab to the left side of her face. Blood was running freely out between her fingers as one of the technicians supported her. The blood dripped down on to the smooth floor as the patient, her face still detached from her skull, slumbered on in blissful ignorance of the mayhem around her.

Bedlam broke out in the gallery as confusion reigned below.

'Quiet, everyone! Quiet, please!' requested the theatre sister. The injured woman surgeon looked up at the gallery and then back at the table before murmuring audibly to the sister, 'Can you do something about my face?'

'You'll have to get a move on,' said the anaesthetist.

The surgeon, her face now obscured by the theatre sister who was applying butterfly stitches to the cut, did not reply. She waited until the sister had finished and then said, 'Now tape it, quickly!'

'Time is getting tight,' said the anaesthetist, as the first uneven blip from the monitor probed everyone's nerves.

Adhesive tape was applied over the line of the cut on the surgeon's face. Freeman's body was removed from the theatre and his assistant stepped up to the table to continue. She seemed a little unsteady.

'Forceps!'

Despite the sympathy the gallery felt for the woman, they gasped sharply when they saw her fumble and drop the forceps. 'Forceps!' she repeated. Her voice reflected the tension she felt. Another pair of forceps were slapped into her hand.

'Christ, her hands are shaking!' said a whispering voice in the gallery. The others could see that the speaker was right. Silently they implored the woman to get a grip on herself. Take it easy . . . take it easy and everything will be fine. The surgeon started to pull the patient's face up over the new prosthesis and they saw it tighten dramatically.

'The optic nerve! For Christ's sake, the optic nerve,' said the voice in the darkness again. 'She's going to blind her!' said another.

ONE

'I thought your piece on corruption in the health service was first class,' said the figure at the bar.

'Praise from Caesar,' smiled the younger man beside him.

'Credit where credit's due. There's plenty who would give their eye teeth for a story like that, and some of them aren't a million miles from here.' The speaker made a face as a third man came up and joined them.

'Good story, Kincaid. How do you do it?' asked the newcomer. He spoke with a lisp and his voice contained a hint of sarcasm.

'Talent, Conroy,' snapped the older man, before Kincaid could reply. 'That's T-A-L- . . .'

'Oh, very droll, Fletcher. When are you going to learn that it's circulation figures that count?'

The third man minced away and Kincaid and Fletcher went in search of a table.

'Good story,' said a voice, as they passed a group of four men.

'Thanks,' replied Kincaid.

'The praise of one's peers,' crooned Fletcher, as they found a place to sit. 'Nectar of the gods.'

'You've had plenty in your time,' replied Kincaid. 'And now you're editor of a paper that Conroy couldn't even read, let alone edit.'

'Perhaps Conroy's right. Maybe we should pay more attention to quantity rather than what we see as quality.'

'Nonsense!' exclaimed Kincaid. 'What does Conroy know?

Spends his life waiting for vicars to drop their trousers in the wrong place. Call that journalism?'

'It's what the great British public want. There's nothing like a bit of titillation from the Sundays before getting the missus bare-arsed among the toast crumbs.'

'You have a tongue of silver, Fletcher.'

'Talking of silver tongues, I hear the health minister has announced the next phase of his master plan.'

'Health in our time – Carlisle doesn't stay out of the news for very long, does he?'

'Charisma,' said Fletcher. 'Not that plentiful in our politicians, but Carlisle has it. Apart from that, anyone who makes a success out of a health job in the government has to be quick on his feet, and he's made it look easy.'

'Makes you wonder why all the others made such a mess of it,' said Kincaid.

'They say he cares. Maybe that makes all the difference,' said Fletcher.

'A politician who cares? Whatever will they think of next? Same again?'

Fletcher nodded and read his copy of the evening paper until Kincaid returned. He said, 'I see everyone has picked up on your story. How did you get on to the scam in the first place?'

'An old friend of mine tipped me off that Carlisle's investigation into the health service in his area was making certain members of the local health boards turn pale. I took the hint and started poking around. An analysis of past purchasing contracts proved embarrassing to say the least. A glut of motorcruisers suddenly hit the market.'

'Sometimes I wonder if there's a single honest bugger in this whole damned country,' said Fletcher.

'Of course there is . . . me.'

'I've read your expense claims.'

'*Touché.*'

'I had a word with our illustrious proprietor on the phone this afternoon,' said Fletcher tentatively.

Kincaid looked at his editor with just a hint of suspicion on his face. 'And?' he asked.

'Apparently Carlisle phoned him after the story broke.'

'Offering his congratulations, no doubt,' said Kincaid, still on his guard.

'Not exactly. I don't think you could expect that after the shit you dumped in his back yard,' said Fletcher.

'Then what?'

'Apparently he was very reasonable about the whole thing. He said that the case in point just illustrated how much the service was in need of a good shake-up. He pointed out that that's just what he intends giving it.'

'And?'

Fletcher smiled uncomfortably at Kincaid's persistence. 'All right,' he conceded, 'Carlisle did say that it was about time he was given some credit for his achievements, and why didn't the press concentrate on the good things about the health service for a change.'

'A traditional air,' said Kincaid.

'He has a point. I hear his Northern Health Scheme has been a big success. The man even had the political nous to start his reform of the service in your neck of the woods. They say College Hospital in Newcastle is now one of the most modern in Europe.'

'It's going to take more than a refurbished hospital to change the way folks vote up there.'

'Maybe, but he's going to stick with it, I hear. The next part of the scheme involves community health care.'

'I think that means us,' said Kincaid, 'but no doubt I'll hear all about it this weekend.'

'You're going up to see your daughter?'

Kincaid nodded.

'Time for another drink?'

Kincaid looked at his watch and shook his head. 'I'm off. I've got a train to catch.'

'How is she?'

Kincaid shrugged. 'She's happy enough in her way.'

Fletcher didn't inquire further. He knew it was a touchy subject.

Kincaid said, 'I think I'll take a look at College Hospital while I'm there.'

'Mr Carlisle will be pleased,' said Fletcher.

'No,' corrected Kincaid. 'I'm intrigued by the story of the surgeon who died at the operating table, Sir Martin Freeman.'

'Tragic business.'

'It's what happened to his patient that interests me,' said Kincaid.

'His assistant completed the operation and the hospital said she was okay,' said Fletcher.

'But no one has been allowed to see her,' said Kincaid. 'Our tabloid friends have been denied taking pictures. There's a rumour going around that the operation may have blinded her.'

'I think we would have heard if there had been anything seriously wrong,' said Fletcher.

'Maybe,' said Kincaid. 'Who covered it for us?'

'A stringer called Grant.'

'Remember anything about the patient?' asked Kincaid.

Fletcher shrugged and said, 'Just that she was called Greta Marsh and that she had spent most of her life in an institution. Harrington Hall, I think it was called.'

'Why were we covering it in the first place?' asked Kincaid, as an afterthought.

'Freeman had called a press conference after the op.'

'Why?'

'Presumably to furnish the press with details of the operation; I understand that it was pretty advanced. I assume he wanted a bit of publicity for himself and the new improved health service.'

'I think I'll take a look for myself,' said Kincaid.

Kincaid settled into his seat for the journey north and accustomed himself to the smell of warm diesel. Outside on the platform people were saying their last goodbyes and a stooped porter in an ill-fitting uniform, decreed more by his shape than any tailor, scuffed his way up the side of the train, slamming open doors shut as he went. It was a familiar scene for Kincaid.

He made the journey north as often as he could, and never less than once a month, to visit his daughter who was a patient in a home for mentally handicapped children. As always, he would stay with his widower father in Newcastle. Usually he just stayed on Saturday night and travelled back to London on the Sunday. This time he might stay longer. The corruption story had taken a lot out of him. The paper owed him some time off.

Raindrops peppered the glass and fought their way down through the grime as the train pulled out of the station. As always, but particularly when the weather was bad or the train more dirty than usual, these circumstances conspired to play devil's advocate and question his reason for going. She doesn't even know you; it doesn't make the slightest difference whether you go or not. That's what the doctors said.

So why did he keep going? Because he didn't believe them; that was the simple, inescapable truth and in that he was agonisingly alone. His ex-wife, Julie, Kerry's mother, had long given up the pilgrimage and still lived in the north, remarried to a quantity surveyor, whatever that was. Probably a damned site more secure than being married to a journalist, Kincaid reflected.

No one had come to sit in the seat opposite so he stretched out his long legs and moved his head into a more comfortable position where he could watch the telephone wires rise and fall against the night sky as the train gathered speed. He watched until his eyelids insisted on closing.

Kincaid's features relaxed as he fell asleep. He was thirty-six and looked it, despite an athletic build inherited from a family that had known nothing but hard manual work in the mines and shipyards of the north. His features, though not coarse, were certainly not refined, and he would not have looked out of place in the crowd leaving a factory at five o'clock, or lining up on a rugby league pitch shortly before kick off on a Saturday afternoon. He was the one exception in the family, being the first of the Kincaids to get a university education and escape the drudgery of the factory whistle. He had taken a degree in English at Newcastle

University and, having no heart for a career in teaching, the line of least resistance for most of his peers, he had opted for journalism. Like many quiet-natured people, he always saw more than he ever admitted. He understood human nature better than most because he watched people more than most. This was of minor importance in the early days when he covered marriages and church fêtes, lost dogs and cats up trees, but as he progressed and moved south, as ambition decreed he must, it became an increasingly important factor in establishing himself as an investigative journalist. His Geordie accent, although softened by education, had never completely left him and when combined with an understated charm and a smile that put people at their ease, he was well equipped to gain their confidence.

Kincaid woke briefly when some noisy youths passed through the carriage. Two were carrying beer cans in their outside hands while they supported a third boy between them. The vomit stains on the front of his T-shirt said that he was being taken to the toilet too late. Kincaid looked up briefly to the smiling-faced advert for rail travel, then closed his eyes again. When he awoke it was six o'clock in the morning and the train was coming into Newcastle.

The early morning cold lurking inside a grey fog made Kincaid shiver when he stepped out on to the platform and paused to rub his hands. Morning dew had condensed on the painted pillars of the station, running down in tortuous rivulets to the dirt-stained concrete where a black cat, its back arched against some unseen foe, moved slowly in its own jungle. The promise of warmth and the smell of steaming coffee made Kincaid head for the yellow lights of the station buffet. The coffee tasted bitter, but had the saving grace of being hot; it was the perfect foil for a bacon sandwich that was too salty.

As usual he would walk to his father's house so that he would not arrive much before eight o'clock. This suited them both, for it gave the old man time to get up and Kincaid the opportunity to walk the streets of his youth and flirt with memories in the quiet of the early morning.

18

The smell of the Tyne before the air filled up with petrol fumes was something special. He was sensitive to the different smells places had, and found them much more effective in evoking memories than any photograph. In truth, he supposed that they must be cocktails of many things, but in their way they were still specific. The Middle East had a distinctive smell, as did the countries of the Mediterranean. Paris had a scent of its own, so did Madrid, even London. But here was the unmistakable smell of the Tyne on a misty morning in April, as he slung his bag over his shoulder and walked along the road between the towering, empty warehouses.

At first his legs were stiff with having sat down for so long, but he soon loosened up. There was no escaping the evidence of decay and neglect near the waterfront. Seagulls wheeled above him and he could almost hear their wings flapping in an area that had once reverberated to rivet hammers turning steel into ships. The lack of people around made the walls seem darker and the pavements harder. He paused to read a hoarding that had been erected since his last visit, which said that this was to be the site of three new blocks of retirement flats. An elderly couple was depicted – smiling, with their arms round each other – above details of the price range. He wondered idly if builders built flats for anyone other than retired folk these days.

The back door to his father's terraced house was open, as he knew it would be. The drainpipe running down the side looked to be on its last legs; rust and a green film of algae had spread out over the bricks where water was slow to dry on a north-facing wall.

'Hello, you old bugger,' said Kincaid softly, as he pushed the door open to find his father frying bacon in the tiny kitchen.

The old man's face broke into a toothless grin and he gave a chesty laugh. 'Want some?'

'No, I've had something. How are you doin'?'

'Same as usual, man. You'll have a cup of tea tho'?'

Kincaid nodded.

The old man poured tea into a dark brown mug and handed it to Kincaid, who added his own milk and then sugar from an open bag.

'What time are you goin' to see the lass?'

'Not until this afternoon.'

'I thought we might have a few pints tonight? There's a bit of a cabaret at the club.'

'I'm not sure,' said Kincaid, 'I may have to go out.'

'Please yourself.'

There was a short silence which Kincaid interpreted as disappointment. 'We could have a couple this morning?' he suggested, 'Club's open all day, isn't it?'

'Aye, fine by me,' said the old man.

They moved into the small living-room and sat down. 'It's a bit cold in here, man,' said Kincaid, rubbing his arms.

'I don't usually put the fire on till later.'

Kincaid hesitated, knowing that he was stepping on to thin ice, then said cautiously, 'Look man, if it's a question of money . . .'

A look of anger clouded Jack Kincaid's face and he turned on his son. 'I've told you before, I don't need your money and I don't want your money. I've got my pension and my benefits and I've got my pride, so don't bring up the subject again. Understood?'

'You're an obstinate old so and so.'

'Maybe, but I'm me own man.'

Kincaid admitted defeat.

Jack Kincaid broke into a coughing spasm, brought on by his outburst.

'Are you taking anything for that?'

'I was down the doctor's last Thursday. He gave me some tablets, bugger-all use if you ask me.'

'Did he say what's wrong?'

'Bronchitis. I'm just gettin' old, man.'

Kincaid looked at the cigarettes and matches on the table.

'Don't you even start,' said his father.

'I hear you've been makin' a name for yourself with tales of corruption in high places,' said Jack Kincaid, as they walked down the hill to the club later on.

'Not very high places,' said Kincaid. 'Who told you?'

'The social worker who calls to see if I'm all right. She reads that kind of paper.'

Kincaid smiled at the reference to his newspaper and said, 'A few health service managers were on the take, that's all.'

'That's hardly news, man. I've never known a manager yet who wasn't.'

Jack Kincaid's club had been built twenty years ago, for the social needs of the employees of the shipbuilding firm he worked for. The shipyard had now closed but the club lingered on, its membership predominantly retired or unemployed men. There had been no money for refurbishment for over a decade and it showed. Plastic-covered seating and formica tabletops were arranged around a hall with nicotine-stained walls and incongruous-looking chandeliers. The whole place smelled of cigarette smoke and stale beer. Kincaid bought two beers from the bar and brought them over to the table where his father had sat down. At eleven-thirty in the morning the club was already about three-quarters full.

'Quite a few in,' said Kincaid.

'Saturday dinner-time,' replied his father, 'there's always a stripper.'

Kincaid didn't say anything but wondered about the outer reaches of show business. As if reading his mind his father said, 'I can remember when Shirley Bassey played here.'

At noon a red-faced man holding a microphone walked out in the front of the hall and started speaking. He read from a scrap of paper which he had to hold at arm's length to see with middle-aged eyes. 'And now the star you have all been waiting for,' he announced, enunciating every syllable like a schoolboy reading out a poem in class. 'The lovely . . . Monique!'

Music blared out from the speakers at a volume which made Kincaid wince. A slight, pale-skinned girl ran out and began dancing. She was dressed in a cowgirl outfit which Doris Day might have sported in the Fifties, only the length of the skirt had been modified for the job in hand.

21

'I'm just a girl who can't say no . . .'

The girl put a finger to her lips to appear seductive, but only succeeded in looking like the lead singer in a primary school concert.

'Jeesus!' said Kincaid's father.

The girl continued through a pathetic routine until she was stripped down to her bra and pants. After a few jerky attempts at appearing coy, she removed her bra and flung it over her shoulder.

'I've had bigger boils on my arse!' said a man at the next table.

'Get them down!' shouted a man at the front with more volume than originality.

'No, keep 'em up!' yelled another man, this time to roars of laughter.

Monique suddenly stopped dancing and stood looking at the audience, her eyes flashing with anger, her chest still rising and falling with the exertion. The music stopped untidily and there was a moment when performer and audience were locked together in silent anticipation. 'Yer all bastards!' she cried, and ran off stage with her hands crossed over her naked breasts.

Jack Kincaid looked at his son. 'Times change, man,' he said.

It rained in the afternoon. Kincaid was soaked to the skin by the time he had walked from the bus stop up the tree-lined drive to the home.

'Not the best of days, Mr Kincaid,' said the Matron.

Kincaid attempted a smile but it was hard. He didn't like the woman. In previous meetings she had sat smugly behind her uniform and spoken down to him, patronised him, humoured him as she did all those outside her profession. She was not an intelligent woman and consequently mistook vocational knowledge for intellect. To Kincaid she was the female embodiment of the military mind; an original thought had never sullied her outlook or devotion to duty.

Taking off his coat and leaving it in the vestibule to drip water on the tiled floor he asked, 'How is she, Mrs Wilton?' Kincaid avoided the use of 'matron' as much as possible, believing it to carry a degree of respect he had no wish to give way to.

'Much the same as usual, Mr Kincaid,' replied Ethel Wilton, her heavy breasts resting on folded arms and her square face made to seem even more so by her uniform cap.

'Any sign of improvement?'

The matron looked briefly exasperated before saying, 'I don't really think we can expect much improvement, Mr Kincaid. I think you were told that by the doctors?'

'Yes Matron, that's what they said,' Kincaid smiled wanly. 'But I keep hoping. You see, it was once the experts' view that the earth was flat. Even common sense was on their side. After all, we would all fall off if it was any other way, wouldn't we . . . ?'

The matron replied with an acid look. She pointed to a ground floor door and turned away.

Kincaid found Kerry playing with some plastic bricks in a room with five other children and two nurses. She looked up briefly when he walked in but showed no sign of recognition and her attention was quickly diverted. Kincaid sat down beside her and passed her a few bricks. She took them without acknowledgement, but Kincaid was conscious of her fingers touching his when she took them and clung to the sensation. He smoothed the hair away from her eyes and said, 'Hello, Kerry.' The girl moved her head back out of the way.

'Who's that, Kerry?' said one of the nurses, whom Kincaid had not seen before. She tried to lift the child away from her bricks but Kerry resisted and struggled strongly.

'It's all right,' said Kincaid to the nurse. 'Just leave her.'

'Does she know you?' asked the nurse.

The words cut through Kincaid, but he remained outwardly impassive. He said quietly, 'She doesn't know me but I know her. She's my daughter.' He continued watching the child play. There was no logic in what she did with the bricks but he repeatedly collected them when she spread them around and muttered words of praise when she balanced one on top of the other. There was a moment when her eyes met his and he imagined he saw some kind of recognition there, but the moment passed and he feared he was seeing merely what he wanted to see. He inwardly cursed his reverence for realism. It would have been nicer to believe that she had acknowledged him. When it was time to go he whispered, 'I'll see you again soon, Kerry.' He ruffled her hair gently and patted her shoulder, but there was still no sign of recognition from the child.

Kincaid got on the first bus that was heading towards the city. He had no real idea of where he was going or why, but for him it was an age-old scenario. Other people went home, sat down and had a think about their problems; he had to keep on the move. He needed the distraction of constantly changing scenery in order to concentrate just like some school children needed loud pop music to study by. He got off the bus when he felt like it and took another and another, always sitting on the top deck, looking out of the window at what was going on around him.

The problem was now defined inside his head and could be faced in simple terms. Kerry wasn't getting any better in the home and the situation wasn't going to change. If he couldn't convince anyone that what she needed was constant stimulation, then he would have to do something. He would take her away from that place and look after her himself. He would find a way to get through to her again. When he had done that, things would start to get better. At the moment, all Kerry had was a prison with benevolent jailers. He would have one last try at getting her condition reassessed with a view to moving her to a more stimulating environment. But if that failed, as it had twice before, then it would be up to him.

It was dark outside. He got off the bus when it reached the centre of town and went in search of something to eat. He had to dodge in and out of the evening traffic which was now heavy with home-going shoppers, and the air was redolent with exhaust fumes which hung in palls round the traffic lights. The neon sign of a fast food place attracted him and he was happy to settle for a hamburger and a Coke in surroundings of contrived American geniality.

'I'm Gina, how may I help you?' said a girl with a broad Geordie accent. It made Kincaid stifle the kindest of smiles.

24

He was considering going home when he saw a bus pull up with 'College Hospital' on its destination board. He hadn't intended visiting the hospital until the following day, but on impulse he boarded the bus. He might as well have a quick look at the jewel in the health service crown.

The bus pulled away leaving Kincaid looking up at the high concrete frontage of the hospital, now studded with lights along every floor. He paused at the gate to read the signs and associated arrows giving directions to a variety of clinics and departments. Consciously grateful that he had no need of any of them, he walked round the outside of the hospital, noting where it had been extended and by how much. It now looked like any other modern hospital, he thought, large, square and impersonal.

As he rounded the last corner he saw a pub across the street. A lit sign featuring a full-masted sailing ship said that it was called The Flying Dutchman. Its position would make it the local for hospital staff. Pubs were always good places to pick up gossip.

At eight o'clock on a Saturday evening the bar was busy. Kincaid ordered a whisky and a bottle of Newcastle Brown beer, and settled himself at the end of the bar where he could watch the clientele and listen out for snippets of conversation. The pub itself, he guessed, had survived the expansion and modernisation of the neighbouring hospital although most old houses in the area had not. Many of the people present looked as if they might have some connection with the hospital, but a few older men in dark clothes and flat caps looked as if they didn't. The old street regulars, thought Kincaid. When one of them came up to the bar to order a round he decided to find out. 'Big changes in this area,' he ventured.

'You're not from round here, then?' said the man.

'I used to be. I was brought up not far from here. Scarcely recognised the old place.'

'They pulled a lot of it down when they modernised the hospital.'

'Shame,' said Kincaid.

'Best thing that ever happened,' replied the man. 'There's many that reckon we get the best medical treatment in the country up here since the changes. There's none of this waiting for hours in draughty corridors for a bit of attention. Everyone gets appointments. It's like goin' private, man.'

'Sounds good,' said Kincaid.

'You'll be voting Tory next, Davey,' said one of the other men with a bronchitic laugh.

A group of young women came into the bar and from their conversation Kincaid learned that they were nurses.

'Have you been invited to the do next week, Susan?' asked one.

'It's only sisters and staff nurses,' replied a short, blonde girl. 'You'll be going, Eve?' she said, to a slightly older girl who nodded.

Kincaid thought the blonde girl too young to be drinking but then conceded that it was probably he who was getting old.

'The health minister is coming up specially from London.'

'Whoopee,' said the girl called Eve.

'Come on, you have to hand it to Carlisle, he's better than the rest. Things have definitely improved.'

'I don't trust politicians, any of them.'

Kincaid could not smile openly but he held a lot of sympathy for the view being expressed. Years of professional prying into the behaviour of his fellow men had done little to endear them to him, and had particularly jaundiced his opinion of the variety who sought to 'serve' in a political capacity. He had long since concluded that the best way to motivate a politician was to present him with an angle with which to further his career.

'How's Sir Martin's patient today?' asked the tallest of the four girls.

Kincaid, almost unable to believe his good luck, pricked up his ears, but pretended to be totally preoccupied.

'She's fine. She'll be going home soon.'

'There's been a lot of speculation in the newspapers about her.'

'They're like vultures, these reporters, but they'll be allowed to see her before she goes home.'

'What does she look like?'

'She looks quite normal.'

'Then the operation was a success?'

'Absolutely.'

'I wish I worked in Sir Martin's unit,' said one of the girls. 'You get all the glamour. All I seem to get is cleaning the bloody sluice.'

'Your turn will come,' said the older nurse.

The four girls saw a table being vacated and left the bar to take it. Kincaid was left to look after them thoughtfully. He had watched the older nurse when she was answering her friends' questions and one thing had struck him; she had averted her eyes every time she had spoken. For whatever reason, he was sure she had been lying.

Kincaid was pondering on this when he saw a serious-looking young man come into the bar and order a half-pint of beer. His accent was southern and educated. Maybe he was one of the administration people from the hospital, or perhaps even a houseman if he was really lucky. Kincaid gambled on the latter, moved nearer the man and said with a smile, 'You're one of Freeman's housemen aren't you?'

'Actually, no. I'm on Professor Grimble's team.' The young man nearly added 'sir' but didn't. He was still trying to place Kincaid.

Kincaid pretended not to notice. 'Oh, that's where I've seen you. I hear Freeman's patient has made a complete recovery.'

'Really?'

'Yes, she'll be going home soon.'

'That's good news. I'm glad for Claire Affric's sake. I thought there might be problems.'

'Claire Affric?' asked Kincaid tentatively.

'Sir Martin's assistant at the operation . . . but you must know th . . . who are you?' asked the young man, suddenly filled with suspicion.

'My name is Kincaid . . .'

'Christ, you're a journalist?'

'Yes, I am,' replied Kincaid.

27

The houseman dropped his head in frustration and muttered, 'You underhanded . . .' His face was flushed with anger when he looked up. 'Always skulking around, always digging for dirt. Trash! That's what you are.' His voice, being suffused with anger, took on an almost girlish quality.

'That's a bit of a sweeping generalisation,' said Kincaid, keeping his cool but feeling angry none the less. 'You should be grateful I don't apply the same attitude to your profession.'

'What the hell do you mean?' snapped the young man.

Kincaid looked at him with cold eyes. 'Three years ago my daughter was taken into hospital for an appendicectomy. By the time the medical profession had finished with her, half her brain had been destroyed and she hasn't recognised me since. Accidental oxygen starvation, they said . . .' Kincaid stood up from the bar and pulled up his collar. Still without visible emotion he said, 'Good-night, Doctor,' and left the bar.

Kincaid was glad of the cold night air on his face, for anger was still lurking beneath his cheeks, despite the fact that he had kept his temper. He maintained a purposeful stride through the dark streets although he had no such purpose. He was even oblivious to the icy rain that had started to fall because he was still preoccupied with thoughts of the doctor back in the pub.

There had been a time when he would have laid out the houseman without hesitation, a time when the mere mention of the medical profession or a hint of their self-satisfied arrogance would have been enough to push him over the edge. He had since learned to control his bitterness, but that did not mean the feeling had gone. Kerry was a living reminder to him. He had a particular interest in exposing the shortcomings of the people that had destroyed his daughter's life and then fought tooth and nail to cover their tracks. He had long since quenched the primitive desire for revenge, but should the opportunity arise to expose feet of clay in a profession he considered to cause as many problems as it cured, he would do so. He found another bar and set out to ease the pain.

*   *   *

Shortly after eleven o'clock in the evening a dark green Jaguar car slid out of Belgravia and started heading north. It was to be two hours before it turned off the motorway and another half-hour before its fat tyres crunched on to the gravel drive of a country house where several other cars were already parked.

Despite the lateness of the hour the door was opened almost immediately and the driver shown inside. He was led downstairs into a room which could have been the boardroom of a city merchant bank. The other men in the room, eight in all and seated at a long table, waited until the new man had opened his briefcase and brought out some papers before turning to face their chairman.

'Gentlemen, it is now one year since we met last and agreed what had to be done,' said the chairman. 'At that time we were faced with one of the hardest decisions we have ever had to make, but we faced up to our responsibility and we meet here tonight to receive a report on progress. I now call for the report.'

The man who had arrived last got to his feet and finished shuffling his papers. He ran his finger briefly round the inside of his collar before starting to speak. 'Gentlemen, I am pleased to say that the targets for the year were met in full. The pilot scheme which we agreed on a year ago has been an unmitigated success. It is my recommendation that the expansion we spoke about in that first meeting be carried out. It is time to implement phase two.'

'I think we should delay,' said one man.

'We agreed on one year for the pilot. A year has passed.'

'The recent publicity changes things. It was messy.'

'It was just bad luck,' said a third man. 'The fool lost his nerve. He was going to ruin everything. We had to do it.'

'But so publicly?'

'We had no choice. We only found out about his intentions at the very last moment. If it hadn't been for the quick thinking of our colleague everything we've worked for would have been lost.'

'I still think we should wait a little to make sure there is no more press interest.'

'There's no need. The matter has been tidied up. The story is already being used to wrap fish and chips.'

'Can we have a vote?'

The chairman nodded. 'All those in favour of waiting?'

Two hands were raised.

'I think we have our answer. We press on.'

'What adjustments are necessary, Mr Chairman?'

'I have the figures.' The speaker handed out a sheet of paper to each man.

The chairman turned his attention to another of the men. 'Has the notification programme been made compatible with these targets?'

'Yes Mr Chairman, the returns will automatically match comparable industrial areas in Scotland and Wales.'

'Excellent. What about on-site administration?'

'No problems.'

'You are absolutely sure that this is necessary?'

'Yes.'

'I would like to see an updated forecast.'

'Very well. Perhaps we can see the latest computer predictions?'

'Certainly, Mr Chairman.'

At the opposite end of the room from the chairman two wooden doors slid back to reveal a screen. A button was clicked and a slide appeared.

'This is what our population will look like in four years' time. You will note the imbalance.'

There were gasps of dismay all round. The slide changed.

'This is the effect that the spread of Aids will have on people under thirty-five. The slide changed again. 'And these are the predicted figures for seven years hence.'

More gasps.

'Suppose the computer is wrong?'

'The computer predictions are based on the best figures available to anyone. If anything, they are optimistic.'

'They might have a cure for Aids within a couple of years.'

'They might not.'

The slide was changed.

30

'This will be the projected cost to the exchequer based on the predictions you have just seen.'

The room fell silent.

The chairman said, 'I think that this can only strengthen our resolve, gentlemen. There is no one sorrier than I that these steps have to be taken, but things have gone too far. We have to do something.'

A murmur of agreement filled the room.

TWO

Kincaid found the house in darkness. At first he thought it was empty, but the sound of coughing from the bedroom indicated that the old man was home and already in bed.

'Poor old devil,' he muttered, taking off his coat and hanging it behind the kitchen door. The sound subsided after a few moments and the house was restored to silence. Kincaid searched for a glass. He found one in a cupboard over the sink, rinsed it out and poured himself a large whisky from the bottle he had brought with him. He added a splash of water from the kitchen tap and sat down in front of the gas fire, but left it unlit.

The chair was uncomfortable because the springs were worn and the arms were threadbare. He could feel the coarse hessian irritating his palms, but it was a link with the past and he had an affection for it which overrode other considerations. By family tradition it had been his mother's chair. The lasting memory he had was of her sitting in it with her glasses sliding down her nose as she followed a knitting pattern.

The knitting had invariably been for someone else; Mrs Smith's youngest or Mrs Elton's Harry in Ellesmere Street. But at precisely ten o'clock she would put it down and go to the kitchen to make toast for the four of them, a nightly ritual that now brought a smile to his face as he remembered it. Whatever disagreements and arguments there might have been before ten o'clock would be forgotten with tea and toast, and the importance of being a family would be emphasised.

Kincaid had a sister, Lisa. She was four years younger than

32

him and was married to Kevin Hardesty, an insurance clerk with Standard Life. Kevin was one of these people who suddenly become middle-aged at the age of twenty-six; a nice enough bloke but without imagination, Kincaid thought. Lisa loved him however, and that was what was important. Kincaid had a great regard for his sister. She wasn't as clever as he was, or as worldly wise, but for him that made her a much nicer person.

He occasionally wondered if this was because she had never been exposed to the workings of human nature as he himself had. She'd never seen politicians manipulate situations for their own self-seeking ends, or watched industrialists throw hundreds of people out of work because it was economically opportune to do so. Regrettably, he concluded, he could not blame it all on that. Lisa was genuinely a much nicer person.

People always liked Lisa and she, amazingly to Kincaid's way of thinking, always seemed to like them. She never had a bad word to say about anyone. After six years of marriage she and Kevin were still childless, but a month ago she had announced that she was pregnant at last. Everyone was delighted, not least their father. Thinking about Lisa made Kincaid resolve to go and see her this time before he went back.

A row of dusty books along the back of the sideboard caught his eye, in the way that familiar objects sometimes do when seen from odd angles. He got up and examined them. There was a 1965 edition of *Pear's Encyclopedia*, a tattered copy of *Kidnapped* by Robert Louis Stevenson, three books in identical covers from a long-defunct book club and two leather-bound volumes about the British people at war. Kincaid remembered the war books. He had been brought up with them; they had been there as long as he could remember. He took them back to the chair and leafed through them slowly, each photograph triggering off a fresh wave of nostalgia, not for Atlantic convoys or the rubble of Leningrad as depicted on the pages, but for his childhood and the way things were.

When he reached the last page of the first volume he put down the books and looked around the room slowly. It had once been filled with warmth and love. Now it was cold and dim and his father coughed again in his sleep. His mother had been dead for two years; Lisa was married and away. Julie had gone on to a new life and Kerry was stuck in that home. The amount of alcohol Kincaid had consumed was making him maudlin.

If only these idiots hadn't done what they had to Kerry it might all have been so different. Maybe he and Julie wouldn't have broken up. Maybe they would have built a warm loving home where the old man could have come at weekends and played with his granddaughter. A place where he could have come and stayed at Christmas, where they would have spoiled him, eaten too much and watched television together. 'Crap,' he muttered, scratching his forehead before swallowing what was left of the whisky. 'Utter crap.'

Kincaid was woken at six o'clock by the sound of his father coughing again. It went on so long that he got up and went next door. 'Are you all right, man?' he asked.

His father tried to swear in his frustration but only succeeded in making things worse. Kincaid watched until concern turned to alarm. He said, 'I'm going to call the doctor. Where do you keep the number?'

The old man pointed vaguely to an old bureau and Kincaid opened it to riffle through odds and ends before he found what he was looking for, a dog-eared old notebook. He dialled the number.

'It's Sunday, you know,' said the voice at the other end of the telephone.

'You mean the Hippocratic oath doesn't apply on Sundays?' answered Kincaid.

'I was merely about to point out that the practice uses a covering agency at the weekends,' said the woman's voice, sounding offended. 'Your father's own doctor will not be the doctor who comes out.'

'As long as he has a medical degree,' said Kincaid, wondering where doctors found these damned women.

'Kincaid ... 17 Claydon Street, coughing fits and chest pains.'

'That's right.'
'Doctor will call as soon as he can.'

Fifteen minutes later Kincaid answered the door to a man who introduced himself as Dr Neil Tolkien. He was wearing a tan leather jacket and had a mop of dark hair that flopped over his forehead, obliging him to push it back at regular intervals. These intervals were made more frequent by a stooped stance which Kincaid found unusual in a man who could not have been more than thirty.

'As in hobbit?' asked Kincaid.

'That's right. Where is he?'

Kincaid showed Tolkien into the bedroom and stood by while he examined the old man.

'You didn't take long to get here,' said Kincaid.

'Emergency attendance is within ten minutes, non-urgent in under thirty.'

'That's pretty good,' conceded Kincaid.

'The Emergency Service has been computerised. Everything is a lot better.' Tolkien had a long sheet of paper in his hand and Kincaid looked over his shoulder to see that it was a computer print-out. It carried details of his father's medical history.

'You didn't keep your last appointment with your own doctor,' said Tolkien.

'No, Doctor,' replied Jack Kincaid sheepishly, without offering any excuse. He coughed again.

Kincaid smiled at the old man's air of deference, a legacy from another generation.

Tolkien looked at the sheet again. 'You were prescribed ampicillin tablets. Did you take them?'

'Yes, Doctor.'

'All of them?'

'Yes, Doctor.'

A slight suggestion of disbelief crossed Tolkien's face and Kincaid found himself sharing the doctor's scepticism.

'I'm going to give you something to calm the coughing and something to help you sleep, but tomorrow morning I want you to go up to College Hospital and they'll take some X-rays of your chest. All right?'

The old man nodded and Tolkien wrote out a note which he gave him to take to the hospital.

'I'll also contact your own doctor.'

'Thank you, Doctor.'

Tolkien snapped shut his case and got up to leave. Kincaid followed him out of the bedroom and closed the door behind him. There was something wrong, he could sense it in Tolkien's demeanour. 'You think it's something more serious, don't you?'

'He is being treated for bronchitis,' replied Tolkien.

'But you don't think it's that?'

Tolkien hesitated, smoothed his hair back and then conceded, 'No, I don't.'

'Then what?'

'I think your father may have lung cancer.'

'Shit.'

'I may be wrong, but even if I'm not it needn't be the end of things. There's a lot we can do these days.'

'But curing it isn't one of them.'

'We can extend life quite a bit.'

'I'm sorry, I didn't mean to be rude.'

'That's all right. Do you live with your father, Mr Kincaid?'

Kincaid shook his head. 'I work in London; I'm a journalist.'

This struck a chord with Tolkien. 'You're not James Kincaid?' he asked.

Kincaid nodded.

'I've read your work. It's good.'

'Thanks.'

'Is there any more family to look after the old man?'

'I have a sister, but she's going to have a baby.'

'Then the social services will have to be alerted, because your father is going to need quite a bit of help, one way or another.'

Kincaid nodded again.

'How long are you staying?' asked Tolkien.

'I'd planned on a few days but I'll go with the old man to the hospital and see what they say, then play it by ear.'

'It's a very good hospital,' said Tolkien.

'So I keep hearing,' said Kincaid.

'Believe it. Health care up here has improved out of all recognition.'

'But not for my kid,' said Kincaid.

Tolkien asked what Kincaid meant and was told about Kerry.

'I'm sorry, but reorganisation takes time. Major hospital care has been the first priority over the last year but now that that is on a sound footing the General Practitioner Service is to be the next to benefit from upgrading. The health minister is to open the new computerised pharmacy service for us GPs next week.'

Kincaid remembered the nurses' conversation in the pub. 'Do you think they will get round to upgrading homes like the one Kerry is in?' he asked.

'I'm sure they will,' replied Tolkien. 'Mr Carlisle has committed himself to upgrading every aspect of health care in the region.'

'Who would be the best person to ask about future plans?' asked Kincaid.

Tolkien scratched his head and confessed that he didn't know. 'Why don't you attend the official function next week?' he suggested. 'There will probably be lots of bigwigs there to answer your questions.'

Kincaid thanked Tolkien for coming.

'All part of the service,' said Tolkien. He took out a notepad and wrote a number on it. 'I think he'll be all right now, but if not call me at this number.'

The old man had just fallen asleep when the telephone rang, and Kincaid cursed as he hurried to answer it before it woke him up. It was Fletcher in London. They exchanged pleasantries and then Fletcher said, 'I thought I'd better tell you that Greta Marsh, the patient you were interested in at College Hospital, is to be released this afternoon. Apparently she's perfectly all right, so there's no need for you to pursue the story.'

'I heard last night that she was okay,' said Kincaid.

'The hospital are allowing the press to see her this afternoon at three o'clock. Our stringer is going to cover it so he'll get us a nice picture and a merry quip.'

'Good,' said Kincaid.

'How's Kerry?'

'Much the same.'

The conversation petered out and Kincaid put down the telephone.

Kincaid had planned to spend the afternoon with Kerry, but when he got there he found that she had been in one of her 'difficult' moods and was resting. She was subject to occasional violent bouts of temper, as if in response to some inner frustration which she felt but could not express. She would become quite disturbed and lash out at whatever or whoever was nearby, and the staff had taken to sedating her when this occurred.

Kincaid had been angry the first time he found out about it because he felt that Kerry was trying to make contact with people and should be encouraged rather than put to sleep, but he had failed to convince anyone in authority that this might be the case and sedation had continued to be applied. He looked down at her sleeping form and ran his fingers gently and silently along her forehead.

'She'll be out for several hours,' said the nurse.

Kincaid nodded and said, 'I'll sit with her for a bit.'

The nurse left and Kincaid sat motionless, watching Kerry sleep as if the silence might unite them. The minutes passed and he found himself quite unconsciously breathing in harmony with her. She looked so pretty and yet so vulnerable when she was asleep. There was nothing to suggest that she was anything but a normal little girl. Surely if there was a god who cared she would wake up, smile and say hello, and run off and play. But she wouldn't. When Kerry opened her eyes the haunted look would be there and the coldness and the detachment, the devastating lack of recognition.

Somewhere in the building a door slammed and jolted Kincaid

out of his preoccupation. He stopped looking at Kerry and instead examined the room. It was painted white and the plain walls were unadorned, save for a single print of trees in autumn. The bed was the only item of furniture except for a small wooden cabinet. A single window with two bars across it looked out to the windswept garden. Kincaid looked back at Kerry with sadness in his heart and whispered, 'Things will get better soon, love, I promise. There has to be a way to reach you and I'll find it.'

As he got up to leave a clipboard hanging on the end of the bed caught his eye and he unhooked it. Under 'Next of kin' it said, 'Parents divorced. In case of emergency, contact father.' It gave his name, address and telephone number in London. He put the board back on its hook, got up, leaned slowly forward and kissed his daughter. 'See you soon, Kerry,' he whispered, and left.

As he walked down the drive to the gate he glanced at his watch and saw that it was twenty minutes to three. If he had a mind, there would be time to go to the College Hospital for Greta Marsh's release. There didn't seem to be much point, but he kept thinking about the behaviour of the nurse in the pub when she had been telling her colleagues about Greta Marsh. It disturbed him. Maybe it was irrelevant, but he was still sure that she had been lying.

Kincaid arrived with a few minutes to spare and found about a dozen reporters and cameramen assembled in a seminar room on the ground floor of the hospital. A hospital spokesman, a tall, painfully thin man wearing a striped suit that only accentuated his gauntness, was seated at the centre of a long trestle table which had been hastily adorned with a white cover and a vase of flowers. He was flanked by two of the medical staff and two senior nurses. Kincaid sat down and became another face in the crowd.

The grey-suited spokesman got to his feet and introduced himself in a strong, articulate voice which belied his appearance. 'Good afternoon. I am Gordon Fields, hospital manager at College Hospital. Miss Marsh thanks you for your interest in her, but regrets that she will be unable to answer too many questions. She hopes, indeed we all hope, that after today you will respect her privacy by letting her get on with re-building her life in peace.'

'Can't she speak, then?' asked one of the journalists.

'She can, but her jaw is still painful from the operation.'

'Will she return to Harrington Hall?'

'She will not return to Harrington Hall,' replied Fields firmly. 'She will be moving to accommodation in the city where the social work department will help her make the transition to independence and aid her return to normal life.'

'Whereabouts in the city?' asked a young reporter. The question got snorts of disbelief from his older colleagues.

'I'm not at liberty to say,' said Fields, with just an edge of irritation. 'What Miss Marsh needs more than anything at this juncture is peace and quiet, to get on with her new life. I hope you appreciate that, gentlemen.'

Fields nodded to one of the nurses and she walked to the door at the end of the room and opened it. A nurse, who Kincaid recognised immediately as the girl called Eve from the pub, brought in Greta Marsh. She was dressed in a tweed skirt with a dark green blouse and a cardigan which had been left undone. She looked down at her feet as she crossed the floor and held on to the nurse's arm, more for moral support than through any physical need, thought Kincaid. She turned to face the reporters and cleared her throat.

'You're looking well, Miss Marsh.' said one of the reporters. There was a general murmur of agreement.

'How do you feel, Miss Marsh?' asked another.

'Sore,' replied the patient, with some difficulty, although she managed a smile at the ensuing laughter. The atmosphere became relaxed and a flood of inconsequential questions followed, with Fields intervening whenever he thought it necessary. The nurse remained at Greta Marsh's side throughout. Kincaid watched her and noticed that she seemed troubled. He moved closer to the front, and when there was a lull in the questions he held up his hand and said, 'How many fingers, Miss Marsh?' The room fell silent.

Greta Marsh turned slowly towards Kincaid and said, 'Four.'
'No trouble with your eyes?'
'None.'
'No ill effects at all?'
'A sore mouth.'
Everyone laughed again at the laboured way she said it, but
this time it was muted, as the implications of Kincaid's question
were considered.

Another man asked a question and Kincaid switched his
attention back to the nurse. He stared at her until she became
aware of him. She tried to avoid eye contact, but in the
end Kincaid's relentless gaze made her look fleetingly back
at him. In that instant Kincaid saw something other than
embarrassment in her eyes. It looked like fear.

The photographers moved in to take pictures and a few minutes
later Fields called an end to the interview. The journalists
trooped out of the room but Kincaid hung back. There was
something wrong with the Greta Marsh story. He didn't know
what it was, but there was a skeleton in the cupboard, of that
he was sure.

He was joined by the local reporter who had been assigned
by his paper to cover the story. 'I know you, you're James
Kincaid. I didn't think you would come to this sort of thing,'
said the man.

'I had some time to fill,' said Kincaid. 'I thought I'd see for
myself.'

'Did you see the pictures of the woman before the operation?'
Kincaid shook his head.

'She was repulsive; a complete monster, and now she looks
like anybody's aunt. Pretty amazing, huh?'

'Absolutely,' replied Kincaid, but without conviction because
he was preoccupied with thoughts of the nurse. 'You don't
happen to know which ward Greta Marsh is in?'

'Some of the boys tried to find out but she didn't seem to
be in any of the surgical recovery wards. I think they must
have been keeping her under wraps somewhere. Probably in
Sir Martin's surgical unit.'

'Where's that?'

'In the west wing, but forget it. It's strictly no interviews.'

Kincaid smiled and nodded. He wasn't really interested in interviewing the patient.

Kincaid had to wait three hours before he saw the nurse again. She wrapped her cape tightly around her as she emerged from the special surgical unit and made for the nurses' home. Kincaid followed and quickly caught up. 'I wonder if I might have a word,' he said. She was startled by his sudden appearance and gasped out loud. Kincaid apologised.

'You!' she exclaimed. 'What do you want?'

'I want to talk about Greta Marsh.'

'You know all there is to know. You were at the conference, and Miss Marsh is no longer a patient here,' said the girl. She started to walk on.

'There's more,' said Kincaid.

The girl turned again. 'What do you mean, "more"?'

'There's something we are not being told. I want to know what it is.'

The girl looked Kincaid in the eye but did not say anything. She turned once more to walk on.

'You are not happy about it, either,' said Kincaid. 'I can see it in your eyes. It's eating away at you. Why not make a clean breast of it, Staff Nurse Laing?'

The girl paused at the mention of her name, which Kincaid had read on the badge pinned to her uniform, but then walked on.

Kincaid caught up with her and said, 'When it gets too much for you, call me.' Kincaid pressed a card into her hand with his name and telephone number on it.

The girl disappeared into the nurses' home and Kincaid turned away with a shrug. He thought some more about the press conference. Both the medics attending had been men. That meant that the surgeon who completed the operation on Greta Marsh had not been there. Why not? He remembered that the houseman in the pub had mentioned her name: Claire Affric.

He found his way back to the hospital administration block.

'Dr Affric is on leave at the moment,' said the clerk, pulling out a none-too-clean handkerchief and blowing his nose loudly.

'Any idea where?'

'No.'

Kincaid stopped at the hospital gate. With the nurse saying nothing and the surgeon and patient out of reach, there was not a great deal he could do, besides, it had just started to rain. He pulled up his collar and left.

It was still raining the following morning. Kincaid was up early, partly because he didn't sleep well and couldn't settle to read anything, but mainly because he had to take his father to the hospital for X-rays. As he waited for the kettle to boil he watched the rain cascade down the broken gutter outside the kitchen window. It bounced off the lid of a disused coal box to splatter untidily on to the ground below, where it had created a small but ambitious pool. He made a mental note of one more thing to attend to when he had the time.

The kettle began to sing and the sound of coughing came from the bedroom. Kincaid put his head round the door and asked his father if he wanted tea. The old man nodded in between coughs. Kincaid saw him reach out to the bedside table and fumble for his cigarettes.

'Jesus man, you can't be serious.'

Jack Kincaid made a weak attempt at laughter and said, 'I think the horse has already bolted.'

So the old man knew, thought Kincaid, as he returned to the kitchen to make the tea. Maybe it was for the best. Keeping the truth from him would have been difficult. He poured the tea and started foraging for bread with which to feed the toaster.

'Mr Jack Kincaid!' said a pretty nurse, holding a clipboard.

'I don't believe it. We've only been here five minutes,' said Kincaid. 'I thought we'd have to wait for hours.'

'Perhaps you would like to wait here,' the nurse said to him. 'We'll look after your father.'

Kincaid took a seat in the waiting area and tried to concentrate on a succession of magazines without success. He gave up and went to look out of the window, not that he found much to cheer him there: the overcast sky and the rain had bestowed a greyness on everything. Across the way two porters were transferring a wheelchair-borne patient to the back of an ambulance. He watched the embarrassment and anguish on the patient's face as he was manhandled into the vehicle. To be so dependent on others was not a happy prospect. Forty minutes later a nurse returned his father to the waiting area.

'How'd it go?' asked Kincaid.

'They took some pictures, said I could have a cup of tea while they processed them.'

'Let's go and get one, then.'

The cafeteria was bright, plastic and modern. Kincaid collected their tea and scones from the self-service counter and took them to a table by a window. It had a red plastic top and Kincaid noticed as he laid the tray down that his father's knuckles were very white against it. Condensation on the inside of the window had made it impossible to see out.

'You know what they're going to find on the X-rays, don't you?' said Jack Kincaid.

Kincaid felt his throat tighten. The old man had caught him off guard. 'What do you mean, man?'

'I know it's the big C, man. I could see it in the doctor's face when he examined me yesterday.'

'He doesn't have to be right, you know. He just thought it was a possibility.'

Jack Kincaid looked down at the table and said quietly, 'It's all right, man, I can handle it. Did he say how long he thought I'd got?'

'It might not even be cancer,' said Kincaid, but his father held up a restraining hand. 'Let's assume it is. How long?'

'He couldn't say for sure but he stressed that there's a lot they can do these days.'

'Every day a bonus, like?'

'Dr Tolkien seemed to be talking a lot longer than that.'

Jack Kincaid sipped his tea in silence for a few moments and then said, 'It's all right, you know. I'm sixty-eight; I've had a good innings and with your mother gone now my number is about due to come up.'

'It's not up yet,' insisted Kincaid.

Jack ignored him and continued, 'It's not as if it was a young life like Kerry's. Now that's a real tragedy.'

Kincaid ignored the attempted diversion. 'It's too soon to talk about death,' he insisted. 'With chemotherapy and remissions you could be around for a long time yet. Don't forget you have a new grandchild on the way. That's what you should be thinking about.'

Once again Jack Kincaid ignored what had been said. He was locked on to a train of thought and would not be moved. He said, 'You know, it's a funny thing, but ever since I can remember I always said when my time came I wanted to be cremated, and now . . .'

'Now what?' Kincaid asked quietly.

Jack looked at his son and said, 'I want to be buried. I want to be buried in St Mary's churchyard up in Hollybank. What do you think?'

Kincaid swallowed and said, 'Have you ever been to that church before?'

His father shook his head and said, 'I sit on a seat up there in the summer sometimes. It's the most peaceful place I know.'

Kincaid moved uncomfortably in his seat. 'I'm sure something could be worked out,' he said, hoping that the lie did not show on his face.

His father leaned across the table and put both his hands on top of his. 'I'd like that, man,' he said. 'I'd really like that. You will do your best, won't you?'

Kincaid nodded and said, 'I promise.' He looked at his watch. 'I think we should be getting back.' He noticed that his father's hands were shaking as he put his cup and saucer on top of the plate.

The doctor spoke to Kincaid alone after he had seen his

father. 'I'm afraid I have some rather bad news for you,' he said.

'I've been expecting it,' said Kincaid, but his insides still reacted.

'Your father has a large growth on his left lung and the lab says it is malignant.'

'Is there anything you can do?'

'We'll have to operate to remove the affected area and then we'll take it from there. We'll have a better idea of how far the tumour has spread when we open him up.'

'Where is he?' asked Kincaid.

'Next door, having a few more tests before we admit him to the ward. You can see him in a moment.'

The nurse left Kincaid and his father alone together for a few minutes. Kincaid felt awkward; he didn't know what to say. They had both known what the outcome of the tests would be, and yet having a third party say it out loud seemed to change everything, make it infinitely more final, although 'infinitely' was definitely the wrong word to use. That was the difference, thought Kincaid. The doctor had made his father's life finite. It had had a beginning, a middle and now it had a clearly-defined end.

His father looked smaller as he sat in an upright chair with his legs crossed. It was as if the news had diminished him somehow. His highly polished shoes, in which he had always taken a great pride, now seemed faintly ridiculous, as did the Sunday-best suit and the tie with the overly-big knot. His skin seemed paler and there was a suggestion of sparse stubble around his chin, despite the fact that he had shaved only a few hours before.

'How are you feeling?' asked Kincaid, instantly regretting every syllable of the stupid question, but he had to say something.

'I've felt better, lad,' was his father's generous reply.

'The doctor says you'll be coming in right away.'

'Aye.'

'Is there anything you want me to get you?'

'I don't think so. The nurse phoned your sister. She's bringing in my pyjamas and toothbrush. I don't think I need anything else.'

'I'll come back this evening and see you when you're settled.'

'You're not going back to London, then?'

'Not just yet,' said Kincaid.

'Don't stay on my account. You've got your life to lead and I'll be fine, really I will.'

'I'll see you later,' said Kincaid, getting up to leave.

Kincaid found his sister Lisa at the house when he got back. She put her arms around him and they held each other for a long moment without saying anything. 'I came round to pick up his pyjamas,' said Lisa as she broke away.

'I guessed as much.'

Lisa looked into Kincaid's eyes for a moment and then burst into tears. Kincaid did his best to comfort her.

'He's going to die, isn't he?'

'He has lung cancer and it's true there's no cure, but the doctors seem confident that he has a while to go yet. They're going to operate to remove the tumour. They'll know more then.'

Kincaid put his arm gently around Lisa's shoulder as he saw the tears start again and said, 'He's going to be around to see his new grandchild, that's for sure, so don't go upsetting yourself. You've got your baby to think about.' He made some tea which they drank before Lisa said she was leaving for the hospital. Looking at her tear-stained face Kincaid said, 'Hang on, I'll come with you.'

Neil Tolkien arrived for morning surgery at ten past eight. Officially, he wouldn't start seeing patients till eight-thirty, but as always he had paperwork to catch up on. He undid the four locks that secured the heavy front door and pushed it open with his shoulder. In this area the locks were necessary. He heard the sound of mail being swept across the floor and stooped to pick it up, two bills and half a dozen bits of advertising literature.

It was cold, but then it nearly always felt cold in the old house he used as his surgery. A great deal of the property in the street had been allowed to fall into such a state of disrepair that it was now council policy to demolish the whole area in the not-too-distant future, so there was no question of installing central heating. It was a case of starting from scratch every morning. A cleaner came in three mornings a week, but this was not one of her days.

Tolkien laid the mail down on an old dresser in the hall and searched for matches to light the gas fire before taking off his overcoat. He sniffed the air and detected again the stale, musty smell that haunted the place.

He carried out a brief tidying up operation in the patients' waiting-room, stacking old magazines neatly into piles on the dining-table that occupied the centre of the room and emptying the waste-paper bins. He turned on the electric fan heater and straightened the chairs. A child had left a lollipop on one of them and it had welded itself to the fabric. He cursed and went to get a wet cloth to free it. He was doing this when his receptionist arrived.

'Good morning, Dr Tolkien,' said the newcomer, a woman in her early thirties with auburn hair that did not look entirely natural.

'Morning, Mrs Prosser. Cold again.'

'It's bitter,' replied the woman rubbing her hands against her sleeves and hugging herself. She was wearing the traditional white overall of the receptionist but had donned a large, purple Shetland cardigan over it. 'I think that smell's getting worse, you know.'

'It's not getting any better,' agreed Tolkien.

'You're in early this morning.'

'I'm hoping to get away sharp to attend the do at the hospital this afternoon.'

'Oh yes, I heard about that. Another excuse for a sherry party on the rates.'

'A new era in health care for all of us,' replied Tolkien, repeating the blurb that the local papers had been carrying and stifling a yawn.

'Late night, Doctor?'
'I was called out at three this morning; Mrs Lawton's baby.'
'Serious?'
'Wind.'

Tolkien got on with his paperwork before the first of the day's patients arrived. It was largely a case of tidying up the card index and filing lab reports that had arrived in the post. He looked at the new computer monitor sitting on his desk and considered that from tomorrow what he was doing now would be a thing of the past. All patients' files and records would be available from the central computer based at College Hospital. Tolkien could not see himself trusting the computer entirely from the word go. It would have to prove itself before he got rid of all his little record cards.

The sound of the front door opening and shutting at intervals told him that the waiting-room was filling up. He cleared his desk and pressed the bell for the first of his patients to enter.

A slight woman in her early sixties with narrow shoulders that seemed weighed down with anxieties entered the room and sat down at Tolkien's invitation. She folded her hands in her lap and looked at her knees as if reluctant to speak.

'It's your husband,' said Tolkien. 'You can't cope.'

The woman looked up at him as if he had read her mind. 'That's right, Doctor,' she said, in a surprised and almost imperceptible whisper.

'It's nothing to be ashamed of, Mrs Harrison,' said Tolkien softly. 'Your husband is totally dependent on you for everything and it's just getting too much for you.'

The woman's face was etched with the torment of guilt. 'He's just so heavy, and getting him on and off the toilet . . .'

'I know,' nodded Tolkien.

'We've been married for forty-two years and I love him dearly, but I don't know what I'm going to do.' The woman broke down in tears.

Tolkien was seeing an all too familiar picture. 'Don't upset yourself,' he soothed. 'We'll have to find Harry a place in a home where he will be looked after properly.'

'But we promised each other that there would no homes while the other was fit and able . . .'

Tolkien held up his hand and said, 'You have nothing to be ashamed of. You have done more than any loving wife could be expected to do and now you can't cope. You're making yourself ill. It will be better for Harry, too. You'll be able to visit him every day if you want to. Now, will you let me see what I can do?'

The woman nodded silently, still clutching her handkerchief to her face.

Most of Tolkien's patients were in their sixties and seventies, testifying to the increased life expectancy of the population. They were presented with all the usual problems of old age. He dealt with them almost on autopilot, having to remind himself constantly that this was something he should not do. Complacency was the constant enemy of the GP, and while it might be understandable because ninety per cent, if not more, were absolutely routine ailments, fate had a way of slipping the odd joker into the pack. This was the case with his next patient.

Tolkien's patient announced himself as Frank Golightly, aged forty-five. He had never had a day's illness in his life, but was now feeling constantly tired and even ill.

Tolkien mentally marked him down as a case of acute middle age, but examined him and noted that there were areas of slack skin about his body. 'You've been losing weight recently,' he said.

'Yes I have,' agreed Golightly. 'Pressure of work, I suppose.'

'What do you do, Mr Golightly?'

'Sales Rep. Fork-lift trucks.'

'Travel abroad much?'

'A fair bit.'

Tolkien's attention had alighted on a series of small spots about Golightly's body. At the beginning of the examination he had been prepared to find an overworked businessman whose body was beginning to protest at too much travel and too many irregular meals, but now he was seeing something quite different and it chilled him. He carried on with the examination, not that there was much doubt in his mind; he needed time to think and work out how best to handle the situation. Each question he asked brought an answer that only served to confirm his fears, before he asked, 'Are you homosexual, Mr Golightly?'

Golightly reacted with barely disguised outrage. 'No, I'm bloody well not! I'm married. What's that got to do with anything?'

Tolkien said simply, 'Just a routine question, Mr Golightly.'

There was a long pause before Golightly suddenly said, 'Oh, my God . . .' He went deathly pale and said in a barely audible voice, 'You think I've got Aids, don't you?'

Tolkien was taken aback. He hadn't expected Golightly to read his mind. He considered stalling but then decided against it. He said gently, 'I think you should be blood-tested. I'm worried about these spots on your body. I think they may be a condition called Kaposi's sarcoma. It's one of the commonest problems associated with Aids.'

'But I'm not a bloody queer, Doctor, honest. It's always been birds for me.'

Tolkien nodded and said, 'I'm sorry, but you can get it through heterosexual contact too. It's not as common but it happens.'

Golightly suddenly became angry. 'Bloody German bitch!' he ranted, 'I'd like to cut her bloody throat!' He leaned across Tolkien's desk, eyes blazing, but all he found there was a numbing hint of sadness in Tolkien's eyes. The words died on his lips and he sank back into the chair. 'What does it matter? Oh Christ, what does it matter . . .'

Tolkien said, 'I'm not going to pretend that it's any less serious than you think it is, but we can do something. We can treat the sarcoma and there's a drug called AZT; it's not a cure but it can slow down development of the disease dramatically and who knows, with all the research that's being carried out . . .'

Golightly no longer heard what Tolkien was saying. For the moment he was in a nightmare world of his own.

THREE

Kincaid followed the arrows and found himself in the Sir Mortimer Huxley Memorial Hall of College Hospital. There was an almost familiar coldness and impersonal aura about the place; it brought back memories of school assembly halls and of university ceremonies where gowned figures, round-shouldered with the weight of their dignity, would expound their views of life and how it should be lived.

He examined his present surroundings and his eyes settled on a stone bust, which he surmised must be the titular Sir Mortimer. He could not verify this because it was on the other side of the hall from the seats allotted to the press. As far as he could determine Sir Mortimer had not been God's gift to women, being fat-faced, bald and somewhat short of a neck. His severe expression made Kincaid wince even at a distance. 'Not over-burdened with the milk of human kindness, I'd say,' he said to his neighbour.

The man smiled and said, 'Not many of them are. I suppose you have to be a bit arrogant to deal with other people's lives the way they do.'

'True,' said Kincaid.

'I just wish they wouldn't treat the rest of us like mental defectives with no right to know anything about our own bodies,' replied the other reporter.

'The mushroom syndrome,' smiled Kincaid. 'Keep 'em in the dark and feed 'em bullshit.'

The conversation came to a halt and a hush fell over the hall as the platform party took their places. Once again, Kincaid

52

found himself watching the hospital manager, Gordon Fields, step up to a microphone.

'It is my very pleasant duty to welcome you all here to mark another big step forward in health care in this region,' Fields began. 'As you all know, it was the good fortune of the north of England and in particular College Hospital, to be chosen by the minister of health, Mr John Carlisle, to spearhead his new health initiative, something that has benefited the hospital and indeed, the people of this region beyond all expectation.'

Applause.

'It is only fitting, therefore, that we have with us today, to inaugurate the next phase of health care, the minister himself, Mr John Carlisle.'

Genuinely warm applause filled the hall as the minister, immaculate in a dark blue suit with a white carnation in his buttonhole, stepped forward to take over from Fields. 'Thank you, Mr Fields, and may I say how delighted I am to be here at College Hospital again. Little did I think a year ago that we would be able to proceed with the next improvement to health care in the region so soon, but thanks to the good sense of my colleagues in government – and to the Russians for allowing us to reduce our defence spending' – laughter – 'we are now in a position to press ahead. In my book, the health of our nation is a number one priority.'

More applause.

'While I am health minister, there will be no compromise. Our people deserve the best and that is exactly what they will get, and I mean everyone. There will be no "two tier system" while I am in charge, no one service for the rich and one for the poor. The finest medicine will be available to all.'

Prolonged applause broke out and Carlisle had to hold up his hand for quiet before he could continue. 'We had to start somewhere, and where better than the north?' More applause. 'Today it gives me the greatest of pleasure to extend the computerised pharmacy facilities at the hospital to all general practitioners in the region. But before I do so, I would like to introduce to you the people who are really responsible for the revolution in health care in this area, the specialist management team at College Hospital, Mr Gordon Fields, Mr Charles French and Mr Paul Schreiber.'

Carlisle joined in the applause himself and then turned back to the microphone. 'And now I declare the second phase of the Northern Health Care Scheme open.'

Kincaid exchanged glances with his neighbour. It had been some time, excepting party conferences of course, since he had heard such applause for a politician.

A man speaking with the first regional accent of the day stumbled through a vote of thanks to the minister, not appearing to know where to look for any length of time. His head moved backwards and forwards between the platform party and the audience like a Wimbledon spectator following a rally. He thanked all and sundry, 'For making it all possible,' then he reminisced about medical care when he was young. He ended by announcing that there would be a sherry reception in the adjoining suite to which all present were cordially invited. Afterwards, it would be possible for those interested to visit the computer centre. Staff would be on hand to answer questions.

Kincaid looked for familiar faces in the crowd at the reception and saw Tolkien. Unlike almost all the others present, Tolkien was not wearing a suit. Instead he favoured a brown corduroy jacket with elbow patches and grey corduroy trousers which had gone baggy at the knees. He was standing alone, sipping sherry and looking a bit out of place among the practised cocktail party conversation that surrounded him.

'Hello again,' said Kincaid, as he edged up to him.

'So you managed to come,' said Tolkien.

'I took your advice,' said Kincaid. 'I thought Carlisle was impressive.'

'I agree. How's your father?'

'You were right. The hospital have admitted him. They're going to operate tomorrow.'

Tolkien nodded and took a sip of his sherry.

'What I don't understand is how his own doctor thought it was bronchitis,' said Kincaid, looking at Tolkien.

'You don't expect me to say anything, I hope,' said Tolkien.

'I suppose not,' agreed Kincaid. 'When it comes to closing ranks you lot are in a class of your own.'

'Don't be too hard. We're all human,' said Tolkien. 'It's just that our shortcomings tend to be more obvious than most, when they occur.'

Kincaid conceded in silence. 'So you've got yourself a computer, then,' he said, changing the subject.

Tolkien smiled and said, 'I certainly have. Like the man said, we all have. It sits on my desk in the surgery where my paper knife used to be.'

'Progress.'

'I suppose.'

'Do you think it'll work?'

'The new system? Everything else has, so we'll have to give it every chance.'

'No reservations?'

'Lots, but nothing I can articulate sensibly.'

'What do you mean?' asked Kincaid.

'I feel like a field marshal who has been told that there aren't going to be any more wars. I think I've become so used to arguing and fighting with health boards that I'm going to miss writing to the papers about government neglect and complacency. In short, I've got nothing to complain about any more and I feel at a loose end.'

'The British are brought up to believe in having to struggle for everything. They feel guilty when things go well without having to suffer.' said Kincaid.

'The efficacy of any medicine is in inverse proportion to the sweetness of its taste,' said Tolkien.

'Exactly,' smiled Kincaid. He looked around the room and asked, 'Who should I talk to if I'm to find out more about future plans?'

Tolkien nodded towards a group in the corner and said, 'These chaps are on the regional board. They must know something.'

'I'll give it a try.'

Kincaid went in search of more sherry first. The talk in the crowd was all about Carlisle and what a difference he had made to the failing fortunes of the government.

Carlisle was a relative newcomer to the front benches but his rise had been 'meteoric', to use the word the papers always favoured. Overnight success always captured the popular imagination. He was seen as a caring man of the people, never an easy accolade for a politician to attain.

Kincaid approached the group that Tolkien had pointed out and introduced himself. 'I wonder if I might have a word with you about future plans?' he asked.

'One of the men held out his hand and said, 'I'm George Mellor, acting press officer for the board. How can I help you?'

The other men drifted away, leaving Kincaid alone with Mellor.

'I was wondering if you had any plans for improving care for the mentally handicapped in the area?'

'Indeed we do,' replied Mellor. 'Is this a particular interest of yours, Mr Kincaid?'

'I have a personal interest,' confessed Kincaid. He told the man about Kerry.

'I understand that the management team have appointed a mental health director. He will start within the next week or so. This is a new post and it will be his job to implement any changes he sees fit to benefit patients.'

'This is good news,' said Kincaid.

'This is the Northern Health Scheme, Mr Kincaid,' said Mellor.

Kincaid felt good as he followed the throng to the computer control centre. His chances of having Kerry reassessed must now be better than they had ever been. His step was light as he followed a couple along the main hospital corridor who looked as if they were dressed for a royal garden party, the woman sporting a hat with a brim wider than her shoulders. The smell in the pastel green corridor was of ether and antiseptics, the smell of hospitals all over the world, thought Kincaid. The party turned left at the appropriate sign and was channelled through swing doors which gave access to a fly-over bridge, connecting the main hospital with the computer and pharmacy centre. Below him Kincaid could see the ambulance depot with two vehicles waiting on the departure grid. One of them was the specially equipped unit which responded to major road accidents. Long may you sit still, thought Kincaid.

The visitors were led into a large, low-ceilinged room where Kincaid counted fourteen people working at computer terminals. A sign told them that this room was the administration centre of the hospital. It reminded him a little of Mission Control at NASA but here the programmers had pallid skin and the accents were northern.

'This is the main operations room for the service,' explained the man who had been introduced on the platform as Charles French. He had an air of authority about him which Kincaid found compelling. Although there was a fair amount of chatter among the group that packed into the room it ceased as soon as French started to speak. He wasn't a large man and he wasn't speaking loudly but Kincaid, standing at the back, heard every word he said. French's accent was definitely not local. Kincaid guessed at Oxbridge.

'Four of our people here are engaged in updating the main computer's database through lab reports and other medical information received. The others are engaged in supplying information from the files to doctors and to developing the service in general.'

'Where is the main computer?' asked the woman with the floppy hat.

'Through there,' replied French, pointing behind him.

'Can we see it?'

'Of course,' replied French. 'There won't be room for everyone at once so have a good look round and feel free to ask anything you want until it's your turn.'

Kincaid, who had no interest in looking at a main-frame computer, was happier with French's last suggestion. He took a slow walk round the operations room and looked for an approachable programmer. He decided on a man in his late twenties who was sucking the end of his pen as he gazed at the screen in front of him.

'Hello, can I ask you a few questions?' he asked.

'Of course,' answered the man with a smile. 'What do you want to know?'

'Can we start with what you're doing?'

'I'm working on the transfusion service at the moment.'

'Blood?' asked Kincaid tentatively.

The man nodded and explained, 'I'm developing a computer programme which will deal with all aspects of blood management in the region. The idea is to feed all the data about blood donors in the region into the computer, along with their groups and sub-groups, and correlate this with the needs of the blood bank in the hospital. When stocks are getting low, the computer will automatically send out cards to appropriate donors requesting that they come in to make a donation.'

'Sounds like a great idea,' said Kincaid.

'Details of all surgery in the area will also be made available to the computer so that it can anticipate the need for blood and act accordingly. It's also going to collect data from patients undergoing blood tests in the hospital for other reasons, and suggest to the ones with rare blood groups that they might consider becoming donors.'

'I didn't think patients were routinely blood-grouped,' said Kincaid.

'They're not in other regions, but here a whole range of tests are performed on patients when they come into hospital for whatever reason and the data sorted in Micky.'

'Micky's the computer, I take it?'

'An acronym derived from Medical Information Coordinator.'

'I see,' replied Kincaid, with as much enthusiasm as he could muster for acronyms; some months before he had resolved not to give any more money to charities who used acronyms.

'Do you want to talk to him? Ask him a question.'

Ignoring the masculine gender that had been bestowed upon the computer, another of Kincaid's pet hates, he asked, 'What sort of question?'

'Micky is in charge of medicine here, so ask him anything you like.'

'How many babies were born in the region last Thursday?'

The operator's fingers leapt over the keyboard and almost instantly information leapt on to the screen:

January 14
Live Births: Eighty-four
Male: Forty-six
Female: Thirty-eight
Press 1 for delivery site.
Press 2 and enter password for names and addresses
Press 3 and enter password for medical data

'I'm impressed,' said Kincaid. 'But what medical data can you possibly hold on newborn babies?'

'Let's pretend that you are a doctor on the staff of this hospital.' The operator entered a password on the keyboard and then pressed 3. A list of names was displayed alphabetically on the screen along with results of blood and biochemical tests. 'All newborn babies in the region are subject to an automatic range of tests and the data fed to Micky so that they are known to him from day one of their lives. If in three years time one of them should run out into the road and get knocked down and subsequently require a blood transfusion, Micky will tell the surgeon exactly the right blood-type to give the child, and if by any chance it should be a rare group and none available, Micky will supply the names of suitable donors along with their names and addresses.

'Makes a lot of sense,' said Kincaid. 'My father has just been admitted as a patient here at the hospital. What have you got on him?'

'I'm sorry, I can't show you that. Patients' files have to be confidential and are only available to medical staff.'

'Don't be sorry,' said Kincaid, 'I would have yelled blue murder if you had.'

'You're not an inspector, are you?' asked the man, with a smile that was tinged with unease.

'No, I'm not. I'm a journalist.'

'Even worse,' said the man.

'I wasn't trying to catch you out,' said Kincaid. 'I'm just interested.'

The programmer looked unconvinced. 'You hear such horrendous stories about journalists these days and what they can do to ordinary people.'

Kincaid nodded and said, 'I know. It shouldn't be that way, but it is. A few bad apples in the barrel and we all start to smell.' He held out his hand and introduced himself.

The man seemed more relaxed and took Kincaid's hand. 'Dave Holland,' he said.

'Dave, tell me about the new pharmacy service. How is that going to work?'

'It's quite simple, really. When a patient visits his doctor and the doctor makes a diagnosis, the doctor will enter all details into his computer link along with his recommendation for treatment. The computer here at the centre will evaluate all the information and pass on the request for drugs to the pharmacy. They will supply the medicine and it will be delivered to the patient's local chemist within three hours. When the patient next visits his doctor his progress on treatment will be relayed to the computer. The computer will not only assess how successful it has been but can also compare the information with all the other files of patients who have been given similar treatment.'

'Sounds impressive,' said Kincaid.

'It is. It's like an automatic, clinical trial of all treatments which the computer will constantly update and make recommendations on.'

'How about costs. Does the computer keep track of that too?'

Holland shrugged his shoulders and said, 'I'm really not sure about that.' He swivelled round in his chair and asked if any of the others knew. No one did.

'Someone must,' said Kincaid.

'Of course,' said Holland. 'We can ask Mr French when he comes back.'

The first group returned from viewing the main-frame computer and Holland asked French if he could spare a moment to answer Kincaid's question.

'Of course,' replied French. He shook hands with Kincaid, smiling as he looked him straight in the eye. 'How can I help you?'

'I was asking about costs, Mr French,' said Kincaid.

'Costs?'

'I was asking your programmer here if the computer kept track of costs.'

'Of course it does,' replied French.

'None of your staff seemed to know anything about accounting for the service,' said Kincaid.

French smiled, but Kincaid thought he saw a flash of annoyance cross his face. 'The people here are concerned with the medical aspects of the service. Accounts, although done by the computer, are passed directly to the DHSS in London.'

'Isn't that a bit unusual?' asked Kincaid. 'Aren't health budgets controlled locally?'

'This is still an experimental scheme,' said French. 'The DHSS therefore has a direct involvement.'

'I see,' said Kincaid.

'Good,' said French. 'If there are no more questions we will proceed to the pharmacy department where Dr Schreiber will be happy to show you around.'

The smell in the pharmacy department was different from the computer centre, which had an aroma of ozone and plastic; the pharmacy smelled more like the hospital. Paul Schreiber, a chubby-faced man with thinning fair hair and square-rimmed, metal-framed glasses, introduced himself and gave a brief talk on how the service operated. He spoke in carefully measured phrases as if he had suffered from a stammer in early life and speech therapy had cured it.

The substance of the talk was more or less what Holland had told Kincaid. A man in Kincaid's group who introduced himself as a local GP asked how many people worked in the pharmacy.

'Two,' replied French.

'Only two?' replied the doctor, clearly taken aback at the reply.

Schreiber smiled at his reaction and explained, 'That's all we need. We have an arrangement with chemists in the area. They supply us with standard packs of all the commonly prescribed drugs, so there is no need to dispense them on the premises. Our two in-house pharmacists are here to deal with any problems and out-of-the-ordinary requests.'

'By out-of-the-ordinary, do you mean expensive drugs?' asked another man in the visitors' group. He was also a GP and Kincaid thought he detected a tinge of hostility in his voice.

'No, I don't,' smiled French. 'I mean any drug which we don't keep routinely. For example, a patient returning from abroad might develop a tropical illness which requires a medication not normally kept on the shelves. The computer would allocate such a request a special file and this would be passed on to our pharmacists, who would order the drug and dispense it themselves.'

The GP did not seem entirely satisfied and Kincaid sensed he had a point to make.

'Earlier today,' said the doctor, 'I prescribed Elocin for one of my patients. Your computer altered my request and supplied Kalocin instead. I would like to know why.'

'Kalocin is cheaper,' said French, matter-of-factly.

A look of triumph appeared on the doctor's face. 'So you admit it,' he said triumphantly.

'Absolutely, Doctor,' replied French. 'Where a cheaper alternative exists, the computer will supply it.'

'If there are any journalists here I hope they are taking note,' said the GP, now red in the face. 'This is deliberate interference by the government for financial reasons. It's monstrous!'

Schreiber, still calm and collected, smiled and said, 'The reasons are not entirely financial, Doctor. Kalocin is just as good as Elocin or the computer would not have altered your prescription.'

'I am the judge of what is best for my patients,' said the doctor, just a little pompously, thought Kincaid.

'The computer deals in hard facts, Doctor. It doesn't require judgement, and what's more it isn't subject to the wiles of glossy advertising as we mere mortals are. Come here, everyone, and watch.'

Schreiber led the party to a computer terminal and typed in the request, Elocin v. Kalocin. The computer responded with the results of several clinical trials on both drugs and finished with the mathematical conclusion that there was no difference in terms of clinical response. 'That's why the computer gave your patient Kalocin,' said Schreiber, 'because it's cheaper and is just as effective.'

The GP was left looking embarrassed and wishing, Kincaid suspected, that he had never opened his mouth.

The party were taken on a tour of the giant stock-room where drugs were stored in convenient quantities, all ready to slide down chutes to the staff below who would see them on their way to their destination. There were several questions about how dangerous drugs were stored and the security of the building, and then the tour was over.

Kincaid had a cup of tea in the hospital canteen and then went up to the ward where his father was, hoping that the sister would let him in outside visiting times. There was no problem. He was shown into the ward where he found his father lying on his side facing away from the door. Kincaid thought he might be sleeping and tip-toed over, but then he saw that the old man's eyes were wide open. 'How are you doing?' he asked.

'All right, man.'

'Worried about tomorrow?'

'Wouldn't you be?' replied Jack Kincaid.

Kincaid confessed that he would, annoyed with himself that he seemed to have developed a talent for saying stupid things to his father. He wanted to get close to the old man but couldn't. He constantly found himself floundering in platitudes. 'Things will start to get better as soon as they find out what's what.'

'D'you reckon?'

'If you have to be sick there's no doubt about it, this is the place to be. I've just seen their new computer centre.'

'No bloody tea.'

'What's that?'

'I didn't get my bloody tea. Something to do with the operation tomorrow.'

'Oh, I see,' said Kincaid, pleased that the old man was showing signs of spirit.

'I think the buggers want to starve me to death, save them the cost of the operation.'

Kincaid smiled. 'It's for your own good,' he said. 'You've got to have an empty stomach in case the anaesthetic makes you vomit.'

Jack Kincaid turned over and faced his son. He said, 'If anything should go wrong tomorrow you won't forget about St Mary's, will you?'

Kincaid said, 'Nothing's going to go wrong, man.' His father kept waiting for an answer. In the end Kincaid said, 'No, I won't forget.' He put his hand on his father's shoulder and squeezed it gently before getting up and saying, 'I'll see you when it's over.'

Kincaid left the hospital feeling that his father had started out on a journey that could have no happy ending. With the old man's admission to hospital the first step had been taken, and somehow, regardless of the outcome of the operation, things would never be the same again. He remembered that this had been the case with his mother. There was something about the first time that a person with a terminal illness went into hospital, something which changed them, distanced them from their families. No matter how hard the others might try to recapture the way things were, the patient seemed to drift out of reach. After that, the gap could only widen.

Kincaid decided to walk for a while, despite the drizzle which soft-focused the streetlights and settled gently on his hair. He opted for the quieter back streets where the noise of traffic would not distract his thoughts. He had gone about half a mile when he started to feel uneasy. This feeling was connected with the brief glimpse of a figure in a dark raincoat. He had caught sight of the man previously when he turned his head before crossing a street. His subconscious reminded him that he had seen the same figure courting the shadows outside his father's ward. The hairs began to rise on the back of his neck: he was being followed.

Kincaid tried to dismiss the notion as ridiculous, something that only happened in films. For God's sake, you're a journalist, not Phillip Marlowe, he told himself. He walked on for a bit and then turned sharply to pretend to look in a shop window. Not a convincing move, he had to admit; the window belonged to a plumber's workshop and it displayed a solitary sink covered in cobwebs.

Once again, he caught a glimpse of someone behind him. The figure merged into the shadows. A mugger, perhaps? There was still half a mile or so to cover before he reached the lights of the main road. Prudence said he should increase his pace, but natural, maybe professional curiosity, disagreed. He felt in his pocket and filled his right fist with a handful of coins.

There were a number of lanes leading off the road he was on. Kincaid ducked down the first one and broke into a sprint. He found a deep doorway and slid quickly into it. If he really was being followed he would soon know, because the only light in the lane came from a streetlamp up on the main road. Anyone entering the lane would cast a long shadow.

There was a deathly silence as he waited with his cheek pressed up against the rough stone at the side of the doorway. He was aware of the pulse beating in his neck and the smell of cats' urine in the lane. Suddenly the walls were alive with a dancing shadow. Someone had started down into the lane. There was no sound of footsteps. Whoever it was, was moving stealthily. Kincaid tensed himself and prepared to hit out.

The shadow disappeared and Kincaid became anxious. He strained to hear something but nothing disturbed the stillness in the lane. Had his follower stopped because he suspected something? Perhaps he had a knife. Kincaid had a sudden mental image of himself lying on the foul-smelling cobbles with his life-blood staining the stones black in the neon light. It made him swallow hard and then regret it as he considered it might have been audible to his pursuer. He thought he heard something and raised his fist again.

The seconds passed and the tension became unbearable.

Inside Kincaid's head he feared the worst. The man must suspect an ambush, otherwise why would he move so slowly? With the element of surprise taken away, he felt hopelessly vulnerable. He heard a breath being taken, a small shallow one, but very near. A shadow started to cross the doorway and Kincaid shot out his arm to curl it round the neck that followed. He secured a headlock and brought up his knee into the small of the man's back. 'Why are you following me?' he demanded.

Warning signals flooded into Kincaid's head as perfume and softness filled his senses. A squeal and feminine splutters of protest made him instantly relax his grip. 'What on earth?' he exclaimed, as he allowed the writhing figure to break free.

'You could have choked me!' exclaimed an outraged girl, rubbing her neck.

'I thought you were a mugger!' protested Kincaid. 'Why were you following me? What do you want?' He was more embarrassed than angry.

'Do I look like a mugger?' asked the girl.

Kincaid had to admit that she did not. The dark raincoat was a nurse's Burberry and the 'mugger' was a slim, attractive girl with auburn hair and soft, brown intelligent eyes. What was more, he knew her. It was Staff Nurse Eve Laing.

FOUR

Tuesday night was Neil Tolkien's night in attendance at a drug rehabilitation centre that he and two colleagues had set up on the large sprawling council estate near their practices. With the decline of industry in the north and the consequent rise in unemployment in the early Eighties, the scene had been set for social disaster. Many young people were faced with no prospect of a job and thus no access to the pleasures of the consumer society others enjoyed. They had fallen easy prey to the drug barons from the south, who had been quick to see their opportunity and exploit it. Heroin, which in previous decades had been a substance confined to American film-sets, became the everyday currency of socially deprived areas of the country. Crime and prostitution had risen to satisfy the Fagin-like demands of increasing addiction.

The centre itself was a prefabricated cabin of the sort used by building firms on construction sites. It stood on the edge of a green area which was used more by dogs than children, the children preferring to play in the tunnels and alleys of the concrete landscape which corralled them.

Gavin Mitchell, a red-faced GP in his early fifties wearing a tweed jacket and checked shirt, looked up as Tolkien entered the office. 'Just in time, Neil,' he said, nodding towards a shorter, female colleague who was unwrapping a bottle of wine. The woman, Dr Mary Cunningham, smiled and said, 'Not Dom Perignon, I'm afraid, but it will have to do at short notice.' She handed the bottle to Tolkien and asked him to open it.

Tolkien took the bottle of Spanish cava and asked, 'What are we celebrating?'

'We have been officially recognised,' replied Mitchell.

'We have?'

'Indeed we have,' smiled the woman. 'The health board have decided that we can come in from the cold. In short, our clinic now has an official blessing. We have even been given our own computer terminal on line to the main one at the College Hospital.'

'Well, well,' sighed Tolkien. 'What can I say?'

'There's more,' said Mitchell. 'Free and plentiful supplies of needles and condoms for us to distribute as we see fit.'

'Why the change of heart?' asked Tolkien, only too aware of the problems the clinic had had in the past with regard to supplies and funding.

'The Northern Health Scheme,' said Mary Cunningham. 'We are to be part of it. Mr Carlisle wants a completely integrated health care programme for the region. There are to be no more poor relation fringe groups.'

The wine cork popped and Tolkien filled the glasses that were held out. He began to feel elated at the prospect of no longer having to battle for resources with a reactionary health board who thought drug addiction could be tackled by lectures on 'pulling yourself together'. A ready supply of free needles would enable them to tackle the nightmare of needle sharing, which they all knew was responsible for the rapid spread of HIV infection and consequent Aids among drug addicts. Being able to give prostitutes supplies of condoms would help protect them and their clients from the sexual transmission of Aids.

'What's more, we are going to be allowed to use AZT prophylactically if we choose to,' said the woman.

Tolkien's eyes widened. 'But what about the cost?' he asked.

AZT was one of the few drugs found to be effective in treating Aids patients. It did not cure them but it slowed down the progress of the disease. American research had suggested that patients given AZT as soon as they were diagnosed as carrying the HIV virus fared much better than patients who received it later on. The prohibitive cost of the drug had prevented similar trials in the UK and only patients recognised as having crossed certain clinical boundaries received it.

'Health care comes before money,' replied Mitchell, 'that's what Mr Carlisle said.'

'I'm beginning to think it's Christmas morning,' said Tolkien, 'but the money must be coming from somewhere.'

'Personally, I'm not even going to ask,' said Mitchell.

'Neither am I,' agreed Mary Cunningham.

Tolkien thought he heard a noise outside the cabin. He turned to look out of the window. 'I think we have a customer,' he said, seeing a figure in a leather jacket approaching. 'I'll look after him.'

Tolkien felt as if he had seen the figure in front of him all too often before. The boy was twenty years old yet looked thirty-five, thanks to general emaciation and bad skin. His eyes had the hunted look of an addict and his hands never stopped moving as he fidgeted with each finger in turn.

'They said you could help me?'

'I hope so,' said Tolkien.

'I want to come off.'

'Good. What's your name?'

'Terry. Terry Feenan. I mean it,' said the boy.

'Yes.' Tolkien's reply was matter-of-fact. Long association with addicts had taught him to observe certain ground rules and number one was, never believe what an addict says. Always look for an angle.

The boy seemed taken aback at Tolkien's lack of reaction. 'What more do you want?' he asked, with just a hint of aggression.

'A reason,' replied Tolkien.

'A reason?' exclaimed the boy. 'Isn't it obvious, for Christ's sake? It costs a bloody fortune.'

'So you want to get off for financial reasons?'

'That's right.'

'You're wasting my time,' said Tolkien.

The boy reacted angrily. 'What's the use?' he exclaimed. 'Doctors? You're all the same. You don't give a shit. If I'm driven to crime it's your fault, and don't fucking well forget it!' He got up to go.

Tolkien watched the performance calmly. 'Driven to crime?' he mimicked. 'Driven to crime? Where did you get your script? You'll be telling me next you've been financing your habit to date with a paper round. I think I'm looking at a gram a day. Am I right?'

The boy calmed down and nodded.

'Roll up your sleeves.'

The boy complied and Tolkien looked at the track marks on his arms. 'Now your trousers.'

Tolkien whistled when he saw the backs of the boy's legs. 'What a mess,' he murmured. 'How long?'

'Three years,' replied the boy.

'If you go on like this you're going to lose your legs.'

The boy nodded.

'Are you going to tell me why you really came here?' asked Tolkien.

'It's my girlfriend, Karen.'

'She's on it too?'

'Yeah. We got a baby, see. Judith, she's two. It was her birthday yesterday. Karen had got her a cake and I was just sitting there watching her play when I thought, maybe this is the last time, maybe Karen and I won't see her next birthday. Maybe we'll both be dead and who'll look after her then? I wanted Karen to come here too but – she's working.'

Tolkien asked the question with his eyes and the boy nodded and dropped his head. 'Yeah,' he said. 'She's on the game. We need the money.'

'Who's looking after Judith tonight?'

'Me mam.'

'Who's your own doctor?' asked Tolkien. The boy told him. 'Did you go to see him?'

The boy nodded.

'What did he say?'

'Told me to piss off.'

It was Tolkien's turn to nod, knowing the doctor in question.

He felt sure he wouldn't have used those words, but the bottom line would have been the same.

'All right,' said Tolkien. 'We'll give it a go.'

'What happens?' asked the boy.

'I'm going to change you to a drug called methadone. It's a heroin substitute. You take it orally so there will be no more injections, track marks or collapsed veins from now on. It's supplied on special daily prescription which I'll arrange for you. Central Pharmacy will supply it through your local chemist if you tell me who that is.'

'Jackson in Alberley Street,' said the boy.

Tolkien noted it down. 'I think I should see Karen and the baby,' he said.

'I'll try to persuade her,' said the boy. 'But she doesn't trust anyone, see.'

'Try,' said Tolkien.

The boy got up to go.

'There's one more thing,' said Tolkien. 'I need some blood for testing, assuming I can find a vein that you haven't knackered already.'

For the third time, Kincaid, still feeling embarrassed, asked Eve Laing if she was sure she was all right.

The nurse looked at the concern on Kincaid's face and relaxed. 'I suppose it was my fault, really, I wanted to talk to you.'

'Talk to me?' exclaimed Kincaid.

'Without anyone knowing,' she added.

Kincaid felt the hairs rise on the back of his neck. 'About Greta Marsh?' he asked.

'Yes,' replied the girl. 'You were right. There is something wrong.' She looked about her and Kincaid took the point. The lane was wet and cold and it smelled bad.

'Why don't we find a pub?' he suggested.

Eve Laing shook her head and said, 'I don't want to be seen talking to you in public. I could lose my job.'

Kincaid thought for a moment.

'How about your hotel?' suggested Eve.

Kincaid told her that he did not have one. He was staying at his father's house.

'Can we go there?'

Kincaid hailed a taxi when they got to the main thoroughfare and held the door open for Eve.

They exchanged a word or two about the weather, but mostly they sat in awkward silence as the cab weaved through the city streets, it's wipers continually flicking away the persistent drizzle that looked as if it might turn to more rain before long.

The taxi pulled up outside Kincaid's father's house and Kincaid paid off the driver. 'It's not the Ritz,' he said, as he unlocked the front door and fumbled with the light switch, 'and it's cold.'

With the gas fire creating a semi-circle of warmth and steaming mugs of coffee in their hands, Kincaid looked at Eve. He observed her hands in detail, noting her long, elegant fingers. He imagined her sitting at a piano. She was nervous and her eyes still had the troubled look that he had seen at Greta Marsh's press conference. When she spoke it was with a pleasant, even voice which held no trace of an accent that Kincaid could detect. 'Now then,' he said, 'what's all this about?'

'I think something awful has happened to Greta Marsh,' said Eve.

'She seemed all right at the press conference,' said Kincaid.

'I don't think that was Greta Marsh.'

Kincaid's mouth fell open. 'Say that again,' he said, slowly.

Eve had become even more nervous. She shifted uncomfortably in her seat and twisted her scarf into ever-tightening folds. 'I don't think the woman you saw was Greta Marsh,' she repeated.

'So who was it, then?' asked Kincaid, struggling to come to terms with what he was hearing.

'I don't know.'

'Suppose you start at the beginning?' suggested Kincaid.

Eve took a sip of her coffee. 'I was one of the nurses who looked after Greta Marsh when she came back from the operating theatre. Her face was heavily bandaged, of course, so I never saw her face, but I did see the rest of her.'

'And?' prompted Kincaid, noticing that Eve was beginning to have second thoughts about telling all.

'Greta had a small birthmark on the inside of her left ankle. It was shaped like a heart. The woman I bathed yesterday and saw the bandages removed from today did not have that birthmark.'

'But can you be sure it was a birthmark and not just a faded bruise?', asked Kincaid.

'It was a birthmark, I'm certain.'

'Anything else?' asked Kincaid.

'Greta Marsh was seriously ill after her operation. She was in intensive care for four days and still very ill when I last saw her. For her to have made such a complete recovery in just over four weeks is nothing short of miraculous.'

'You weren't with her when she recovered?' asked Kincaid.

'None of us were,' replied Eve.

'I don't understand.'

'Last Wednesday Greta was moved out of Sir Martin's unit. We were told that she was being taken to a private nursing home for some specialised tests.'

'Is that so unusual?' asked Kincaid.

'College Hospital is very well equipped. I can't imagine what the tests were that we couldn't do, and no one offered to tell us. Greta came back at the weekend. She was conscious, although still heavily bandaged. I asked Sister Grey what treatment Greta had been having, but she didn't know either. Later, when I was bathing Greta, I saw that her birthmark had gone.'

'So you think the woman in the bandages wasn't Greta Marsh at all,' said Kincaid, thoughtfully.

'That's about the size of it.'

'Have you said anything about this to anyone else?' he asked.

'No.'

'Not even to Sister Grey?'

'No. People were just so pleased that Greta had made such a wonderful recovery – we all were – if she really did.'

Kincaid looked at Eve. 'So it's all down to a birthmark,' he said. 'What made you tell me this?'

'I had to tell someone, it's been preying on my mind.'

'Why not your colleagues?'

'I suppose I didn't want to be seen as a troublemaker. I might lose my job. I thought, as you were a journalist, you could investigate without involving me.'

'I see,' said Kincaid.

'What are you going to do?' asked Eve.

Kincaid shrugged his shoulders and said, 'I don't know. There's not much to go on. A missing birthmark. Besides, why would they do this?'

It was Eve's turn to shrug. 'Embarrassment?' she suggested. 'The hospital is very conscious of its image.'

Kincaid looked doubtful.

'Think about it,' said Eve. 'Sir Martin invites all the press along to witness his operation and it all goes horribly wrong. Bad publicity is bad news, as far as the management team is concerned. Mr Fields insists that the hospital be presented in the best possible light. All the staff have to work at it. We have to look smart and be polite at all times.'

'Doesn't sound too bad to me,' said Kincaid. 'It's a damned sight better than sullen indifference.'

Eve moved her head from side to side to indicate both agreement and disagreement. 'Perhaps I'm explaining it badly,' she said. 'The problem is that we can't have a real conversation with the patients any more. We are obliged to project an image of cheerfulness at all times.'

'Like, "Have a nice day"?'

'That sort of thing.'

'Or else?'

'We get the sack.'

'How about the patients?' asked Kincaid.'

'They seem to like it.'

'Maybe that's the bottom line,' said Kincaid.

'Perhaps,' Eve conceded, but her voice held reservations.

'Tell me more about the hospital management,' said Kincaid.

'When the government introduced the new health scheme and modernised the hospital, control was virtually taken away from the regional health board. A management team was put in from London.'

'Didn't the regional council object?' asked Kincaid.

'They didn't seem to. I think extra money was invested in the hospital.'

'I see. Who pays the piper calls the tune?'

'A short-sighted view, if you ask me.'

'Why so?'

'Every time the scheme expands the local council will have less power and central government more.'

'Maybe that's not such a bad thing, if the patients get a better deal,' suggested Kincaid.

'I tend to think that centralised control of things is bad in principle. Too few people end up having too much power.'

'Maybe you're right,' said Kincaid, unwilling to get into a political argument, 'but to get back to Greta Marsh . . .'

'I'm sure the woman you saw at the press conference was not Greta Marsh,' said Eve.

Kincaid saw that Eve was sincere in her belief. He said, 'All right, so who was she, then? And what happened to the real Greta Marsh?'

'I can only guess,' said Eve.

'So guess.'

'I don't think Greta recovered from surgery. I think they had someone stand in for her to avoid bad publicity before the health minister's visit.'

'Good God,' said Kincaid.

'I know it sounds crazy,' said Eve, 'but it's the only way they could have done it.'

'How can we prove it?' asked Kincaid.

'Find the real Greta, I suppose.'

'I'm listening,' said Kincaid.

'I thought you journalists knew about finding people,' said Eve.

'We usually get help.'

'I do have one suggestion,' said Eve.

'I'm listening.'

'Fingleton Grange.'

'That's an asylum,' said Kincaid, who knew of the place.

'Yes, but patients who are badly brain damaged, with

little or no chance of recovery, usually end up in Fingleton Grange.'

Kincaid put Eve Laing in a taxi, paid the driver and told him to take her back to the nurses' home at College Hospital. He watched the cab drive away and waited till it had turned the corner at the end of the street before going back inside. He was still reeling. Fifteen minutes later he had decided there was nothing to be gained by deliberating any more. He would visit the asylum.

Fingleton Grange was a bleak reminder of the past, a Victorian workhouse that might have changed its name and acquired a few modern signs, but nothing to alter its forbidding façade and the legacy of misery that generations of shamed inhabitants had left locked up in its dark, stone walls. The turreted skyline of the place did little to fill Kincaid with enthusiasm for the job ahead. He walked up the drive, keeping close to the shadow of the trees.

Years of experience had taught him that there was nothing to be gained from trying to do things the way the establishment liked when there was an easier, more direct alternative. The simple truth was that the establishment didn't like anyone doing anything at all, and existed largely to stop things happening and maintain the status quo. The fact that alternative action was usually illegal did not deter Kincaid. The offence involved was usually of such a minor nature that the penalty, should it be invoked – and it seldom was in the long run – was a minor consideration. This time he was going to enter Fingleton Grange and attempt to find the real Greta Marsh.

Kincaid circled the building in the darkness and counted the entrances. There were four including the main one, which was out of the question, being at the head of a flight of stone steps, well lit and with a formidable front door that looked as if it had been designed to withstand assault by battering ram.

The kitchen door seemed to offer his best chance of access. Apart from its convenient location at the back of the building, near to clumps of berberis which offered good cover, it had another attraction. Kitchen staff had a notoriously high turn-over rate: such jobs were the mainstay of the casual labour market and unfamiliar faces were the norm.

Kincaid checked his watch and deduced that the activity he could see was concerned with the patients' supper. Trolleys were being loaded with metal-covered dishes and wheeled out into the hall for collection by porters. All he needed was the right kind of overall. He waited until the two porters he could see near the door had moved off. He crept closer to the door and tried to get a good look at the corridor. It appeared to be empty. Better than that, he could see a number of brown overalls hanging up on pegs just inside the door.

His fingers were on the handle when his luck ran out. An inside door to the main kitchen suddenly swung open and a man dressed in a chef's hat and clothing pushed a trolley into the corridor, cursing as the powerful brake on the door fought against his attempts to fend it open. For a moment the light from inside the kitchen caught Kincaid full in the face. He ducked down below the glass panel, holding his breath.

Kincaid stared at the door handle, fully expecting that at any second the chef would open it and raise the alarm. It didn't happen. The man had not seen him. The kitchen door closed again and the corridor returned to dimness. Kincaid let himself in quickly but took time to close the door quietly behind him. He lifted one of the overalls from its peg and put it on. It was a tight fit, but it would do.

Avoiding making any noise, he took the loaded trolley and wheeled it away, heading for the main hospital. He came to a junction with the main ground floor corridor and paused to look out furtively in both directions before committing himself. To the right he could see a kitchen trolley parked outside one of the wards. To the left he could see the same thing. The porters he had seen leave the kitchen earlier were servicing the ground floor. He looked back along the way he had come and saw the lift. The decision was made; he would start at the top of the building.

As the lift climbed to the fourth floor, Kincaid picked up one of the metal lids on the trolley. Potatoes and brown sludge lay underneath. He replaced the lid with a slight grimace of distaste and prepared to move out into the top corridor.

Beige walls and dull brown linoleum did nothing to brighten a badly-lit corridor which ran the entire length of the top floor of the building. Kincaid glanced at his reflection in one of the tall windows as he pushed the trolley along and decided that he looked enough like a porter to chance his luck and approach one of the staff for directions. He paused in front of a locked glass door leading to a ward and looked in. A broad-shouldered man wearing a white smock with blue epaulettes looked back at him without smiling. He got off his chair and came to the door.

Kincaid did his best to look apologetic as the door was unlocked. 'Sorry, I'm a bit lost,' he said. 'First day on the job, – you know what it's like. Is this for you?'

The man looked at the trolley and still without smiling said, 'Where's the list?'

'List?'

'The patient list. It comes with the trolley,' said the man sourly.

'I'm sorry, I didn't know,' said Kincaid. 'Where do I get that?'

'The chef, of course.'

'Sorry, I don't seem to have one.'

The broad man moved some of the plates on the trolley and withdrew a card. 'What do you think this is?' he snorted, and handed it to Kincaid who read it and said, 'Ward seven?'

'Seven?' exclaimed the man, raising his eyes heavenwards. 'You're not even on the right floor. Ward seven is on level three.' He pointed at the floor with an angry gesture.

Kincaid smiled weakly, thanked him and moved off. He had hoped for a more productive encounter, but he could see that trying to engage the surly male nurse in light conversation was a non-starter. He had learned one thing, though. There was a patient list on all the trolleys. As the lift descended he looked at the list of names in ward seven. Greta Marsh was not among them but then, he reasoned, she was hardly likely to be. If she was really being held in Fingleton it would never be under her own name, but perhaps there would be some clue in the list.

Kincaid could hear the sounds of arguing as he neared the kitchens and knew immediately that he must be the cause. The chef was questioning the two porters about the food for ward seven. They, of course, were denying all knowledge of it.

Quietly, Kincaid parked the trolley beside the service lift and tip-toed across the corridor to hide in a broom cupboard until the matter was resolved. He only had to wait a few moments before the rattle of trolley wheels told him that the porters were setting off with new loads.

'Jesus Christ! There it is!' exclaimed one of the men as he turned the corner and saw Kincaid's trolley.

'What berk put it there!' asked the other.

'Search me.'

'We'd better tell his nibs.'

'Suppose so.'

The two men left their trolleys by the lift and returned to the kitchen. Kincaid seized his opportunity and left his hiding place to snatch a look at the patient lists on each trolley. Still no clue. Maybe it was too much of a long shot. He waited until the porters had returned and gone up in the lift before going back to the kitchen. After a wait of two or three minutes, the door opened again and a small tray was placed on the rack outside. As soon as the door closed once more Kincaid moved towards it and read the card. It said, 'Special Unit 2' and there were two names on it, John Leadbetter and Miss Harrington. Kincaid remembered that Greta Marsh had spent most of her life in Harrington Hall.

All Kincaid needed now was the location of Special Unit 2 and he felt sure that he would find Greta Marsh. But he wasn't going to find a floor plan conveniently pinned up on the wall so there was nothing else for it, he would have to brass it out and ask again. He lifted the tray and headed once more for the main corridor.

There were surprisingly few people about for such a large building, thought Kincaid. His footsteps echoed on the floor and the tension grew inside him. He considered that it must have something to do with the nature of the place. Ward doors were locked and staff and patients would be largely contained within those areas, while the corridors would remain deserted.

Somewhere up ahead he could hear the sound of one of the ward doors being unlocked. A smartly-dressed woman stepped out and began to walk towards him. When she got nearer he could see the stethoscope sticking out from her pocket.

Kincaid said, 'Excuse me Doctor, I'm a bit lost, my first day, you see. I'm looking for Special Unit 2.'

The woman looked at him with an expression he was only too ready to construe as suspicious. She replied, 'Didn't they even tell you what floor the special units are on?'

Kincaid shrugged. 'I thought they said ground floor but I probably got it wrong.'

'You certainly did. They're on level two. Turn right when you get out of the lift.'

'Thanks, Doctor,' said Kincaid. He turned and headed for the lift, aware that the woman was still staring at him. He was relieved when the lift doors closed and contact was broken.

SPECIAL UNITS, said the sign, underlined by an arrow. Underneath was a reminder to staff of the the need for security and vigilance when dealing with severely unbalanced patients. Kincaid read it and wondered for whose benefit Greta Marsh had been imprisoned in such a place. He reminded himself that as yet he had not proved that she was here. He followed the arrow and came to a locked glass door which was reinforced with wire mesh. He pressed the bell at the side and waited. Two thickset men in white uniforms came out and unlocked it.

'Who are you?' asked one.

'Harry Geddes. I just started today,' said Kincaid.

'Where's the other tray?'

'The other tray?' Kincaid repeated weakly.

'You've only brought two meals. We have four patients.'

'Sorry, they only gave me two.'

'Shit, this place gets worse.'

'I'll get the others,' said Kincaid, and then he improvised. 'Oh and Chef says you've still got one of the lunch trays up here. He asked me to bring it back.'

'No we haven't,' said one of the nurses, looking for confirmation to his partner.

'That's what he said,' lied Kincaid.

'Better have a look, Norm. I'll check the duty room. Come in and wait here,' he said to Kincaid.

The door was locked again with Kincaid on the inside this time, and the two nurses went to look for the missing tray. As soon as they left him alone Kincaid grabbed his chance and slipped in through the access door to the unit itself. He closed it quietly behind him and found himself in another dimly lit corridor. It was quiet, as if the door was soundproof, but a soporific hum was coming from the air conditioning grills set at regular intervals in the ceiling. It was claustrophobically warm, but his eyes had now adjusted to the gloom.

He started to move along the corridor and came to a metal door which had a peephole set in it. He slid it back as quietly as he could and saw that it was a padded cell. In the brightly lit interior a man was pacing up and down, totally engrossed in himself, whose eyes betrayed a terrible torment. Kincaid felt himself go cold just looking at him. He hoped sincerely that he might never experience what was going on inside that man's head.

There were two more patients occupying padded cells, one sat in a corner shaking his head rhythmically from side to side, the other was kneeling as if examining some tiny insect on the floor. Kincaid came to the fourth and last cell in the line. The card in the frame outside said, Miss G Harrington. Kincaid looked through the peephole and saw that the lights inside this cell had been dimmed. In the corner of the room he could just make out a sleeping form under a blanket and protruding from the blanket, at the end nearest him, he could see the back of a head swathed in white bandages.

Suddenly Kincaid became aware of agitated voices and knew that the male nurses were hitting the panic button. In a moment they would find him. He tried the door and to his relief it opened. He slipped inside.

'Miss Marsh . . .' Kincaid whispered.

The woman in the bed did not respond.

'Miss Marsh!' he repeated urgently.

Outside he heard one of the male nurses curse and say, 'He's not bloody here!' His companion replied with an oath and the opinion that 'he' must have gone back to the kitchen.

'And locked the door, leaving the key on the inside?' asked the other, with derision.

Kincaid knew that he only had moments to find out what he had to. He was standing over the sleeping form and she seemed to be breathing as if in a deep sleep. Slowly he loosened the blanket from her feet and drew it back to expose her ankles. What was it that Eve Laing had said about Greta Marsh's birthmark? It was on the inside of her left ankle, and was shaped like a heart? The woman was lying on her left side with her right leg obscuring what Kincaid was trying to see. He moved it as gently as he could and examined her left ankle. There, plain to see, was a small strawberry birthmark in the form of a heart. Eve Laing had been right: the woman at the press briefing had not been Greta Marsh at all.

The sleeping woman suddenly turned her head and sighed. Kincaid saw her bandaged face turn towards him. He could make out nothing save the eyeholes and a dark slit in the white bandage where her mouth would be. 'Miss Marsh?' he whispered 'Don't be afraid, I mean you no harm. I'd just like to ask you a few questions. You are Greta Marsh, aren't you?'

The woman raised her right hand slowly and weakly beckoned to Kincaid to come closer. He complied and bent down so that his ear was near her mouth. He touched the outstretched fingers, finding them cold and damp. 'Miss Marsh, my name is Kincaid and I . . .'

Kincaid did not finish the sentence. He was suddenly jerked off his feet when Greta Marsh's fingers flew to his throat. She pulled his face down on hers. He could smell her breath; it was like warm onions. It competed with an unpleasant antiseptic smell from her bandages. He was so close that he could sense the very wetness of her mouth in the jagged cut in the bandages.

She swept her other hand over and drew her fingernails down

his left cheek, leaving four trails of blood before Kincaid could finally break free. Greta Marsh's maniacal laughter was ringing in his ears as he staggered backwards across the room. He was off balance and in no position to avoid the heavy swing-door as the two male nurses burst into the room. The door hit him on the back of the head and pain filled his world briefly before nothingness took over.

When Kincaid awoke, he felt as though he had been hit over the head with a hammer. He lay still for a moment, trying to remember what had happened, but even the very act of thinking seemed painful. He remembered about the birthmark and the mad laughter as Greta Marsh had sunk her nails into his cheek. Gingerly he brought his hand up to his face and felt the crust of dried blood – it was real enough. The whole thing had not been a nightmare. He really had found Greta Marsh; she was deranged and being held in Fingleton Grange. But where was he? He remembered being hit on the back of the head. But why was he cold, and why was it so dark?

Very slowly, Kincaid tried to sit up. The pain inside his head increased until nausea threatened to overwhelm him. He sank back down again on to one elbow. He was not only cold, he was wet. He was wet because he was outside. He was lying on some kind of grassy bank and it was raining because he could feel it on his cheek. He moved his fingers and felt wet grass and mud beneath them.

Suddenly a rushing started in his ears. It grew louder and louder until he thought his head must explode. The darkness was suddenly torn apart by hundreds of lights flashing, as an express train thundered past his feet at a speed of over a hundred miles an hour.

The noise and the lights, coupled with Kincaid's involuntary reaction to draw up his knees, pushed the pain level in his head beyond all toleration. He threw up helplessly as the last carriage tunnelled furiously off into the night.

Kincaid now knew where he was. He must have been brought from Fingleton Grange while still unconscious and dumped on a railway embankment. What if he had rolled down on to the track? He shuddered at the answer. What in God's name did they hope to achieve by doing this, anyway? Did they imagine that he was going to forget all about Greta Marsh and go home, or was it conceivable that he had been meant to roll down the embankment on to the line? Kincaid's sense of proportion rebelled at the thought. Someone at the Grange must have panicked, he concluded, someone who didn't want to read the story that he was now going to write.

FIVE

Before Kincaid could do anything at all he would have to get out
of his present predicament. The urge to throw up overcame him
again and once more he succumbed, much to his disgust. His
disgust turned to frustration when he attempted to stand up
and fell over helplessly to slide further down the embankment.
There was something terribly unreal about his situation, but
when he tried to put his finger on it he found that he could
not concentrate for long enough to work out what it was. He
had been transported to an alien planet where gravity and the
laws of physics were different. He looked up at the night sky.
He could see a few stars through a gap in the clouds, but he
couldn't focus on them; they were going round and round,
just as if he had had too much to drink.

The thought alarmed Kincaid, because he suddenly realised
that he could taste whisky! Drunkenness was the feeling he
couldn't understand; he was drunk – and yet he hadn't had
anything to drink. But he must have done. When he vomited
it was whisky he tasted. How in God's name . . . ?

'There he is!' said a voice somewhere above him. A torch beam
swung round and Kincaid felt it stop on his face.

'Ye gods, what a state,' said the voice. 'Can you hear me down
there?'

Kincaid opened his mouth to reply, but nothing coherent
came out.

'Pissed out of his bloody mind,' said the voice above. 'Hold
the torch, Stan; I'll get down there.'

Kincaid could only continue to look up at the stars while he heard the sound of cursing as someone slid down the embankment towards him. A few moments later a figure joined him in the torch beam; it was wearing a police uniform.

'I've got him!' shouted the man. 'Better tell the station.'

Somewhere above him Kincaid could hear the crackle of a two-way radio, then a voice asked, 'Do we need an ambulance?'

Kincaid tried to protest as rough hands began to examine him. 'I was hit on the head,' he tried to say, but it came out slurred.

'Hold still,' said the policeman, ignoring Kincaid's protests. He jerked Kincaid's head forwards, forcing him to retch involuntarily.

'Jesus Christ!' exclaimed the policeman angrily. 'What a mess. Stan! Get down here, give me a hand.'

Kincaid felt himself being dragged bodily up the embankment and then allowed to slump down again as they reached the top.

'He's got a bad gash on the back of his head,' said one of the policeman. 'We'd best call an ambulance. Don't want him dying on us.'

Kincaid was aware of what was happening, but everything in his world was still revolving. He could not speak without slurring his words. His mouth felt as if it were paralysed, a bit like the lingering effects of a local anaesthetic used by dentists. He tried to discipline himself into rational behaviour, first attempting to focus on objects in the ambulance like the oxygen cylinder strapped to the bulkhead, but it was no use. After a few seconds his head began to swim again and he gave up.

'What a state,' he heard an ambulanceman say to one of the policemen. 'Where did you find him?'

'A woman reported seeing a drunk man fall down the railway embankment. She was afraid he had fallen on to the tracks.'

'He was lucky he didn't,' replied the ambulanceman. 'He doesn't even know what day of the week it is.'

'Issh Choosday,' said Kincaid, weakly.

'Of course it is,' said the policeman patronisingly, 'and come Wednesday you'll be standing in court.'

The Accident and Emergency unit was bright and full of bustle. Although Kincaid could not see much of it, because he was screened off in a small cubicle, he could sense it and snatches of conversation broke through to him. The curtains opened and two people came in, temporarily blocking the light and allowing him a brief glimpse of their features. One was a young man with the vestiges of teenage acne on his face and a pair of spectacles which were too large for his thin features. The other was a nurse, somewhere in her mid-thirties, although with plump-faced women it was always difficult to tell. She could have been eighteen.

The houseman shone a pencil torch into his eyes and then asked a series of questions in a voice devoid of emotion. His attempts at answering were not acknowledged, and Kincaid felt as if he was taking part in a High Street marketing survey. The interview was over and the nurse dressed the back of his head. Outside the cubicle he could hear a voice, the houseman's he thought, saying, 'I'm not convinced it's only booze. We'd better empty his stomach and I'll get biochemistry to run a barbiturate check.'

'But he smells like a distillery,' a female voice protested.

'Better safe than sorry. Pump him out.'

'Empty my stomach,' thought Kincaid. As if it wasn't empty enough. A large, red-faced woman entered the cubicle and started issuing instructions to a nurse who answered, 'Yes, Sister,' at appropriate intervals. The older woman donned a plastic apron before turning to Kincaid and saying, 'Now then, we are going to be a clever boy and do our best to swallow this tube, aren't we?' Kincaid felt that he was in no position to argue. He nodded dumbly.

A plastic tube was pushed into his mouth and after some adjustment was fed down directly into his stomach. The continual urge to retch was barely held in check throughout the procedure, and the feeling when fluid was poured down into his stomach in order to wash out the contents was vile beyond description. In his nightmare stupor he imagined that this was how rape victims must feel, a complete violation of their person. Relief when it was over and the accumulated effects of physical and nervous exhaustion made him feel very drowsy, but he was kept awake for some time before being transferred to a ward and allowed to fall into a deep sleep. He was out cold for nearly seven hours.

'So you're with us again,' said a smiling face, when he opened his eyes and then closed them again because of the sunlight coming through the window of the ward.

'Where . . . ?'

'You are in ward four of College Hospital,' said the nurse. 'That was some party you had yourself last night.'

Kincaid groaned at the pain in his head. He put his hand up to it and felt bandage.

'You have a cut on the back of your head,' said the nurse.

'No kidding,' replied Kincaid sourly.

'Well, I hope it was worth it because I think the reckoning is about to be paid. The police are here to see you and I don't think it's to sell raffle tickets.'

Kincaid groaned again. Why were so many nurses Irish, he wondered.

The nurse left the room and he started to consider what he should tell the police. He thought about telling them the truth; that was the easiest thing to do, in his present state. But could he simply tell them that he had entered Fingleton Grange illegally and discovered the brain-damaged Greta Marsh? Then, for his pains, that he had been knocked out, force-fed whisky and dumped unconscious on a railway embankment? 'God almighty,' groaned Kincaid. He put his hand to his head. He could hardly believe it himself, let alone expect the police to. What was the alternative? Plead guilty to being drunk and disorderly and causing a public nuisance?

In itself it wasn't that serious a charge, but it could be damaging and rival papers might decide to have a field day. An investigative journalist could lose a lot more than a fifty pound fine in the dock: he could lose all credibility. But if he persisted with his story and the police were forced to check out Fingleton Grange, would Greta Marsh still be there? Of course not. That was the inevitable conclusion to be drawn. They would have moved her after last night.

The door opened before he had decided what to do and two uniformed policemen came in. Kincaid was pleased to note that there was no detectable air of antagonism about them.

'Thank God I'm not in your head this morning,' said one of them.

Kincaid attempted a smile and failed.

'Perhaps you could furnish us with a few details about last night's escapade?'

Kincaid stalled for time. 'It's all a bit hazy,' he said.

'I thought journalists could hold their booze,' said the policeman.

'I wasn't drunk,' said Kincaid, feeling that he had just taken the first step on a long, uphill journey.

'That's what the doc said,' agreed the policeman, to Kincaid's complete surprise. 'He reckons you had a drink after a fistful of sleeping tablets. You spilled more on your clothes than you actually drank. You're lucky to be alive old son, or are you?'

Kincaid looked up at the policeman and saw the question repeated in his eyes. 'No, it wasn't a suicide attempt,' he assured the man.

'To be quite frank,' continued the policeman, 'we were all ready to throw the book at you, but considering what the doctor has said, we're prepared to take a more lenient view and regard it as an unfortunate accident.'

Kincaid felt as near to good as was possible in his condition. 'I'm very grateful,' he said contritely. 'I've been working under great strain recently. I think I must have taken my pills twice or something. I won't be that stupid again.'

Kincaid could hardly believe his luck. The police involvement removed, he was relieved of the embarrassment of court action and its attendant publicity. He was now free to pursue the Greta Marsh story in his own way. As soon as the police left he got out of bed and started looking in cupboards for his clothes. He was cursing his lack of success when the Irish nurse returned.

'What do you think you're doing?' she demanded.

Kincaid, with a sigh of frustration at being asked the obvious, told her.

'And where do you think you are going?'

Kincaid looked at the ceiling and gave a silent prayer for patience. 'I am leaving, Nurse,' he said. 'I am exceedingly grateful for your care and attention, but now I am leaving.'

'Who says so?' demanded the nurse, maintaining her air of outraged officialdom.

'I do,' snapped Kincaid.

'But Doctor hasn't said you can go.'

'No Nurse, I say I can go, now where are my clothes?'

'You'll have to sign a form.'

'I'll sign a confession to murder if you'll just get me my clothes.'

The nurse left the room, to return with Kincaid's clothes and the ward sister. The older woman was carrying a form which she held out for Kincaid to sign. 'You're very foolish, you know,' said the sister, 'that's a nasty bump on your head.'

'I'll be okay, Sister,' replied Kincaid, starting to get dressed. 'Thanks for everything.'

Outside in the daylight Kincaid became aware of his dishevelled appearance. He was wearing the clothes that he had been admitted with, and they bore clear and extensive witness to his sojourn on the embankment. He did his best to brush them with his hands and then flagged down a passing taxi to take him to his father's house. Fumbling for the key in his pocket when he got there, he suddenly had the uneasy feeling that there was someone behind him. Fear gripped his stomach; he was in no fit state for a fight. Slowly he turned round.

'Where have you been?' asked Eve Laing.

Kincaid nearly fainted with relief. He closed his eyes and let out a long sigh. 'Thank God,' he crooned. 'I thought . . .'

'You thought what?' asked Eve.

'Forget it,' said Kincaid, and turned round to open the door.

'You look terrible,' said Eve.

'I feel terrible,' said Kincaid, sinking slowly down on to the couch and resting his head on the back with his eyes closed.

'You went to Fingleton Grange, didn't you?'

Kincaid gave an affirmative grunt.

'And?' asked Eve.

'You were right. Greta Marsh is there. She's been brain damaged.'

'I knew it. I just knew it.'

Eve lit the gas fire and then made coffee, while Kincaid told her everything that had happened the night before. He saw her eyes grow wider as the tale progressed.

'But that's incredible!' said Eve. 'What was the point of drugging you and leaving you on a railway embankment unless . . .' she baulked at finishing the sentence.

'I've been asking myself that, too,' agreed Kincaid.

'But that's the sort of thing that happens in films!' Eve protested.

'Maybe some fool panicked and didn't think of the consequences.' said Kincaid.

'What did the police say?'

'I didn't tell them,' said Kincaid.

'You what?' exclaimed Eve.

'They wouldn't have believed a word and I can't prove a damned thing.'

'But you found Greta Marsh! Surely that . . .'

'They must have moved her by now,' said Kincaid.

Eve looked about her in restless frustration. 'But you can't simply let them get away with it,' she protested. 'You must print in your paper what you saw.'

'I can't do it without any proof,' replied Kincaid. 'And we don't know who "they" are. The paper would be sued out of existence without proof.'

'You mean we have to find Greta all over again?' asked Eve.

'Or find out who engineered this and why.'

'Any ideas?'

'No. You?'

'Not really,' confessed Eve.

Kincaid thought for a moment, then said, 'I could try to frighten some people into talking.'

'Go on.'

'You said that Greta was removed from your unit. On whose instructions?'

'I don't know. I suppose Dr Affric was in charge.'

Kincaid groaned as a wave of pain filled his head.

'Forget about all this for the moment,' said Eve. 'You have to get some proper rest. I'll run you a bath and then you can get into bed.'

Kincaid offered no protest.

When Eve returned from the bathroom Kincaid asked her what time it was.

'Ten o'clock. Is there something you have to do?'

'My father is being operated on today. They said it will be over by four this afternoon. I have to be there.'

'I'll set your alarm,' said Eve.

'You're on duty today?'

Eve nodded. 'I'll be off at seven-thirty.'

'Could we meet?'

'If you like.'

'Dinner?'

'All right.'

When Eve left, Kincaid climbed into the bath and relaxed for a moment before his mind insisted that he make some plans. He would have to get in touch with Fletcher and let him know that he wasn't coming back to London. He also needed a place to stay if, as seemed likely, he was going to be up here for some time; somewhere comfortable and somewhere away from the agonising emptiness of his father's house. He would also need transport. He started to work out a time-table. Sleep would have to wait.

The telephone in the hall was dead when Kincaid picked it up. He cursed it and put on his jacket. There were two panes of glass missing from the public call box at the end of the street, so Kincaid found his conversation with his editor interrupted by traffic every few seconds. He tried turning his back in an attempt to block out the noise coming through the broken squares, but it did not make much difference.

'Are you standing in the middle of the M1?' asked Fletcher.

'Sounds like it,' agreed Kincaid.

'Want to tell me what all this is about?'

'Not yet.'

'Suit yourself, but how long is it going to take?'

'A week, maybe two,' replied Kincaid. 'It's hard to say.'

'I think you'd be better off employed down here,' said Fletcher.

'I'm due some time.'

'Suit yourself,' conceded Fletcher. 'There's a rumour going round Westminster that Carlisle is going to be persuaded to challenge for the leadership of his party soon.'

'There are always rumours at Westminster,' said Kincaid.

'This one has a certain ring of truth to it. The smart money thinks that if the next set of trade figures triggers off another rise in interest rates, there's going to have to be a change.'

'That won't bring down the interest rates,' said Kincaid.

'That's what common sense would say, but people are remarkably immune to that commodity. They will be only too keen to believe in magic; Carlisle's reforming of the health service in the north, at apparently no extra cost to the taxpayer, has got them talking about the Midas touch. Cometh the hour, cometh the man.'

'Did you say at no extra cost?' asked Kincaid.

'I did. The question was raised in the House yesterday and that was the substance of the reply.'

'Good God,' said Kincaid, 'he'll be turning water into wine, next.' He pressed another coin into the slot. 'That's my last one,' he said.

'Give me the number,' said Fletcher.

Kincaid read out the number from the wall in front of him and put down the receiver. He turned to watch a particularly heavily-laden lorry belch out black smoke as it laboured by. The telephone rang.

'Is there anything you need?' asked Fletcher.

'A car, and I'll have to find somewhere to stay.'

'I thought you were at your father's place?'

'The old man's in hospital. I just don't want to stay there.'

'Let's keep it modest, shall we?'

'Don't I always?' smiled Kincaid.

'Forgive my mirth.'

'About bloody time an' all,' muttered an old woman in a shapeless coat, her face half hidden by a headscarf, when Kincaid left the call box.

'Sorry, I didn't see you waiting there,' said Kincaid.

'All the same, you're all the same,' continued the woman as she bustled past Kincaid into the booth. 'Thoughtless.'

'Have a nice day,' murmured Kincaid, as the door swung shut. It sounded different with a Newcastle accent.

'How long will you be requiring the vehicle, sir?' asked the blazer with the clipped moustache at the car-hire firm. Kincaid wanted to substitute 'needing the car', but restrained himself.

'A week, maybe two.'

'Clean licence?'

'Yes.'

'How long?'

'Fifteen years.'

'Business or pleasure?'

'Bit of both.'

The blazer stopped filling in the form and looked up from the counter. 'What kind of business are you in?' he asked, with overtones of suspicion.

'Stock car racer.'

'What!'

'A joke. I'm a journalist.'

'I see,' replied the blazer with a weak grin. 'Size of car?'

'Medium.'

'Sierra? Cavalier? Dedra?'

'What was the last one?' asked Kincaid.

'A Lancia Dedra, sir.'

'I'll have that.'

'Group six insurance.'

'I'll pay.'

'Sign here.'

Kincaid signed the form and was led out into a courtyard where half a dozen cars were parked. An old man in dungarees was polishing one of them. 'This is yours,' said the blazer, opening the door of a white Lancia.

Kincaid turned the key. The tank was full. He was mobile.

The letting agencies posed more of a problem. None of them wanted to cater for short-term lets. Kincaid was about to leave the third when the man added, 'Unless you fancy a cottage?'

'A cottage?'

The agent read from the paper in front of him, 'Haddow Cottage, Rose Lane, Otterby. Two bedrooms, all mod cons, nice garden.'

Kincaid thought for a moment. Otterby was only a ten mile drive; he used to go there on family picnics when he was a boy. 'How much?' he asked.

The agent screwed up his face in thought and said, 'The previous tenant had to leave a couple of months early. That means the cottage will be empty for a month. There's not much chance of renting it in the normal way for that length of time, so shall we say two hundred?'

'Fully furnished?'

'Everything except linen.'

'I'll take it.'

'Don't you want to look at it first?' asked the agent.

'I trust you.'

Kincaid picked up some sheets and towels from his father's house and then drove out to Otterby. Although it wasn't far from the city in terms of distance, it took longer than he thought it would to get there because the road narrowed and became very twisty as it contoured the river valley which separated the peripheral suburbs of Newcastle from the green belt. A particularly steep section leading down to the bridge which crossed a ravine had Kincaid almost changing his mind about living outside the city.

He liked the cottage as soon as he saw it. It was very old and had not been all that well maintained, but it did have a lot of character and a garden that would have done justice to *The Wind In the Willows*. He stood still in it for a few moments and listened to the sounds of the country.

The door knocker was made of heavy wrought iron. Kincaid examined it closely and discovered it was in the form of a snake wound round a stick. There was a matching boot scraper to the left of the front door. Kincaid tried it out and wondered about the people who must have preceded him. There was an open hearth fire in the living-room and a three-piece suite covered in loose chintz covers. There was a basket of logs by the hearth and a note saying that there were more in the shed outside. Kincaid sat down and felt at home. He picked up the telephone.

'College Hospital. Can I help you?'

'The hospital manager, please.'

'Who is calling?'

'My name is Kincaid.'

'Can you give me some idea what it's about?' asked the woman.

'No.'

'One moment.'

Kincaid looked at his watch while he waited. It was lunchtime and he was hungry. He hadn't eaten breakfast.

'Fields,' said the voice, 'what can I do for you, Mr Kincaid?'

'I'd like to arrive and talk to you about Greta Marsh,' said Kincaid. He said it calmly but his palms were sweating.

'I'm not sure I understand,' came the uncertain reply.

'I'm a journalist. I'd like to talk to you about Greta Marsh.'

There was a pause, then Fields said, 'I don't think there's anything to discuss, Mr Kincaid. Miss Marsh has left hospital to begin her new life and has no wish to see the press.'

'Miss Marsh was lying in Fingleton Grange last night with scrambled egg for a brain,' said Kincaid.

'This is preposterous!' exclaimed Fields.

'I agree,' said Kincaid.

'The drunken intruder!' exclaimed Fields. 'There was a report of a drunken intruder at Fingleton last night. It was you!'

'I was the intruder,' agreed Kincaid, 'but I wasn't drunk.'

'My information is different, Mr Kincaid. I was informed that a drunk was found wandering around the asylum last night. He fell down and knocked himself out, but while the staff were waiting for an ambulance to arrive the man came to and wandered off into the night. I understand the police found you some hours later, still drunk.' Fields managed to endow the last word with a lot of distaste.

'I was drugged, Mr Fields.'

'Really.' said Fields, in a bored voice.

'I was given the drugs at Fingleton Grange, Mr Fields, to make it appear as if I was drunk.'

'I can only suggest you are taking hallucinogens, Mr Kincaid. I've never heard such a ridiculous story.'

'I think the public will find the Greta Marsh story a great deal more outlandish.'

'There is no story, Mr Kincaid. Why don't you be a sensible fellow and admit that you had too much to drink, made rather a fool of yourself and have now concocted some outrageous tale to excuse your behaviour.'

'Because we both know that that isn't true, Mr Fields, and before I'm through I'm going to get to the bottom of all this.'

'A word of warning, Mr Kincaid,' said Fields.

'I knew it couldn't be far away,' said Kincaid.

'We will take a dim view of any nonsense you may print which damages the good name of this hospital. We will not hesitate to use the full powers of the law to seek redress. Be very sure of what you say.'

'I intend to be, Mr Fields. I also intend to find Greta Marsh – both of them.' As Kincaid hung up, he noticed that his hand was shaking. He put it down to lack of food and set off to find the local pub.

Kincaid arrived at the College Hospital a few minutes before the operation on his father had ended. He was still preoccupied with thoughts of Greta Marsh when he saw a man coming towards him. The surgeon was in his early thirties, fair-haired, bespectacled and still wearing his theatre garb, although the gown and mask had gone. A green, short-sleeved shirt exposed his hairy arms as he sat down, resting them on the table in front of him.

'Mr Kincaid?'

'That's right. How is he?'

'He's fine. The operation went well and he was stable throughout. No problems. No complications.'

'Good.'

'The good news is that the tumour was confined to one lobe of the left lung. I removed it. There was absolutely no evidence that it had spread anywhere else.'

'Does that mean he's cured?'

The surgeon moved his body in a gesture designed to convey ambivalence. 'Yes and no,' he said. 'In cases like this it's really a question of how long before it returns.'

'And how long would you say?' asked Kincaid.

'Well, with no obvious signs of spread I'd guess at at least a year, maybe as much as two. If we put him on chemotherapy, and I think we should, the future is looking quite bright.'

'When can I see him?'

'I'd leave it till tomorrow,' said the surgeon. 'He's going to be very drowsy for a while, then he'll benefit most from a good night's sleep.'

Kincaid nodded and offered his thanks. There were three hours to kill before he was due to meet Eve, so he decided to visit his sister. Having the car made it easy to get across town to the housing estate where she lived, although the evening rush hour traffic slowed him down. Lisa hugged him and led him inside. 'The hospital said he'd come through it all right,' she said. 'I phoned half an hour ago.'

'I've just come from there,' said Kincaid. 'They say it went well.' He saw that Lisa had been knitting something for the baby. 'Sticking to safe colours, I see,' he said, when he saw the wool was lemon-coloured.

'Kevin's sure it's going to be a boy,' she laughed, 'but I thought it best to play safe, like you say.'

'And what about you?' asked Kincaid.

Lisa smiled and said, 'The truth is, we're both so delighted after all this time that it doesn't matter a hoot whether it's a boy or a girl.' The smile faded from her face and she asked, 'They're not lying about Dad are they, I mean, he is going to be around for a while yet, isn't he?'

'Yes, of course,' said Kincaid, taking his sister's hands in his and feeling upset at her distress. 'They're talking in terms of years before any more signs of trouble arise.'

Lisa wiped a tear from her eye with the tips of her fingers and said, 'It's just that I want him to know his new grandson, that's all.'

'Or granddaughter,' said Kincaid.

Lisa smiled and agreed. 'How's Kerry these days?' she asked.

'She's getting big,' replied Kincaid.

Lisa looked at her brother until he admitted that he knew that wasn't what she meant. 'All right,' he said. 'She's not showing much sign of improvement, but she will. She just needs a bit of encouragement.'

Lisa put her hand on his arm and squeezed. 'Do you think it would help if I visited more often?' she asked. 'I could try, you know.'

'You have enough on your plate with the baby on the way,' said Kincaid. 'Besides, it's specialist help she needs. A child psychologist, something like that.'

'If there's anything I can do you will tell me, won't you?' said Lisa.

Kincaid smiled and nodded. 'Of course I will. Thanks. Now where's that husband of yours?' He looked at his watch. 'Shouldn't he be home about now?'

'Not on a Tuesday. He has a couple of beers with his pals before he comes home. Would you like something to eat? I'm just about to make supper.'

Kincaid declined, telling Lisa that he had a dinner date.

'Somebody nice?' asked Lisa.

'A nurse I met at the hospital.'

'Serious?'

Kincaid laughed. 'Give me a chance, I've only known her a few days.'

'It would be nice if you met someone. It's been a while since you and Julie broke up.'

'You're behaving like a sister,' Kincaid complained.

'All right, I'll stop,' said Lisa. 'But a good woman is probably just what you need.'

'I'll bear it in mind,' smiled Kincaid.

Eve Laing was standing by the entrance to the nurses' home when Kincaid swung his car through the gates of the hospital. She had no way of recognising the Lancia so Kincaid had to lean across the passenger seat to attract her attention.

'Nice car,' said Eve, holding the hem of her dress as she eased herself in.

'Nice dress,' replied Kincaid, with an admiring glance at what Eve was wearing. This was the first time he had seen her dressed up, and he liked what he saw.

'Thank you. How is your father?'

'They say he came through it well and there was no sign of metasta-something.'

'Metastasis; it the means spreading of the tumour to other sites.'

'I gathered that,' smiled Kincaid.

'I'm glad.'

'The doctor said they would start him on chemotherapy as soon as possible, and with a bit of luck it could be a while before any more trouble breaks out.'

'Good.'

They lapsed into silence and after a few minutes Kincaid, who had been concentrating on moving through heavy traffic said, 'Tell me about yourself.'

'What's to tell? I'm twenty-seven. I have a degree in psychology and I'm a qualified staff nurse at College Hospital. I was born in Kenya but my parents came home to England when I was two. I was brought up in Stroud in Gloucestershire where I went to school. I went to Durham University and got an upper second.'

'You didn't use your degree?' asked Kincaid.

'Briefly. I worked for an American company for a year in their personnel department. It was my job to screen potential employees and assess their suitability.'

'You didn't like it?'

'No, I didn't. It was the kind of job that anyone with a modicum of common sense could have done. The company just wanted someone with a psychology degree for window dressing. I got out and got myself a real job.'

'At half the salary, I'll bet.'

'At one third,' corrected Eve.

'A vocation?' asked Kincaid.

Eve laughed and said, 'That always sounds terribly grand. Let's just say I think I was meant to be a nurse.'

'Boyfriend?' asked Kincaid tentatively.

'I'm married.'

'Oh.'

There was a long pause before Eve added, 'We're separated.'

'I see.'

'How about you?'

'Divorced. I have been for quite a long time.'

'Children?'

'I have a daughter, Kerry.'

'So she stays with her mother?'

'Kerry was brain damaged. She stays in a home here in Newcastle.'

'I'm sorry. I didn't mean to pry.'

'You're not.'

'Where are we going?' asked Eve as they turned off the main road and started twisting through a series of back streets.

'The best Greek restaurant in the north,' said Kincaid, adding as an afterthought, 'I hope you like Greek food?'

'Love it.'

Being midweek, the restaurant was less than half full.

'Well, put me out of my misery. I'm all ears,' said Eve, as they sat down at their table.

A waiter intervened to light a candle. Kincaid waited until

he had finished, then said, 'What do you want me to tell you?'

Eve's eyes opened like saucers. 'Greta Marsh, of course. What's been happening?'

'I called Fields. I couldn't budge him. He denies all knowledge of a substitution. I'm just a drunk who dreamed the whole thing up.'

'But they can't possibly get away with it!' exclaimed Eve.

'Someone is pretty confident that they can,' said Kincaid. 'That means they've got the real Greta somewhere well out of the way.'

Eve's frustration was beginning to show. 'You can't just do nothing,' she exclaimed. 'You must expose them. They can't be allowed to get away with it.'

'I have to think,' replied Kincaid.

'It's action that's required!' said Eve.

Kincaid held up a restraining hand. 'No it isn't,' he said firmly. 'You don't take on the establishment like a bull at a gate, because you'll lose. Nothing is more certain. You circle it cautiously, you prod it, you weaken it, and then and only then, if you are absolutely sure of your facts, you can have a go. That way you have an even chance.'

'But . . .'

'No buts I know, I've done it before.'

Eve sighed and then conceded defeat. 'So where does that leave us?,' she asked.

'Greta lived in an institution before her operation,' said Kincaid.

'Harrington Hall,' said Eve.

Kincaid was thinking out loud. 'The fact that she had no relatives must have been the factor that convinced the hospital they could get away with it. No one was going to request access to her. But it occurs to me that there must have been someone at Harrington Hall who was fond of her, someone who would like to see her now, settled in her new life.'

'I think I heard that the matron up there was very fond of her,' said Eve.

'Good,' said Kincaid. 'Then maybe I'll take a trip up to

Harrington Hall. Perhaps I could persuade her to request Greta Marsh's new address from the hospital.'

'But they would have to refuse,' said Eve.

'Exactly.'

Eve looked puzzled. 'Then what's the point?' she asked.

'The point is that their refusal would make a story. The human interest angle. The public are quite happy to accept that the press should be kept away from Greta, but an old friend is a different story.'

'Prodding,' said Eve.

'Pressure,' replied Kincaid.

'So you think that the hospital might be forced to allow the matron to see Greta?'

'Absolutely, and then they would have to come up with the fake Greta again.'

'And the matron would be sure to know the difference?'

'Precisely.'

Kincaid was shown into the matron's office at Harrington Hall by a domestic assistant dressed in a pink, candy-striped dress and a matching cap. The woman had a speech defect and Kincaid noted that she had an artificial left arm. She had to cross her right arm across her body to open the door. She stood aside to let Kincaid enter and he thanked her. Anna Keats put down her pen and smiled.

'Good of you to see me at such short notice, Matron,' said Kincaid.

'When you said that you had news of Greta I could hardly refuse. I haven't heard a thing since the operation,' replied Anna Keats, who to Kincaid's way of thinking looked every inch the perfect grandmother. She was slightly plump, had a beautiful head of silver-grey hair and a smile that instantly put him at his ease. There was no trace of the nervousness he thought he had detected earlier in their telephone conversation. She was a woman totally in command of herself.

'I am afraid you are going to find all this a bit hard to believe, Matron,' said Kincaid.

'I don't think I understand, Mr Kincaid.'

Kincaid took a deep breath and made a tentative start along a difficult road. 'I'm afraid that Greta's operation may not have been the success we have all been encouraged to believe, Matron.'

'But the newspaper report said . . .'

There was no easy way. Kincaid swallowed and took the

plunge. 'Matron, I have reason to suspect that the woman pictured in the press reports was not Greta Marsh at all.'

Anna Keats looked bemused. She spread her hands as if appealing for help from some unseen deity and exclaimed, 'Mr Kincaid, what on earth are you talking about?'

Kincaid told her about the attempt to cover up the failed operation, watching her face all the time with trepidation and seeing incredulity being stretched to the limit. When he had finished there was a very long pause before Anna Keats said, 'Are you seriously asking me to believe that Greta was mutilated and brain-damaged by the operation, and is now being held prisoner somewhere?'

'Yes, Matron.'

'But this is outrageous! For goodness' sake, why? And why haven't you gone to the police?'

'Frankly, I don't know why, but I'd like to find out,' said Kincaid. 'As for going to the police, I don't have any proof to offer them as yet.'

'If what you say is true, and I am not saying I believe you for a moment, why do you need me?' asked Anna Keats.

'Greta has been hidden away somewhere. She doesn't have any relations to ask after her and the press are barred. That leaves you. By all accounts you are the nearest thing to a friend that Greta ever had. If you were to ask to see her, the authorities would be under some pressure to comply.'

'And if they should still refuse?'

'That's where I come in. If they turn your request down my paper would run the story until the pressure on them becomes unbearable.'

'I see,' said Anna Keats, gently rubbing her cheeks with her fingertips while she thought. At length she stopped and said, 'Pardon me for saying this, Mr Kincaid, but this could all be an elaborate subterfuge of yours to gain access to Greta for your own reasons. An exclusive, isn't that what you call it? The new life of the woman with no face.'

'It could be but it's not, Matron. I promise you.'

Anna Keats looked at Kincaid, searching his face for clues.

'All right,' she said, with some reluctance, 'what do you want me to do?'

Kincaid relaxed and said, 'Ask to see Greta.'

'Whom should I ask?'

'Fields, the hospital manager at College Hospital.'

Anna Keats picked up her phone and dialled the number. As she waited for a reply there was a knock on the door. It was the domestic in the candy-stripes. One-handedly she wheeled in a trolley loaded with coffee and cups into the room. She had difficulty when the wheels baulked at the carpet near the desk, and Kincaid started out of his chair to help, but the acid look he received made him sink back down again. The domestic set out the coffee cups while Anna Keats finally got through to Gordon Fields.

Kincaid watched the woman pour the coffee while listening to one end of the conversation. He wondered how well the matron was going to handle Fields' refusal. Anna Keats interrupted herself to cover the mouthpiece with one hand and say, 'Thank you, Tilly.' The domestic mumbled something in reply, looked aggressively at Kincaid and then left. Kincaid watched her leave, then turned round again to see Anna Keats replace the receiver.

'I'm sorry about Tilly, Mr Kincaid. She's a law unto herself.'

'What did Fields say, Matron?' asked Kincaid.

'He said that there would be no problem,' replied Anna Keats.

Kincaid's eyes opened wide. 'He agreed?' he exclaimed. 'How on earth is he going to manage this?' He saw that Anna Keats was looking at him with rekindled suspicion and said, 'I assure you, Matron, that what I told you is absolutely true. Fields must be hoping to deceive you like he did the press. But surely you would know? I mean, even with a different face you would know the real Greta Marsh, wouldn't you?'

'Yes, Mr Kincaid. I'm sure I would.' said Anna Keats solemnly.

'Did you arrange a date for the meeting?'

'Mr Fields said that he would have to check with Greta but

he thought that Thursday afternoon would be all right. 3 pm at the hospital. It's my half-day.'

'I'd like to be there,' said Kincaid.

Anna Keats thought for a moment and then said, 'No.'

'No?'

Anna Keats said, 'I do believe that you're not after a story, Mr Kincaid, but all the same I must insist that I see Greta alone in the first instance.'

'Very well, Matron,' said Kincaid.

Eve ran from the nurses' home to the waiting car and got in, flicking the rain from her shoulders. 'What a day!' she exclaimed. She searched for the end to her seatbelt and then finding it, she asked, 'Well, what happened?'

Kincaid told her.

'But how can they possibly hope to get away with it?' said Eve.

'I haven't worked that out, yet,' replied Kincaid. He switched on the fan heater to help clear the windscreen, which the rain had turned into a condenser for their breath. He had to resort to clearing it ineffectually with his hand as they stopped at the hospital gates and waited for a suitable gap in the traffic.

'Where are we going?' asked Eve.

'My place.'

Shortly before they came to the village the rain stopped and the wind fell away to nothing. When Eve got out of the car it was absolutely still and only the sound of water, dripping from the trees and running along the gutters, broke the silence. Eve looked around her. 'Charming. I had no idea this place existed,' she said.

Kincaid smiled and said, 'My father used to bring us here for picnics when my sister and I were kids. There were only two buses a day so we got the first one out and the last one back.'

Eve smiled. 'Where did you have your picnic?' she asked.

'In the field behind the church. It runs down to the river. I remember my old man always insisted on bringing a paraffin stove. It took him half the day to light it and my mother always took delight in pointing out how long she had been waiting for a cup of tea. "You wouldn't have to be dying of thirst on this picnic," she'd say. "In a jiffy, pet," he'd reply, "In a jiffy,".'

'And now you're living in the place after all these years,' said Eve.

'Life's rich pattern,' smiled Kincaid. 'We're here.' He opened the garden gate and let Eve go through.

'It's nice.'

Kincaid paused for a moment before opening the front door to allow Eve to examine the garden, not that much could be seen in the darkness.

'It feels nice,' she said.

'I'll put the kettle on.'

Eve came inside and settled down on the sofa, tucking her legs beneath her.

Kincaid returned while he waited for the kettle to boil.

Eve was looking at a photograph of Kerry that Kincaid had put on the table by the fireplace. 'Tell me about her,' she said. She saw the muscle in Kincaid's left cheek tighten and then relax again.

'She was a normal little girl, and then suddenly one day she wasn't. She was brain damaged through oxygen starvation during a routine operation. She's been in a home ever since, stuck there, like a vegetable.'

'What's the prognosis?'

'The official prognosis is that she won't get any better.'

'But you don't believe it?' asked Eve, interpreting the tone of Kincaid's voice.

'Let's say I don't altogether accept it.'

'What have you done about it?' asked Eve.

'I keep pressing for a reassessment of Kerry's condition and for rehabilitative treatment.'

'Any success?'

'Mostly it's been flat refusals, but I think all that's about to change.'

'Really?'

'I understand that a new mental health director is being

appointed for the region as part of the Northern Health Scheme. Patients are going to get a better deal.' said Kincaid.

'That's good news,' said Eve cautiously. She added, 'But it's possible that the new chap might agree with the original assessment.'

'In that case I'm going to take Kerry away from that place.'

'But how will you look after her?'

'I'll find a way,' replied Kincaid. 'She needs stimulation, someone to care about her enough to give her the time and attention she needs.'

'What about her mother?' asked Eve.

'She has a new life. Kerry's my responsibility.'

'But your job would make it impossible,' said Eve.

'Then I'll give it up,' said Kincaid.

'Can you do that?' asked Eve, just a little overawed by Kincaid's determination.

'I've got some savings and I can do some freelance writing from home.'

'You must love her very much,' said Eve.

'She's my daughter. I remember how she used to be.'

Eve watched Kincaid's features relax at the thought. It was the first time she had seen him without tension or anxiety in his eyes. She liked what she saw.

'When do you expect to hear about a reassessment?' asked Eve.

'The man I spoke to said that the new director has been appointed; he'll be starting in the next week or so.'

Kincaid went to get the coffee and Eve replaced the photograph. She asked if Kincaid would be accompanying Anna Keats to the College Hospital.

'No, I don't think Miss Keats trusts me entirely. She wants to go alone.'

'Well, you can't blame her,' said Eve, sipping her coffee.

Kincaid gave her a sidelong look. 'What do you mean?' he asked.

'You're a journalist,' said Eve, matter-of-factly.

'What does that mean?' asked Kincaid, beginning to sound annoyed.

'Well, let's face it. Journalists come a poor second to used-car salesmen in the honesty and integrity stakes.'

'Of all the . . .' began Kincaid, and then he saw that Eve was smiling out of the corner of her mouth. 'You're winding me up!' he exploded.

'And it was so easy . . .' smiled Eve.

Kincaid tousled her hair and then stopped, his fingers still holding it. Eve looked at him with the smile still on her lips but her eyes were questioning.

Kincaid brought his fingers slowly down her cheek and guided her chin towards him. He kissed her gently on the lips and then harder as he felt her respond. When they finally broke apart Kincaid murmured, 'About this husband of yours . . . ?'

'He's in the past,' said Eve.

'Good,' said Kincaid. He settled down beside her on the couch and put his arm round her. 'Are you going to tell me about him?' he asked.

'What can I say? Gavin left me two years ago.'

'I'm sorry.'

'Don't be. We were never happy. Gavin was a public school-boy who never grew up. Like many men with that background, he was uneasy with women. Some end up treating us like whores, others decide we're madonnas. Gavin was the madonna type. Unfortunately I'm not. I found the strain of playing Mary Poppins just too much. In the end I told him to bugger off and be done with it.'

Kincaid wanted to laugh but did not know whether he should or not. He looked at Eve out of the corner of his eye and decided it might be all right. 'You didn't really, did you?' he asked cautiously.

'I did,' replied Eve.

They both laughed.

Tolkien arrived a little late for evening surgery and glanced into the waiting-room. He saw that it was nearly full. An old man, coat collar still up, muffler over his ears, was coughing into a dirty handkerchief. His eyes were watering and his face was going red with the effort. A child was crying on his mother's knee as she tried, ineffectually, to shush it. Another, older child sat at her feet, gazing up at her with expressionless eyes. Most people sat with their heads buried in magazines. *Country Life, Vogue, What Car?* Another world, or maybe they didn't see it that way. After all, it was only a football coupon away. Eight crosses in the right places and it would be them in the black Porsche 911, the warm winds of Paris blowing through their hair. Smiling air stewardesses, head waiters and cab drivers were all out there somewhere waiting for them. Poverty, unemployment and illness were just temporary setbacks along the way.

'Good evening,' said Tolkien.

The response was uneven and unharmonious; it always was. He was about to close the door again when a young man in the corner caught his attention. He had been staring at the floor but lifted his eyes when Tolkien came in. There was something familiar about him. At first Tolkien couldn't place him, and adopted a half-smile as cover for his embarrassment; then he remembered. It was the boy from the drug clinic, Terry Feenan. What he was doing sitting in his waiting-room was the question that still occupied Tolkien as he took off his coat and settled down into his chair.

Tolkien flicked through the pile of mail on his desk and discarded more than half without opening it. Circulars were the bane of his life. He opened the envelope he knew would contain the lab reports and digested the contents. Three positive pregnancy tests and one negative. He now checked the reference numbers against his patient files. Two of the positives would be welcome but not the third; she was an unmarried, teenage girl. Tolkien sighed; a bit of heartache to come, he thought. Ironically, the negative result would come as a big disappointment to the lady concerned. She was thirty-one and had been trying for a baby for the last seven years; maybe he should pencil her in for possible *in vitro* fertilisation if a place on the programme became available.

Tolkien thumbed through some routine biochemistry reports

before stopping as he came to one from the special lab at College Hospital. He had been right about Frank Golightly; his blood was HIV positive and he had full-blown Aids, a high price for his German adventure. Tolkien switched on his computer monitor and took the dust cover off the keyboard. Golightly would need immediate supplies of AZT to slow down progress of the disease as much as possible. After that he would be referred to College Hospital for treatment of his sarcoma and Aids management. This would be Tolkien's first opportunity to try out the new computerised pharmacy system. He typed in details of the patient from his record card and then answered the questions as they appeared on the screen:

'TREATMENT RECOMMENDED?' Tolkien typed in AZT.
'AFFIRMATIVE,' replied the monitor.
'DOSAGE?' Tolkien typed in the figures.
'AFFIRMATIVE. COLLECTION POINT?'

Tolkien asked the computer to have the drug sent to the surgery. Golightly could pick it up when he came in for the result of his tests. Tolkien checked; Golightly was due to come in on the following morning.

'FURTHER ACTION?'
Tolkien typed in, 'Referral to College Hospital Clinic.'
'AFFIRMATIVE.'

Three patients were to come and go before Terry Feenan came into the room. 'I hope you don't mind me coming here,' said Feenan.

'You're not on my list,' replied Tolkien. 'The clinic is open house, but for anything else you really should attend your own doctor.'

'He doesn't give a stuff,' snarled the boy.

Tolkien decided that a lecture on medical ethics would be wasted. 'What's the problem?' he asked.

'It's Karen and the kid.'

'Go on.'

'I tried to persuade her to come down the clinic but she won't.'

'Why not?'

'Hates doctors.'

Tolkien shrugged and said, 'Then I don't really see what I can do.'

The boy leaned forward and placed his hands on Tolkien's desk. 'I thought . . .' he began uncertainly, 'I thought if I came here to tell you . . . you might come an' see her. Make her see reason, like?'

Tolkien's body language left the boy in no doubt that this was being received as a bad idea. 'I know, I know,' he continued, 'it's probably against all the rules but it's the only way, believe me, it's the only way. Please help?' Feenan looked down at the floor. He brushed the back of his hand quickly across the corner of his right eye.

Tolkien considered in silence for a long moment. All his instincts were telling him to refuse, but the thought that he might really be able to help the girl was preventing him from saying so. He scratched his forehead in an agony of indecision. Common sense started to gain the upper hand again. 'No,' he said, 'it's out of the question. She must come to the clinic.'

'It's no good. Please, just this once, have a word with her?' pleaded Feenan.

Tolkien lost the struggle with his conscience. He picked up his pen. 'Give me your address. I'll come along after surgery.'

Tolkien's next patient was Mrs Harrison, the old woman who was finding it hard to cope with an ageing and very dependent husband. She was looking haggard. Tolkien came round from behind his desk and helped her into the chair.

'I came to see if there was any word about a place for Harry,' she said.

'Not yet,' said Tolkien, wishing he could give her better news.

'I see,' said the woman slowly. She was wringing her hands in her lap and trying not to show her face.

'It's very bad?' asked Tolkien.

The woman nodded. 'Yes, Doctor.'

Tolkien had an idea. He said, 'Look, I'll ask if the geriatric unit at College Hospital will take him for a few days, give you a bit of a break, shall I?'

The old woman's eyes lit up. 'Do you think they really would?,' she asked. 'I'm sure if I could get a couple of nights sleep I would be able to cope again.'

'I can make the request right now,' said Tolkien, turning to the computer. This was going to be another first and he knew that it would not be easy. He was quite used to sweet-talking staff at the hospital into taking on patients; it gave relatives a brief respite from the hell that caring for the chronically sick and elderly could become. But reasoning with a computer was going to be difficult. He typed in Harry Harrison's details and waited for the prompt:

'REQUEST?'
'Hospital Admission,' typed Tolkien.
'DIAGNOSIS?'
'Clinical Assessment.'
'REQUEST MORE INFORMATION.'

Tolkien smiled. The computer was betraying evidence of its having been programmed by health service administrators. It had always been a favourite delaying tactic of theirs to 'request more information' or alternatively, demand 'clarification'. He decided to ignore the request and repeat his own. 'Hospital admission,' he typed.

'Assessment,' repeated Tolkien, as if he were playing chess. It was not uncommon for old people to be admitted to hospital for a short period, to be assessed for their ability to cope with living on their own. Tolkien was gambling that the computer might accept this in Harry's case.

Ten seconds passed before the screen showed, 'ADMIT TO WARD 17, COLLEGE HOSPITAL.'

Tolkien grinned and said to Mrs Harrison, 'College Hospital will take Harry in for a few days. Who knows, maybe by that time we will have word of a permanent place for him.'

'Doctor, I don't know how to thank you,' sobbed the old woman.

'There's no need,' said Tolkien. 'You must have a break.'

'When will they take him?'

Tolkien returned to the computer and asked for an admission time. He was told ten o'clock the following morning.

'Request ambulance.'

'AFFIRMATIVE,' said the screen.

Mrs Harrison left and Tolkien felt pleased with what he had managed to achieve so quickly and without moving from his chair. He had taken to the new computer system like a duck to water.

Surgery was finished by eight-thirty, but Tolkien did not feel his normal sense of relief that the working day was done because tonight it wasn't over yet. He still had to go and see Karen; he had promised he would. He locked up the surgery and tested the front door with his shoulder before deciding that it was secure. He fumbled in his pocket for his car keys and then walked to the lane where he parked the car during surgery hours.

He took pleasure from the fact that it still seemed to be intact. This hadn't always been the case. When he first took over the practice, door mirrors had been snapped off, his radio aerial had disappeared and on one occasion he had found a wheel missing and the car propped up on a pile of bricks. As time had passed he seemed to have been awarded some kind of immunity against such happenings. He wasn't quite sure how this worked, but he wasn't questioning it either. He and his insurance company were both grateful.

The Feenans lived in a tower block. Tolkien parked the car on the concrete apron fronting the building and walked over to the entrance. Dogs were barking somewhere nearby and a game of football was continuing, despite the darkness, at the back of the block. He glanced up at the tower and decided that it looked better at night than at any time during the day. A fifteen-storey tower of lights was not at all unattractive; in some ways it symbolised the modern world.

The reality of living there, however, was quite different, as he knew only too well; but when he thought about it, the unhappiness and despair that such places engendered was difficult to understand. The notion of vertical villages had seemed a sound one at the outset, but it had never worked out that way. He didn't think that anyone could have predicted how bad such places would be in practice, but he had prescribed enough valium to the inhabitants over the years to know that they were, undeniably.

One of the lifts was broken. He did not think that he could recall a time when this had not been the case; the other smelled of urine. Tolkien tried to hold his breath as the ribbed metal box, specifically designed to be as user-unfriendly as possible to graffitti artists, took him to the the ninth floor. The doors moved apart sluggishly and he stepped out on to a landing where the smell of cooking took over from the urine in the lift; fried onions, if he wasn't mistaken. The door to the Feenans' flat was dark blue, but looked as if it had been kicked a great deal; the lower half was scratched and dented to expose the wood below. Tolkien pressed the bell.

Terry Feenan answered the door. Although he didn't smile when he saw Tolkien standing there, he did look relieved. Tolkien guessed that smiling was a thing that Terry did not do a lot of. He was shown into a sparsely-furnished room, where a girl in her early twenties sat watching television. She was eating potato crisps.

'Karen, this is Dr Tolkien. I want you to listen to what he has to say.'

'Christ! What is this?' demanded the girl.

'Dr Tolkien can help us,' insisted Feenan.

'You didn't tell me he was coming here!' said the girl, shrugging off Feenan's attempts to placate her.

The girl turned to look at Tolkien; her expression was one of total hostility.

'He's all right,' insisted Feenan. 'He wants to help us, honest he does.'

'Why?' demanded Karen. 'What would the likes of him be doing helping us? Answer me that.'

'Face it, Karen,' said Feenan. 'We need help. We've got to trust someone and I'm telling you, he's okay. For Judith's sake, eh? Talk to him at least.'

116

Karen let out her breath slowly and calmed down. 'All right, I'll listen,' she said. 'But no promises.'

Tolkien, who was used to histrionics from drug abusers, had stood quietly by throughout the argument, not that he was pleased that his visit had come as a surprise to the girl. Now that Karen had calmed down he spelled out just what the future would hold for her, her boyfriend and the baby. 'Where is the baby?' he asked.

'Sleeping.'

'Can I see her?'

'Suppose so,' replied Karen, sullenly.

Karen brought the baby through from the room next door and Tolkien took her in his arms. He asked her age. The answer seemed to match the weight he was guessing at; the child was not undernourished. She was wearing clean clothes too, and he could smell baby lotion.

'She seems contented,' he said to Karen.

'She is,' Karen replied, softening a little with talk of her baby.

'Terry's going to try coming off drugs, Karen. It would be a lot easier for him, for both of you in fact, if you tried together'.

'I can't. I know I can't.'

'You can try,' said Tolkien. 'I know it's not easy, but think of Judith, surely you can try for her? Who is going to cheer at her school concerts if you don't?'

Karen looked at Judith and stayed silent.

'Give it a go, Karen,' urged Feenan.

'Just think what it would mean,' said Tolkien. 'You and Terry could become a real family. Judith could grow up being proud of her parents. What do you say?'

Karen looked first at Tolkien and then at her husband. Their combined efforts won the day. 'All right,' she said, 'I'll try.'

'Good,' said Tolkien. He was now glad he had come. 'First I'll have to write down some details, then I'll examine you, and then we'll see about getting you on to methadone. You'll be registered as a patient of the clinic, just like Terry.'

Terry said that he would wait next door while Tolkien

examined Karen. Tolkien opened his case and took out his stethoscope and sphygmomanometer cuff.

'What the hell's that for?,' asked Karen, anxious to re-establish some aggression in her demeanour.

'To check your blood pressure.'

'It looks like some of the equipment the punters use.'

Tolkien ignored the comment and wrapped it round Karen's upper arm. He inflated it and took the reading. 'Not too bad,' he said. 'Take a deep breath . . . and again.'

Tolkien examined the track marks on the insides of Karen's arms without comment. There was a severely discoloured area of skin near one of them, and he traced his thumb round it.

'Went septic,' said Karen.

'Do you ever share needles?' asked Tolkien.

'Only with Terry.'

'Never with anyone else?'

'Not recently.'

'And in the past?'

'Sure, lots of folk.'

Tolkien nodded but didn't say anything. He continued his examination.

'What's wrong with your back?' Karen asked, out of the blue.

'What do you mean?' replied Tolkien, trying to sound matter-of-fact, but the question had got to him like an armour-piercing bullet.

'The way you stand, a bit bent-like.'

'I have a problem; it's called spondylitis.'

'Oh,' replied Karen. 'I had a hunchback punter once.'

Tolkien stiffened involuntarily; the girl sensed it. 'Oh shit! I didn't mean . . . I didn't mean that you . . . shit!'

'It's all right. I'd like a specimen of blood from you. We'll get the lab to check it out and they'll make sure you're not anaemic or anything like that.'

Karen watched as Tolkien inserted the needle into a vein in her arm and withdrew 20cc of blood. He ejected it into a small plastic specimen bottle and secured the cap.

'Pretty good,' said Karen admiringly, 'I didn't feel a thing.'

'Good,' said Tolkien. 'From now on, no needle goes into your arm without a doctor or a nurse on the other end of it.'

Terry came back into the room. 'All right?' he asked.

'Fine,' said Tolkien, fastening his bag. 'I'm off. You and Karen can collect your methadone tomorrow at your usual chemist.'

'Thanks, Doc,' said Terry, as he opened the door for Tolkien.

'You're welcome,' said Tolkien. 'It's an old cliché, but remember, tomorrow is the first day of the rest of your life, believe it.'

Tolkien paused on the balcony landing and looked out across the city. The girl had noticed his back. That must mean that it was getting worse.

Thirteen months had passed since he had first realised what was happening to him and had it confirmed at College Hospital. He could still recall the feeling. Suspecting what was wrong had been bad enough, but there had been a terrible finality about seeing it written down on the report. Emptiness had been followed by panic and then anger, and lastly by an uneasy acceptance of the inevitable.

An initial notion to give up medicine and see something of the world before it was too late had to be abandoned when he found out just how much medicine meant to him. It came as a surprise, but it actually meant more than seeing the Pyramids and the Holy Land; more than anything else, in fact. Nothing would change; he would continue in medical practice as long as he could. He had no wife or family to worry about; medicine was all he had.

Tolkien moved towards the lift. The pain in his back was getting worse; it was time for another pill.

SEVEN

The telephone rang at four o'clock in the morning. Kincaid took a few moments to accustom himself to the darkness of a strange house; he fumbled for the receiver. 'Yes?' he said sleepily.

'Mr Kincaid? It's College Hospital here.'

Kincaid's heart sank. There could only be one reason for calling him at this time in the morning. 'Yes?'

'It's your father, I'm afraid,' said the female voice, 'he's taken a turn for the worse.'

'I'll be there in half an hour,' said Kincaid.

'There's no immediate cause for concern, but Dr Leslie thought you should be informed.'

'I'll come.'

There was little traffic around in the early hours of a cold but dry morning, and the Lancia ate up the miles. Kincaid swung the car in through the hospital gates and left it just clear of the ambulance bay outside Accident and Emergency. Parking problems he could deal with later. The hospital corridors had an eerie silence; his footsteps echoed as if he were alone in the building. He could have been in a deserted castle were it not for the smell of ether. He opened the glass door leading to the ward where his father lay. The night staff nurse put her head round the duty room door and asked, 'Mr Kincaid?'

'Yes.'

The nurse came towards him. 'I'm afraid your father has developed complications,' she said.

'What sort of complications?'

'An infection. Doctor will explain; he'll be with you in a moment. Perhaps you would like to wait in here?'

Kincaid was shown into a small room and left alone. There were a number of odd chairs, a glass-top table with a few magazines lying on it and a large calendar stuck up on the wall with various dates crossed off in blue marker pen. He tried to spot the logic but couldn't concentrate for long enough.

A young man, white coat flapping open and stethoscope slung round his neck, came into the room. He adjusted his glasses with one hand and closed the door behind him with the other. 'I'm Dr Leslie,' he announced.

'James Kincaid.'

'I'm afraid we've hit a snag.'

Kincaid had the distinct impression that Leslie was deliberately lowering the tone of his natural voice to create an illusion of maturity beyond his years. He couldn't have been more than twenty-four. 'The nurse told me my father has an infection. What sort of infection?'

'Pneumonia, I'm afraid. He's rather ill.'

'How ill is "rather ill"?'

Leslie said, 'We've put him on antibiotics, so there's every chance he'll pull through, but I thought you should be informed at once.'

'Thanks,' said Kincaid. 'Can I see him?'

'Of course,' said Leslie. 'He won't be able to talk to you but you can sit with him if you like.'

Leslie took Kincaid to see his father. They did not speak on the way. When they got there the old man had his eyes closed. Plastic tubing emerged from his nostrils and a thicker tube from his mouth. Endless spikes drifted across the green, glowing face of an oscilloscope on a trolley by the bed, and an electric relay clicked on and off. The atmosphere seemed stiflingly warm.

'Good God,' muttered Kincaid under his breath. He was shocked by how frail his father looked.

'I'm afraid that post-operative infection is all too common in cases like this,' said Leslie.

'Why?' asked Kincaid. The question flustered the young

doctor, who was more used to relatives hanging on to his every word.

'I don't know why, exactly,' he stuttered. 'It just is. Old people are more susceptible to infections, I suppose; it's just one of those things.'

'You said that you'd started treatment?'

Leslie nodded and said, 'Penicillin, so there shouldn't be a problem.'

Kincaid could not take his eyes off his father. In his present surroundings he seemed so small. It was hard to believe he was the same man who could have the men down the club in hysterics with stories of times past in the yards.

'You will call me if he get's worse?'

'Of course,' said Leslie.

Kincaid called his sister at ten o'clock in the morning after checking with the hospital that there had been no deterioration in their father's condition. He found himself using the same platitudes that Dr Leslie had earlier employed for his benefit. 'It's just a bit of a set-back; the antibiotics will sort it out in no time.'

'Are you sure?' Lisa asked. 'You're not keeping something from me, are you?'

'Of course not,' said Kincaid, with more conviction than he felt. The old man had looked so weak in his unconscious world of tubes and electrodes. 'I'll call you if there's any change.'

'Maybe I should go in this morning,' suggested Lisa.

Kincaid managed to persuade her that there would be no point. It would be better to wait for a while. He hoped that the delay would give the antibiotics time to fight the infection so that the old man would at least be conscious when she went in to see him. He had just put down the phone when Eve rang. 'Can you meet me for lunch?' she asked.

'Of course, is something wrong?' Kincaid asked, thinking that she sounded upset.

'I can't talk now,' said Eve.

They arranged to meet at twelve-thirty.

*   *   *

Eve, who had a arrived a few minutes before him, smiled when she saw Kincaid, but he sensed that she was troubled. 'What's the problem?' he asked.

Eve opened the newspaper she had brought with her. She pointed to the picture of a woman half-way down one of the middle pages. 'Who is that?' she asked.

Kincaid took the paper and read an article headed, 'Local Actress Dies'. The name didn't mean anything to him, nor did the photograph. The story said that Moira Gaines, a Gateshead-born actress who had once appeared in several episodes of a television soap opera some years ago, had died in College Hospital after a short illness. She was forty-two. 'I'm sorry,' said Kincaid, 'it doesn't mean anything.'

'Look again,' said Eve.

Kincaid did so.

'Picture her with her hair down and combed to the left over her forehead.'

'Oh my God,' said Kincaid, as he saw what Eve was getting at, 'Greta Marsh!'

'The woman who played Greta,' said Eve. 'She was an actress.'

'And now she's dead,' murmured Kincaid.

Both of them looked at Moira Gaines' picture in silence for a moment.

'Apparently she just collapsed and died,' said Eve quietly.

Kincaid's face was full of doubt. 'And Anna Keats was due to meet her tomorrow afternoon,' he said hoarsely.

'I'm frightened,' said Eve, 'I've got such a bad feeling about all this.'

Kincaid shook his head and said, 'I know what you mean. Things are getting out of all proportion.'

Eve tried covering bits of the photograph at a time. She screwed up her eyes to gain new perspectives. 'Maybe it's not her,' she said. 'Maybe it's just someone who looks like her.'

This was a straw that Kincaid would have dearly liked to grasp, but couldn't. 'I think we both know different,' he said.

'The funeral is tomorrow afternoon,' said Eve. 'I'll be on duty, but maybe you should go along?'

'You think so?'

'Perhaps you'll find someone to tell you when Moira last worked,' said Eve.

Kincaid agreed that it might be worthwhile.

As Kincaid drove Eve back to the hospital he told her about his father.

'I'm sorry,' she said. 'It happens.'

'Tell me about post-operative infection,' said Kincaid.

'It's not as common as it used to be but it still happens,' said Eve.

'Exactly the kind of reply I would have expected from the medical profession,' said Kincaid.

Eve ignored the jibe, giving Kincaid the benefit of a little licence through being upset. 'It's not an easy question to answer,' she said, 'there are so many individual variables, the age of the patient, the degree of debilitation, luck . . .'

'And sheer incompetence,' added Kincaid.

'Stop it!' snapped Eve.

Kincaid was taken aback by Eve's sudden outburst. He didn't get a chance to say anything before she continued, 'I'm becoming heartily sick of your sarcasm and self-pity.'

'Self-pity?' questioned Kincaid.

'Self-pity,' repeated Eve. 'I'm sorry about what happened to your daughter, but it does not give you the right to label the whole medical profession as incompetent charlatans. It simply isn't true!'

Kincaid was reeling, but he wasn't ready to give in. 'Good God, they were treating my old man for bronchitis!' he exclaimed. 'He had cancer of the lung and his GP was giving him Smarties for his cough! That doesn't exactly . . .'

Eve interrupted him. 'The chances are that your father's GP would have diagnosed his condition correctly at his next visit.'

Kincaid kept his eyes on the road ahead, smarting angrily but saying nothing.

Eve continued, 'There are a lot of good people in the hospital. They are doing their best for your father and everyone else who happens to need them. Don't you dare go on dismissing them in this way!'

Kincaid brought the car to a halt. He kept both hands on the wheel, lowered his head and took a deep breath. 'I'm sorry,' he said. 'You're right. I carry this knot around inside me and sometimes it stops me seeing the good things. I always look for the bad, I can't explain it. I'm sorry.'

Eve said nothing until Kincaid turned his head to look at her. 'All right,' she said, 'I understand, I really do.'

Kincaid started the car again and they drove away from the kerb. A few minutes later Kincaid said, 'Tell me about Sir Martin Freeman.'

'He was a typical surgeon,' said Eve, 'loud, pushy, extrovert, larger than life, you know the type.'

'But brilliant?'

'I suppose so,' replied Eve uncertainly.

'There's some doubt?'

'He certainly got a lot of publicity,' replied Eve. 'Some would say more than he deserved.'

'How so?'

'Well, it may be sour grapes, but I've heard other surgeons suggest on occasion that Freeman wasn't quite the innovative genius he made himself out to be. Take the Greta Marsh operation, for example . . .'

'What about it?'

'One of the nurses I work beside is engaged to a surgeon, and he told her that the operation wasn't new at all. It had been done before.'

'But Freeman called a press conference, didn't he?'

'Yes,' agreed Eve.

'He would hardly do that if the procedure was common-place.'

'I don't think anyone was suggesting that the operation was commonplace,' said Eve, 'just that it had been done before.'

'Sounds awfully risky to steal someone else's thunder like that,' said Kincaid.

'I agree,' said Eve, 'but I suppose surgeons are used to taking risks.'

'Not with their own lives,' said Kincaid.

Eve shot him a warning glance and Kincaid smiled. 'Sorry,' he said, 'they're all very warm, wonderful human beings.'

'Just people,' said Eve, determined not to let Kincaid get away with anything.

They drove in silence for a bit before Kincaid asked, 'Why do you think Claire Affric screwed up so badly when she took over from Freeman?'

'She had just had her face slashed open with a scalpel. Will that do?'

'I'm sorry, I didn't realise,' said Kincaid. 'I didn't mean to sound critical, I was only asking.'

Eve said, 'It's my turn to be sorry. I over-reacted. It must have been a nightmare for her, poor woman; we all felt so sorry.'

'Have you seen her since the operation?' asked Kincaid

Eve shook her head.

They arrived at the hospital and Eve got out. Kincaid watched her disappear through the hospital gates. He found himself wishing that she would turn and look back because he wanted to see her smile again, but she didn't. It was early days, he thought, but he was beginning to think an awful lot of Staff Nurse Laing.

The chapel at the crematorium was cold and smelled of lysol. There were about twenty people scattered among pews which could have accommodated ten times that number. The congregation included one man who seemed vaguely familiar to Kincaid; this was because he had seen him on television at some time or other. He couldn't remember in which programme or in what context but it didn't matter; it fitted with the fact that Moira Gaines had been an actress. There didn't seem to be a husband in evidence, or anyone who fell easily into the category of close relative. Likewise there did not seem to be any children. Everyone present was over thirty.

As they waited for some sign of a priest, Kincaid tried to picture Moira Gaines' life. The mournful tones of an electric church organ did nothing to disabuse him of the notion that it had not been too wonderful. Only twenty people at her funeral, nineteen if he didn't count himself and he hadn't known her at all. What was more, none of the other people present seemed to know each other. He had not seen any nod of recognition pass between them. He had expected at least a small nucleus of women, those who had been Moira Gaines' closest friends, to be present, but this was not so.

The organ tune changed to the twenty-third psalm and a priest, adjusting his surplus round his ample body, appeared from a side door near the front. He seemed slightly out of breath and looked dishevelled, but Kincaid knew at first glance that he was the type who would always look like that. He had known men in his time who would look immaculate after spending the night in the gutter and conversely he had known those who would always look as if they had just emerged from the bottom end of a refuse chute.

The priest was one of the latter; his hair stood up at a variety of angles from his head, despite the obvious application of some greasy substance which had only made matters worse. His spectacles seemed to sit diagonally on his face, being much higher on the right than on the left, and the excess flesh around his neck seemed to flow unevenly over his collar, giving the impression that he was being strangled. There was a large wart on his left cheek; Kincaid imagined him shaving round it every morning. He could only surmise at the sartorial nightmare he felt sure lay under the untailored folds of the tent-like cassock.

Kincaid deduced that he was one of the 'duty priests' attached to the crematorium, those who were detailed to see off those customers who had no recent affiliation to any church. He had to fight off unpleasant thoughts concerning his father as he watched the priest flick through his order of service book with fingers that seemed to function more like thumbs.

Sounding like a man who had done the same all too often before, the priest intoned his way through the basic rudiments of the Church of England service in a high-pitched whine. He thanked God for the life of Moira Gaines, said a prayer, sang a hymn and pressed a button. The plain, pine coffin with a solitary wreath sitting on its lid, slid slowly back on unseen rollers and disappeared behind a purple velvet curtain.

The mourners began to leave the chapel and Kincaid took an interest in a well-dressed woman wearing a figure-hugging suit in black. She had an easy elegance that Kincaid associated with Parisian women ever since spending a weekend in Paris in his early twenties. A small black hat seemed exactly the right size for her hair style and a half-veil acted as the perfect foil for her perfect complexion. Kincaid tried to get a better look at her face, thinking that he might recognise her; this was based on an unconscious assumption that she must have something to do with the stage or show business.

As he worked his way nearer, the woman turned her head and he barely stifled a grimace as he saw that the other side of her face was marred by an unsightly and recent scar.

The woman had almost reached her car in the gravelled car park, which was situated near the gates of the crematorium, when Kincaid sidled up beside her. 'Dr Affric?' he said. 'It is Dr Affric, isn't it? Dr Claire Affric?'

The woman put her hand to her face, an almost unconscious gesture born of vanity, thought Kincaid.

'I'm sorry . . .' she said, 'I don't seem to . . .'

'My name is Kincaid.'

'Yes?' replied the woman, still puzzled.

'I'm a journalist.'

Despite the veil Kincaid saw her eyes fill with uncertainty. She didn't know which way to turn. 'What do you want?', she stammered.

'The truth,' said Kincaid. 'Now that we've been to the funeral of one Greta Marsh, tell me about the other one.'

Claire Affric seemed a little unsteady on her feet. She put both hands on the roof of her car and rested for a moment with her head hanging down. 'All right,' she said, with an air of resignation, 'I'll tell you everything.' She put away her car keys and said, 'Can we walk?'

Kincaid agreed. They walked towards the gardens attached

to the crematorium and started out along the path, their feet crunching slowly on the gravel.

'I should have known that it was a ridiculous idea, but I'm afraid I wasn't strong enough to protest. Mr Fields, the hospital manager, thought he could save my career with what he called a simple and harmless deception. Looking back it was an absolutely crazy notion, but I was very upset at the time.'

'Go on.'

'I made a complete mess of finishing the operation. My hands were shaking, I could feel the blood on my face from the cut and I knew I was going to be marked for life.'

'Not an ideal state for a surgeon to be in,' conceded Kincaid.

'Afterwards I couldn't stop shaking. I was in shock. I didn't realise what a mess I'd made until Gordon Fields told me. I was sent on sick leave and then he called and told me what he planned to do. At first I protested, but he insisted that the damage had been done as far as Greta was concerned. No amount of scandal in the newspapers would help her. He convinced me that his plan would hurt no one, my career would be saved and the hospital would avoid the unwanted attentions of the gutter press.'

'I see,' said Kincaid.

'I should have known we wouldn't get away with it,' said Claire.

'You say that your career would have been destroyed if the truth had got out. How so? Surely people would have understood the state you were in at the time?'

'That's not the way the human race works, Mr Kincaid,' said Claire. 'Certain people are not excused mistakes in this life, whatever the extenuating circumstances. Airline pilots are one, surgeons are another. Think about it; if you were lying in hospital waiting for your operation and your surgeon turned out to be Claire Affric, the one you had read about in the *Sun* as having left a woman without a face or a brain, what would you think?'

Kincaid conceded the point silently.

'Well, it's all academic now. My career *is* over. The question is, what other price has to be paid?'

'Who was responsible for putting me on the railway embankment?' asked Kincaid.

'Sorry about that,' said Claire. 'The people at Fingleton Grange didn't know who Greta was, just that she was a patient who had been referred from College Hospital. They called Mr Fields to say that some "nut", to use their word, had broken into the patient's room and was now lying unconscious on the floor. They wanted to know if they should call the police. He said that having the police all over the place would be a nuisance. Sorting it all out would take time and there would be endless paperwork. The two male nurses you ran into offered to "move" you themselves. They were a bit over-enthusiastic.'

'I'll say,' said Kincaid, ruefully.

They had reached the end of the 'garden of rest' and they paused before turning back. 'Tell me about Moira Gaines,' said Kincaid.

'Gordon hired her to play the part of Greta.'

'Did he know her personally?' asked Kincaid.

'Moira had a heart condition. She's been a patient at College Hospital on and off for the last four years. I knew her well, that's why I'm here today. She's not been able to work because of her illness, so the chance of earning a few pounds was more than welcome.'

'Who paid?'

'Mr Fields arranged it.'

'You didn't pay anything?'

'No.'

'What happens now?' Claire asked, as they started back to the car park. 'Should I leave the country?'

Kincaid could see that the question was serious, but he ignored it. 'Where is Greta Marsh now?' he asked.

'She's in a residential home in the Midlands; she'll be well cared for.'

'But she won't get better?'

'No,' said Claire quietly. She stopped walking and turned to face Kincaid. She said, 'I'd change places with her if I could, but I can't. Greta has to stay in the home and I'll have to live the rest of my life with the nightmares.'

Kincaid nodded.

'I can't even begin to tell anyone what it feels like,' said

Claire, her eyes bright with the pain of the memory. 'I don't think I've had a night's sleep since it happened. I doubt if I will ever again.'

They reached the car park. Kincaid held open the door of her car while she got in. 'How long before your readers get their story?' she asked.

'Maybe they won't,' said Kincaid.

Claire seemed stunned. She stopped fastening her seatbelt. 'Are you serious?' she asked quietly. 'Did I understand you correctly?'

Kincaid, still leaning on the open car door, looked down at Claire and said, 'Nothing I say or do will restore Greta Marsh to normal health. What you and Fields did was more stupid than criminal. I don't want to see your career in ruins over it any more than he does. Why don't you have a holiday, then come back to medicine and start all over again.'

Claire seemed bemused. She tried several times to say something before succeeding. 'I really don't know what to say,' she stammered. 'I can't begin to thank you.'

'Don't,' said Kincaid. 'See you around.' With that, he walked away.

Kincaid stopped the car on the way back and got out; suddenly he needed fresh air. Inside his head he felt cheated somehow, cheated because he wanted to feel good and thought that he deserved to – but instead he felt guilty. What the hell do you think you're doing, his conscience wanted to know. You are a reporter, it accused, it's your job to investigate and report facts, not to make judgement on them. Who do you think you are?

Against this self-inflicted onslaught Kincaid tried to argue with himself that he had a greater duty as a human being. What was so damned important about being a reporter, anyway? Was the public's right to know the truth really so sacrosanct? Damn it, he wasn't an automaton; he had a mind of his own. He had a right to decide which was the greater evil: keeping quiet about an ill-conceived deception or destroying a surgeon's career. He decided on the latter. Rubbish, insisted his conscience. Well, at least Eve will be pleased, he thought with a wry smile. Who would have thought that Kincaid would ever go soft on the medical profession?

Kincaid was sitting staring into space when the telephone startled him. It was Anna Keats.

'Mr Kincaid? I thought I should tell you that I did not meet with Greta today as planned.'

Kincaid was taken aback. Meeting Claire Affric at the funeral had put all thoughts of Anna Keats' planned meeting out of his mind. 'Really, Matron? What happened?'

'Mr Fields was very apologetic. He told me that Greta had a bad cold and had been confined to bed. It was very important for her to be fit by the end of the week because she was going away to start a new life.'

'Did he say where?'

'No, only that Greta sent her regards and said that she would be in touch as soon as she was settled.'

'I see,' said Kincaid. His mind was racing and he was cursing himself for forgetting about the problem that Anna Keats might pose; he had told her everything. 'And what did you say, Matron?' he asked, with bated breath.

'I said that I had reason to believe that all was not well with Greta, and if I did not hear from her within a week I would be taking the matter further. Did I do the right thing, Mr Kincaid?'

Kincaid closed his eyes. What had he done? He could hardly confess to Anna Keats that he had agreed to drop the matter to save Claire Affric's career, not to the only friend Greta had ever had. He felt like a criminal. He couldn't renege on what he had said to Claire Affric, but if Anna Keats was the one to break the story he would be up to his neck in it. 'You did the right thing, Matron,' he said flatly.

'What do we do now?' asked Anna Keats.

'I think we give them a few days.'

'Very well, I'll expect to hear from you.'

Kincaid replaced the receiver slowly and swore under his breath. What the hell was he going to do now?

*　　*　　*

Kincaid picked up Eve at the hospital and they drove to an Italian restaurant where they opted for lasagne and a bottle of Valpolicella. Despite the Mediterranean ambience and the cheerful bustle of the waiters, Eve could sense that something was wrong. She let Kincaid tell her in his own time.

'I met Dr Affric at the funeral.'

Eve raised her eyebrows; she saw that Kincaid was avoiding meeting her eyes. 'Did she confess?' she asked.

'Yes.'

'You're kidding,' exclaimed Eve.

Kincaid shook his head and said, 'No, she told me everything. It's as we thought. Fields hired Moira Gaines to play the part of Greta Marsh. He did it to save Claire Affric's career as a surgeon and to avoid an outbreak of horror stories about the hospital.'

'I see,' said Eve, but she saw that there was more to come.

'I said I'd keep quiet.'

'You did what?'

Kincaid looked Eve straight in the face for the first time. 'It's true,' he said. He told Eve his reasons.

'Well,' said Eve, with an air of resignation, 'who would have thought?'

'You think I've done the wrong thing, don't you?'

Eve looked down at her plate and toyed with her fork. 'That's not for me to say,' she said kindly. 'I can see both sides of the argument, always an unhappy position. I think that's why Liberal Democrats always look so miserable . . .'

Kincaid smiled at Eve's attempt at lightening the atmosphere. He said, 'I thought you'd be pleased that I hadn't automatically gone for the throat when I saw a medic on the run.'

It was Eve's turn to smile. She said, 'I hope that what I said the other night wasn't the reason for your decision.'

'You were right to say what you did,' Kincaid assured her. 'Unfortunately now I have the problem of Anna Keats.'

Eve put her hand to her mouth. 'Of course!' she exclaimed. 'She knows the truth. You told her.'

'And I can't un-tell her.'

'Couldn't you say that you were mistaken?' suggested Eve.

She instantly realised how weak her suggestion sounded. 'Of course you couldn't.'

Kincaid was reluctant to consider any scheme involving lying to Anna Keats, because he knew that the moment he did so he would become part of the whole deception over the fate of Greta Marsh. The thought irritated him.

'It's true what they say about lying,' said Eve. 'It starts with a small one, but that leads to another, then another and another.'

Kincaid gave her a less than appreciative look and reminded her that he hadn't lied to anyone.

'I'm sorry,' she said, placing her hand on his. 'I know that what you have decided is for the best and I respect and admire you for it. I hope Claire Affric appreciates just how much this means.'

'I think so,' said Kincaid.

'Let's walk for a bit,' suggested Eve, when they left the restaurant. Kincaid agreed. She made several attempts at conversation but they were all fated to peter out into silence.

'You are not a happy man, James Kincaid,' she said. 'I wish I could help.'

Kincaid squeezed her arm and apologised for being so preoccupied.

'Still thinking about Anna Keats?'

Kincaid nodded and said, 'I suppose so. I should have remembered about her involvement before making any rash promises to Claire Affric.'

'Tell her the truth,' said Eve. 'You said that she was a nice woman and that you liked her. Tell her the truth; let her decide what's best. The chances are that she will see it the way you do and let sleeping dogs lie.'

'I hadn't considered that,' confessed Kincaid. He liked the idea.

On the following morning Kincaid checked with the hospital. He was told that there had been no significant change in his father's condition. He called his sister, only to find out that she already knew this; she had checked with the hospital too.

'I'm going to visit him this afternoon,' said Lisa.

Kincaid didn't argue. He said, 'There's probably no point in our both going in together. I'll spend the afternoon with Kerry and check with you afterwards. If he's showing signs of coming round I'll see him in the evening. With this agreed, Kincaid called Harrington Hall to ask for an appointment with Anna Keats. His mouth went dry as he waited for the telephone to be answered.

'I'm afraid Miss Keats has a long weekend off. Can I help?' asked the voice.

'No, I'll call back,' said Kincaid, feeling deflated. He made himself an instant coffee, resolved to buy himself a cafetière, and had a slow walk round the garden. He cradled the mug in both hands. He had been reprieved for the weekend. Reprieve was the wrong word, he decided; limbo had been extended. He went indoors again and read his two morning papers.

The health minister, John Carlisle, featured prominently in both, having won a cabinet battle to extend the new health service sooner than anticipated on the grounds that it had been so successful in the north, and was even more cost effective than anyone had dared to hope.

Opposition coming mainly from within his own party had centred on matters of political philosophy rather than practicality. Centralisation of services was something that some members had spent their entire political career opposing; they found it difficult to change horses. Opposition spokesmen contented themselves with pointing out that the government was only implementing what they themselves had advocated all along. Kincaid smiled at the fact that some things never seemed to change. He was about to leave for the city when the telephone rang; it was his editor.

'Long time no hear,' said Fletcher.

'I'm sorry.'

'How's the story coming?'

'It's not.' Kincaid felt a creeping pang of guilt in his head; it was becoming a regular visitor.

'Pity,' said Fletcher, leaving a pause for Kincaid to elaborate.

'Just one of these things,' said Kincaid. 'You know how it goes.'

'Yes, they can't all be gems,' said Fletcher.

Kincaid thought he could detect a note of suspicion, perhaps even disbelief, in Fletcher's voice, but had to concede that this was probably born of his own discomfort at lying.

'You'll be back soon, then?'

'My father's ill. I'll wait till he's a bit better.'

'Suit yourself, but the car and the house . . .'

'I know,' said Kincaid. 'I'll take over the expenses. What's happening down there?'

'The grapevine's still alive with rumours of Carlisle going for the leadership before summer.'

'I see he managed to get the health scheme extended early,' said Kincaid.

'The more cynical among us might suggest that some MPs saw which way the wind was blowing and decided to collect some brownie points from a future PM.'

'Perish the thought,' said Kincaid.

'We're going to do a feature on Carlisle next week. Anything you care to contribute?'

'I don't think so, I don't know anything about the man; I don't even know where he comes from.'

'Not many people do, that's why we're doing it. How's Kerry?'

'I'm going to see her this afternoon.'

'Good, let me know when you're coming back.'

Kincaid drove into the city and went shopping. His first stop was a supermarket, where he loaded a trolley with anything that took his fancy, including three different brands of coffee and a plastic cafetière. He would have preferred a metal one but that would have meant going elsewhere. Shopping was not his favourite pastime. He did however steel himself to park near the centre of town and go in search of a toyshop. He wanted to buy some things for Kerry.

As he left the shop and started back to the car he became

aware of the smiles of passers-by. He was puzzled for a moment, but then realized that it was the large blonde doll that was attracting attention. He reflected on the fact that the world seemed a much nicer place when people smiled. He put the toys in the boot of the Lancia before looking at his watch and deciding to have something to eat before going up to the home.

'Well, Mr Kincaid, it appears that you are to have your way after all,' said Ethel Wilton.

'Really, Matron?' said Kincaid, affording her the title for once, 'In what way?'

'A working party set up in advance by the new mental health director for the region, Dr Sutton, have agreed to your request for reassessment for Kerry.'

Kincaid could see that the woman thought it a complete waste of time because she had not smiled once in giving him the news. It didn't matter, he was delighted. Kerry was to be given another chance.

EIGHT

Tolkien sat quietly with Frank Golightly and let him come to terms with the news. He was pleased that he seemed to be taking it well, perhaps better than he had expected, but then the man had had some time to think about it. The initial anger and despair had disappeared to be replaced with almost calm resignation, albeit suffused with an air of hopelessness.

'How long?' asked Golightly.

Hard to say,' replied Tolkien. 'A couple of years, maybe longer.'

'What will happen to me?'

'The Aids virus destroys your immune system; this leaves you very susceptible to infection. We can still fight infection, of course, where and when it arises. The hospital will use radiotherapy for your Kaposi problem and you'll be on AZT to slow down progress of the virus.'

'What kind of infections can I expect?' asked Golightly.

'There's no way of knowing which bugs you will be exposed to but there are a few diseases which are more common than others in Aids patients. Top of the list is Pneumocystis pneumonia; tuberculosis is also a frequent opportunist, but we can fight these things when they happen.'

'How about diet? Exercise? Those sort of things?'

'There's some evidence to show that the fitter you keep yourself the more able you will be to fight infection when it occurs.'

'But no sign of a cure.'

'Not yet,' said Tolkien quietly. The nurse-counsellors at

138

College Hospital will help you come to terms with all this and give you support and advice.'

'Social workers,' snorted Golightly.

'They're nurses who are specially trained in this field. You'll find them very helpful.'

'If you say so,' said Golightly, sounding unconvinced. He got up out of his chair.

'I'd like to make an appointment for you now,' said Tolkien.

Golightly hesitated, then decided not to argue. 'Go on, then,' he said.

Tolkien made the request through the computer. Golightly was given an appointment at three o'clock that afternoon.

'Have you told your wife?' Tolkien asked.

Golightly shook his head. 'I've tried a number of times,' he said, 'I just can't seem to do it.'

'Talk it over with the people at the clinic.'

'I will,' said Golightly.

Golightly left and Tolkien continued to stare at the door. He hadn't lied to Golightly, but he hadn't told him the whole truth about Aids either. He had not fully described the nightmare that the HIV virus would bring to him. A body without an immune system in a world full of bacterial and viral predators was like a defenceless lamb in the jungle, only death would not be as kind nor as quick. The legions of the microbe world would unleash a merciless attack until his body was reduced to a suppurating skeleton with fungus invading every orifice and tumours seeking out every organ.

Medicine was Tolkien's life, but sometimes he felt it was such an unequal struggle. This was one of these times. Experience had long replaced his simple, once-held view that man would progressively wipe out disease through improvements in living conditions and medical research. He had come to recognise that there were other factors at work in the great scheme of things, factors which didn't play by the rules. It almost seemed that for every disease that disappeared, another, even worse one would arise to take its place. In this order, the Aids virus was truly something special. Not since the great epidemics of typhus, cholera and black death had man had to face something so awesomely well equipped to destroy him completely.

Aids, which people in general seemed determined to ignore, believing it to be a pestilence confined to the outer fringes of society, was making its presence ever more felt. It was spreading now into the heterosexual community through cases like Golightly. There must be a real risk that Golightly's wife was also HIV positive. She might even be one of these people who believed that Aids was a million miles away from her life, or even someone who vociferously condemned Aids sufferers as people who had brought misfortune upon themselves. How many more travelling salesmen would bring home more than a sense of guilt before the community realised the extent of the problem?

The pain in his back was bad today. Tolkien had noticed before that there seemed to be a correlation with mood; the lower he felt the worse the pain would be. A good day would be one where the majority of patients he saw could be given treatment to cure their condition. Conversely, a bad one would be one where he was faced with a stream of people he could do very little to help. The latter kind was fast becoming the norm. He reached into his desk drawer and brought out the bottle of painkillers; he took two and called in the next patient.

Madeline Bell was five years old and a Down's syndrome child. Her mother, Angela Bell, had been in her early forties when she became pregnant, and because of her age had been tested by amniocentesis for any foetal abnormality. Down's syndrome had been diagnosed and the question of abortion raised. Angela had been adamant that she would not contemplate abortion in the circumstances, maintaining that Down's children could still have a worthwhile life. She had gone to full term and Madeline had been the result. There was no doubt that Angela doted on the child and Tolkien was happy to admit that, in the circumstances, the right decision had been made.

'How are we today?' he asked Madeline.

'She's not very well, Doctor,' replied her mother. 'She's had a bit of a cold and now I think she's getting a chest infection.'

As if on cue, Madeline demonstrated her cough.

Tolkien made playful tutting noises and put his stethoscope to his ears. He sounded Madeline's chest.

The child struggled a bit on her mother's knee at first, but then settled and Tolkien listened to both back and front. 'Deep breaths, Madeline,' he coaxed, taking one himself as a demonstration. The child, seeing this as a game, took one enormous breath and held it, her eyes sparkling with mischief.

'Come on, be a good girl,' encouraged her mother.

As the novelty of the situation wore off the child began to lose interest in Tolkien and his stethoscope. He was able to get some soundings. 'You're right,' he said to her mother, 'she's a bit bubbly. We'll give her something for that.' He asked Angela which chemist was best for her and then put his prescription through the computer. 'You can pick it up in an hour,' he said.

Whenever Tolkien felt that cynicism was beginning to colour his view of life too deeply, he took heart from people like Angela Bell. She restored his faith in human nature. She obviously doted on her child and was determined that Madeline should have the best quality of life possible. It was something he found entirely admirable because the odds were against her from the outset, and being an intelligent woman, she had known it.

Although he found it admirable, he did not find it all that understandable. He often came up against a conflict between his regard for nobility of spirit and plain logic. The logical scientist in him said that Angela Bell should have had her pregnancy terminated when the ante-natal tests had shown Down's syndrome, but she hadn't, and she had been proven right. There was a lot of love in that family.

Love was a force to be reckoned with, if not understood. It was the same force that made old Mrs Harrison look after her Harry long after her ability to do so had declined. It was behind Terry Feenan's concern for Karen and Judith. Yet it was often taken for granted. People gave and accepted it without a second thought. It was only people who did not have it who noticed; people like himself.

Tolkien had been an only child, born at a time when his parents had long given up thoughts of having children and had settled into a comfortable lifestyle for two people. Although they had given him everything a boy could want in material terms, there had been a lack of real affection in his childhood; plenty of adherence to parental duty, but little in the way of spontaneous hugs and kisses. Books had been his real companions; they had been his escape route from the solitude and the quiet of a house where the plants had rivalled ageing parents in displaying emotion. He had been praised, of course, when he did well at school, but only at the level of a smile and perhaps a present rather than anything more.

The location of the family home at some distance from the school and neighbouring houses meant that he did not have any close friends of his own age. Not being any good at games had decreed that he did not have Saturday morning soccer or rugby matches to explore peer-group relationships. Being rather small and unprepossessing in appearance, with ears that stuck out, he had not been a target for the interest of teenage girls later on, either.

Tolkien had been a virgin when he went up to medical school and had left it the same way. It was not that he was unpopular, more that he was invisible, a quiet, bookish student to whom everyone said hello but not much more. It hadn't bothered him too much at the time because he had never known any kind of emotional relationship, but he had become aware of how nice it must be to have someone care for you in a more physical sense.

It was not until his second term as a houseman in a general hospital in Birmingham that the delights of the opposite sex were revealed to him. A pushy young social climber of a nurse had decided to capture herself a doctor, and Tolkien had been her target. He had not been first choice by any means, but he wasn't willing to admit that at the time. She flattered him into wining and dining her and even believing that he was in love with her, not too difficult in a young man who knew nothing of the wiles of women or anything else about them, save for the physiological data he had been taught at medical school.

After a well-planned campaign during which she allowed him to progress from good-night kisses to fondling her breasts, to making exploratory forays into her underwear, she allowed him to make love to her. A few weeks later she announced that she was pregnant; when would Tolkien marry her?

Tolkien, filled with a sense of duty, agreed at once to the wedding and even managed to convince himself that it was what he wanted; marriage wouldn't be too bad and it was what all his contemporaries were doing. He bought a ring, received the congratulations of his colleagues and set about making plans. A few weeks later, he arrived unexpectedly one evening at his fiancée's flat to find her in bed with his senior registrar. Tolkien, true to his philosophical nature, had not been angry, just bemused. The marriage was called off, Claire admitted that she had never been pregnant and left the hospital to seek new hunting grounds.

Tolkien was first surprised and then relieved to find that he wasn't at all heart-broken. He had had a narrow escape. Perhaps being single wasn't so bad after all. Perhaps that was what he had wanted all along.

Tolkien looked at the sheet of paper his receptionist had handed him; it was a list of the patients who had requested house calls. There were seven and none of them looked too serious. With a bit of luck he should be finished by one-thirty and have the afternoon to himself. He had been meaning to visit the art gallery and take in a current exhibition of French Impressionist painting, if he got the chance.

At two-thirty in the afternoon, Tolkien found the art gallery surprisingly but welcomely quiet. He had half-expected there to be crowds, as this was the second day of the exhibition and it was scheduled to last for only a week. Perhaps he had overestimated the cultural appetite of his fellow citizens, or maybe it was because it was raining heavily. He found himself alone in a small room with seven paintings by Monet and rejoiced at the prospect. He sat down on the bench facing the first and began to enjoy it.

Trees and flowers were reflected in a small pond, the leaves and petals on the water being imperceptibly but definitely different from those above. Tolkien marvelled at the blend of colour, the perfection of nature being conveyed unerringly by a master craftsman. But there was more to it than visual pleasure, important though it was; he could feel the shade of the overhanging tree, he could feel the heaviness of summer, almost smell the scents as they rivalled each other for the attentions of insects whose buzzing was inside his head.

'Beautiful, isn't it,' said a voice behind him.

Tolkien was startled; he had been totally preoccupied with the painting. He turned round to find James Kincaid standing there. 'Yes, it is,' he replied, regaining his composure. 'Are you a fan?'

'I'm the other one,' said Kincaid, alluding to the fact that they appeared to be the only two people in the gallery.

'I'm not complaining,' said Tolkien.

'Me neither,' agreed Kincaid.

'How's your father?'

'Not so good, he's developed pneumonia.'

'I'm sorry.'

'How is computerised medicine?'

'It's fine,' said Tolkien. 'I've no complaints at all, which means I'm getting exactly what I want. I'm completely self ish.'

'I think it's called human nature,' said Kincaid, sitting down on the bench beside Tolkien.

A uniformed attendant appeared in the arch of the doorway and looked at the pair of them sitting there. Kincaid's baleful stare made him retreat and pretend to be about some other business.

'Why do they make these places so gloomy?' complained Tolkien, unhappy with the artificial light. 'If you ever get the chance, go and see Monet at his best in the Musee D'Orsay in Paris, or have you been already?'

Kincaid said he hadn't

'It used to be an old railway station. When they converted it they kept the glass roof. Sometimes the French can be quite brilliant. The result is that you can view the paintings in real daylight and see them as the artists must have done in their studios instead of in this gloomy crypt.'

Kincaid pointed to a small watercolour of a young girl in a vineyard. He said, 'She looks like my daughter. I think I told you about her?'

'She was brain damaged; you wanted the authorities to reassess her?'

'That's right, they've finally agreed to do it.'

'Excellent, I'm very glad for you,' said Tolkien.

'The matron at the home told me today.'

'Who's doing it? Did she say?'

'Someone called Sutton. He's to be the new mental health director for the region.'

'Can't say I've heard of him,' said Tolkien. 'He can't be a local appointment.'

'Apparently quite a few kids are going to be reassessed with a view to formulating new plans for the education of the mentally handicapped in the area.'

'Things are getting better every day,' said Tolkien. What we need now is for Carlisle to wave his magic wand and come up with some new geriatric units, particularly psycho-geriatric units. I'm seeing more and more old people with dementia problems, and there's nowhere to put them.'

'Why's that?'

Tolkien shrugged his shoulders and said, 'People are living longer. The more old people we have in the community, the more old people's problems we have. It's as simple as that.'

'A legacy of progress,' smiled Kincaid.

'You could say.'

'I've often thought that more research should be carried out into improving the quality of life rather than the prolonging of it, but the money always seems to go on fighting killers rather than maimers, if you know what I mean?'

'Very well,' said Tolkien. 'Cancer gets big bucks; arthritis gets peanuts.'

'That's it exactly,' said Kincaid, pleased that Tolkien agreed with him. 'I don't see the point in living till you're ninety if you're blind, deaf, incontinent and doo-lally.'

'Unfortunately that's something that happens to other people as far as the public are concerned. They'll buy flags in the High Street for heart transplants, but they're not too concerned with deafness. Brain tumours are serious but incontinence is a joke.'

'Why is that?' asked Kincaid.

'I don't know,' smiled Tolkien. 'Maybe some research should be done on it?'

Both men were smiling as they agreed to end the conversation and enjoy the paintings while they had the chance. Kincaid said that he would leave Tolkien to enjoy the Monets on his own and move next door. As he got up to leave, two old ladies dressed in fur coats and hats came in to the room; they were carrying shopping bags and had obviously decided to pop in out of the rain. Kincaid turned and shrugged his shoulders at Tolkien as he left. Tolkien smiled in reply.

'What are you so pleased about?' asked Eve when she met Kincaid at seven o'clock.

Kincaid told her the news about Kerry.

Eve said that she was pleased, but Kincaid could not help but notice that her enthusiasm was a bit muted. 'What's the matter?' he asked.

Eve put her hand on his arm and said, 'I'm sorry, it's great news, it's just that I'd hate you to build up your hopes too high. Kerry has been assessed before . . .'

'But they were wrong last time!' insisted Kincaid. 'This time it'll be different.'

'Who's doing the assessment?' asked Eve.

'The new mental health director, a man called Sutton. He's not local.'

'Why not?' asked Eve.

Kincaid found the question strange. 'I don't know,' he said, shrugging his shoulders, 'Isn't it usual to bring in people from outside?'

'No,' said Eve, 'it isn't.'

'Then maybe it's part of the new scheme of things.'

'It's absolutely amazing,' said Eve.

'What is?'

'The way that London has taken over everything to do with health in this area. Faceless men whom nobody knows just seem to appear from nowhere and start running things.'

'Maybe it's a good thing,' argued Kincaid. 'Maybe that's why everything is working so well? They've cut out the dead wood and put in people who know what they're doing.'

'I prefer accountability,' said Eve.

'Right now I'll settle for efficiency.'

Eve smiled and decided to give up the argument, seeing that Kincaid was too pleased about the prospect of his daughter's reassessment to be objective. 'What are we going to do?' she asked.

'First I have to call Lisa. If my old man's better, I'd like to call in and see him.'

'Of course,' said Eve.

Kevin Hardesty, Lisa's husband, answered. He said that Lisa had called from the hospital half an hour before to say that her father was worse and that if Kincaid called he was to tell him to come to the hospital. She was staying there for the moment.

'Not good?' said Eve, when she saw Kincaid's face.

'I think he's dying.'

As they drove Kincaid became impatient when they got caught up in traffic and seemed to catch every red light in town. Eve put her hand on his as he rubbed his palm against the gearstick at yet another hold-up. She didn't say anything, but then she didn't have to.

'I wanted there to be more time,' he said. 'There's so much that should be said before . . . I wanted to . . .'

'You want to tell him that you love him,' said Eve.

Kincaid took one hand off the wheel and rubbed it against his forehead. 'Something like that,' he said.

'Exactly that,' corrected Eve. 'It's all right, you know, grown-up men are allowed to say things like that. You wouldn't have any trouble if you were a Frenchman or a Spaniard or an Italian, but because you're a big Geordie lad you think it's sissie.'

'Him too,' said Kincaid.

'Tell him,' said Eve. 'As soon as we get there, tell him.'

147

'Assuming there's time,' said Kincaid, coming to another stop.

'I'm afraid he's very poorly,' said the nurse as they entered the ward. 'Your sister's with him.'

Eve gave Kincaid an encouraging pat on the arm and he went through into the side ward where his father lay. Lisa turned round and got up from where she had been sitting at the head of the bed. Kincaid kissed her lightly on the cheek and asked, 'How is he?'

'He hasn't come round at all. I've just been sitting here looking at him and remembering all the things we used to do together when we were kids.'

Kincaid brought over a chair from the corner and sat down on the opposite side of the bed from Lisa.

'Do you remember that holiday we had at Blackpool when you kicked the beach ball into the sea and Dad went in after it?'

Kincaid smiled as he remembered. 'There was a big hole in the sand he didn't know about.'

'And he went right under!' Lisa put her hand to her mouth at the thought.

'And his language when he got up,' said Kincaid.

'Mum went bright red.'

The old man moved slightly and groaned.

'Do you think he heard?' asked Lisa hopefully.

'They say that hearing is the last thing to go when you lose consciousness and the first to come back,' said Kincaid. 'Dad, can you hear me? It's Jim and Lisa.'

The old man moved again as if surfacing from some deep dream.

'We came to tell you . . . that we love you.'

After fifteen minutes or so, Kincaid suggested to Lisa that she should take a break and maybe get a cup of tea. He took her outside to the waiting area and introduced her to Eve, who said she would accompany her. Kincaid returned to sit with his father. As he watched him fight an unequal battle with

failing resources he began to think of an Alastair Reid poem
which dealt with the death of the poet's own father. He tried
to recall the lines:

> *There is so much might be said,*
> *Dear old man, before I find you dead;*
> *But we have become too separate.*
>
> *I am not ready*
> *To be without your frail and wasted body,*
> *Your miscellaneous mind-way.*

Kincaid could tell that his father was getting weaker all the
time. His cheeks grew more hollow and his breathing shallow.
At times, it was almost imperceptible. On one occasion when
he thought it had stopped altogether he leaned closer to see, as
Reid had put it, 'If the butterfly of his breath had fluttered clear
of death'.

Lisa returned and asked the inevitable question.

'It can't be long now,' replied Kincaid.

Tears appeared at the corners of Lisa's eyes and Kincaid
reached over to take her hand. He placed both their hands
on top of the old man's right hand which lay across his chest.

The fingers moved briefly and stiffly but it was a sign of
contact which made Kincaid and Lisa smile at each other. They
sat like that until the old man's breathing suddenly changed.
Kincaid felt Lisa's fingers tighten on his own as the old man
took a series of increasingly rapid breaths and then gave one
long sigh. His head fell to one side on the pillow.

Lisa began to sob and Kincaid came round to her side of the
bed and put his arms around her. 'He's gone, love,' he said. 'It
was painless and we were both with him.'

Eve took charge of consoling Lisa while Kincaid spoke to
Dr Leslie.

'I'm sorry,' said Leslie. 'He was just too old to fight the
infection.'

Kincaid thanked him for his efforts.

Eve volunteered to take Lisa home while Kincaid dealt with

the formalities at the hospital. Kincaid agreed, assuring Lisa that he would deal with all the arrangements for the funeral. She was not to worry about anything. He was concerned that Lisa should be upset as little as possible in her pregnancy. He knew that she had desperately wanted the old man to live long enough to see and, if possible, to know her first child, but it was not to be.

Kincaid sat patiently in Leslie's office while the young doctor adopted an air of solemnity which Kincaid could imagine him practising in front of a mirror. Each time he asked a question, Leslie would lean forward solicitously in his seat and nod gravely as if contemplating every syllable. One day, he thought, when computers are well enough developed, they will look and behave exactly like Leslie. For the moment he had to grin and bear it. He signed forms when and where he was told. A nurse came in and put a plastic bag down on the desk. 'These are Mr Kincaid's things,' she announced.

Kincaid lifted the bag off the desk and put it down by his feet. It was made of clear plastic; he could see the old man's toothbrush through it and his slippers. He wanted to destroy it, to throw it away, burn it. At this instant it seemed totally offensive, an insult. There was a separate, smaller envelope which the nurse had brought; Leslie handed it to Kincaid. 'His wedding ring,' he said solemnly.

Kincaid accepted it and put it in his pocket without comment. He felt claustrophobic; he had to get out of this place.

Leslie adjusted his spectacles and held out his hand to Kincaid as they neared the door. 'My deepest sympathy,' he said.

Kincaid wanted to tell Leslie how bad his performance was but he settled instead for, 'Thank you, Doctor, I'm sure you did your best.'

Kincaid took a deep breath of fresh air as he got outside and looked up at the night sky. He was carrying the plastic bag with his father's things in it and had started to look around for a bin to put it in when Eve drove through the gates in the

Lancia. He got in and threw the bag in the back, 'You drive,' he said.

'Where to?'

'A funeral parlour.'

'Which one?'

'Any one.'

'Will they be open at this time?' asked Eve.

'They have a night service,' said Kincaid. He had an image of a vulture sitting in a tree in the darkness, waiting, just waiting.

Night Bell, said the message on the brass plate. Kincaid rang it and put his arm round Eve's shoulder as they waited. He wanted to thank her for being there and to tell her how much it meant to him, but for the moment the words wouldn't come. A man answered the door and said, 'I'm sorry, do come in.'

They were led along a narrow corridor lit by a solitary bulb which couldn't have been more than sixty watts, thought Kincaid. The man turned into a small room and seated himself behind a desk, switching on a table lamp and indicating that he and Eve should sit down. 'Perhaps I could have some details of the deceased?' said the man.

Kincaid noticed that there was egg at the corner of the man's mouth and surmised that he had been disturbed at his supper. He wondered if he would go back to it when they left. He supposed that he would, but it would be cold. Maybe his wife would re-heat it and ask about the interruption. 'It's always the same,' she'd say. 'Every time you sit down to a meal that damned bell will go.'

Kincaid realised that he had been asked a question. He had not heard it but both the man and Eve were looking at him. 'I'm sorry?' he said.

'Cremation or burial?'

'Er . . . Burial.'

'You're sure?' asked the man.

'Yes.'

'Did your father have a minister?'

'No.'

151

'Then where, might I ask . . . ?'

'I'll call you with the details tomorrow,' said Kincaid, thinking ahead to the problem over St Mary's.

'Very well,' said the man, reaching down into his desk drawer and bringing out a catalogue. 'Perhaps we could decide on the other things?'

Eve saw the muscle in Kincaid's cheek harden as he watched the man open the book. This is our range of coffins. Perhaps you would care to look through them and decide on something you think suitable?' The man smiled, looked over his glasses at Kincaid and Eve in turn and turned the book towards them.

'This one's fine,' said Kincaid, pointing to the first one on the first page. He slid the book round again on the desk.

'Our standard pine model,' said the man, as if the words pained him. 'If you're sure . . .'

'I'm sure.'

'Very well, now perhaps we could decide on what handles and . . .' The man began to leaf through the pages of the catalogue.

Kincaid interrupted him. 'Look,' he said, 'you must have a simple, straightforward pine coffin that people get buried in?'

'Well, yes, but . . .'

'Then that's what I want. I don't want air conditioning and a stereo. I don't want fitted carpets and I don't want double glazing, just a plain pine box to bury my father in. All right?'

'Very well,' said the man, obviously offended but resolving to act in what he considered a professional manner.

Eve looked at Kincaid out of the corner of her eye. Her look was both critical and adoring.

'Bloody buzzards,' said Kincaid, as they left the premises.

'They have a job to do,' said Eve, taking his arm.

Kincaid snorted.

'I just can't believe that you are as untainted by human failing as you pretend,' said Eve.

'I don't pretend for one moment that I'm any such thing!' protested Kincaid.

'Oh yes you do,' insisted Eve. 'Not in so many words, but

every time you give the rest of us a bad time that's what you are inferring.'

Kincaid tried to rally a reply but failed and the corners of his mouth began to break into a smile. 'You are good for me,' he said.

'At last, we agree,' smiled Eve.

Kincaid looked at his watch; it was ten-thirty. The streets were busy, then he remembered that it was Saturday night. His father had died and the world hadn't noticed. Life was going on as if he had never been there. People were laughing, joking, driving around. They were watching television and putting the kettle on. There hadn't even been a hiccup in the scheme of things. That's how it was for his father, that's how it would be for him. That's how it would be for everyone.

'What are you thinking about?' asked Eve.

'Nothing.' replied Kincaid.

Across the city, in a semi-detached house in a long-curving crescent lined with cherry trees which would blossom in the next six weeks or so, Frank Golightly intertwined his fingers and freed them again in a continuous sequence as he pretended to watch television. He had been doing that almost incessantly since he had come in from the pub half an hour beforehand. He hadn't actually gone to the pub; he had been wandering round the streets wondering how to tell his wife what he had to.

Mary Golightly gave him an irritated look. 'Whatever is the matter with you?' she asked.

'Nothing,' lied Golightly. He changed to smoothing his thinning hair over his scalp.

'Yes there is. What aren't you telling me?'

'Mary, I . . .'

'Well, out with it.'

'I don't know where to begin. It's so awful.'

Mary Golightly put down her knitting and felt her heart miss a beat. Something was seriously wrong. She couldn't remember a time when Frank had looked and behaved this way. Maybe when her mother had died and he had taken the telephone call, but even then his eyes had been filled with concern, not with what she saw now. This look was quite different and quite terrible.

'I love you Mary, I always have, but just occasionally when I've been abroad . . . well, it's different for a man. We see sex differently from women, and . . .'

'What are you trying to say?' said Mary slowly, with an air of trepidation that made her body seem so heavy she was unable to move.

'On my last trip to Germany there was this girl, and . . .'

Mary Golightly's world was turning upside down. 'Are you trying to tell me you've fallen for another woman?' she demanded.

'No, no, nothing like that,' said Golightly, shaking his head.

'Then what?'

'I slept with her. There was nothing in it, but I slept with her . . . and she gave me . . .'

'Oh my God!' exclaimed Mary, putting her hands to her cheeks. She gave you one of these diseases, a venereal disease! And you have given it to . . . oh my sweet Lord. Oh God! How could you!' Mary Golightly buried her face in her hands and started to sob.

Golightly felt a great weight on his chest which threatened his breathing as he prepared himself to utter the last line. 'No,' he croaked, 'I'm afraid it's worse than that, she gave me Aids.'

For a few seconds time stood still. Mary stopped sobbing and there was a terrible silence which challenged Golightly's sanity. When his wife looked up at him he thought he was looking at a stranger. He had never seen her look that way before in his entire life. 'You bastard!' she said, in a voice he barely recognised that cut him to the quick. 'You absolute bastard.'

NINE

St Mary's was a pleasant church in a pleasant area. A middle-class congregation ensured that it was kept water-tight, well cared for in terms of building fabric and surrounded by tended lawns where the deceased lay beneath rows of erect, flower-fronted headstones. It was the sort of place where Sunday mornings brought lines of parked BMWs and Volvos and the sound of voices raised in song, determined to thank somebody for something and please God, if you've anything left over, help the rest.

Kincaid read the noticeboard by the gate. It was no ordinary noticeboard; its rectangular plainness had been disguised by making it into a little house. It even had a slate roof above it, a bit like a wishing well. The information on the board told him that the vicar was one Nigel Rees, and that he lived in St Mary's vicarage in the street adjoining.

Kincaid was still not sure how he would go about making the request; he decided to walk round the churchyard to court inspiration before seeking out the vicar. He came upon the seat that his father had mentioned, and sat down on it himself. The old man had been right; it was a beautiful spot. Trees and grass, shrubs and bushes, all seemed to blend together, bringing pleasure to the eye and calm to the spirit. It evoked memories of the Monets he and Tolkien had so much admired. He sat stock still for a full five minutes before reminding himself that he still had one enormous hurdle to cross if the old man's request was to be granted. At length he concluded what he already knew; there was no easy way.

*   *   *

155

The doorbell was answered by a woman Kincaid presumed to be the housekeeper. Wives didn't wear overalls, housekeepers did. They occasionally, as this one did, kept their hats on indoors.

'Yes, what is it?'

'I wonder if I could have a few words with Mr Rees, please,' said Kincaid.

'Is he expecting you?' asked the woman, her face slightly flushed and bearing testimony to the effort she had been putting into using the brush that she still held in her hand. Her irritated attitude reminded him of the maid he had come across on his visit to see Anna Keats. What was it about him, he wondered, that brought out the worst in these women? He settled for the hypothesis that they were hostile to everyone, he shouldn't take it personally.

'No,' Kincaid confessed, admitting to himself that he had not actually foreseen a problem in getting to talk to the vicar.

'What name?'

'Kincaid.'

The woman disappeared to come back a moment later. 'This way,' she said.

Kincaid followed her into the house and immediately noticed that it smelled like a library; wood panelling, old paper and dust. There was an umbrella stand in the hall made out of an elephant's foot. He wondered if anyone living in the house had ever thought about it; He could not avoid seeing the image of a three-legged elephant in the jungle as the housekeeper announced him.

A short, squat, balding man got up from a chair and held out his hand. 'Nigel Rees,' he said in a Welsh accent, 'I don't think I've had the pleasure.'

Kincaid shook the outstretched hand and admitted that there was no reason for the vicar to know who he was.

Rees made a joke about being relieved that he had not failed to recognise one of his parishioners, then asked, 'How can I help you, Mr Kincaid?'

'You have a very beautiful church here, Vicar,' said Kincaid.

'You are not the first one to have made that observation,' smiled Rees. 'I'm very lucky.'

'My father died on Saturday night in College Hospital.'

'I'm sorry to hear that.'

'His last wish was that he be buried here in St Mary's churchyard.'

'Was he a member of this church?' asked Rees.

Kincaid said that he was not.

Rees fell silent and Kincaid knew that rejection was in the air. It was just being packaged for easier consumption.

'Mr Kincaid,' Rees began, appearing to struggle with the words, 'I am afraid I have to say no. Your father was not a member of our congregation and if I were to grant this request there's no telling where it would end. I hope you can see that?'

'It would end with my father being buried in your yard, Vicar,' said Kincaid. 'There's no reason to believe it would set any kind of precedent.'

'No, but there's a principle involved,' said Rees. He had picked up a cat from the floor and was stroking it.

'That no shipyard workers be buried at St Mary's?' suggested Kincaid.

'Really, Mr Kincaid! I must protest. It's nothing like that at all. There is simply not space enough for everyone who would like to be buried here, and that's an end to it.'

'How many requests have you received from outsiders, Vicar?' asked Kincaid.

Rees took a deep breath, clearly niggled by Kincaid's persistence. 'Actually, none,' he said quietly.

Kincaid felt compelled to explain his behaviour. He said, 'I have to be single-minded about this Vicar, I am not asking for everyone to be buried here. I promised my father I would do my best for him so I'm here to give it my best shot. Anyone else can make their own arrangements.'

'I understand, Mr Kincaid, and I do sympathise, but I must refuse, I'm sorry.'

'I had a walk round the churchyard before I came along here, Vicar,' said Kincaid.

Rees shrugged his shoulders uncomfortably.

'You're not short of ground . . .'

'That's as may be, but . . .'

'In fact you've hardly started on that lower plot of land. There must be room for, what? One hundred more graves? Two?'

'Mr Kincaid, that is neither here nor there, it's the principle that's important. The matter is closed.'

Rees got up from his chair meaning it as a signal that Kincaid should leave.

The angry gesture triggered off some half-forgotten memory in Kincaid's head, an angry Welsh vicar, mouth turning down at one side, fending off news and cameramen. It was the flash of temper that had done it. Maybe a little more prodding and it would come back to him. He looked at Rees and said, 'Perhaps if you have an adjoining stable we could bury him there?'

Rees put down the cat and said angrily, 'I must ask you to leave.'

Kincaid remembered. He said, '1984, wasn't it? Or maybe 1985?'

Rees went deathly white. 'I don't know what you're talking about,' he said. 'Please leave this house.'

'Winchester, as I remember? A boy scout camp and two twelve-year-olds?'

Rees sank down into his chair again, all signs of anger gone, 'How on earth did you get on to that?' he asked.

'I didn't,' said Kincaid truthfully, 'it just came to me this minute. I'm a journalist, I tend to remember stories.'

'I was acquitted,' said Rees.

'So you were,' agreed Kincaid, 'but you had to move on. Presumably the parish council here knows all about your . . . acquittal?'

The look on Rees' face said otherwise.

Kincaid's pulse was racing. It was true that he had only just realised at that moment who Rees was, and his unpreparedness was bringing him dangerously close to blackmail. He was almost afraid to say another word. His memory had just shown him how to get something he wanted badly. But at what cost?

'I was innocent,' said Rees, 'those wicked boys made it all up.'

'And you were acquitted,' agreed Kincaid.

'But the stigma remains,' said Rees. 'No smoke without fire, isn't that how it goes?'

'A bit like labouring all your life,' said Kincaid. 'You may be perfectly respectable but nice folks still don't want to know you.'

'Where do we go from here?' asked Rees.

Kincaid held up his hand and said, 'Before you get the wrong idea, I have no intention of mentioning this to the parish council or to anyone else, for that matter. I promised my father that I would try to get him his wish and I have tried, but you have said no, and that's an end to it.'

Rees gave him a long hard look and said, 'I think I believe you.'

'The court said you were innocent. That's good enough for me.'

'Thank you, Mr Kincaid, but I have changed my mind. I will bury your father. Give me some details, then we can go and choose the spot.'

Later, as Kincaid left the churchyard, he turned at the gate and said, 'Just out of curiosity, Vicar . . .'

'You are going to ask if I still go to scout camps? I do not, Mr Kincaid, nor do I attend scout meetings, outings, jamborees or any other functions involving small boys, for one simple reason.'

'What's that?'

'After what they did to me, Mr Kincaid, I hate the little bastards.'

Kincaid left the vicarage uncertain in his own mind about whether or not he had been guilty of blackmail. Was his assertion that he would have kept quiet anyway, even in the event of a refusal to bury his father, genuine, or had it just been a ploy on his part to cover up the semblance of a crime? Kincaid was happy to conclude that it did not deserve too much thought.

He had achieved what he had suspected might be impossible; his father would be buried in St Mary's churchyard and the thought gave him a warm glow as he walked down the avenue to where he had left the Lancia. When he got back he called the undertakers and made the final arrangements, then he called Lisa. She was delighted at the news. 'How did you manage it?' she asked.

'The vicar was a very understanding man,' said Kincaid, feeling a bit like a Mafia boss.

'What a bit of luck, I never thought you'd manage it.'

'The ways of the Lord are strange,' said Kincaid, feeling perhaps that he was in danger of over-playing it. He told Lisa that he would be in touch soon and hung up. With a definite date set for the funeral, Kincaid now knew when he would return to London and the paper. He called Fletcher in London to tell him about his father's death. Fletcher offered his sympathy but said that he would be glad to see Kincaid back in harness.

'How's the piece on Carlisle coming along?' Kincaid asked. 'I haven't seen it in the paper yet.'

'Nor will you for a while yet,' said Fletcher, ruefully. 'We're having trouble finding out anything about the man.'

'What about Central Office?'

'We can get plenty of stuff from the time he entered parliament, but his early life is very sketchy. He seems to have been invisible at school and university. No one remembers him as anything other than a charming, amiable bloke who didn't seem to shine at anything in particular.'

'A late developer,' said Kincaid.

'Maybe. I don't suppose you'd fancy having a crack at it?'

'No thanks,' replied Kincaid. 'I find political biographies about as interesting as telephone directories.'

'Thought you'd say that,' said Fletcher.

'See you next week.'

The smile on Kincaid's face faded as he thought about the forthcoming meeting with Anna Keats. How friendly and understanding would Fletcher be if he ever found out that he had covered up a perfectly legitimate story? He wondered, yet all the time he knew the answer.

Neil Tolkien let out a long sigh; it was Sunday evening and his weekend off was nearly over. Not that he had done anything with it, but it was nice to know that the locum service was covering any calls from patients until Monday morning. It had been a bad week for the pain in his back, not that it had been agonising, but it had been persistent, a constant, nagging ache that, even when he wasn't conscious of it, would alter his demeanour and make him irritable and prone to depression.

The pain killers had not been too successful in dealing with it. Tonight he would give them some help by adding a few whiskys to the prescription. It was something that he would never allow patients to do, quite the reverse. It was so dangerous to mix drink and drugs but, by God it was also effective. It was as good as morphine and not so addictive. First, he would have a long, hot bath.

There was a small transistor radio on the windowsill in the bathroom which Tolkien listened to in the morning while he shaved to catch up on the day's news. He had been meaning to get new batteries for it for the past few days but had forgotten; he turned it on. The music was scratchy when he found Radio Three and he repositioned it to get the best reception. Alfred Brendel was playing Schubert, but it sounded like he was doing it inside a biscuit tin.

Tolkien settled down into the water and lay back to let the suds lap up over his shoulders and whisper in his ears. He had just closed his eyes when the telephone rang. He resolved to ignore it but finding this easier said than done he got out of the tub and padded out of the bathroom, leaving a trail of wet prints behind him.

'Tolkien.'

'Doctor, I'm sorry to bother you . . .'

Tolkien was about to consider how rich he'd be if he had a pound for every time he'd heard that expression when he recognised that there was real distress in the voice. 'Who is this?' he asked quietly. It was always important to get a name or an address early in this situation in case the person concerned hung up.

'My name is Mary Golightly,' said the voice.

Tolkien's mouth tensed. It was Frank Golightly's wife. He must have told her. 'How can I help you, Mrs Golightly?'

'It's Frank . . .'

'What about him?'

'I've stabbed him . . .'

Tolkien couldn't hide the gasp. 'You've done what?' he whispered.

'I've stabbed him; I think he's dead.'

Tolkien's unwillingness to believe the horror of what he was hearing evaporated in an instant. 'I'll be right there,' he said. 'Do what you can to stop the bleeding.'

'No!'

'You must!' insisted Tolkien.

'I won't touch him!'

Tolkien slammed down the receiver, swore twice then picked it up again to call the emergency services. He spoke to the ambulance service first, giving them Golightly's address and saying what had happened. 'There's one more thing,' he added.

'What's that?' asked the controller.

'The patient is high risk.'

'Understood,' murmured the controller.

Tolkien spoke next to the police, giving them the same information.

He struggled into his clothes, a task made more difficult by the fact that he had not dried himself properly, but there was no time to lose. He picked up his bag and headed for the door, leaving the bath water a stagnant pond with curls of steam moving slowly over the surface like autumn mist. The flat lights were left on and Alfred Brendel was still playing Schubert inside the biscuit tin.

Tolkien did not have to look at the house numbers, an ambulance had already arrived. He parked behind it and got out as the squeal of tyres behind him announced the arrival of the police.

162

'How well do you know the woman?' asked the inspector in charge.

'Not well,' said Tolkien. 'She's on my list but I can't recall seeing her in the last year or so.'

'It sounds like she's gone berserk,' said the policeman.

Tolkien shook his head and said, 'No, nothing like that.'

'But she's stabbed her husband. I can't afford to take risks with the men's lives.'

'I don't think there's any risk to other people,' said Tolkien, 'not from violence, but blood is another matter.'

'Yes, I heard. The men have been instructed to wear gloves.'

'Let me try first,' said Tolkien, 'he may still be alive.' Tolkien knocked on the front door and called out, 'Mrs Golightly? It's Dr Tolkien.'

There was no need to repeat the exercise. The door opened slowly and framed in the hallway was Mary Golightly, her dress covered in blood and a hollow look in her eyes. 'He deserved it,' she said.

Tolkien turned and saw that the policemen were reluctant to approach. He could understand it; Mary Golightly was drenched in blood. Their rubber gloves seemed woefully inadequate. The ambulancemen were donning suits and visors. Tolkien moved past Mary Golightly and found her husband lying on the floor of the living-room in a pool of blood.

There was also a great deal of blood over the walls and furniture, indicating that he had not fallen to the floor immediately but had staggered around the room first, knocking over ornaments and pulling one curtain from the window. He still clutched it in his right hand. His eyes were open but Tolkien knew that they saw nothing; the prospect of eternity was the only thing facing Frank Golightly. He put on a pair of surgical gloves and checked for a carotid pulse. There was none.

Tolkien looked up and saw Mary Golightly in the doorway watching him. The policemen were behind her but still kept their distance.

'Is he dead?' she asked.

'I'm afraid so,' said Tolkien.

She gave a small, wry smile and then looked up from the

163

body so that Tolkien could see the agony that lurked in her eyes.

The hellish scene was made all the more surreal by the ordinariness of the room. There were pictures of the family dotted around the furniture, a football coupon, Mary Golightly's knitting lying on a chair. Freshly-ironed shirts were hanging on a clothes stand, unaware that their owner would now never wear them. Things would never be the same again in this house. Even when new occupants came the neighbours would still talk about it in hushed tones. People would point it out to strangers. Children would be afraid of it.

'Sit down, Mrs Golightly,' said Tolkien, gently.

Mary Golightly complied without looking at Tolkien. Her eyes were fixed again on the body on the floor. As soon as she sat down the police inspector appeared in the doorway and beckoned Tolkien.

'What the hell are we going to do?' he asked, in an urgent whisper.

'What do you mean?' asked Tolkien.

'Christ, look at her man, she's covered in the stuff.'

'We'll have to clean her up.'

'I don't think that . . .'

'I'll do it,' said Tolkien. 'Have someone run a bath will you, and we'll need the community health people over here with a decontamination squad.'

The inspector moved back, taking his men with him. In the background Tolkien heard him issue instructions. He sat down opposite Mary Golightly.

'What will happen to me?' she asked, still staring at the corpse of her husband.

'I don't know, Mary,' confessed Tolkien.

'I'll go to prison, I suppose.'

'Maybe not. You were very upset. It must have been a terrible shock.'

'When will I know if I have Aids?'

'You'll be blood tested for the presence of the HIV virus, but even if you test positive that doesn't mean to say you will get Aids; some people don't. If you do test positive there's usually a period of time before full-blown Aids develops.'

'Do you think I will have it?'

'It's possible,' replied Tolkien.

'Thank you,' said Mary Golightly.

Tolkien looked at her questioningly.

'Thank you for not lying to me.' Mary Golightly explained. She reached down at the side of her chair and brought up a sharp-pointed kitchen knife. The blood on it said that it was the one she had used to stab her husband.

Tolkien stopped breathing, mesmerised by the sight of the knife.

'You'll be wanting this,' she said, and laid it down by the body.

Tolkien breathed again.

Mary Golightly had come out of her trance-like state and was now conscious of what was going on around her. She looked at her bloodstained dress and then at Tolkien. 'I must be a danger to everyone,' she said.

The statement brought a lump to Tolkien's throat. He could see the kind of person Mary Golightly really was before circumstances had pushed her briefly outside the bounds of sanity. She was reverting to the ordinary housewife she always had been.

Tolkien said that a bath had been run for her; she should bathe and change as quickly as possible.

'What about . . . ?' Mary looked down at her dress.

'Plastic rubbish sacks,' said Tolkien. 'Do you have any?'

'In the kitchen.'

Tolkien watched the police car take away Mary Golightly. Her husband's body was removed in a sealed bag by men wearing overalls and visors and shortly afterwards the decontamination squad arrived to start making the house safe again. They had to wait while the police forensic team finished their work, but the circumstances of the murder had reduced the demand for their expertise to a minimum.

'What a mess,' said the inspector, as Tolkien closed his bag and prepared to leave. 'People never fail to amaze me.'

'Me neither,' said Tolkien sadly, and wished him good-night.

Kincaid spent Monday morning clearing his father's house. It was something that had to be done, but a job that he approached with a heavy heart. He had agreed with Lisa that there was nothing either of them wanted to keep with regard to the furniture, so it was just a case of gathering together personal effects before inviting the social services to take what they wanted and then arrange for clearance of the rest.

Kincaid had to steel himself not to dwell on any object too long. He knew that the house was full of things which would trigger off memories if he let them, and he had decided to fight sentimentality rather than give in to it. This only worked up to a point; it was impossible to avoid all allusions to the past. He came across a battered spectacle case which held his mother's glasses; his father must have hung on to them. He couldn't help but see her wearing them. There was a dog-eared pack of playing cards with tartan backs, which he remembered the family playing snap with when he and his sister had been very young. He could almost hear the excited squabbling, feel the tension as more and more cards were played without a call.

Kincaid systematically emptied drawers and cupboards and packed several tea chests with the contents before he decided that he had done all he could. It had started to rain; he became aware of water trickling out through the broken gutter on to the stone flags outside. He went over to the kitchen window to look. He had planned to fix that bit of guttering, but now there was no need. Soon it would be someone else's problem.

Kincaid drove over to see Kerry in the afternoon. Mrs Wilton was off duty but her deputy said that there had been no word as yet about reassessment dates. This didn't worry Kincaid unduly and he took the view that if he had waited this long another few days would not make much difference. It was a view with which he even surprised himself, but the truth was that he was still euphoric about Kerry being granted reassessment at all.

Kerry was sitting alone. There were other children in the room and two members of staff, but Kerry seemed content to sit on her own, ostensibly to examine her feet. Kincaid nodded to one of the nurses and pointed to Kerry with a questioning look in his eyes. The girl replied with a smile and a nod of affirmation. Kincaid went over to Kerry.

At first she did not acknowledge him but after a few moments she stopped pulling at her toes and looked up. Kincaid smiled and to his utter joy, Kerry smiled back spontaneously. She returned to playing with her toes but stopped again to look at Kincaid and he felt she was trying to communicate something. He knelt down beside her and started to count her toes, one at a time.

'This little piggie went to market, this little piggie stayed at home . . .'

Kerry looked at her toes, spellbound.

'This little piggie had roast beef and this little piggie had none.'

Kerry had not moved.

'And this little piggie . . .' As Kincaid paused before the tickle he felt Kerry shy away and curl up. He looked at her, almost frightened to believe what he was seeing. Kerry knew! She remembered! She remembered what came next!

It was Kincaid's turn to be spellbound. For Kerry the moment had passed and she had now become intent on slapping her thighs, but for Kincaid the moment lived on. Kerry had shown clear signs of having remembered something from her past and also the capacity to anticipate what was coming next. 'I was right,' he whispered. 'I knew it all along.'

'Is everything all right, Mr Kincaid?' asked a nurse standing at his shoulder.

'Everything is just fine, Nurse,' he replied, without looking at her because he was still watching Kerry. 'Just fine.'

Kincaid tried to elicit some other sign of recognition from Kerry, but without success. She had grown interested in the toys the other children were playing with and moved over to join them.

*   *   *

Kincaid could hardly wait to tell Eve when he met her in the evening. 'She actually knew!' he insisted.

Eve laughed at having to cope with Kincaid, who was behaving like a Labrador puppy. 'I'm delighted,' she said. 'That is really fantastic news.'

'I'm sorry, I should have asked how your day was,' said Kincaid.

'Just fine,' smiled Eve. 'Now tell me more about Kerry.'

Kincaid went through the story again, as much for his own benefit as Eve's. 'This must mean I am right,' he insisted. 'Kerry does have the ability to improve. Her condition is not final.'

'I think you're right,' agreed Eve, 'I really do.'

'It's just a question now of convincing this Sutton character when he arrives.'

'I checked up on him,' said Eve. 'He is being sent from London.'

'And you still disapprove?' asked Kincaid.

'I do,' said Eve, determined to stick to her guns. 'Sutton is being sent here to take charge of all matters relating to mental health in the region, without any reference at all to the local health board. London is now effectively controlling all health matters in the north; the people up here have no say at all.'

'We've had this argument before,' said Kincaid. 'If the service is good does it really matter?'

'If they can do it with something good they can equally well do it with something that's bad,' insisted Eve.

'Believe me, I can understand your point of view,' said Kincaid. 'But if you are arguing on grounds of principle why do we not hear complaints from the regional council and the health board? Surely if they thought a principle was at risk they'd be shouting their heads off?'

'Why not indeed,' said Eve. Her reply had a cryptic content that Kincaid insisted she explain.

'The council have been encouraged to see the London influence as an extra commitment on the part of the government to the region. All the people they second to the region are paid directly by London and they have their own budgets, again funded directly by London. There is no cost to the region.

Ostensibly the council still runs the service with its usual budget, but London has effectively taken control by funding key posts and filling them directly as "extras".'

'So the council see it as getting the same money but having to pay for less?' said Kincaid.

'Exactly.'

'What about the health board, surely they are the losers if control has been taken away from them?'

'I would say so, yes.'

'So why aren't they complaining?' asked Kincaid.

'Precisely. Why aren't they?' said Eve.

For a moment Kincaid was puzzled, then he saw what Eve was getting at. 'You're not suggesting that they have been bought?' he said incredulously.

'I'm saying nothing of the sort. I'm just asking the same question you did.'

'Maybe they are far-sighted enough to see that what's happening is the best for the region and the people,' said Kincaid.

'Maybe,' said Eve, but her tone suggested otherwise.

Kincaid privately shared her doubt. He had never known any kind of political animal relinquish power without a struggle.

'You're the journalist, why don't you ask them?' said Eve.

'Who do you suggest I ask?' said Kincaid.

'The chairman is a man called Peter Gilmore. You can get his address from the book.'

'Can you get me the names of the other board members?'

'Tomorrow,' said Eve.

TEN

As soon as he entered Harrington Hall on Tuesday morning Kincaid knew that something was amiss; there was an atmosphere about the place. It was particularly noticeable because on the occasion of his last visit he had been struck by the air of bustling efficiency and signs of how well the staff worked together. At the time he had interpreted it as a sign of good leadership on the part of Anna Keats. Staff motivation was all-important in a hospital. He was uncertain as to how to take the current atmosphere, but he did not have time to contemplate things before he was shown in to Anna Keats' office.

'I trust you had a pleasant weekend, Matron?' said Kincaid, hoping that he appeared and sounded relaxed, when in truth he felt the complete opposite. His stomach was in knots.

Anna Keats glanced up at him but ignored the pleasantry. 'I have come to a decision over the last few days,' she said, looking back down at her desk.

'Yes, Matron?' said Kincaid, fearing the worst, that she had decided to go public on her own.

'I have decided to abandon my request to see Greta Marsh.'

Kincaid was stunned for a moment. This was exactly the outcome he had hoped to achieve, but only after presenting a reasoned argument. Here was Anna Keats suggesting it on her own. He almost had to choke back the plea he had been ready to make on behalf of Claire Affric's career. He took a moment to compose himself and then, when he had recovered sufficient aplomb, felt obliged to ask why.

'I just don't feel that I want to pursue the matter any further,' said Anna Keats, still keeping her eyes glued to the desk. She sounded upset and her reply seemed weak and puzzling to Kincaid, but he was not going to push his luck. If the firing squad did not want to pull the trigger, who was he to argue? He was aware of the ticking of an old clock on the wall and how it was out of synchrony with the beating of the pulse on the side of Anna Keats' neck. After what he thought was a suitable pause he said quietly, 'Very well, Matron, if that's your decision then of course I'll respect it.'

Anna Keats looked up at him for the first time and he was disturbed at the expression in her eyes. There was a strange mixture of emotions there; tiredness, relief, pain, perhaps? Something had upset her deeply and it was quite obvious that she could not cope with the Greta Marsh problem on top of everything else, whatever 'everything else' was.

Kincaid asked, 'Is there anything I can do to help, Matron? You seem distraught.'

'Thank you, Mr Kincaid, but no. If you'll excuse me . . . ?'

Kincaid got up to leave. 'If you're sure, Matron?' he asked.

'Quite,' replied Anna Keats.

Kincaid left the room feeling uneasy. He liked Anna Keats and, despite his relief at being let off the hook over Greta Marsh, he was genuinely concerned about her. He wondered whether or not he should try again to offer help, but finally decided against it. The one-armed domestic had been watching him suspiciously as he deliberated outside Anna Keats' door. He smiled but got the expected frosty response.

There would be no point in trying to find out anything from her, but some of the other staff might know what was wrong with the matron. On reflection, he was almost certain that they would and that that knowledge was responsible for the air of gloom he had noticed on the way in.

As he neared the front entrance he looked around for someone to talk to. There was only one nurse to be seen and she was heading off in the other direction. That left the staff at the reception desk and he was reluctant to approach them, because experience had taught him that they would be the least likely to give anything away. They were trained to be obstructive.

Outside in the garden he could see two gardeners digging over a long, narrow flowerbed. The ground seemed wet and heavy and the earth clung tenaciously to their spades like sticky goo, forcing them periodically to shake it off. One of them put a hand on his back and paused to rest on the handle of his spade. His partner said something and they both smiled. Kincaid decided to pass the time of day with them.

'Looks like hard work,' he said cheerfully as he stopped beside the men.

'Feels like it, too,' said the older man, who had been massaging his back.

'Not the best of soils,' said Kincaid.

'Holds the water like a sponge, man.'

'What you need is one of these machines,' said Kincaid, making a circular motion with his hands, 'A rotovator, I think they call them.'

'I'll speak to Matron,' laughed the man.

'But not today,' said Kincaid, grasping his opportunity. 'She's not exactly in the best of moods.'

'It's her dog,' said the man.

'Her dog?' Kincaid asked, innocently.

'Her dog was killed at the weekend,' explained the man. 'She loved that animal.'

'A car?' asked Kincaid

'An axe,' said the younger of the gardeners.

Kincaid thought that he had misheard. 'A what?' he asked.

'An axe. Some bastard cut the poor mutt's head off.'

Kincaid was lost for words.

'Bloody yobs,' said the old man.

'Want their bloody heads looked at if you ask me,' said the younger man.

'It was all she had in the world.'

'Tragic,' said Kincaid.

Kincaid needed a drink. He looked at his watch and saw that it was nearly lunchtime; the pubs would be open. There was one at the corner of the junction with the main road, the Duke of Northumberland, if he remembered rightly.

There were only three other customers in the bar, all drinking beer. Kincaid ordered a gin and tonic and took it to a seat where the sunlight was coming in through a stained-glass window depicting a military coat of arms. At this time in the day the copper ashtray on the table in front of him was clean and shining. He turned it round slowly so that the sun caught its dimples as he thought about the events of the morning.

There was no way he could have foreseen that a mutilated dog would play a role in the outcome of his meeting with Anna Keats. It was an image he did not care to entertain, but it kept recurring. It wasn't just the straightforward horror of such a mindless act that bothered him. There was something else, a feeling of unease, a feeling that he should be making correlations, but his only desire was to suppress them. He decided not to order lunch and left the pub.

Neil Tolkien was having a bad morning. It had got off to the wrong start when he had to delay the start of surgery while he dealt with paperwork and police questions relating to the events of Sunday night. When eventually he got round to opening his mail he found that both Terry Feenan and Karen had been found to be HIV positive by the special lab at College Hospital, where he had sent their blood samples. 'Christ, what a mess,' he said under his breath as he read the report. The baby was still negative; the chances were that she had been born before Karen had contracted the Aids virus. If that were so then she would probably remain negative, but her future seemed to be already mapped out. She was destined to become an orphan.

Tolkien ordered supplies of AZT via the computer link to the College Hospital pharmacy. The prescriptions were agreed without question. His problem now would lie in convincing the pair of them that they should start the treatment. He suspected that their effort at coming off heroin would now be a lost cause. There was probably no way that they, or anyone for that matter, could cope with the combined effects of hard drug withdrawal and the news that they were infected with the Aids virus. Terry Feenan had promised to attend the drug clinic on Tuesday evening. Tolkien had till then to think about it.

There was a courtesy letter from the consultant in charge of ward eleven at College Hospital, saying that Harry Harrison had contracted bronchitis since being admitted and was being treated for it. He would be detained a bit longer than the week he had originally been admitted for. The longer the better, thought Tolkien,: it would give Mrs Harrison an extra break from looking after him.

It was eleven-thirty before Tolkien started to make his house calls. There were four this morning; three were routine but the fourth was a request from Angela Bell that he call and take a look at Madeline. He saw Mrs Bell standing anxiously at the window as he pulled up outside.

'I'm so glad you're here,' she said, 'Maddy's not well at all.'

Tolkien followed her into a bright, airy bedroom where Madeline lay. She was surrounded by toys and the wallpaper told the story of the three bears. Madeline lay on her side, very pale and quiet. One arm was outside the covers and Tolkien could see that it was damp with sweat. He sat down on the edge of the bed and smoothed the hair back from the child's forehead. 'Now then, what's the matter?' he asked gently.

The child did not respond. He did not expect her to, and her mother filled in the details. Madeline had seemed all right on the previous evening but at some time during the night she had developed a fever and had been sick more than once. When she had shown no improvement by morning and no interest in eating anything, Angela had called the surgery.

'You did the right thing,' said Tolkien, sounding the child's chest. 'She's not well at all. You did get the pills from the chemist I prescribed?'

'Yes, Doctor.'

There was no need to ask Angela Bell if she had been giving them to the child. She was probably the most conscientious mother in the city.

'I think we'd better have her admitted to hospital,' said Tolkien.

Angela Bell was visibly upset. 'Is that absolutely necessary?'

she asked. 'Couldn't I look after her here if you tell me what to do?'

Tolkien shook his head. 'She needs hospital care,' he insisted. 'It's best when all the facilities are to hand, then whatever happens, they can cope.'

'Is it serious, then?' asked Angela Bell.

'Her chest infection has definitely got worse and Down's children like Madeline don't respond so well to treatment.'

Angela Bell put her hands to her face and turned away so that her daughter wouldn't see that she was upset. Tolkien got up to comfort her.

'I don't know what I'd do without my baby,' she sobbed.

'The sooner we get her into hospital the better, then,' said Tolkien.

'The phone's in the hall, I'll get her things together.'

The ambulance arrived within ten minutes and two pleasant ambulancemen moved Madeline out into the vehicle and did their best to cheer her mother up as they helped her into the back. Tolkien said that he would follow in his car. As they drove across town he reflected on the sudden downturn in Madeline's condition. He had felt quite certain when he first saw her that the child only had a mild chest infection which would be cleared up in no time with the ampicillin treatment he had prescribed. For some reason, the drug was having little or no effect at all on the infection. This was unusual; he made a mental note to ask at the hospital for a copy of the lab report when it became available.

The ward sister in children's medical was plump and jovial and exuded a warmth which made children think of fairy godmothers and inspired confidence in their parents. She invited Angela to help get Madeline into bed, while Tolkien had a word with the admitting houseman. Tolkien gave him details of Madeline's treatment and recorded his surprise at how suddenly her condition had deteriorated.

'It sometimes happens this way with Down's children,' said the hospital doctor. 'One minute they're as right as rain, the next they're fighting for their life.'

175

'The ampicillin seems to have made no improvement at all,' said Tolkien.

The houseman nodded and said, 'We'll give cephalexin a try.'

With Madeline safely in bed and a change of antibiotic on its way up to the ward from the pharmacy, Tolkien offered Angela Bell a lift home. She was reluctant to leave at first, but the combined efforts of the ward sister and Tolkien persuaded her that there would be very little point in her hanging around. Someone would call her if there was any change in Madeline's condition.

On the way back Tolkien tried to persuade her that there was every chance that Madeline would make a complete recovery, but he could sense that he was batting on a losing wicket. Angela Bell was a very worried lady. He dropped her outside her house and headed back to the surgery.

The afternoon post had arrived by the time he got in. He made himself a couple of cheese sandwiches and a cup of tea for lunch, and sat down to open it. Mostly routine stuff, circulars, a free appointment diary from a drug company, an invitation to a seminar on modern diabetes treatment. Wine and cheese would be provided, courtesy of yet another drug company. There was an official letter informing him that a patient he had treated on weekend locum duty had subsequently died after developing post-operative infection at the College Hospital. His name was Kincaid.

'Shit,' said Tolkien, recognising the name, 'James Kincaid's father.' He would have even less regard for the medical profession now. The last letter he opened was even more depressing; the blood test on Mary Golightly was positive. Her husband had given her Aids.

Kincaid checked the address he had written down for the chairman of the health board and found he had not forgotten it. He didn't think his chances of getting an interview by just turning up on the doorstep were good, but he decided it was worth a try. The alternative of telephoning to make an appointment would just give his subject time to prepare himself.

The house was an imposing Victorian villa standing in mature gardens which had been planted in an age when the cost of horticultural help had not been a consideration. Quite a bit of the shrubbery had been allowed to run wild and modern-day care stopped short at mowing the lawns and keeping the rest at bay. Tolkien was encouraged to see two cars parked on the drive. One was a dark green Rover, the other a Ford Fiesta. He suspected he was looking for the driver of the Rover. His feet made plenty of noise on the red gravel path but did not seem to excite any interest from within; he rang the bell and waited.

The door was answered by a teenage girl with long blonde hair who was desperately trying to control an energetic golden Labrador puppy who seemed hell-bent on leaping up at Kincaid.

Kincaid smiled and bent down to make a fuss of the dog.

'Sorry about that,' said the girl, pushing her hair back.

'No problem,' replied Kincaid. 'Is Mr Gilmore in?' he asked.

'Yes, who should I say is calling?' asked the girl as she took charge of the puppy again.

'James Kincaid.'

The girl returned a few moments later, accompanied by a man Kincaid took to be her father. He was dressed casually but expensively, Kincaid noted, in slacks and sweater which managed to suggest both athleticism and wealth.

'I'm Gilmore,' said the man. 'I don't think I've had the pleasure.'

'We haven't met,' confessed Kincaid. 'I'm a journalist, I was in the area doing a piece about how good the new health service up here is and I wondered if you might have a few moments free to talk to me?'

'This is really a bit irregular,' said Gilmore. 'All requests for press interviews should go through the board secretary.'

'I appreciate that,' smiled Kincaid. 'I apologise for the intrusion. I'll make my request in the usual way.' He smiled again and turned to leave, knowing that he had put down the bait. Right now Gilmore would be thinking, where's the harm? This man is impressed with the job we're doing up here, a little good personal publicity never did anyone any harm . . . .

Kincaid started his walk to the gate when Gilmore called him back. 'Just a minute, Mr Kincaid,' he said amiably. 'Let's not bother with all the red tape. Ten minutes okay?'

'That's very generous, Mr Gilmore.'

Kincaid was shown into a room that would have passed as a Victorian sitting-room. Display cases lined the walls; they were full of interesting bits and pieces, but Kincaid could detect no common theme in the collection. The man was a magpie but he would have liked to have spent an hour or two browsing through the objects. The walls were decked in heavy flock paper and a series of rather dark paintings in ornate, gilt frames were spaced out at regular intervals. A superb grandfather clock stood in one corner and its ticking was the only sound in the room until Gilmore, who had excused himself for a moment without saying why, returned and sat himself down behind the large pedestal desk that occupied the bay window space.

'Now, Mr Kincaid,' smiled Gilmore, 'what would you like to know?'

'I would like to know why the health board in this area seems to have abdicated all control and responsibility for health in the region to incomers from London,' said Kincaid pleasantly.

The smile faded from Gilmore's face, leaving a mixture of confusion and anger. 'What exactly do you mean?' he snapped. He didn't wait for an answer. 'It's Wheatfield, isn't it? He put you up to this, didn't he? Self-righteous pillock!'

Kincaid was bemused by Gilmore's outburst. He tried hard to get a word in, eventually managing to ask, 'Who's Wheatfield?'

Gilmore seemed to realise that he had gone over the top and did his best to minimise the damage. Making a conscious effort to control his temper, he said, 'I don't know what your game is, Kincaid, but the health board is quite able to manage its own business and does so. There is no question of control being handed over to London or anybody else. The people up here have the finest health service in the country bar none. Why don't you write about that, instead of stirring up political trouble?'

'Gordon Fields was appointed by London, was he not?'

'Yes, but . . .'

'Charles French? Paul Schreiber? London appointments?'

'Yes, but you must realise that our new health scheme is experimental. The regional budget could not have funded it. We are very lucky to have central funds allotted to us. If they had gone to Surrey instead, people here would have been up in arms about it. Under these circumstances you must see that with so much extra money coming to the region a degree of external influence is to be expected.'

'I suppose so,' agreed Kincaid.

Gilmore seemed to be taken by surprise at Kincaid's apparent capitulation. He paused for a moment, then said, 'Well, there you are then. We all have the best interests of our people at heart.'

'Indeed we do,' smiled Kincaid pleasantly. He got to his feet. 'I am grateful to you, Mr Gilmore, for giving me so much of your time.'

'Not at all,' smiled Gilmore, his composure now fully recovered. He was obviously pleased to have won the day.

'One more question,' said Kincaid. 'Did the board appoint Dr Sutton?'

'Who?' asked Gilmore.

'Sutton.'

'I'm afraid the name doesn't ring a bell, but then I don't know every appointment personally,' replied Gilmore.

'Of course not,' smiled Kincaid. 'Thanks again.'

Gilmore saw Kincaid to the door and waved as Kincaid turned round once while walking down the drive.

Kincaid stopped at the nearest telephone box and called College Hospital. He asked for Eve's ward and then asked to speak to her.

'Yes, who is it?'

'It's Jim, sorry to bother you on duty but I've just been to see Gilmore.'

'How did you get on?'

'I think you may have a point. I smelled a rat.'

'Did you indeed?'

'Have you managed to get a list of the names on the board?' Kincaid asked.

'Hang on a moment.'

There was a rustling of paper in the background before Eve's voice began to read out a series of names.

When she had finished Kincaid felt disappointed. 'No Wheatfield?' he asked.

'There was,' replied Eve.

'What does that mean?'

'Earnest Wheatfield was a member of the board but he resigned four months ago.'

'On what grounds?'

'Ill health.'

'Do you have an address for him?'

'117, Manor Drive.'

'Thanks, I'll see you later.'

Kincaid felt good as he drove across town to Manor Drive. He was back on the job again with the bit between his teeth. He was amazed at how quickly he had become converted to Eve's way of thinking. She was quite right; there was something irregular about the way the local health authority had kept quiet over who was controlling what in the region. It wasn't until he had read the list of appointments, ostensibly for Gilmore's benefit, that he had come to realise that the hospital and its administrative infrastructure was practically controlling the entire region's health service. The three people controlling College Hospital were Fields, the manager, Schreiber, the computer controller and French, the pharmacy director; all London appointments with no regional accountability. They were shortly to be joined by Sutton, who would have control of matters relating to mental health in the region. Another London appointment. Gilmore hadn't even heard of him.

Earnest Wheatfield lived in the ground floor flat of a Georgian house that had been converted into three apartments. Kincaid noticed that there was a wheelchair parked in the vestibule when he rang the bell. An elderly woman answered.

'I wonder if Mr Wheatfield is in?' he asked.

'Who wants to know?'

'My name is Kincaid. I'm a journalist.'

'A journalist?' exclaimed the woman. 'What on earth would a journalist want with Earnest?'

'I'd like to speak to him about the regional health board.'

'I see,' said the woman. She said it slowly as if she was thinking at the same time. 'My husband is not a well man, Mr Kincaid. I don't want him being upset.'

'I understand, Mrs Wheatfield. I have no wish to upset him.'

The woman seemed to be weighing something up in her own mind before she came to a decision and said, 'Wait here a moment.'

It was fully two minutes before she returned and said, 'Mr Wheatfield will see you.'

Earnest Wheatfield was in bed. From what Kincaid could see he was a large, stout man with a florid complexion and a mane of white hair. There were various bottles of pills on the table beside his bed along with a bottle of orange squash and three paperback books. There was an electric bell-push within easy reach. He struck Kincaid as a man who would use it quite a lot.

'What d'you wanna know?' he said gruffly.

'I want to know why the health board handed over control to London without a whimper.' said Kincaid.

Wheatfield threw back his head and started to laugh, but this induced in him a fit of coughing which brought his wife scurrying in to the room to take charge. She threw an accusing look at Kincaid. 'I told you,' she said.

Her husband recovered and waved her away with his arm. 'What took you so long?' he demanded.

'So long?' repeated Kincaid.

'You're the first one to have asked that question. What took you so long?'

'I work in London,' said Kincaid.

'Oh, a journalist with brains, eh?'

'I don't know about that,' said Kincaid.

'Our esteemed health board relinquished control of our health care in the best interests of our people,' said Wheatfield, with a smug smile that inferred he didn't believe a word of what he was saying.

Kincaid waited for him to continue.

'That's what our glorious chairman told us when I asked him what the hell was going on.'

'Gilmore?'

'The very fellow.'

'And you didn't believe him?'

'Believe him? Greedy Gilmore? You must be joking!'

'But the chairman couldn't concede control on his own,' said Kincaid.

'Of course not,' agreed Wheatfield. 'He had Sanderson and Stanner with him.'

'So why do you think they allowed it to happen?' asked Kincaid.

'Got a pencil?'

Kincaid nodded and took out his notebook.

'Gilmore has a brother-in-law, Frank Kennedy. Recognise the name?'

'The builder?'

'Correct. Ask who got the contract for the new day-clinic?'

'Frank Kennedy?'

'Top of the class. Now we come to the supply and maintenance of ambulances and emergency vehicles for the region. Would you believe Sanderson Motors?'

'But surely he couldn't have . . .'

'Correct. Sanderson sold the business. He couldn't have such a blatant conflict of interests.'

'So why . . . ?'

'He sold after he was assured the contract was coming his way. That put up the value of the business by more than forty thousand pounds.'

'Can you prove this?' asked Kincaid.

Wheatfield shook his head and said, 'No more than I can prove that Stanner has a financial connection with Northern Foods, who supply groceries to College Hospital.'

'Did you ever voice these beliefs?' asked Kincaid.

'To their faces lad, but never in public. I'm not a wealthy man. I can't prove it, so they would sue my arse off.'

'Were you never approached in any way?'

Wheatfield snorted and said, 'An anonymous little fart in a double-breasted suit came up to me one day in the car park and remarked on the age of my car. He said it was a shame a man of my ability wasn't driving around in a new Rover.'

'I asked him what the hell he was getting at and he suggested that that very thing might be possible if I were to help smooth the way for some of the changes that were going to benefit us all anyway.'

'What did you say?'

'I told him I didn't know what his game was, but if he didn't piss off I'd take his combination-locked briefcase and shove it up his arse sideways.'

Kincaid grinned broadly and the recollection brought on another fit of coughing in Wheatfield. His wife came back and said, 'I think you'd better leave, Mr Kincaid.'

Kincaid agreed and got up to go. Wheatfield's wife escorted him to the door. 'Harry was never the same after he left the health board,' she said. 'That business broke him. He's been going downhill ever since.'

'I'm sorry,' said Kincaid. 'He's a nice man.'

'And a good one,' said his wife.

Kincaid found it hard to analyse his feelings as he walked back to the car. True, he had uncovered yet more graft and corruption and that could be said to be his job, but he took little comfort from it. It was just too depressing; another story of dishonesty and greed in public service. Perhaps the public would soon come to regard it as the norm, just like they did in some South American countries. Perhaps they already did, for that matter. Maybe it was really just human nature; had people always been that way? Honesty and integrity were just values instilled in the gullible, while the realists in life got on with the business of shafting everyone else.

'Ye gods, Kincaid,' he cautioned himself, 'you're a cynical bastard.'

Kincaid met Eve at seven o'clock and they had a drink before eating dinner. He told her all about his day and what he had learned from Earnest Wheatfield.

'Are you going to do the story?' Eve asked.

'It would need a bit of work to prove Wheatfield's allegations,' replied Kincaid.

'But it could be done?'

Kincaid nodded. 'I think so. The question is very much a case of, is it worth the effort?'

'And you don't think so,' said Eve, interpreting Kincaid's mood.

'I'm not sure,' said Kincaid thoughtfully.

'What's the problem?'

'There's a *quid pro quo* problem,' replied Kincaid.

'Explain,' said Eve.

'According to Wheatfield, at least three members of the board took bribes, but from whom? And what did they give in return?'

'They relinquished control of the health board,' said Eve.

'But why?' Kincaid persisted. 'And who exactly is doing the bribing?'

'Central government,' said Eve.

Kincaid looked at her and she conceded that it was a strange notion.

'You see the problem,' said Kincaid. 'How can we suggest that central government bribed the local health board to stay out of the way while they got on with giving the region the best health service it's ever had?'

'Put that way,' agreed Eve, 'there is a problem.'

'It doesn't make sense,' said Kincaid.

'Maybe Wheatfield made it up. You said he was sick,' said Eve.

'But not in the head,' replied Kincaid. 'Besides, Gilmore looked as guilty as sin when I brought up the subject.'

'So maybe central government did do it; there's precedent,' said Eve. 'The sale of Rover Cars was not without it's "incentives", if I remember rightly.'

'Good point,' agreed Kincaid. 'But the government was getting rid of an albatross; it wasn't trying to buy one.'

'Then why?' said Eve.

Kincaid said, 'I'm damned if I can see it at the moment, but somewhere in the answer to that question lies the biggest story of the lot.'

Eve gave a little shiver.

'Cold?' asked Kincaid.

Eve smiled a little uneasily. 'No,' she replied. 'For some reason I felt a little afraid.'

Kincaid took her hand and kissed her fingers lightly. 'Eve, I want you to know that . . .'

Eve interrupted him and put her finger to her lips.

Kincaid conceded that this might be the wrong time. He said, 'I'm going back to London after the funeral. I'm going to see what I can dig up about who controls what up here. I'll be back soon, in any case for Kerry's assessment. Perhaps we could meet again?'

Eve smiled and nodded. 'Of course,' she said, 'I'd like that. But let's not waste the time we've got.'

ELEVEN

Jack Kincaid's funeral was held on the following morning. Kincaid, his sister Lisa and her husband, Kevin, travelled in the first car behind the hearse as principal mourners. Kevin comforted Lisa who sobbed quietly into her handkerchief, while Kincaid concentrated on what he could see through the glass partition separating them from the driver. He did this to avoid looking out at people looking in. He hated the expression people wore when they saw a funeral procession pass by, a kind of thoughtful resignation followed by a strange look he could never fathom. He could see on the speedometer that their car, an old Daimler Limo, had done sixty-three thousand miles. He tried converting that into numbers of funerals but gave up; the car had seen a lot of black and a lot of tears in its time.

As they arrived at the church Kincaid was surprised to see the number of people who had turned up, many of them still in their working clothes, suggesting that they had taken an hour or so off work to attend. It made the vicar, Nigel Rees, comment on how well regarded Jack Kincaid had been in life.

Kincaid was pleased with the service. Rees managed to translate the details he had given him at their initial meeting into a homely service which gave the impression that he had known Jack Kincaid personally. This obviously pleased Lisa, who nodded her head at intervals at what Rees said.

The weather was kind too, a particularly important point where burial was concerned. Rain turning earth to mud was never a prospect to lighten the heart. Jack Kincaid was laid to rest with the birds singing, the sun shining and the trees in the the churchyard moving in a gentle breeze. Kincaid left the grave with a feeling of well-being. He had given his father what he wanted.

With the last of the mourners making their way to the gates Kincaid turned to Nigel Rees and thanked him. 'That was a nice service' he said. 'I'm grateful.' He held out his hand.

Rees hesitated for a moment, then took the outstretched hand with a half smile. As Kincaid turned to leave Rees said, 'I trust your mother is well?'

Kincaid stopped in his tracks. Without turning round he said, 'Sleep easy Vicar, she's dead.'

Kincaid was about to get in the car to join Lisa and Kevin when he caught sight of his ex-wife, Julie. She was standing by the open passenger door of a car on the other side of the road, looking over at him, as though wondering whether or not he would notice her. Telling Lisa that he would only be a moment, he crossed the road.

'I didn't realise you were here,' he said. He felt the awkwardness of speaking to someone he had once been very close to in a manner he would use for acquaintances.

'Jack drew quite a crowd,' said Julie.

'I'm glad. It was a nice send-off.'

'Yes.' Julie seemed ill at ease; it made him aware that there was someone waiting for her inside the car. He bent down to look inside and saw a man wearing a Barbour jacket, drumming his fingers on the steering wheel. He was wearing the kind of cap Kincaid associated with royalty enjoying weekends in the country. Julie said hastily, 'Jim, this is Mark. Mark this is Jim.'

Kincaid said hello and Mark nodded and allowed the briefest of smiles to cross his lips. He then looked at his watch and said, 'Julie, I think we should be going.'

Kincaid straightened up again and said to Julie, 'The health board are going to reassess Kerry.'

'Oh, that is good news,' said Julie, half getting into the car. 'You must let me know how she gets on. I must rush.'

Kincaid opened his mouth to say something but stopped himself. There was no point, Julie was itching to be off. 'Take care,' he said. Julie shut the door and gave him an exaggerated wave as Mark started the car. Kincaid nodded in reply and walked back to join his sister and her husband.

'That was Julie, wasn't it?' asked Lisa.

'Yes.'

'Nice of her to come.'

'Yes.'

Kincaid met Eve at eight o'clock and gave her a report on how the day had gone. She was pleased to hear how many old friends and colleagues had turned up to pay their last respects to Jack Kincaid. This had obviously made Jim happy. She had half-expected him to be a bit sad and withdrawn and understandably so, but this was not the case. The funeral was over, he had given his father the burial he wanted and every-thing had worked out for the best. Kincaid seemed relaxed.

'Our last evening,' said Eve.

'I'll be back soon,' said Kincaid.

'I hope so.'

'Rely on it,' said Kincaid, turning to look at her and then putting his arm round her shoulders.

'Where are we going?' asked Eve, as they got into the car.

'The sea.'

'Oh really,' smiled Eve.

'I'm serious,' said Kincaid. 'The weather forecast said that it's going to be a clear night, there's a full moon and we're going to an inn by the sea. It's about an hour's drive from here and they're expecting us. What do you say?'

'Sounds good,' said Eve, 'but are you sure you want to? I mean, with your father and all . . .'

'I want to,' insisted Kincaid.

They lingered over dinner for two and a half hours and then walked along the beach afterwards. 'What a wonderful place,' said Eve.

'It's a special place,' said Kincaid. 'I only bring special people here.'

'I'm flattered,' said Eve.

'I discovered the village by chance in my early twenties and decided to keep it a secret between me and people I care for. Most folk don't know it exists. I hope it stays that way.'

They walked on in silence for a bit, then Eve said, 'You must have brought your wife here.'

'A long time ago. I saw her today, she came to the funeral.'

'Any lingering regrets?'

'None,' said Kincaid.

'Sure?'

Kincaid stopped and kissed Eve. 'None at all,' he said.

'You will take care in London, won't you? You don't really know what you might be getting into.'

'I will,' Kincaid promised.

'Look at that moon,' sighed Eve, as they started up the path that led to the cliff tops.

Kincaid paused when they got to the top. He said, 'I came here just before I went to London to work for the first time. I wanted to look at the view, store it, remember it, so I could summon it up whenever I felt down or lonely.'

'I can understand why.'

'Do you know Matthew Arnold's poem, *Dover Beach*?'

'The sea is calm tonight . . .'

'That's the one,' said Kincaid, pleased that it was something he shared with Eve. 'It's beautiful, and equally well applies to this place.'

They looked at the moon on the water for a while before Kincaid asked, 'Eve, does anyone at the hospital know that you've been seeing me?'

'I haven't told anyone,' replied Eve. 'Why?'

'Good. I think it best if you keep it that way for the time being. I don't want anyone associating you with me in case I start annoying the wrong people.'

'If you think it's best,' said Eve, with concern in her voice.

'Just a sensible precaution,' said Kincaid.

They walked on for a bit, then Eve said, 'I've been thinking about it a lot. It was awfully fortuitous that Anna Keats' dog was killed just when she was thinking of causing a fuss over Greta Marsh. Don't you think?'

Kincaid felt a hollowness creep into his stomach. He had indeed considered briefly that it was an amazing coincidence, but he hadn't wanted to believe that it was anything else. Now Eve was going to make him face up to a different possibility. 'What makes you say that?' he asked.

'Suppose for a moment that it wasn't just a bunch of yobs who did that to her dog.'

'Go on,' said Kincaid, with the sinking feeling getting worse.

'Suppose it was some kind of warning to her to keep her mouth shut about Greta?'

'A warning from whom?' asked Kincaid, prepared to argue in the hope that he could convince himself rather than Eve.

'I don't know.'

'I can't see Gordon Fields going around cutting off dogs' heads, can you? Besides, Anna Keats would hardly be likely to assume that the death of her dog was connected with the Greta Marsh affair,' protested Kincaid.

'No, she wouldn't. Someone would have had to spell it out for her,' said Eve.

'She didn't say anything about threats or warnings,' said Kincaid.

'She wouldn't if she was scared witless,' pointed out Eve.

'No, she wouldn't,' agreed Kincaid. 'I'll have to think about that.'

'But not just now,' said Eve.

'No,' agreed Kincaid.

It was three-thirty in the morning when Kincaid finally said goodbye to Eve and started back to the cottage. Clouds had rolled across what had been a star-filled sky, and it started to rain as he cleared the outskirts of the city and set off along the winding road that led to the village. He slowed down as he came to the narrow viaduct bridge which spanned a deep gorge.

Repair work was being carried out on the bridge parapet and temporary traffic lights had been positioned at either end. The red glow of the stop-light was reflected in the patches of rainwater on the white bonnet of the car; he waited for what seemed an eternity before the reflections changed to green and he eased the Lancia into the narrow lane between the parapet wall and a row of plastic cones.

He was close to the centre of the bridge when he was suddenly blinded by headlights. They were high off the ground so he deduced that it was not a private car. 'Idiot,' he murmured, concluding that a heavy lorry had parked at the other end of the bridge with its lights on full beam. He slowed to a crawl and flashed his own main beams to alert the other driver to the problem, but there was no change. The lights continued to dazzle him and he held his forearm up to the windscreen.

Kincaid had been forced almost to a halt when he realised that the lights were not static. They were moving! They were coming towards him! 'What the hell?' he stammered, as the sound of a powerful diesel engine continued to increase in volume. 'Of all the stupid . . .,' Kincaid stopped the car and looked behind him, but a combination of the darkness and the fact that his eyes were still affected by dazzle prevented him from seeing his way to reverse back. He looked to the front again and could now see that the vehicle approaching was not a lorry but a JCB digger. 'Bloody clown! What the hell do you think you're doing!'

Kincaid undid his safety belt and prepared to get out to tell the driver of the JCB exactly what he thought of him, but as he gripped the door handle he suddenly became paralysed by the sight of the digger's blade being lowered. 'What the . . .' Kincaid thumped the heel of his hand down on the horn. 'Are you bloody blind?' he yelled at the top of his voice, but the digger continued inexorably on its collision course, giving Kincaid only a second to cry out before the steel blade tore into the front of the Lancia and started pushing it, like a spoilt child sweeping away a toy with its forearm. The angle of the blade ensured that the car was pushed sideways towards the parapet of the bridge.

Kincaid frantically tried to open the driver's door, but it was now too close to the parapet wall and the metal scraped along the stone with only a few inches of space showing. The car stopped moving as it was jammed hard up against the stonework and a cloud of diesel smoke rose up in the air from the digger. Its driver was increasing engine revs to cope with the task of pushing the Lancia clean through the wall and over the edge.

Kincaid flung himself across the front seat and snatched at the door handle on the passenger side. He released it but was suddenly flung backwards as the car was lifted up off the ground on that side. Kincaid hit his head as he was thrown back, but fear enabled him to ignore the pain and he scrambled up to reach the passenger door again; it now jammed tight because its pillar had been deformed. Desperately he pressed the electric window-wind, but the glass only moved an inch before the motor rebelled and a strong smell of burning filled the car. His last chance of escape was the back door on the same side. The car lurched as the parapet wall gave way and Kincaid was flung to the floor once more although the 'floor' was now what had been the driver's side of the car.

With only seconds to spare the rear passenger door yielded to the strength that blind panic had given him. It swung open and Kincaid clambered out clumsily on to the bodywork. He leapt from the car as its centre of gravity passed the point of no return, and in an almost lazy roll it left the bridge to plummet down to the rocky ravine below.

Kincaid landed on the broken edge of the parapet and struggled to regain his balance as his feet hit the rubble of masonry lying there. There was a moment when he thought he was going to be all right, but the crumbling edge suddenly gave way and he felt himself fall outwards. His hands clawed frantically at the air for anything solid. His right hand made contact with a smooth, round steel bar. It was a scaffold tube that extended under the bridge from the parapet work on the other side. He was now hanging over the ravine by one hand.

He heard the digger's engine falter and die as he desperately tried to get a grip on the scaffolding with his other hand. He made it on the third attempt and allowed himself a moment's respite, hanging like a trapeze artist, at rest in the eerie silence above the void. Up on the bridge the digger's lights had gone out and there was no sound save for that of the wind as it moaned through the valley beneath his feet.

The knowledge that the digger's driver would look over the edge at any moment to find him hanging there spurred Kincaid on. A surge of adrenalin released by the sheer terror of his situation helped him swing his legs up on to the bar and at least take some of the strain off his arms. He worked his way along the metal pole like a Koala bear until he made contact with the main frame of the scaffold and pulled himself up to sit on it. He heard feet moving on the road above his head and knew that his assailant was looking over the edge. Would he believe that he had fallen to his death?

Kincaid remained motionless and absolutely silent, fearing that even the beat of his heart might give him away. The scaffolding pressed painfully into the backs of his thighs, imploring him to move, but he dared not. It had stopped raining and the sky was clearing. Far below him in the moonlight he could see the river tumble through the ravine like a silver thread. The wreckage of his car was strewn over the gorge like some toy that had been crushed underfoot and scattered. The fact that there was only a metal bar between him and death made him grip more tightly than ever. He heard the boots above him move back from the edge and then the sound of a door being opened. The driver was climbing back into the cab.

Kincaid looked up at the damp stone arch a few inches above his head and silently gave thanks. The digger's engine spluttered into life and he was free to move again. He felt the circulation return to his legs as he edged his way along the steelworks, believing that it would be safer than attempting to climb up on the damaged side. He paused at the far end and waited for the digger to move off before leaving his hiding place.

The sound of the diesel engine faded, and Kincaid waited a few more minutes before coming out of the shadow of the arch and pulling himself up on to the planking below the parapet on the outside of the bridge. His hands rejoiced in the firm feel of the stone as he hauled himself up on to the roadway and fell to his knees in exhaustion. Anguish, more mental than physical, suddenly overcame him. He was filled with a feeling of nausea and did nothing to suppress the urge to vomit. He had voided the contents of his stomach and was still kneeling on the road when he heard the sound of a car approaching. He looked up and saw a white saloon car with a blue flashing light on its roof come slowly over the bridge towards him.

Kincaid looked up into the faces of two policemen and their expressions told him how he must appear. His clothes were torn and covered in dirt, and he was kneeling over a pool of his own vomit.

'Just like they say, man,' said one of the policemen, 'there's no honour among thieves.'

'Fall out with our mates lad, did we?' the other asked Kincaid with a hostile sneer.

'What the hell are you talking about?' croaked Kincaid.

'I suppose he's going to tell us he was just an innocent passer-by, Harry.'

'Probably tried to stop these nasty villains, no doubt.'

One of the policemen bent forward from the waist and looked right in to Kincaid's face. 'You're nicked, pal,' he crowed. 'Now, let's be sensible. Who were the others?'

The anger that welled up inside Kincaid came out as a fit of coughing. 'Idiots!' he managed to get out between bouts.

'Up you get!' snapped a policeman, grabbing Kincaid roughly by the scruff of the neck.

Despite his exhaustion, Kincaid reacted angrily and started to struggle. 'Get your hands off me, you cretins' he fumed, then winced as they both moved in to subdue him; his right arm was twisted up behind his back.

'Not resisting arrest, are we?' sneered the policeman, applying pressure on it.

'You don't understand!' Kincaid gasped through the pain. 'Someone has just tried to kill me. He pushed my car over the edge. I damned nearly went with it.'

'Car? What car?'

The policeman relaxed his hold and moved slowly over

to the damaged section of the bridge to look over the parapet.

'Careful!' urged his partner.

Kincaid stopped struggling and an eerie truce was declared as the policeman inched towards the edge.

'Jesus Christ, he's telling the truth. There's a car down there.'

Kincaid felt the policeman, who was still holding him, relax his grip. 'What exactly happened here?' asked the voice behind him.

Kincaid broke free and started to dust himself down. He told them who he was and what had happened. The two policemen exchanged embarrassed glances.

Realising that they had approached from the direction the digger driver had driven off in, Kincaid said, 'You must have seen him.'

'We found the digger. It's in a ditch up the road.'

'And the driver?'

'No sign.'

'Who the hell did you think I was?' asked Kincaid.

'One of the gang, I suppose,' answered one of the policemen sheepishly.

'The gang?'

'Stealing heavy plant machinery is big business. Do you realise how much one of these JCBs costs?'

'I've never considered buying one,' replied Kincaid acidly.

'Gangs steal them at one end of the country and ship them to the other, and a new plant hire business is born.'

'I see, and you think that's what happened here?'

'Almost certainly, but God knows how you came to get caught up in it. You must have just slipped through before they erected the signs.'

'The signs?' asked Kincaid.

'Diversion signs. The gang put up diversion signs at both ends of the road to ensure that they wouldn't be disturbed, that's why we're here. Someone telephoned the station to ask about the diversion and we had no knowledge of it. We came out to see what was going on. As I say, we found the digger in a ditch and then we found you crawling about in the road. We thought you were one of the villains and had fallen out with the others.'

Kincaid considered the possibility in silence.

'You didn't happen to get a look at any of them, I suppose, sir?'

Kincaid shook his head. 'I was under the impression there was only one and I couldn't see him for the head-lights.'

'There would be more than one, sir. They would have had someone at either end of the road and someone to drive the transporter.'

'Transporter?'

'For the digger, sir. It's not the fastest of get-away vehicles.'

'Neither is a transporter, presumably. I take it you've put out an alert for it?'

'First thing we did when we found the digger, sir.'

Kincaid walked slowly over to the edge of the bridge and looked down at the wreckage of his car. 'They were prepared to murder me simply because I interrupted the theft of a bloody digger?' he said incredulously.

'People have been killed for a lot less, sir. I think you've been very lucky.'

Kincaid turned and looked at the policeman. He smiled wryly before saying, 'Yes, Officer, very lucky.'

The police drove Kincaid home, an unpleasant journey with the competing smells in the car of plastic trim and disinfectant, ensuring that he still felt nauseous when he got out. The staccato crackle of the radio and the clipped, single syllable replies throughout had done little to reorientate him to normality, and it was a relief to step out of the car into the fresh air outside the cottage. The policemen said they would be in touch if there were any further developments. They would also deal with the business of recovering the wreckage of the Lancia. Kincaid gave them details of the hire-car's documents and closed the door.

He paused for a moment with his back against it until he heard the police car move off, then let out his breath in a long, slow sigh. He made for the cupboard where he kept the whisky.

He splashed a good measure into a glass and swallowed the contents down in a single gulp; he was pleased at the fiery sensation it created. He repeated the exercise and then moved upstairs to run a bath. He was so tired that taking off his clothes demanded most of his remaining capacity to concentrate, and when he found that he had left one of his shirt-cuff buttons fastened and it was stopping him pulling the shirt off, he ran out of patience and wrenched it free, sending the button flying across the room.

Kincaid lowered himself gingerly into the water and rejoiced in the feeling of warmth and security it gave him. He lay back and let the water lap round his chin. He got round to thinking about what the police had said.

Did it make sense? He supposed that it did, but he was certainly in no mood to accept it without question. Coming so soon after what Eve had said about Anna Keats, there was one thing that disturbed him about the incident more than anything else. If there had been a man at both ends of the road, as the police had proposed, presumably they were in touch by radio. How had they missed his car and put up the diversion signs with him inside the section?

Kincaid could think of no comforting answer. He was left with a scenario that made him go cold: the diversion signs had been deliberately put up after he was inside the section. They had been put up for that very reason and at that very time, because the purpose of the exercise had not been to steal machinery at all. It had been to kill him.

The thought made Kincaid shiver. Who would want him dead and why? He looked up at the bathroom window. They, whoever they were, were still out there. Had he locked the door of the cottage? It was still very dark outside. He wished the daylight would come.

Kincaid relaxed a little when he realised that his attacker must be under the impression that he was a corpse lying at the bottom of the ravine. That at least gave him some time. He got out of the bath and dried himself. He felt better when he was doing something. He wouldn't go to bed. That could wait until he was back in London. He would catch the first train south.

As the Inter-City train sped towards London, Kincaid wrestled with the puzzle until it filled him with frustration. He was unable to see any sense or logic in it. If someone had gone to the length of murdering Anna Keats' dog to keep her quiet, that might mean that his earlier flirtation with death on the railway embankment might have been a real attempt to kill him. But why? Surely not just to save Claire Affric's career and avoid a scandal? That seemed ridiculous.

Apart from anything else, he had already agreed to say nothing about the affair, so why kill him? Unless, of course, he was on the wrong track and there was some other reason for wanting him dead. He started to think about Gilmore and his colleagues on the health board. Would they consider murder to stop him investigating the sordid little deals that had persuaded them to relinquish control of the board?

As he stared out of the window at the countryside flashing by in the early morning light, Kincaid concluded not. It was the people on the other side of these deals that mattered. They must think that he was getting too close to finding out something that he himself, as yet, knew nothing at all about. It must be something big, something big enough to warrant murder and terror tactics. But who were these people? At last a question he could answer. Surely the people controlling the Northern Health Scheme were . . . Her Majesty's Government? A dark cloud passed over the sun and turned the landscape grey. Kincaid suddenly felt very vulnerable.

Tolkien was washing his hands after seeing off what he thought was the last patient of evening surgery when there was a quiet knock on the door. It was Mrs Harrison. She seemed even more slight and frail than usual.

'I'm sorry, I didn't realise you were in the waiting-room,' Tolkien apologised.

'That's all right, Doctor. I've just come from the hospital.'

'How's Harry?' Tolkien asked.

'Harry died this evening,' said Mrs Harrison quietly.

Tolkien was filled with compassion for the old woman. He could see that she was devastated. She had lost the man who had meant everything to her for many years of her life. 'I'm so sorry to hear that,' he said. 'The hospital didn't tell me.'

'It only happened an hour ago. I came straight here.'

'I see,' said Tolkien.

'The hospital said I should come and see you.'

Tolkien nodded and said, 'I'll give you something to help you sleep tonight, and tomorrow I'll arrange for someone from the social work department to come and help you with the formalities.'

'Thank you, Doctor.'

Tolkien sensed that she needed someone to talk to. It was his night for the drug clinic but he felt sure his colleagues would understand if he was a bit late. 'Why don't you and I have a cup of tea?' he said. He got up from the desk and went next door to plug in an electric kettle he kept by the small instrument steriliser.

Mrs Harrison smiled when he returned. 'Harry was a lovely man,' she said. All the girls fancied him when we were courting.'

Tolkien smiled at the look that had come to the old woman's eyes. It gave him an idea of how she must have looked when she was a girl.

'You should have seen him in his uniform, tall, straight, handsome; he must have frightened the life out of them Germans. I can see him now, walking down the middle of our street with his kit bag across his shoulder and all the little lads falling in behind him. Harry would whistle the British Grenadiers and they'd all keep in step. The kids loved him.'

'You didn't have any of your own?' said Tolkien.

'No,' said Mrs Harrison, shaking her head. 'I couldn't have children and the work for Harry was never steady enough for us to be able to adopt any.'

'That's a pity,' said Tolkien.

'Harry would have made such a fine father.'

'And you would have made an equally fine mother,' said Tolkien. 'As it was you were as fine a wife as Harry could ever have hoped to find.'

'I let him down at the end,' said Mrs Harrison, looking sad.

'No, you did not!' insisted Tolkien. 'Believe me, I know.'

Mrs Harrison gave a faint smile. 'Maybe in time, Doctor,' she said, getting to her feet. 'Thanks for everything.'

'If you want to talk you know where to find me,' said Tolkien. He gave her the tablets and saw her to the door.

Tolkien made a note on his pad to contact the social work department first thing in the morning. He entered the fact that Harry Harrison had died in his patient record file. As yet he did not know the cause of death. He would learn that from the hospital in due course. He locked up and set off for the clinic.

As chance would have it the clinic was busier than usual. The publicity given to Aids in the local papers over the Golightly murder had awakened fears in many who had been lulled by the silence of the national press and media over an unpopular subject.

Tolkien, as usual, was appalled at the lack of knowledge some of the kids he was seeing had about the disease and how it was transmitted. There was still a widespread belief that Aids was something that homosexuals alone suffered from. He had to convince them that the virus didn't give a damn about the sexuality of its victims. Infected blood and semen had to be avoided. He didn't waste time with lectures or philosophy. The message to get across was clear and simple: don't share needles; use condoms.

Terry Feenan came in just after nine o'clock, when things were beginning to quieten down. Tolkien told him the bad news.

'So that's it, then,' said Feenan. 'Karen and I are going to die anyway.'

'The baby is clear,' said Tolkien, playing the only good card in his hand. 'You've got to consider her.'

'What's the point?' said Feenan bitterly. 'What's the bloody point?'

'The point is,' said Tolkien, 'that some HIV positive patients are alive five years after diagnosis. A lot can happen in five years. A cure isn't out of the question. You mustn't give up hope, you owe it to your daughter.' He could see that Feenan was desperately trying to believe him.

'You really think there could be a cure?' asked Feenan.

'Lots of good researchers are working on the problem and five years is a long time,' replied Tolkien.

'This could be the last straw for Karen,' he said quietly.

'Then it's up to you to convince her that you must give it your best shot. I've got a course here of a drug called AZT; it slows up progress of the disease. I want you both to start on it right away, and then you'll be referred to the College Hospital clinic. Okay?'

Feenan nodded and accepted the drug packs that Tolkien handed him.

'Is Karen "working"?' Tolkien asked.

Feenan shook his head. 'Not since we started the methadone,' he replied.

'Good, it's more important than ever that she doesn't go back to it.'

Feenan nodded and left.

It was the last Tuesday in the month and as always, Tolkien and his colleagues met after the clinic closed to discuss progress. It made sorry listening. The number of HIV positive clients on the books was now at such a level that prevention of the spread of Aids had to take precedence over getting them off drugs.

'As it stands, forty per cent of the heroin addicts attending the clinic are HIV positive,'said Gavin Mitchell.

'Does that include the figures for prostitutes?' asked Tolkien.

'It includes prostitutes who are also addicts,' replied Mitchell. 'The best figure we can come up with for prostitutes in general is that between fifteen and twenty per cent of prostitutes in the city are carrying the virus.'

'A time bomb,' said Mary Cunningham.

Tolkien and Mitchell concurred.

'Perhaps we should circulate information to all GPs in the city, to warn them about the inroads the virus will be making into the heterosexual community in the very near future,' suggested Tolkien.

'If it's not there already,' said Mitchell.

'How are our HIV positive clients doing in general?' asked Tolkien.

'Not good,' replied Mitchell. 'All those diagnosed HIV positive in the last six months and referred to the College Hospital special clinic have now developed Aids-related diseases.'

'All of them?' exclaimed Tolkien and Mary Cunningham in unison.

'Afraid so.'

'What's the breakdown?' asked Tolkien.

Mitchell referred to his notes and said, 'Sixteen with pneumonia, eleven with tuberculosis two with unidentified septicaemia.'

'Deaths?'

'Ten,' said Mitchell.

'Ten out of twenty-nine within six months,' said Tolkien.

'It seems that our addicts are much more susceptible to the Aids virus than other patients,' said Mitchell.

'Their general state of debility, I suppose,' said Mary Cunningham.

Mitchell and Tolkien agreed silently.

Tolkien looked at his watch and saw that it was eleven o'clock. He stretched his arms in the air and said, 'This has been one god-awful day.'

'There seem to be more and more of them, nowadays,' said Mary Cunningham. No one disagreed.

TWELVE

Kincaid went straight from the railway station to the newspaper's offices. It was raining heavily and his hair got wet while he searched his pockets for money to pay off the taxi. Right now he didn't want to see anyone except Fletcher, but knew that this wouldn't be possible. He would have to walk through the newsroom to reach Fletcher's office. He took a deep breath and pushed open the swing doors.

He acknowledged the friendly calls and accepted the proffered sympathy with all the good grace he could muster and without breaking his stride. Luck was with him. He managed to walk through the entire room without stopping and without being overly rude to anyone. He went straight in to see Fletcher.

'Good to see you back, sorry about your father,' said Fletcher, getting up to shake hands.

'Thanks. We have to talk.'

Fletcher was taken aback by Kincaid's intensity. He turned to the girl sitting in front of his desk with notepad and pen and said, 'Leave us for a few moments, would you Jill?'

The girl left and Kincaid took her place on the chair. 'I'm on to something,' he said.

'Big?' asked Fletcher, lighting a cigarette.

'Big enough for someone to want to kill me.'

'Are you serious?' asked Fletcher, failing to make contact with the match.

'Never more so.'

'Then we call in the police,' said Fletcher.

Kincaid shook his head and said, 'There's nothing I would like better right now, but there's no point, I can't give them any proof to go on.'

'I thought the story up there had fallen through,' said Fletcher.

'So did I,' agreed Kincaid, 'but I've had second thoughts. There's something going on; it involves the hospital and its administration.'

'More sticky-fingered managers?'

Kincaid shook his head and said, 'Something bigger than that.'

Fletcher flicked the ash off his cigarette thoughtfully and said, 'You'll want help. What do you need?'

'Information, to start with. I need all the stuff we have on the Northern Health Scheme from the very beginning, including the profile you've been preparing on Carlisle. I also need to know if we have anything on the following people: Gordon Fields, the hospital manager, Charles French, the scheme's computer expert, Paul Schreiber, who's in charge of the pharmacy, and a psychiatrist called Sutton who has just been appointed mental health director. The first three could be career civil servants, maybe scientific civil service.'

Fletcher finished writing down the names and said, 'The background to the Northern Scheme and info on Carlisle I can give you right away. I'll put a couple of researchers on to the others. You look all in.'

'I am,' agreed Kincaid. 'I'm going home to get some sleep. I'll take the gen on Carlisle with me.'

'Fletcher pressed an intercom button and requested the file. The girl who had been in the office when Kincaid arrived brought it in a few moments later. Kincaid took it from her and got up to leave.

'Hey!' said Fletcher, as Kincaid reached the door.

Kincaid turned round.

'You haven't told me what the story is.'

Kincaid shrugged and said, 'I don't know myself yet. I just know there is one.'

*   *   *

204

The rain showed no sign of letting up as the taxi taking Kincaid home crossed London. As they passed over Westminster Bridge he glanced up at Big Ben. For the first time in his life, the Palace of Westminster seemed a forbidding place.

When he got in he found that his flat smelled musty. It was also cold and unwelcoming, having been closed up for the best part of two weeks. He lit the gas boiler and took comfort from the hum of the central heating pump as it started to circulate water through the radiators. He turned on a couple of table lamps to counteract the darkness imposed by the rainclouds outside and switched on the radio. Now it felt more cosy.

Kincaid wondered again if he should call Eve and tell her what had happened last night after he had left her. He had thought about this all the way down on the train, but had failed to reach a decision. Now, on balance, he decided against it.

The other thing that troubled him was whether or not Eve would be in danger after the events of last night. If it had been a genuine attempt on his life it was because he, as an investigator, was perceived as a threat to someone or something. Eve was no threat; even so, Kincaid could not totally reassure himself. He wished that she was here in London.

He made himself a cup of coffee and opened the file on Carlisle. As Minister of Health it seemed unlikely that Carlisle would have anything to do with the day-to-day running of the health scheme, but in this case he was the architect and prime mover of the new service. More than that, the success of the scheme was responsible for his current high profile and perhaps, if the rumours were to be believed, his stepping stone to the highest office in the land. Kincaid had intended to leave reading the file until he had slept, but it seemed so thin that he thought he would have a preliminary look.

Fletcher had been right: getting material about Carlisle had been difficult. He seemed to have suddenly materialised on the political scene from nowhere some eight years before, having been selected as parliamentary candidate for the safe seat of Ryleigh and District in the Cotswolds. Kincaid found this a bit strange in itself. Prospective parliamentary candidates usually had to serve some sort of apprenticeship, often by standing in constituencies where they were on a hiding to nothing. They had to smile in High Streets at people who ignored them, hold babies while mothers berated them, listen to inarticulate nonsense from all and sundry and still appear interested. They had to look concerned that the roof leak at 37 Boghall Avenue had still not been repaired. Character-building stuff.

There was no mention of Carlisle ever having had to do this. He seemed to have been given a safe seat from the start. There was a photograph of Carlisle on the platform after the announcement of his victory, rosette in his buttonhole, right hand held aloft. Par for the course, thought Kincaid, the standard photograph for politicians. He was about to put it down when he recognised someone else in the photograph. It took him a few moments before he could put a name to the face, but then he remembered. Standing behind Carlisle, also wearing the same colour rosette, was Charles French, the computer manager at College Hospital in Newcastle.

'Old pals,' said Kincaid to himself. 'Well, well, well.'

He examined the photograph thoroughly. There were no more familiar faces, but this was a good start. It made up for the fact that he could glean very little from the scanty information that had been gathered about Carlisle's life before he entered parliament. There were three photographs pinned to a sheet of paper in the file. One showed Carlisle as a boy. It was summertime, judging by the rolled up sleeves and shorts he was wearing. The subject was smiling and holding a fishing rod. The second showed him a bit older and wearing school rugby strip, and the last one was a graduation portrait. Kincaid checked the details; Carlisle had obtained a lower second in history at Cambridge.

It struck Kincaid that there was nothing in the file to suggest any outstanding ability in Carlisle. He appeared to have been average at just about everything. He found it strange that there were no clues pointing to the success awaiting him in later life, and was forced to conclude that the man must have been a late developer.

From the moment Carlisle had entered parliament, however,

his career had been anything but average. Everything he touched had turned to political gold. There were glowing reports from his time as a PPS, followed by outstanding success as a junior minister at the treasury, now followed by universal acclaim as health minister, the man to reform the health service and improve it beyond measure. This bit Kincaid already knew, and his eyelids were beginning to come together. It had been a long time since he had last slept and the flat was becoming pleasantly warm.

Tolkien put down the telephone slowly and swore. College Hospital had just informed him that Madeline Bell had died. Her chest infection had proved intractable and she had developed bi-lobar pneumonia from which she had gone downhill rapidly and died. Tolkien knew her mother would be inconsolable; Maddy had been everything to her. What a rotten stroke of luck. He made a note to call round and see her later. The news had come as such a surprise that Tolkien momentarily forgot that he had a patient in the room with him. When he finally emerged from his preoccupation he had to apologise to the lady sitting there.

'Bad news?' said the woman.

'Very,' said Tolkien.

Morning surgery was lighter than usual; he was finished by ten-thirty and was preparing to go out on his rounds when the telephone rang and his receptionist said it was someone who would only speak to him personally. Tolkien shrugged his shoulders and lifted the receiver.

'Dr Tolkien? Derek Hanlon here, *Daily News*.'

Tolkien rolled his eyes. He had had more than enough of the press over the past few days in the aftermath of the Golightly killing.

'About Mrs Golightly,' said the voice.

'I have nothing to say about Mrs Golightly or anyone else,' said Tolkien.

'I just wondered how it happened.'

'How what happened?'

'The death.'

'What are you talking about?' demanded Tolkien.

'You don't know, do you?'

'Know what?' asked Tolkien, who was becoming angry.

'She's dead,' said the voice, 'Mary Golightly is dead.'

'What?'

'It's true. She died in the prison hospital at Granham last night.'

'You mean she committed suicide?' said Tolkien.

'They say not,' said Harmon. 'The official story is that she just fell ill and died. I wondered what was wrong with her, that's all.'

'I see,' said Tolkien, feeling stunned.

'I thought that, as your patient is now dead, Doc, and your obligations under the Hippocratic oath are over, maybe you would like to say something about what happened at the Golightly place last week?'

Tolkien put down the telephone without saying anything. He picked it up again and asked Directory Enquiries for the number of the prison. When he got through he asked to speak to the prison doctor. After some delay a gruff voice said, 'Gallacher here, who is this?'

Tolkien introduced himself and said that he was Mary Golightly's GP. 'I'd like to know the cause of death.'

Gallacher asked Tolkien for his telephone number and then told him to ring off. He would call him back. Seeing this as a sensible precaution, Tolkien complied and the telephone rang after a minute. He knew that his address would have been checked against the number he'd given.

'She died of Aids,' said Gallacher.

'What?' exclaimed Tolkien.

'She was a classic case of *Pneumocystis carnii* pneumonia. We put her on Septrin but she succumbed quickly and died at three o'clock this morning. We've had the press camping outside the gates since eight, hoping for a juicy story. They were disappointed to learn it wasn't suicide. I suspect they're still not convinced.'

'I've had one on the phone,' said Tolkien.

'What did you tell him?' asked Gallacher.

'That I didn't know anything,' said Tolkien pointedly. 'That's why I'm calling you, remember?' He was still smarting from having heard about the death of one of his patients from a reporter.

'We would have been in touch soon,' said Gallacher.

Tolkien moved in his chair until he found a position that was less painful. He took a couple of tablets from the bottle in his desk drawer and popped them into his mouth. It was shaping up to be another rotten day. He reflected on the demise of the Golightlys and what a tragedy it had been. One night with a German prostitute and this had been the result: disease, murder, death. An ordinary couple living in an ordinary suburban house had been caught out by that bloody virus and destroyed.

Angela Bell was sitting by the window when Tolkien was shown in by her sister, who had come to be with her for a few days. She did not look round.

Tolkien stood for a moment in silence, a silence which seemed to be enhanced by the deep-pile carpet in the room. Outside in the garden he could hear a robin chirping. He said, 'I just came to say how very sorry I am, and to ask if there's anything I can do.'

Angela Bell did not turn round; she did not say anything. She just continued to look out of the window.

'Perhaps I could give you something to help . . .'

'Why?' interrupted Angela Bell, 'Why did she die?'

'Her chest infection got worse and there was nothing the hospital could do about it,' said Tolkien.

'Maybe the bloody hospital didn't want to do anything about it!' said Angela Bell.

The tone in her voice shocked Tolkien as much as what she was implying. He had always known her as a gentle, sensitive woman, intelligent and charming. Now she sounded like a different person, bitter, hard, accusing. It unnerved him. 'You're upset. I know how much Maddy meant to you. I really think you should let me prescribe something.'

Angela Bell ignored Tolkien. Through her tears she stormed, 'She was a mongol, she didn't matter. They didn't care if she lived or died. If they had had their way she would have been aborted before she was even born.'

'Of course she mattered,' said Tolkien. 'Everyone loved Maddy. The hospital did everything they could to save her. They tried treatment after treatment. It's just that none of the drugs could save her.'

'I want you to go,' said Angela Bell.

Tolkien stood in impotent silence. He could think of nothing to say that would bring comfort to the woman and it distressed him. He looked around the room for inspiration. There was an upright piano standing with its lid open and Chopin's music on the stand. Tolkien recognised the piece; he could hear it in his head, sad music that didn't help.

'Of course,' said Tolkien quietly, 'but if there's anything I can do . . .'

'Just go.'

Tolkien left the house, wishing that he had never gone there in the first place. He had expected to be met with grief, but Angela Bell's bitterness had taken him by surprise. The pain in his back was now joined by knots in his stomach. As he drove home he saw her in his mind, sitting in the bay window, handkerchief to her face, her world in ruins. She was saying, 'Go, just go.' There had been hatred in her voice. He tried to come to terms with it by rationalising that she had been very upset, and some people did lash out at the nearest person when their grief became too much to bear. Most people got over it quickly but some nurtured hatred, justified or not, for a long time. They learned to control it, suppress it, but it was still there inside, eating away at them like a cancer. There was that journalist he had met a couple of weeks ago, James Kincaid. He had it inside him. He wondered how he was getting on.

Kincaid woke at six o'clock in the evening, feeling better after an undisturbed sleep. He called Eve at the nurses' home.

'I'm just in,' she said. 'What have you been up to?'

210

'I've made a start on getting information about the management up there,' said Kincaid. He was reluctant to tell Eve that he had been sleeping most of the day because he didn't want to have to explain why.

'Progress?'

'Carlisle, the health minister, knows Charles French, the computer manager. French was standing beside him in an election photograph.'

'What does that mean?' asked Eve.

'I don't know. Maybe nothing, but it's a start. What have you been up to?'

'I'm being transferred to theatre work from tomorrow. Theatre Sister is off on a week's holiday. I'm standing in for her.'

'Sounds glamorous.'

I won't say it's not,' agreed Eve. 'I'm a bit nervous, I haven't done theatre work for a while.'

'You'll be fine,' said Kincaid.

'What do you know about it?' laughed Eve.

'Nothing,' agreed Kincaid, 'but I know you. You'll be fine.'

'Claire Affric is operating tomorrow,' said Eve.

'Oh.'

'I hope everything goes all right for her. This is her first op since Greta.'

'I'll second that,' said Kincaid.

'In a way you are responsible for her comeback,' said Eve.

'Let's just wish her well,' said Kincaid. 'I'll call you tomorrow.'

There was no food in the flat and he did not want to go out to eat alone, so Kincaid called a pizza place that delivered. When it arrived it was cold. He heated it up but it tasted like rubber. He discarded half of it and finished the can of beer he had opened. He cleared the table and laid out the information he had on the Northern Health Scheme.

The researchers at the paper had done a good job. The report was comprehensive and contained figures and statistics in abundance. It took Kincaid all of two hours to come to grips with the main aspects.

211

The Northern Scheme, the brainchild of health minister Carlisle, had been in operation now for just over a year. Initially it had been implemented at College Hospital after a period of upgrading and modernisation during which many of the hospital's administrative functions were computerised. Although based on College Hospital, computerised control of administration and pharmaceutical services had been applied to four other hospitals in the region via the College mainframe computer. The scheme had recently been expanded to include general practice patients and now covered a region populated by some two million people.

Comparisons were given to show that the cost of the much-improved health scheme was actually slightly less than the cost per patient in any other region of the British Isles. Waiting time for major operations had disappeared, and the list for smaller operations had been halved. The drug bill for the region had been reduced by twelve per cent, through the computerised selection of generic compounds, wherever possible, in preference to the more expensive proprietary brands.

Kincaid had to admit that Carlisle deserved all the credit he had been getting. The man had pulled off a minor miracle. He looked at the total bill for salaries and noted a slight reduction over the previous year. The explanation was that less administrative staff were needed, thanks to computerisation.

Something made Kincaid check the figure against the money allotted to the regional board for salaries on another sheet. It was the same. He checked again. There was no mistake. The money allotted to the board for wages was the same as the total money paid out in salaries. There was no mention of any extra money coming from central funds to pay the London people, as Eve called them. There was no mention either of special budget money being available to the London managers.

Kincaid felt a tingle of excitement. He had to caution himself not to jump to conclusions. After all, these figures had been compiled by the paper's researchers. This wasn't an official document. There was nothing to say that the calculations of patient cost under the new scheme had been presented to parliament without including the extra funding coming directly from London. The door buzzer went.

Kincaid jumped at the sound. It would take him a while to get over the events of the other evening.

'Yes, who is it?' he said into the entryphone.

'Fletcher.'

'Come on up.' Kincaid pressed the door release button.

Kincaid returned to his papers for a moment while Fletcher climbed the stairs to the third floor. He pencilled in a circle round the figure for salaries in the report.

'These stairs are going to kill me,' said Fletcher, holding his chest and looking red in the face.

'Come in,' said Kincaid.

'You looked so rough this afternoon I thought I'd come round and see how you were.'

'A nice thought,' said Kincaid. 'Drink?'

'G and T.'

Kincaid made Fletcher's drink and handed it to him.

'You're not having one yourself?'

'Not just now,' said Kincaid.

'So, how are you?'

'Puzzled,' said Kincaid. 'Who made up this file?'

'Judy Grimble. Bright kid, know her?'

'Vaguely,' said Kincaid. 'Where did she get the patient costs from, do you know?'

'The parliamentary report, I suppose,' said Fletcher.

'Are you sure?' asked Kincaid, feeling excited again.

'No, but we can ask her. Can I use your phone?'

Fletcher called the paper and asked for Judy Grimble's number at home. He called it. She was in. 'James Kincaid wants a word,' said Fletcher. He handed the receiver to Kincaid.

'I've been reading your report on the Northern Health Scheme,' said Kincaid. 'It's very good.'

'Thank you. How can I help?'

'The figure you quote for costs per patient under the new scheme, where did you get it?'

'From the parliamentary report submitted by Mr Carlisle.'

'You're sure?' said Kincaid.

'Perfectly. Is something wrong?'

'No, nothing,' said Kincaid. He thanked her and rang off. He explained what he had discovered to Fletcher, who was less than excited by the news.

'So they've missed out three salaries in the cost calculation. That's no big deal,' said Fletcher.

'But don't you see? That might be the tip of the iceberg. I know that Fields has an independent budget funded by London, so maybe the other two do as well. If they don't say how much money from central funds is being pumped in to the scheme, we won't know how much it really costs.'

'But why would they pretend it costs less than it does? It doesn't make sense, especially as they want to expand the scheme all over the place.'

'I don't know the answer yet, but I want to find out,' said Kincaid.

'Call the DHSS in the morning and ask how much is being put in from central funds.'

'I intend to,' said Kincaid.

'One of the researchers managed to come up with something on one of the people you asked about,' said Fletcher.

'Charles French?'

'How did you know?' asked Fletcher.

Kincaid showed him the election photograph and pointed to French. 'I recognised him; he's in charge of the computer network at College Hospital.'

'He was a contemporary of Carlisle's at Cambridge, only French was brilliant. He took a double first in Maths and Physics. He was chairman of the Conservative club and seemed destined for big things.'

'What happened?'

'There was some argument over policy. French thought the club was becoming too wet. They in turn thought he was becoming a bit too embarrassing with his extremist views. The upshot was that French left the official club to found a breakaway faction calling itself the Schiller group. He managed to take quite a few members with him and the group became fairly established.'

'I haven't heard of it,' said Kincaid. 'Does it still exist?'

'No,' said Fletcher. 'In 1975 the Schiller group invited a certain white, South African politician along to speak to them. The student left got wind of this and organised a demonstration, during which one of them succeeded in hitting the said gentleman in the face with some overripe fruit. Apparently, French completely lost control and charged after the demonstrator. When he caught up with him he beat the hell out of him. It took half a dozen blokes to pull him off. When they did they found that the student on the ground had lost an eye. He was in hospital for several weeks. French was charged, of course, but managed to get off with a fine.'

'How the hell did he do that?'

'The magistrate was inclined to view the whole affair as student "highjinks" that had got out of hand. Faced with a brilliant student who had now recovered his cool and appeared full of remorse over the incident, he decided to take a lenient view in the belief that French would feel guilty about it for the rest of his life.'

'And does he?'

'Who knows? What we do know is that the incident put paid to French's chances of going into politics for real. A background of causing grievous bodily harm in defence of South African politics was too big a skeleton to carry in the cupboard. The Schiller group was disbanded and French eventually made his peace with the official body. He maintained an interest in politics when he left university, but had to be content to remain a backroom boy. That probably explains his appearance with Carlisle's election team.'

'What's he been doing for a living up till now?' asked Kincaid.

'Computers. He set up a software business when he left university and it's done very well.'

'Name?'

'Deltasoft.'

'So what is he doing working in College Hospital?' asked Kincaid, thinking out loud.

'Maybe his company supplied the software for the new service and he's setting it up for them?' suggested Fletcher.

'He's been there over a year,' said Kincaid.

'Just a thought,' said Fletcher.

'Why would a brilliant man with a successful business go and work in a hospital at setting up a new health scheme?' Kincaid found himself saying again, 'It doesn't make sense.'

'Plenty of successful businessmen do things out of the goodness of their hearts,' said Fletcher.

'Usually when there's a knighthood in the offing,' said Kincaid.

'Maybe you've just answered your own question,' said Fletcher. 'French's company got the Queen's award for industry two years running. Add a touch of community care and concern and it could be, "Arise, Sir Charles"? Especially when you've already got an old university buddy in the government who's rising fast. In fact, this could answer your question about a salary for French. Maybe he's giving his services for free?'

'Maybe,' said Kincaid, without committing himself. He needed more time to think about it. 'Anything on any of the others? Fields? Schreiber, Sutton?'

'Not yet,' said Fletcher, 'but we'll keep at it.'

When Fletcher had gone, Kincaid spread out more notes on the table, poured himself a drink and started to look at them. He thought about Fletcher's idea. Could that really be why French was working up north? Because he was after a knighthood? There would have to be something in it for him, Kincaid decided. A man with French's background of extreme views and violent tendencies wasn't likely to be punching keyboards in a northern hospital *pro bono publico*. But if it wasn't a knighthood, what else could it be? Money? French already had a successful business. That wouldn't necessarily make him honest, just more expensive.

Kincaid looked for clues but couldn't immediately put his finger on any opportunity for graft unless it was in the supply of software. The system's design costs must be worth quite a bit to Deltasoft if, of course, it was their company being used, but once it had been installed there would be no reason for French to oversee it for such a long time. Unless . . . unless it was so complicated that no one else could do it? Or because they didn't want anyone else to have access to it? This last notion entered Kincaid's head as an innocent seedling, but it began to grow.

The big stumbling block to even looking for, let alone finding a scam, was the fact that the government was involved. There was a definite connection between French and Carlisle, but Carlisle was a minister of the crown; the new service was all his idea. Apart from that, how could anyone make money out of providing a vastly improved health service? It didn't make sense. Kincaid threw down his pen in frustration; maybe things would look better in the morning.

THIRTEEN

Eve had not slept well. She was nervous about returning to theatre duty and the fact that today's operation would be Claire Affric's comeback as a surgeon did little to put her at ease. More than anything, she was haunted by thoughts of Greta Marsh and what had happened to her. She accepted that the nightmarish outcome could not be blamed on Claire; she had been an appalling victim of circumstance. No, it wasn't a question of blame, just of fact. Greta Marsh was lying somewhere in an asylum with no face, no sight and a damaged brain.

The thought made Eve very uneasy. She tried to persuade herself that such a thing could not possibly happen again, but she was still glad that today's operation was relatively minor in comparison, a series of skin grafts to a burns victim. Her feelings convinced her that Kincaid had been right: Claire Affric could not possibly have continued to work as a surgeon if the truth about the Greta Marsh case had been made public.

Breakfast for Eve was orange juice and coffee; she couldn't face anything more substantial, not even her usual muesli. She fidgeted a lot, tidied up her room, folded her clothes and put them away, generally seeking physical distraction from mental stress. The hollow feeling in her stomach did not begin to subside until she reached the theatre suite and started to scrub up.

Eve found the chatter in the room therapeutic. Her hope was that once the operation had begun she would quickly get into the swing of things and start to feel a whole lot better. Gloved and gowned, she entered the theatre and started to check and re-check the instrument trays. Normally this would be a routine task but today, in her tight-nerved state, she had to try to anticipate every conceivable request, challenge the boundaries of clairvoyance.

In addition, Eve imagined every conceivable situation that might arise in the course of surgery; the patient going into cardiac arrest on the table, sudden haemorrhage, respiratory problems, oxygen starvation. She positioned emergency equipment to be in exactly the right place should it be called for. She even saw to it that the wheels of trolleys were pointing in the direction in which they would be required to move to avoid 'supermarket syndrome'. Lastly she saw to it that plastic specimen containers were to hand should lab samples be taken.

The hands of the large theatre clock pointed to nine-thirty and the patient was wheeled in. He was a twenty-three-year-old man who had been burned about the face and hands in a garage fire. The car on which he had been working had burst into flames after his welding torch had cut through a fuel line. This was his fourth operation to repair the damage. The skin grafts added at his last operation had failed to take properly and were to be done again.

The patient was drowsy under the effects of pre-medication, an injection of tranquilizing drugs which he had been given to relax him before leaving the ward. He had no real notion of where he was, just that he felt good, as if he were floating. He moved his head lazily and smiled to himself at some secret thought. People in this state always reminded Eve of people at picnics on long, hot summer days. They looked as if they were lying on the grass, with their eyes half-closed against the brightness of the sun in a clear blue sky. The heat had made them drowsy and they were caught in the carefree border between consciousness and sleep.

Eve adjusted the green surgical drapes to permit access to the relevant areas of his skin. The anaesthetist was speaking to him gently but firmly so he could get through the drowsiness as he asked him to start counting. The man had barely reached four before the gas from the mask being held over his face had put him into a deep sleep, the depth of which would now be monitored from the instruments on the trolley at the anaesthetist's elbow.

Claire Affric and the young doctor who would assist her today came into the theatre from the scrub room and seemed to be relaxed; they were chatting. The surgical mask hid the scar on Claire's face.

'Good morning, everyone,' said Claire. Eve noticed that the tone of her voice was confident.

'How is he, Jerry?' asked Claire.

The anaesthetist replied, 'All ready when you are.'

'Everything all right, Sister?'

Eve suddenly realised that Claire Affric was looking at her over her mask. 'Sister Martin is on leave this week, Doctor,' she said. 'I'm standing in for her.'

'I don't think we've worked together before, have we?' asked Claire Affric pleasantly.

'No, Doctor, I'm Staff Nurse Laing.'

'Pleased to meet you,' said Claire.

For a moment Eve imagined that her name may have meant something to Claire; she thought she had seen just a hint of recognition in the eyes above the mask, but then it was gone.

'Everything ready?' asked Claire.

'Yes, Doctor.'

'Good. Let's get started.'

As the minutes passed, Eve was relieved to see that Claire showed no sign of nerves at all as she set about her business. She cut away lifeless skin and shaped replacement grafts with complete surety before positioning them deftly and skilfully over the marked areas. Requests for instruments came thick and fast, but were spoken clearly so that Eve had no difficulty in complying.

Eve glanced up at the clock and saw that an hour had gone by. Her own nerves had disappeared and she was on top of her job.

She signalled to the junior nurse that more swabs were required and lined up another row of instruments in anticipation. Claire Affric, unlike most surgeons, did not speak much during the operation. From time to time she would ask the anaesthetist how the patient was doing, but apart from instrument requests the only other words that passed her lips were occasional comments on progress such as, 'Good,' or, 'That's better'.

Eve thought that she preferred it this way. In the past she had known surgeons speak non-stop about football or sex or politics throughout an operation. She had always seen it as unnecessary bravado, perfectly in keeping with the extrovert personality most surgeons seemed to have, but a pain nevertheless.

Claire Affric made a tutting noise and the mood in theatre changed slightly in anticipation.

'There's some infection here,' she said to her assistant, who duly came closer and bent over the patient to look. Claire Affric lifted a flap of skin with the point of her scalpel and pointed to an area with the probe in her other hand.

'Looks a bit angry,' agreed her assistant.

'We'd better have some swabs for the lab.'

Eve reached behind her and removed a microbiology swab from its sterile tube. She handed it by the stem to the surgeon, carefully avoiding contact with anything on the way. If the swab was to detect bacterial infection in the patient's tissues it was imperative that it should not touch anything else before being returned to its tube.

Claire Affric ran the tip of the swab gently around the infected area, twirling the cotton head so that it would be thoroughly impregnated. She handed it back by the stem to Eve. Eve replaced it in its container and labelled it before handing it to the junior nurse, who placed it in the receptacle for lab specimens.

Claire Affric said, 'I'm sure it's infected. I'm going to cut away this section. 'Scalpel!'

Eve slapped the shaft of a fresh scalpel into the surgeon's outstretched hand.

Claire Affric started to cut away the suspect tissue, holding flaps of skin taut with forceps as she slit along the edge with the scalpel. She seemed to have difficulty with the angle of the cut. 'Too big,' she said. 'Give me a smaller one.'

Eve selected a smaller-bladed scalpel from the tray and held it ready. Without looking up from the patient, Claire Affric held out her hand for the new knife without dropping the old one in the metal discard tray first. The used blade caught Eve in the fleshy area between the thumb and forefinger of her right hand. She gave a brief gasp as blood welled out through the cut in her glove. There was very little pain because the blade was so sharp, but she could sense that she had been cut quite deeply.

'Sorry,' said Claire Affric, 'Can't stop.'

Eve changed places with the junior nurse and wrapped a gauze dressing round her hand. She supervised the supply of instruments by anticipating what would be needed next and pointing to it on the tray. This continued until the end of the operation.

With her assistant tidying up the patient before taking him to the recovery room, Claire Affric came over to Eve and apologised. 'I am so sorry,' she said, removing her mask.

'No real harm done,' said Eve.

Claire Affric removed the gauze from Eve's hand and examined the cut. 'How clumsy of me,' she said 'I'll pop in a couple of stitches. Is your anti-tetanus up to date?'

Eve said that it was.

Claire looked concerned. She said, 'The thing that worries me is the fact that I had just used the blade on an infected area of skin.'

'I've rinsed it well,' said Eve.

'I think you should have some antibiotic cover, just in case.'

'I'm sure it'll be okay,' said Eve.

'I insist,' said the surgeon. 'I'll order something up from the pharmacy. Better to be on the safe side. I really am most sorry about this. I was so preoccupied with what I was doing that . . .'

'It's nothing,' said Eve. 'Think no more about it.'

'To tell the truth, I was a bit nervous about coming back today. It's good to get the first one over.'

'I understand,' said Eve.

The bleeding in Eve's hand had almost stopped when the antibiotics arrived from the pharmacy.

'What are you giving me?' asked Eve.

'The "umbrella" cocktail we give to patients having their wisdom teeth extracted. It gives good cover against most bacterial opportunists,' said Claire Affric. She filled the syringe, expelled the air by holding it upright and pressed the plunger gently. When fluid emerged from the needle she injected the contents of the barrel into Eve's right buttock. She swabbed the area with an alcohol-impregnated swab and said, 'That's it, you'll be okay now. If there's the slightest problem, let me know.'

Eve was conscious of the pain in her buttock as she walked along the corridor away from the theatre suite, but she expected the discomfort. The hypertonic nature of the injection would make it painful until it diffused into the surrounding tissue.

Kincaid paused before opening the front door of the flat. There was a truth to be faced: he was reluctant to leave its confines because he was scared. His fingers were on the handle but remained unwilling to turn it. There was even a suggestion of sweat on his brow, cold sweat. God! This is ridiculous, he told himself. To a man brought up in the finest film traditions of John Wayne, knowing that a man had to do what a man had to do, this was just too much like cowardice for comfort. So what, the John Wayne in him argued. Someone tried to kill you, but so what? It's over now. Your insides don't turn to water over something like that, do they?

'Oh yes they do,' insisted Kincaid. That kind of dicing with death and then shrugging it off was strictly for film heroes. So what *was* he going to do, demanded his inner self.

Kincaid walked slowly over to the window of his flat and looked out at the traffic. He looked at the people passing in the street, ordinary people going about their business, but he could no longer see them as such. He wondered which one of them was looking for him. The taxi driver pretending to be waiting for someone? The window cleaner with the cloth draped over his bucket – what was the cloth concealing? Every briefcase hid a weapon. Every innocent expression was assumed. He examined each parked car in turn to see if a man wearing a raincoat with the collar turned up was sitting there waiting for him to emerge.

Kincaid had always been against firearms. He had invariably been a staunch opponent of any suggestion that the police force be armed, but right now he considered what a comfort it would be to have a pistol nestling in a holster underneath his left arm. He smiled at the thought, not because of a shift in attitude but because it meant that he was weathering the crisis. He wasn't going to run away and hide, he was going to do his job. He had a daughter to consider and in Eve he had a woman he wanted to get to know a whole lot better. But he was going to get to the bottom of things in the north. He was going to do this, in spite of being scared stiff. He set out for the office.

The press officer at the Department of Health and Social Security took Kincaid's number and said that he would ring back when he had the information requested. Kincaid sipped his coffee and tapped his pen on the desk. He hated waiting. He lifted the internal telephone and called one of the researchers that Fletcher had assigned to the job. He asked if there was anything new.

'I think we may have found Paul Schreiber. If it's the same man, he's not a civil servant. He was, until a year ago, chief pharmaceutical chemist with Lander Pharmaceuticals in Kent.'

'Lander,' murmured Kincaid. 'Why does that name ring a bell?'

'They made the news a couple of years ago. They were taken to task by the government over the price of one of their products used a great deal by the health service. It was claimed that the company was making excessive profits and they were forced to reduce the price and in the end pay back quite a large sum.'

'Why did Schreiber leave the company?' asked Kincaid.

'Nothing on that, I'm afraid, although in a sense he didn't.'

'What do you mean?' asked Kincaid.

'Paul Schreiber is still a major shareholder in the company.'

'Is he?' purred Kincaid. He congratulated the researcher on a good job and put down the telephone. He stared at the paper in front of him, mesmerised by it. All the puzzling questions about French's involvement in the Northern Scheme now applied equally to Schreiber. Another successful man gives up the good life to go and work in a hospital up north. Why? Another aspiring knight of the realm? Too much, thought Kincaid.

Once again, altruism seemed to start as a hopeless outsider. If Schreiber was a major shareholder in Lander and the company had a history of ripping off the health service, it hardly seemed likely that he would be dispensing pills for the masses out of the goodness of his heart. The question was, once again, what was in it for Schreiber? Or Lander Pharmaceuticals, for that matter?

Could it be that Lander had been given the contract to supply generic drugs to the new health service? Was that it? Deltasoft supplied the computer technology, Lander the drugs? Maybe Schreiber was an old friend of Carlisle, too.

Kincaid hit another stumbling block. If it was simply a question of old pals being given government contracts, why were French and Schreiber both on site for such a long time? What was, by all accounts, a brilliant and successful research chemist doing running a hospital pharmacy? The telephone rang and startled him. It was the DHSS.

'I have an answer to your question, Mr Kincaid,' said the voice. 'The figures quoted in the report by Mr Carlisle to the House of Commons are correct. No additional money is being put into the service from central funds.'

'Are you absolutely sure about that?' asked Kincaid.

'Quite sure.'

'Then who is paying the salaries of Messrs Fields, French and Schreiber at College Hospital?'

'I think that's a matter for the regional health board to answer,' said the voice.

'Or Mr Carlisle,' said Kincaid.

225

'I beg your pardon?'

'The board say you're paying them and you say the board's paying. Perhaps Mr Carlisle can come up with the truth?'

There was a pause before the voice said, 'I'm sure there must be some perfectly innocent explanation for the confusion,' sounding well-practised at pouring oil on troubled waters. 'Perhaps I can get back to you?'

'Please do,' said Kincaid.

It was three o'clock in the afternoon before the DHSS called back. Kincaid took the call expecting to hear the same press officer he had spoken to earlier, but it was a different voice.

'Mr Kincaid, my name is John Milton-Dunning, I'm parliamentary private secretary to Mr Carlisle. He asked me to contact you and give you any assistance I could.'

Well, well, well, thought Kincaid. They've been on to Carlisle himself.

'I'm interested in the financing arrangements of the Northern Health Scheme, Mr Dunning. There seem to be some discrepancies.'

'Surely not,' said Milton-Dunning pleasantly. 'Probably a misunderstanding.'

'It appears that the scheme is being administered by at least three individuals who are neither appointed by the local health board nor being paid by them,' said Kincaid.

'There's no great mystery there, Mr Kincaid,' said Milton-Dunning pleasantly. 'These key personnel are being paid from a trust fund.'

'A trust fund?' repeated Kincaid.

'Indeed,' said Milton-Dunning smoothly. 'It is by no means unusual for hospitals to receive support from a variety of trust funds for a variety of purposes, you know the sort of things, kidney machines, heart monitors and the like. College Hospital has access to a fund called the Wellington Endowment. Mr Fields, Mr French and Mr Schreiber are being paid, in the short term, from this source.'

'Why?' asked Kincaid.

'Because none of them is occupying a permanent post in the

hospital. Once the new service is completely operational they will return to their former careers and the administration will become more routine.'

'How much are they being paid?' asked Kincaid.

'Ten thousand a year.'

'Ten thousand?' exclaimed Kincaid. 'A ward sister earns more than that.'

'Exactly, Mr Kincaid. These are public-spirited men who believe whole-heartedly in the principles of the National Health Service. They are giving of their talents to support these principles.'

'Aren't trust funds supposed to be for equipment?' asked Kincaid.

'The terms of the Wellington Endowment specify that the money be used to promote advances in health care for the people of the north,' said Milton-Dunning. 'We see no conflict of interests in our interpretation of the terms.'

Kincaid went silent.

'I hope I have managed to answer all your questions Mr Kincaid?' said Milton-Dunning.

'Thank you,' said Kincaid. 'Just one more thing?'

'Yes?'

'Who administers this trust?'

'The trustee is Lady Antonia Freeman.'

'Sir Martin Freeman's widow?'

'Yes.'

Kincaid put down the telephone and Fletcher came in. 'Progress?' he asked.

'Slow,' replied Kincaid. He told Fletcher about the Wellington Endowment.

'Well, that answers your question, doesn't it?' said Fletcher.

'On the face of it,' said Kincaid slowly.

'What does that mean?'

'It means that as far as I'm concerned there's still a strong smell of rat in the air.'

Fletcher lit a cigarette and blew a languid column of smoke into the air. 'Don't see why,' he said.

Kincaid looked into the middle distance and tapped the end of his pen on the desk. 'Charles French, Paul Schreiber . . . ten thousand a year, strong beliefs in the principles of the health service. With their track records?'

'So what are you going to do?'

'Talk to Lady Freeman. I want to know more about this Wellington Endowment.'

'You're going back up north?'

Kincaid nodded.

'What about the attempt on your life?' protested Fletcher.

'I'll take a toilet roll.'

'You've got guts.'

'If I told you how many times I've been to the lavatory today you wouldn't have said that.'

Fletcher smiled.

Kincaid said, 'I don't want anyone to know I'm going back. Stall for me if anyone should call. Tell them I'm sick or out on a job anything.'

'Will do.'

'I'll call you.'

Kincaid returned to the flat, packed a bag and collected his notes, which were still spread out on the table from the previous evening. He checked that he had enough money in his wallet and that his credit cards were there. He turned off the gas and electricity and made sure the front door was secure before running downstairs and stepping out into the back lane where he had parked his car. The car, a red Honda Prelude, had been standing there for three weeks unused, but it was about to have a good run now. He had decided to drive up to Newcastle.

As he walked towards it he fumbled for the keys in his pocket, which had become entangled with his handkerchief. He freed them, looked at the fob and remembered. Ostensibly it was a cheap, souvenir keyring with the word 'Lakeland' on it, but it meant a lot to Kincaid. Kerry had given it to him on a family outing just before the operation which had taken her from him. She had been too young to buy it herself, Julie had bought it for her, but he could still see the look on Kerry's face when she had handed it over. He squeezed it in his palm.

Kincaid saw that the windscreen was dirty from being left in the street for such a long time. He was wondering whether he had a cloth in the car when something else caught his eye. There was a box underneath it. He froze in his tracks as fear paralysed him. His eyes were fixed on the dark box. His imagination was ablaze with orange flame and flying metal. 'Jesus,' he whispered.

Somewhere out on the main street a car blew its horn and made Kincaid jump. He moved slowly towards the Honda and knelt down beside the driver's door to look underneath. There were no wires to be seen and the box did not seem to be made of anything substantial. In fact, it looked like . . . cardboard. It was bashed in where it was wedged against the oil sump, as if it were empty. Kincaid reached in and pulled out a harmless confectionery carton, blown underneath the car by the wind. Most of the writing had been worn away but he could still make out the words, 'Helps you work, rest and play'. He closed his eyes as relief flooded through him. Suddenly he felt very silly.

By nature, Neil Tolkien was an academic. This was a legacy from his childhood, when books had been his nearest and dearest companions. Whenever something troubled him, his first thought was to seek information and help from them. Today his own collection was inadequate to the task in hand; he had come to the University Medical Library to get the data he needed. He wanted to know if there was any reported correlation between heroin addiction and the onslaught of full-blown Aids in HIV positive patients. His colleagues at the Tuesday night clinic had accepted that there must be, if all their referral patients had developed Aids since being diagnosed. He found it surprising; he needed some figures.

Three hours later, Tolkien admitted defeat. He had been unable to find any confirmatory report in any of the medical journals and felt more puzzled than ever. Surely such a clear correlation could not have gone unnoticed. The nature of scientific research and its grant funding systems ensured that even the smallest detail would find its way into print. Cynics might suggest that the scientific journals were full of 'smallest details'.

Tolkien pondered this all the way back in the car. If the link between heroin addiction and Aids development really had been missed then he had better start writing it up for the *Lancet*. This was something that people in the profession should be aware of.

First he would need more information about numbers. He could get that from the clinic at College Hospital. In fact, that information should be available from the computer; public health figures for the region were available to all medical practitioners. As soon as he got in he switched on his monitor before even taking his jacket off. He keyed in his password and started asking questions about the incidence of HIV infection in the region. He took notes of figures from the screen as they appeared.

As the last page came up on the monitor, Tolkien shook his head in disbelief. 'I don't understand,' he murmured, repeating his question to the computer. The same statistics appeared on the screen.

The computer had informed him that the incidence of HIV infection in the region was broadly similar to other comparable regions in the British Isles. This he expected. It also told him that the average time taken for HIV positive patients to develop full-blown Aids was currently two and a half years, although the information carried a reminder that this figure was computed on patients who had not been given AZT as a prophylactic measure. Tolkien then asked what proportion of HIV positive patients were also registered drug addicts. He asked for the development time for these patients. 'Two years, five months, seventeen days,' said the computer.

'The same?' said Tolkien, unwilling to believe what he saw. 'How can they have the same average when all twenty-nine of the clinic referrals had contracted Aids within six months and ten of them had subsequently died! Surely there could not have been such a large number of Aids patients that the clinic cases had been insignificant statistically.

'How many deaths from Aids in the last year?' Tolkien asked.

'NEGATIVE,' said the computer.

Tolkien's eyes opened wide in disbelief, then he remembered that no one died from Aids officially. They died from the variety of diseases that Aids left them open to. This was going to be difficult.

'Deaths from *Pneumocystis carnii* pneumonia?' he asked.

'NOT AVAILABLE,' said the screen.

'Why not?' asked Tolkien.

'LACK OF DIAGNOSTIC CONFIRMATION PRECLUDES ANALYSIS.'

Tolkien had to accept the reason. It was notoriously difficult to prove the presence of the *Pneumocystis* organism in body tissues. He began to see the hopelessness of the task he had set himself. To determine the number of Aids deaths, he would have to gather in numbers from under a dozen or more different causes of death headings and even then he wouldn't have a way of separating out the Aids deaths from the others. 'Crazy,' he complained. Surely there must be some way of getting figures for deaths involving Aids patients. He tried asking for Aids-related deaths.

'NOT AVAILABLE,' came the reply.

'Shit!' said Tolkien. He picked up the telephone and called College Hospital. He asked to speak to the duty computer manager.

'Computer Service. Can I help you?'

'I'm trying to find out the number of Aids-related deaths for the region over the past year,' said Tolkien. 'The computer doesn't seem to want to give me them.'

'Who is this, please?'

Tolkien gave his name, where his practice was and read out his pass number.

The man said, 'Put down the phone, Doctor. I'll call you back.'

Remembering a similar request from the prison doctor, Tolkien complied. The telephone rang.

'These figures are not generally available over the computer network, Doctor,' said the man.

'Why not?'

'There are special problems of confidentiality surrounding Aids, but then I'm sure you are aware of that?'

'I don't see how presenting a broad overall picture is threatening anyone's privacy.'

'It's regional policy not to put out figures on Aids.'

'That's silly.'

'Then you must take the matter up with the regional board, Doctor,' said the man icily. 'May I ask why you need this information? You are a GP, aren't you?'

The man made the comment sound condescending, and Tolkien took a dislike to him. He worked hard at remaining civil. 'I think there may be a connection between heroin addiction and the speed of Aids development. I need some figures to work on.'

'I see,' said the man, 'I'm sorry, we simply don't have them on the computer. Individual case histories are, of course, available.'

Tolkien put down the telephone and cursed. Individual case histories were no good to him at all; he could only call up those he had knowledge of. He needed figures for the whole region. It was almost as if the computer programme had been designed to keep the information from him.

FOURTEEN

Kincaid woke up and felt disoriented; he couldn't remember where he was. His eyes darted round a room lit only by some light coming in through a vee near the top of the curtains; the furniture told him that he was in a motel bedroom. Normally this would be a depressing discovery but today he took comfort from the anonymity of his surroundings. Room 216 would be identical to room 215 or 217. He would be one of the faceless men travelling north or south, wearing dark suits, carrying black cases with numbers on the locks and stopping overnight on their way to sell pumps in Peterhead or knickers in Norwich. This was good. He had no wish to advertise his presence in the area and had, as yet, informed no one of his return. He would call Eve later.

Kincaid got out of bed and turned on the television to watch the breakfast-time news. A well-coiffured woman told him of the closing prices on the Tokyo stock exchange. He filled the electric kettle and plugged it in to its wall-socket. The weather forecast for the area said that it was going to be generally dull with a forty per cent chance of rain. He opened the curtains and saw that it was raining.

With a cup of tea made from a bag that had dried out some weeks before, Kincaid sat down on the end of the bed to watch a presenter being rude to a politician.

'Come, come,' the presenter was saying, 'surely a change in the leadership of your party is inevitable?'

'Not inevitable at all,' countered the politician. 'The Prime

233

Minister is assured of the whole-hearted support of the parliamentary party.'

The kiss of death, thought Kincaid.

'But with respect,' said the presenter without any, 'isn't Westminster alive with rumours of Mr Carlisle, the health minister, taking over the top job?'

'You used the word rumour and I would agree with that,' said the politician smugly. 'The corridors of power are always rife with rumour.'

'The latest opinion polls put your party's chances of re-election at thirty per cent higher with Mr Carlisle at the helm,' said the presenter.

'You cannot pay too much attention to polls,' insisted the politician.

'But surely you can't ignore them?'

'Not altogether,' agreed the politician, beginning to move uncomfortably in his seat.

'So the party will pay some heed to what the people are saying?'

'He's got you by the balls, old son,' muttered Kincaid.

'Naturally we listen, but that doesn't mean to say . . .'

'Would you serve in a cabinet under Mr Carlisle?'

'The question really doesn't arise.'

'But if it did?'

'Let's wait and see, shall we?'

'Then you do concede that there is the possibility of a change?'

'No, no, I repeat, the Prime Minister has the overwhelming . . .'

Kincaid switched off. 'Don't worry, lad,' he said to the blank screen. 'They'll give you a bucket to carry home your career in.'

He showered, dressed and started to plan his day.

It was just before eleven o'clock when Kincaid turned into Leamington Grove, where Sir Martin Freeman's widow lived. Checking the numbers he found that she lived in the last house on the left. It was a substantial, stone-built villa with a large conservatory tacked on to one side where he could see a small, thin woman watering plants. The watering-can seemed tiny, but it had a very long spout. The woman looked to be in her fifties and had fine, patrician features when viewed in profile, as Kincaid was seeing her. He pushed open the iron gate and climbed the three stone steps to the path.

Kincaid decided to chance his luck and approach the woman directly rather than march up to the front door and ring the bell. He adopted a friendly smile and walked towards the conservatory, making sure that his feet made plenty of sound on the gravel. He wanted the woman to hear him coming rather than risk startling her. The glass door which led in from the garden was a bit stiff, but it opened with a shudder at the second attempt. He was immediately aware of how much warmer it was inside due to the morning sun on the glass. It was also very humid and the air was scented with a mixture of blossoms. The woman looked at him imperiously and waited for an explanation.

'Lady Freeman? I do hope you'll forgive this intrusion. I was in the area and I felt I just had to come by and offer my condolences personally. My name is . . . Grant, John Grant. I was a colleague of Martin's some years ago. He and I became quite good friends.'

The woman looked at Kincaid with a vaguely puzzled look which he found hard to interpret, but when she spoke all was explained. She had been drinking.

'I don't think I recall a Grant,' she said, trying not to slur her words. Kincaid noticed that she deliberately clipped her words to this end and deduced that she must drink a lot to have developed the technique.

'I'm not nearly as famous as Martin was,' said Kincaid modestly. 'A man like Martin must have had so many friends and colleagues.'

'Quite so. And what do you do, Mr Grant?'

'I'm a psychiatrist, Lady Freeman. I work with mentally disturbed children.'

'Why bother?' she replied. The question was rhetorical; she continued watering the plants.

The words hit Kincaid like stones, putting him slightly off

balance. Priorities, he reminded himself. He needed information from this woman. He mustn't get on her wrong side. He saw that she was looking at him out of the corner of her eye, waiting to see if he would rise to the bait she had thrown to him. It was all too obvious to Kincaid, but her drunken state was making her less than subtle. Kincaid ignored the comment and pretended to examine the plants nearest him.

'Do you know the human species is the only one stupid enough to keep diluting itself with cripples and misfits?' asked Lady Freeman. 'Soon we'll be absolutely swamped with them. The meek will inherit the earth and destroy it for the rest of us.' Antonia Freeman took a sip from a glass that sat on the staging by the window. It looked like water but Kincaid suspected it was gin.

'Did Martin share these views?' asked Kincaid cautiously.

Antonia Freeman laughed bitterly and said, 'My husband shared any views he thought would further his career, but when it came to actions, that was quite a different story.'

'Martin was a very well-respected surgeon,' said Kincaid, treading as carefully as he could. A drunk with a loose tongue was just what he needed.

'Martin was a windbag. When it came right down to it that's all he was. It makes me so angry to think of it.' Antonia Freeman shook her head in frustration and said, 'He could have played such a big role in reshaping his country and he blew it.'

Kincaid hoped that the excitement he felt inside at what the woman was saying did not show in his face. He strove to maintain a neutral but not unfriendly expression. He nodded slightly at intervals, hoping to infer sympathy with the views being expressed. It was a technique he had seen television interviewers adopt. The woman was angry and bitter. She wanted to talk. She was highly self-opinionated. She needed an audience.

'I didn't know Martin was involved in politics,' said Kincaid, as the woman paused to take another sip from her glass.

'Martin lacked vision, and do you know why that was?'

Kincaid shook his head.

'Breeding. He didn't have it. He wasted his talents pandering to nonentities when, if he had had the breeding, he would have seen the broader picture.'

'The broader picture?' repeated Kincaid tentatively, feeling that the conversation was racing away from him.

Another sip and the woman continued, not appreciating that Kincaid had posed a question. She said, 'He went yellow in the end, blew the whistle, called a bloody press conference! Can you imagine?' She broke into bitter laughter which Kincaid found unnerving. He hoped the woman wouldn't read it in his eyes.

The woman stopped laughing and Kincaid could sense that she was undergoing a change of mood. She drained the contents of her glass and stared at him in silence for a few moments. Kincaid saw a tear run down her cheek. It made him uncomfortable; he felt like the intruder he was. Almost inaudibly he heard her say, 'But they shouldn't have killed him, they shouldn't have done that.'

'Who?' whispered Kincaid.

Antonia Freeman looked up at him as if she hadn't heard the question. She held out her glass. 'It's empty,' she said.

Kincaid took it from her. 'Would you like another?' he asked.

'Through there,' said Antonia Freeman, swinging her arm round to point vaguely behind her.

Kincaid left the conservatory and hurried along the short corridor which connected it to a large ground floor room. Somewhere in the house he could hear the sound of a vacuum cleaner, so they weren't alone. As long as whoever it was kept out of the way until the Freeman woman had talked herself out. He quickly found the gin and replenished the woman's glass; a small gin and a lot of tonic. As he turned round to leave, a framed inscription on the wall caught his eye. It was a quotation written in German, in Gothic script:

Mit der Dummheit kämpfen Götter selbst vergebens.

Kincaid recognised it and translated it out loud, 'Against stupidity the gods themselves are baffled'. It came from the works of Schiller. The name Schiller made him go cold. Charles French, Carlisle, the Schiller group! Had Freeman been involved as well? He hurried back to the conservatory with the gin.

As Kincaid had feared, the interruption had broken the spell and Antonia Freeman now looked at him suspiciously as he handed her the glass.

'What did you say your name was?' she asked.

'Grant, John Grant,' said Kincaid.

'And you're a psychiatrist?'

'Yes.'

The woman looked at Kincaid as if she was examining a laboratory specimen. 'So what on earth did you and Martin have in common? Tell me that. Martin thought that all psychiatrists were charlatans.'

Kincaid decided to take a huge gamble. He said, 'The Schiller group.'

There was a long, silent pause. Kincaid held the woman's gaze without flinching, despite the blood pounding in his temples and the feeling that he had lit the fuse of a bomb without letting go.

After a pause that seemed to go on for hours Antonia Freeman said, 'Why didn't you say so?'

Kincaid breathed an inward sigh of relief. 'I didn't know if you . . .'

'I introduced Martin many years ago.'

'Oh,' smiled Kincaid.

'You are with the people at the hospital?'

'Yes.'

'There's a problem?'

'No.'

'Then why are you here?' asked Antonia Freeman.

'I came about the Wellington Endowment.'

'What about it?'

'You are the trustee.'

'So?'

Kincaid could tell that he was running out of luck. Suspicion was beginning to edge into the woman's voice. 'I wondered if I might just have a look at the current figures for expenditure?'

A black cloud rolled across Antonia Freeman's face. 'Who are you?' she hissed, in an angry rasp. She came towards Kincaid. 'Who the hell are you?' Her voice rose in anger as she repeated the question. She drew back her hand and threw her glass at Kincaid, who ducked and made for the door. It shattered one of the panes, sending shards of glass on to the lawn as Kincaid ran to the gate and vaulted it. He didn't relax until he was safely out of the area.

The sound of a horn and the blaze of headlights from an oncoming vehicle warned Kincaid that he had strayed over the centre line in his preoccupation. He pulled the wheel hard over to the left and ignored the angry gesture from the other driver. 'Jesus,' he said to himself as he slowed down and pulled off the road into a lay-by; his mind was racing.

The most Kincaid had dared hope for from the meeting with Freeman's widow had been some indication of the size of the Wellington Endowment and how much was being contributed to the Northern Health Scheme. Instead he had hit the jackpot.

Antonia Freeman had more or less told him that her husband had been murdered. The Schiller group, which Fletcher thought had been disbanded, was still in existence and up to something, something based at College Hospital. Martin Freeman had been involved but had chickened out. She had said that he had called a press conference but that 'they' had killed him. Who? Fields? French? Schreiber? And how? Freeman had died in the middle of an operation. He had suffered a heart attack . . . hadn't he?

Kincaid caught his breath as he remembered that Freeman *had* called a press conference for after the operation on Greta Marsh! He also remembered that a surgeon Eve had spoken about had thought it strange because the operation had been performed beforehand. Now it made sense. It had not been Freeman's intention to talk about the operation. He had been going to blow the whistle on the Schiller group!

Kincaid rubbed his forehead and put the next brick in place. The group must have realised this at the last moment and killed him. But how? And was that the real reason Fields had been so keen to cover up what had happened to Greta Marsh? It had had nothing to do with Claire Affric's career at all. They didn't want press attention because they didn't want anyone stumbling upon Martin Freeman's murder and whatever else they were up to in College Hospital. Just what 'whatever else' might be now occupied Kincaid's entire attention.

Henry James Harrison had died of *Staphylococcal* pneumonia, said the report from College Hospital. Neil Tolkien read it and turned his pen end over end on the desk while he thought about it. College Hospital had admitted Harry for 'assessment' and he had died of pneumonia a week or so later. He developed a chest infection on the Wednesday, which led to pneumonia on the Saturday, and then he had died. There was nothing too strange in that. Harry was an old man; old men were prone to sudden infections and their immune system was often unable to cope. Then why did it disturb him so? Tolkien found it hard to answer his own question. He had the unsettling feeling that there was something wrong somewhere, but he couldn't quite put his finger on it.

Tolkien knew that this feeling had germinated from the Aids figures for clinic referral patients. He kept returning to them. Ten victims dead within six months of developing full-blown Aids – ten out of twenty-nine. Two of them men had been his own patients at the clinic. Tolkien dug out his case notes on them. Both had been healthy at the time of referral to the special clinic at College Hospital, although one had a small Kaposi's sarcoma on his face. One had died three and a half months later from pulmonary tuberculosis, and the other three weeks after that from *Pneumocystis* pneumonia. Nothing odd in the causes of death, he noted. They just went downhill very quickly, that's all . . . like Harry . . . or like Madeline Bell. Tolkien felt a thin film of sweat break out on his forehead. Just where the hell was this line of thought taking him? What was he suggesting?

Two Aids patients, three, as he remembered Frank Golightly's wife, a frail old man and a Down's syndrome child had all died of the things such people die of, but much quicker than he might have expected. In his mind he could hear Angela Bell, in her grief, say that the hospital hadn't tried to save Maddy. Tolkien put his hand to his throat; it felt tight. He loosened his collar. The pain in his back was getting worse and he was finding it difficult to concentrate on something his subconscious was telling him was too dangerous to contemplate.

Tolkien made himself some coffee and tried telling himself that he was tired and his imagination was playing tricks on him, but it didn't work. He knew he had to investigate further. He needed more information. He began by trying to recall if there had been any other surprisingly quick deaths in the recent past. He remembered Jack Kincaid, the man he had seen while on weekend call. Kincaid had been operated on for cancer but had developed a post-operative pneumonia and died shortly afterwards. He remembered the case clearly because of his son's lack of regard for the medical profession. He also remembered feeling uncomfortable when he learned of the old man's death as he himself had suggested that Kincaid would live for some time after the operation. Another old man had died sooner than would have been expected. Sick old men, Aids patients, expensive people to treat on the health service, drains on the social services. The nightmare suggestion was that the brave new health service wasn't treating them at all. It was killing them!

Tolkien looked down at his hand and saw that it was shaking slightly. He baulked at the enormity of what he was considering. This was England in the Nineties, not Nazi Germany. What he was seeing must be some kind of statistical aberration. He was basing his suspicions on a mere handful of cases. No one else had noticed anything unusual . . . had they? He picked up the telephone and called Gavin Mitchell. He was still thinking about how to broach the subject when Gavin Mitchell's receptionist answered.

'I'm afraid he's out at the moment, Dr Tolkien.'

'I'll call again.'

Tolkien called Mary Cunningham's practice. She herself answered. They exchanged pleasantries and Tolkien said, 'Mary, I'm trying to put some figures together about our clinic patients. Were any of the ten who died in the past six months your patients?'

'Yes, three.'

'Could you give me some details?'

'Do you want their case histories?'

'No, just primary details if that's all right?'

'Of course, give me a moment.'

Tolkien sat ready with pen in hand.

Mary Cunningham came back on the line. 'Agnes Rossen, heroin addict, diagnosed HIV positive on March third last year, referred to College Hospital clinic, developed *Pneumocystis* pneumonia in May, failed to respond to treatment, died June third. Mary Lownes, heroin addict, diagnosed HIV positive in May, referred to College clinic, developed miliary tuberculosis in June, died September fourth. Joan Divers, heroin addict, diagnosed HIV positive in May, died of septicaemia November fourteenth. Is that what you want?'

'Thank you,' said Tolkien.

'What exactly are you looking for?' asked Mary Cunningham.

'I'm trying to establish a link between drug addiction and susceptibility to Aids-related complexes,' lied Tolkien.

'They certainly succumbed very quickly,' agreed Mary Cunningham, 'but as we said the other night, it was probably due to their generally debilitated state.'

'You're probably right,' said Tolkien

'I know it's an awful thing to say, but . . .'

'Go on.'

'It's a blessing in a way. My three girls were all on the game. God knows how many clients they would have infected if they had lived for a couple more years. God, I wish I hadn't said that now; it sounds terrible.'

'You're right,' said Tolkien with a leaden feeling in the pit of his stomach. He wasn't at all sure how to continue probing. 'Mary, can I ask you a question in strictest confidence?'

'Of course, you know you can.'

'What you said just now about it being a blessing . . .'

'Yes?'

'Have there been any other occasions recently when you've thought that?'

'I don't think I understand what you mean,' said Mary Cunningham.

'Have you had any other deaths in your practice when you've felt within yourself that it was probably for the best?'

Mary Cunningham thought for a moment before saying, 'Now you come to mention it, there was a severely handicapped seven-year-old . . .'

'Yes?'

'She had been like that since birth. A couple of months ago she had a cold and it went down into her chest. She was admitted to College Hospital and died a few days later. The post-mortem said that she had picked up a staphylococcal lung infection which was resistant to ampicillin and the other drugs that College put her on. I remember thinking at the time that she hadn't much of a life to look forward to. Is that the sort of thing you mean?'

The parallel that Tolkien had drawn between this case and that of Madeline Bell made him swallow hard before he could reply quietly, 'That is exactly the sort of thing I mean.'

'Why did you ask?'

Tolkien ignored the question and asked one of his own, 'Would you mind giving me the name of the child?'

'I suppose not, she was called Linda Holland. What's wrong, Neil?'

'When I know for sure, Mary, I'll tell you.' Tolkien put down the telephone. He felt unwell. It wasn't the pain in his back, although it was there. It wasn't a physical feeling at all; he was just very afraid.

Afraid or not, Tolkien knew that there would be no going back. He had lots of questions to ask the computer. He wanted numbers, ages, diagnoses, treatments, case histories, post-mortem results and overall statistics for the region. If someone was killing off patients, he wanted to know how many and, most important of all, how they were doing it. Forty minutes later he came to the conclusion that he was going round in circles.

The overall figures for the region for deaths occurring in the groups that Tolkien was interested in were not significantly different from any other comparable region in the United

Kingdom. The causes of death, established at post-mortem for the individual patients he had asked about, were exactly as expected for these people. The only common factor he could determine lay in the deaths of three of them. Jack Kincaid, Madeline Bell and Linda Holland had all died from chest infections caused by *Staphylococcus aureus*, a common enough bug to find in hospitals; but he noticed that the antibiogram obtained from the lab at the time was identical in all three cases. The same strain had killed them all.

Tolkien knew that it was not at all unusual for so-called hospital strains of bacteria to become resistant to various antibiotics. In fact, *Staphylococcus aureus* was implicated more often than any other kind of bug in this respect. What was unusual was that there had been no suggestion in the reports that there had been a hospital outbreak. In the normal course of events, three deaths occurring in the same hospital from the same infection would automatically trigger off an alert, and measures would be taken to trace the source and deal with the problem. Wards would be disinfected and staff would be swabbed to see if they were carriers of the infection. But as far as College Hospital was concerned, there had been no problem.

Tolkien wondered if this was because the three patients had been in hospital at different times and in different wards. Usually, a hospital-based infection would infect a number of patients at the same time and usually in the same ward, where the source would eventually be found. This was possible, Tolkien concluded, but if he could see what was going on from a few questions asked at his terminal surely the mighty computer power of the control centre could come up with the same thing?

The telephone rang; it was Terry Feenan.

'It's Karen, she's sick.'

Tolkien did not bother to ask if Feenan had tried calling his own GP. 'What's wrong with her?' he asked.

'She can't breathe.'

'When did this start?'

'This morning.'

'I'll come.'

*   *   *

Tolkien considered the plight of the Feenans as he drove round to the flats. Not only were they drug addicts and HIV positive, they were now, by his classification, in a new high risk group. They were exactly the kind of people who died quickly in the northern region.

Tolkien waited for the lift with a large woman who must have weighed in the order of fifteen stone, despite a height of no more than five foot. She carried shopping bags in both hands and was breathing hard from the effort of having walked from the shops. There was a film of moisture along her upper lip and she smelled of sweat. She was wearing a heavy brown coat that was buttoned up to the neck.

Two young boys emerged from the lift as soon as the doors opened and nearly bowled the woman over as they charged out. 'Little bastards,' she murmured, sidling into the lift and taking so long that the doors started to close before Tolkien was aboard. He thrust out his elbows against the shutting doors until they relented and let him in. 'Nine, please,' he said, as he saw the woman push the button for her floor.

The woman looked at him with a disgruntled expression and said, 'Are you paralysed?'

Tolkien leaned over and pressed nine. The woman got out on the fifth floor, shaking her head and murmuring, 'Lazy bastard.'

'Heigh-ho,' murmured Tolkien, as the doors closed again.

'She's real sick,' said Terry Feenan, as he opened the door to Tolkien. 'She's in here.'

Tolkien was led into a bedroom that had not seen any cleaning or tidying for a long time. But when heroin and Aids were playing leading roles in your life, he supposed that such considerations did not stand much of a chance. 'Where's the baby?' he asked.

'With Karen's mum.'

Tolkien nodded and sat down on the edge of the bed to examine the girl who had not as yet acknowledged his presence. She couldn't, Tolkien realized, she was having such trouble just breathing. He sounded her lungs, front and back, and knew that she had pneumonia.

'Will she have to go to hospital?' asked Terry Feenan.

Tolkien was on the horns of a dilemma. He knew the answer should be yes. Karen was clearly very ill. She needed the facilities that only a well-equipped hospital could provide. He should pack her off in an ambulance and turn over responsibility, just like he'd done with Madeline Bell. The difference was that when he had sent Maddy to College Hospital he had believed he was doing the right thing. Now it was different. He felt that if he sent Karen to hospital she would not come out alive. She would be another 'blessing'.

'No.' said Tolkien. 'I'll treat her here. You'll have to look after her, day and night. Understand?'

'If you say so, but . . .'

'Just do as I say.'

Tolkien had never felt so exposed in his life, but he could not bring himself to send Karen to her death. He knew that if she died at home he would be blamed and there would be no defence. He would think about that later. Right now he had to decide on treatment. Karen had pneumonia and both lungs were affected. She was HIV positive, but he was going to bet against *Pneumocystis*. The condition had come on too suddenly and progressed too quickly. He did not know how, but he was going to go for *Staphylococcal* pneumonia, the same disease that had killed Madeline Bell and Linda Holland. He was even going to bet that it was the same strain.

From the antibiograms he had seen earlier he knew which drugs he could not use to treat the condition, but he also knew which ones he could. They were not his first choice by any means, but they should do the job if taken in time. He turned to Terry Feenan and said, 'I'm going back to the surgery to order the capsules Karen needs. You can pick them up in an hour. I'm going to start her off with an injection. After that it's up to you to see that she takes the capsules every four hours. Okay?'

Feenan nodded.

'Your main job is to see that she is comfortable. Look after her.'

Tolkien hurried back to the surgery and punched in his request to the College Hospital pharmacy. It was denied.

Tolkien stared at the screen, unable to believe what he was seeing. He repeated his request and again it was turned down.

'NOT DRUG OF CHOICE,' said the screen. 'PRESS RETURN FOR ALTERNATIVE'.

Tolkien pressed the Return key.

'PENICILLIN,' said the screen.

'Strain is resistant,' replied Tolkien.

'NO LAB INFORMATION,' said the computer.

'I'm giving you the bloody information,' cursed Tolkien. He switched off the terminal and called the computer manager at College Hospital.

'But how do you know that your patient is suffering from a penicillin-resistant infection?' asked the duty manager.

'I have good reason to believe that she is suffering from the same infection which has killed three patients, to my knowledge, in College Hospital. They all had the same antibiogram, which said that the infection would not respond to penicillin. Your computer system appears to have missed this,' said Tolkien.

There was a momentary pause before the manager said, 'It does indeed, Doctor. I'm grateful to you for pointing this out. Perhaps you can give me the details?'

Tolkien read out the names and said, 'Perhaps you will now overrule your damned machine and supply the treatment I asked for?'

'Of course, Doctor. Please accept my apologies.'

Tolkien put down the telephone and kept his hand on it. He had succeeded in getting the drugs he wanted for Karen Feenan, but to do it he had had to let College Hospital know that he had been making inquiries. Somebody might not like that. Things were getting out of hand; he had to have help.

Tolkien considered telling his colleagues what he knew, but what could they do? Three amateurs against God knows what? It wasn't just help he needed, it was expert advice. Could he tell the police, he wondered. Tell them what? That he believed someone was murdering the old, the handicapped and the

247

chronically sick? Tolkien screwed up his eyes as he imagined himself talking to the police.

'Oh yes, sir, and how are they doing this?'

'I've no idea.'

'And who is doing this, sir?'

'I've no idea.'

He would need far more than suspicion before he called in the police. This meant discreet, expert investigation, the sort of thing that the London journalist was good at. He would call James Kincaid.

FIFTEEN

Kincaid called Fletcher and had to wait because the editor's line was engaged. His nervousness showed through the impatient drumming of his fingers on the wall of the call box. 'C'mon, c'mon,' he whispered, as he examined the change in his hand. He had to insert his last coin before Fletcher's voice came on the line. Kincaid asked him to call him back on the number he gave.

'Did you see the Freeman woman?' asked Fletcher.

'That's why I'm calling.'

'She was worth seeing, then?'

'Are we sure Eva Braun died in the bunker?' asked Kincaid.

'That nice?'

'All the charm of a snakebite. This thing has got nothing to do with graft or sticky fingers; it's political.'

'Damnation!' said Fletcher, 'That always means trouble. Are you sure you can handle it on your own?'

'At the moment, yes. I'm going to stay up here in the meantime, but I want you to start rattling cages down there. Have the researchers start asking questions around Westminster about the Schiller group. See who shits their pants, particularly among Carlisle's people.'

'But they disbanded years ago,' said Fletcher.

'Lady Macbeth says not. They're running the health service up here.'

Fletcher was quiet for a moment, then he said, 'That's very public spirited of them.'

'If they're anything like Lady M, "public spirited" is the last thing they are.'

'You don't care for the lady, I can tell.'

'The last time I listened to that kind of philosophy it came from a crew cut waving a union jack, with a boot size bigger than his IQ.'

'So what are they doing?'

'Re-shaping the country.'

'That has a familiar ring to it,' said Fletcher. 'But how? Everyone thinks the service up there is the bees' knees.'

'That's my problem. I know who the bad guys are, I just don't know what they're doing. Anything at your end?'

'Nothing on Fields as yet, but talking of Carlisle, one of our researchers has discovered that he has a nickname in certain sections of the Party: he's called "Trojan".'

'Why?'

'I think it's because he looks very nice but has the intellect of a wooden horse,' said Fletcher. 'The thing is, you don't have to be bright as long as you are successful. You only get asked difficult questions if you screw up. In Carlisle's case, the opposition have been reduced to asking him why the Northern Scheme hasn't been implemented more quickly in other parts of the country, and how can his own party criticise him when he's worth twenty points in the opinion polls?'

'I'd better go,' said Kincaid.

'Be careful,' said Fletcher. 'Oh, there was a call for you here at the paper.'

'Who?'

'A man called Tolkien? He said he was a doctor. I told him you were out on a job. He wouldn't say what it was about but he left a number.'

'Thanks,' said Kincaid.

Fletcher dictated the number and Kincaid scribbled it down.

Kincaid tried calling Eve at the nurses' home; she was on duty. No, there was no message.

Kincaid had been driving round in circles on the outskirts of the city since visiting Lady Freeman and decided that he had better eat something. He stopped at the first roadside inn he came to, a large building called The Feathers, whose façade was discoloured by brown rust stains and neglected white paintwork.

The bar was empty on both sides; Kincaid coughed, but did not succeed in disturbing the sound of distant voices. He was in no hurry; he occupied himself by examining the grandfather clock that stood beside the fireplace. It was working and provided the only noise in the room, a pleasantly loud tick. He learned from a brass plate inside the cabinet that it had been built in 1897 by J Cargill and Sons of Newcastle. A teenage girl appeared from the back and took his order, then disappeared again.

The beef dish, when it came, tasted like cardboard, but the apple pie and custard that followed helped combat the hollow feeling in his stomach. He finished with coffee which, although served from a percolator-style jug, was instant. He made a face; he hated being taken for a fool.

So what did Neil Tolkien want? He hadn't called him back immediately because he suspected that he might have been telephoning to give him a glowing report on the Northern Health Scheme. He could do without that, right now. His problem at the moment was that he did not know which way to turn. Lady Freeman had seemed to imply that her husband had been murdered because he was about to give away the Schiller group's plans, but he would need more than the rambling tongue of a drunk to instigate an official investigation. Besides, she would only deny having said it. He could hardly have Freeman's body exhumed on these grounds – and maybe it had been cremated anyway.

The irony was that a great many people had been present at Sir Martin's death, including several gentlemen of the press who had attended the operation at Freeman's request. The event had even been recorded on video. Kincaid's hand froze at the thought, his coffee cup held in mid-air between the table and his lips. Was it conceivable that the video still existed?

More questions flooded into his head. Who would be responsible for making such a recording? Was that something the hospital would do, or would an outside agency be employed to make it? He had no idea, but Eve might know. On the other hand, maybe he would call Neil Tolkien after all.

Kincaid brought out the scrap of paper with Tolkien's number on it. He had difficulty in reading it because the light had been failing dramatically, as what he thought might be thunder clouds rolled across the sky from the west. The teenage girl had not returned to turn the lights on in the bar. He dialled the number at the payphone in the narrow entry hall and heard Tolkien answer as the first roll of thunder confirmed his suspicions.

'Neil? It's Jim Kincaid.'

'Thank God,' replied Tolkien.

The reply took Kincaid aback. Tolkien sounded frightened.

'I have to see you,' said Tolkien.

'What about?'

'Not over the phone.'

'Is it that important?' asked Kincaid, knowing that Tolkien would think that he was calling from London.

'Yes, it's important; I have to talk to you.'

'Can't you give me a clue?' asked Kincaid.

'It's about this bloody health service; there's something wrong.'

Kincaid swallowed. Could this be the break he needed? Maybe a medic could see what he couldn't. 'All right,' he said. 'When?'

'Can you get here by tonight?'

'Yes.'

'Evening surgery will be over by eight, so any time after that. Do you have a pen?'

'Yes.'

Tolkien read out his address and gave directions. Kincaid copied it down. He had to ask Tolkien to repeat part of it when a crash of thunder overhead blotted it out. He hung up as rain started to pour in the street outside.

He returned to the bar to collect his jacket and found the teenage girl clearing away his dishes. 'Was everything all right?' she asked automatically.

'Fine,' said Kincaid, and left.

He stood in the glazed porch of the pub looking out at the rain for a few moments, noting the universal darkness of the sky before turning up his collar and opening the door. It was only a twenty-yard sprint to the car, but he still got soaked. He sat for a moment wondering what to do as water cascaded down the windscreen like a waterfall. He made his decision. He would find a place to stay for the night, then he would call the home and ask about Kerry. The thought that he had been here in Newcastle for two days without going to see her was making him feel guilty.

Kincaid chose another featureless motel on the main trunk road and filled in the registration card using an assumed name. He suspected that this might be erring too much on the side of caution, but it was definitely better to play it safe. Thoughts of the nightmare on the bridge were never very far away. He threw his bag down on the floor and himself on the bed, looked up at the ceiling and listened to the rain. At two-thirty he lifted the bedside telephone and called the home.

'This is James Kincaid, I'm calling about my daughter.'

'Good news, Mr Kincaid,' announced Mrs Wilton. 'Dr Sutton will reassess your daughter next Wednesday.'

'That's excellent news, Mrs Wilton,' said Kincaid, but his heart wasn't in it.

'Three of our children are being reassessed. There is a form you will have to sign. Would you like me to send it to you or will you be up in the near future?'

Kincaid hesitated. His instinct was to say that he was already up in Newcastle and that he would be right over, but prudence won. He simply said that he would be up soon.

Kincaid rang off and sat quietly on the edge of the bed. This was the moment he had fought so hard and waited so long for, but now all he could feel was a sense of anticlimax and worse than that, trepidation. Sutton was going to assess his daughter, but he was one of the London appointments. He remembered what the Freeman woman had said about the mentally handicapped. Why bother? The words rang round in his head like the mocking cries of a children's game. *Why bother? Why bother? Kerry Kincaid is soft in the head, why bother? Why bother?*

Kincaid looked at his watch. Maybe in five hours time, when he met Tolkien, he would understand more about what the hell was going on up here in the north.

At six o'clock Kincaid called the nurses' home and succeeded in contacting Eve.

'I thought you had forgotten all about me,' she complained.

Kincaid apologised for not having called her the night before and told her he was in the city.

'You are?' exclaimed Eve.

'Yes, but I'm not advertising the fact. Can you meet me this evening?'

'Just say where.'

'Do you remember the Italian restaurant we went to a couple of weeks ago?'

'I remember.'

'I'll book a table for a late supper. I have to see someone at eight. Say, ten o'clock?'

'I'll be there.'

The rain had stopped by the time Kincaid left the motel to go to Tolkien's surgery. He knew the area of town, but more by reputation than geography. He had to keep leaning over the wheel to look up at street signs in order to follow the directions Tolkien had given him. He found himself hoping that the rain might start again. It might give him an even chance of finding his car in one piece when he came out.

He found the surgery and parked on the other side of the street. Through the lit bay window he could see two people sitting on hard-backed chairs. He deduced that this was Tolkien's waiting-room and that the doctor was running late. He sat in the car until the second of the two patients got up, leaving the room empty.

From across the road Kincaid could see how depressing the waiting-room was. The inadequate lighting set the tone, while the old furniture and peeling wallpaper matched the ambience of the area.

As the last patient left the surgery Kincaid walked up to the door. He wondered about ringing the bell but decided just to go in as Tolkien's patients had been doing. He found himself in a hallway with a 'Waiting-room' arrow pointing to the room he had seen from the street. The arrow was made of cardboard and drawn in red biro pen. He passed the door and looked to see which one of the three doors ahead was Tolkien's consulting room. The one to his left had a plate on it with Tolkien's name. He knocked gently. There was no reply.

Kincaid knocked again and then opened the door slowly. Tolkien's desk was in front of him but the swivel chair behind it was empty. He took a step forward saying, 'Neil?'

There was a sigh behind him and he spun round to find Tolkien standing behind the door with a scalpel in his hand. Tolkien lowered the blade and said, 'I heard someone in the hall. Thank God it's you.'

Kincaid looked at Tolkien in astonishment. 'Who were you expecting?' he asked.

Tolkien shook his head to avoid giving an answer. He said, 'Sit down.' He opened up the bottom right-hand drawer of his desk and took out a half-full bottle of Famous Grouse whisky. 'Join me?'

Kincaid nodded, still trying to appraise the situation. Tolkien was scared; that made two of them.

Tolkien took a gulp of whisky and attempted a half-hearted smile. 'I don't know where to begin,' he said.

Kincaid was silent for a moment before deciding to take the initiative. He said, 'Then let me tell you what I know. I believe that several people with connections to an extreme right wing faction in this country are in administrative control of the health service in this area. Ostensibly it's offering the best health care in the land, but I suspect that there's more to it than meets the eye.'

Tolkien was looking at him with wide eyes. He was surprised, but there was an element of relief there.

'That's as much as I know,' said Kincaid, 'but that's why I think someone tried to kill me recently. Now tell me what you know.'

Tolkien took another slug of whisky. 'They're killing people,' he said, in a voice that was almost a croak.

It was Kincaid's turn to be shocked. 'Killing people?' he repeated like an automaton.

'The very old, drug addicts, people with Aids, mental defectives. They're dying.'

'Of what?' asked Kincaid, who was shaken and didn't try to hide it.

'Exactly what you would expect them to die of,' said Tolkien angrily, 'only it happens much more quickly.'

'Can you prove this?' asked Kincaid.

'The official statistics say that nothing is wrong.'

'But you know different?'

Tolkien nodded. He brought out the papers he had been working on with details of the patients who had died. 'I'm afraid one of them is your father.'

Kincaid took the papers without speaking and started to read. When he was finished he put them down slowly on the desk. 'You're saying that my father and these people were murdered?'

'I believe so.'

'Jesus Christ Almighty.' Kincaid rubbed his temples in a nervous gesture and pondered the implications. His father might have lived to see Lisa's baby after all. They could have said a lot more to each other; the lunchtime pints needn't have ended where they had. The old bugger could have met Eve and been happy for him. Kincaid desperately wanted not to believe what Tolkien was alleging, but it seemed a far better fit for the Schiller group than anything else he had heard.

'You said a "right wing faction",' said Tolkien. 'Surely the service is being run by the government? This is Mr Carlisle's scheme.'

Kincaid nodded and said, 'You're not the only one who s scared by that thought. Carlisle must be involved, but I don't know who else. The one straw to cling to at the moment is the fact that operational money for the group is coming from a trust fund called the Wellington Endowment, not central government. Heard of it?'

Tolkien shook his head.

'The trustee on paper is Lady Antonia Freeman, widow of Sir Martin Freeman, but she is just a name. Her husband was the original trustee and he was one of the Schiller group. At some point he got cold feet and tried to spill the beans. There's a strong possibility that he was murdered to keep him quiet.'

'Murdered?' said Tolkien in a whisper. 'I thought he died of a heart attack?'

'Right now I can't prove anything, but I'm working on it and so is my paper. They're trying to find out just how big the Schiller group is and where the funding for the Wellington Endowment is coming from.'

'In the meantime what do we do?' asked Tolkien.

'We know who the bad guys are and, thanks to you, we now know what they are doing. What we have to do is find out *how* they are doing it. Have you any idea?'

'Not yet. Old people get chest infections and despite treatment they deteriorate and finally they die. There's nothing intrinsically odd in that. It happens that way. Aids patients get pneumonia or tuberculosis or whatever. They go downhill quickly and die. Again, for Aids patients there's nothing unusual in that. It's the speed with which it is happening that makes it unusual.'

'How so?'

'On average, Aids sufferers survive three or four illnesses with proper treatment, many survive more. In between they recover and lead a normal life again. It's true that eventually they will succumb and in the end they die. Occasionally you will get a patient who succumbs more quickly than the others, for no known reason, but in this region I suspect that all succumb after the first illness. There will be no remission.'

'But surely statistics for the region will show this?' said Kincaid.

'The official figures say that everything is normal.'

'You think that they're altering the figures?'

'They must be,' said Tolkien.

'How do we get round this?'

Tolkien shrugged and said, 'Frankly, I don't know. Unless we gather enough information in the form of case histories from a sufficient number of patients to show a different trend, there's nothing we can do.'

'Is that possible?' asked Kincaid.

'I think not,' said Tolkien. 'We would have to visit every GP in the region and collect details of case histories by hand. Apart from anything else they would be reluctant to divulge that information anyway.'

'But if you noticed that something was amiss,' suggested Kincaid, 'surely others will too?'

'If I hadn't had the extra patients from the Tuesday drug clinic I help run I wouldn't have noticed anything wrong at all. It was the Aids patient figures that started me thinking.'

Kincaid shook his head in frustration. He said, 'Without valid statistics we are like mice in a cornfield. We've no idea how big the field is, or what shape it is, or even if there's a combine harvester coming.'

Tolkien nodded in agreement.

'Kerry!' said Kincaid suddenly. 'She's in danger.'

'Your daughter?'

'They told me that she's going to be reassessed next week along with two other kids.'

'Then she must be considered at risk,' agreed Tolkien. 'But we have some time.'

'We have to find out how they are doing it,' repeated Kincaid.

'There is one clue,' said Tolkien. 'Your father died of exactly the same infection as the two handicapped girls.' He underlined the word 'exactly'. He took out some papers from his desk drawer and showed Kincaid the antibiogram reports from the lab. He said, 'This tells me that the same bug killed all three patients. They were in hospital at different times and in different wards. They were nursed by different staff, but I think that somehow they were deliberately infected with the same strain.'

'How would they do that?'

'Inject them with a culture of the killer organism?'

'Does that mean we are looking for a killer with a syringe?' asked Kincaid.

Tolkien shook his head. 'It's not that simple. There would have to be lots of them and they would have to be all over the place. Some of the patients developed fatal conditions without being admitted to hospital.'

'Wee Willie Winkie runs roon the toon.'

'Pardon?'

Kincaid shook his head and apologised. 'I had a Scottish grandfather. I just remembered a nursery rhyme.'

Tolkien recharged their glasses and said, 'Tell me about the people involved.'

'I just know about the ones at the top. Fields, the hospital manager, French, the computer director, Schreiber, the pharmacy director and Sutton, the latest appointment for mental health services.'

Tolkien's eyes suddenly lit up. He said, 'Tell me about Schreiber.'

Kincaid told him all that he knew.

'That's it!' exclaimed Tolkien. 'The pharmacy! That's why they were so anxious to centralise the supply of drugs for the region. They're doing it from the hospital pharmacy!'

'I'm not sure I understand,' confessed Kincaid.

Tolkien had become very animated. He leaned over the desk saying, 'Don't you see? It's all too simple for them. All drugs prescribed for patients in this region come from the central pharmacy at College Hospital!'

Kincaid now saw what Tolkien was getting at. 'You mean, if the patient is on the hit list he gets the wrong drugs?' he said.

'Yes,' said Tolkien. 'Or maybe not drugs at all!'

'Schreiber sits there deciding who is going to live and who is going to die?'

'My guess is that the computer does it. They must be using a computer programme to selectively kill off certain groups of patients,' said Tolkien.

'But it must be more sophisticated than that,' said Kincaid, 'if, as you say, these patients are dying of the very things you might expect them to die of. How do you explain that?'

Tolkien shook his head as if he was unwilling to continue unravelling a nightmare, then he said, 'Instead of a drug to fight the condition the patient is suffering from, the computer gives him something to make it worse! Suppose I have an old patient with bronchitis; I prescribe ampicillin. The computer decides he is too old and instructs the pharmacy computer not to give him the drug. He gets something that looks like the thing he's supposed to get, but is completely useless or even something that antagonises his illness. His condition deteriorates and then he dies, a logical progression! No one is surprised, and the state is relieved of the burden of caring for a sick old man.'

'That must be what they did to my father,' said Kincaid.

'I think so,' said Tolkien. 'He would have required more and more treatment and help from the social services as his condition progressed. He would have been perceived as a drain on regional resources.'

'Bastards!' whispered Kincaid.

'We still have to prove this,' said Tolkien.

Kincaid thought for a moment, then he said, 'Invent two patients, better still, select two patients from your list with supposedly similar problems. One should be young and normally healthy, the other old and chronically sick. Prescribe the same antibiotic for both and see what the pharmacy sends. I'll get my paper to have the drugs analysed.'

Tolkien nodded and said, 'That might work.'

Kincaid looked at his watch and saw that it was a quarter to ten. He said, 'I have to go, I'll call you tomorrow. Do you have a home number just in case you're not here?'

Tolkien wrote the number down on a card and Kincaid put it safely in his wallet.

'One more thing,' said Kincaid. 'Do you happen to know who makes the video films of surgery at College Hospital?'

'A company called Cinemed make all films and videos for

teaching and illustration purposes at College Hospital. They're based in Sunderland.'

'That's exactly what I wanted to know,' said Kincaid, without explaining further.

Kincaid got to the restaurant at five minutes to ten; Eve had already arrived. He kissed her and held her tightly for a few moments outside the door, just feeling how good it was to be with her again. 'I've missed you,' he said.

'It works both ways,' smiled Eve.

They went inside and were shown to a table in the half-empty restaurant. 'What's been happening?' asked Eve.

Kincaid told her everything and watched her expression change to one of horror. 'You can't be serious!' she protested in a whisper.

'I'm afraid I am,' said Kincaid. He told her of his meeting with Neil Tolkien and how he had worked out that the hospital pharmacy must be to blame.

'But you are accusing them of mass murder!' whispered Eve.

'I think our friends call it, "re-shaping the country".'

'Absolute lunatics!'

Kincaid saw the dressing on her right hand. He asked about it and Eve told him what had happened.

'Claire Affric?'

'She was very upset about it,' said Eve.

'And so she should have been,' said Kincaid.

'These things happen a lot in theatre,' said Eve. 'Cuts and needle-stick injuries are all part and parcel of the job.'

'Did it need stitches?' asked Kincaid.

'A couple. Claire put them in as well as checking my anti-tetanus status and giving me an antibiotic umbrella,' said Eve, amused but also pleased at Kincaid's concern.

'Umbrella?' asked Kincaid.

'To guard against possible infection from the scalpel blade,' said Eve, 'It's a mixture of antibiotics.'

'Good,' said Kincaid. 'It must have been a shock. How are you feeling?'

'A bit tired, but I'll be okay,' said Eve.

Kincaid looked at her for long enough to embarrass her. 'Eat your meal,' she said, 'I'm fine.'

Kincaid did as he was bid but noted that Eve had left half of hers. She asked for a glass of iced water and complained about the heat of the restaurant.

'Eve, I don't want you to go back on duty,' said Kincaid.

'Don't be silly, I must,' said Eve.

'It's too dangerous,' said Kincaid, 'things are going to come to a head in the next couple of days. I want you to stay with my sister Lisa until Tolkien and I get the proof we need. Please, you know it makes sense. You can phone in sick, say you'll be back when you feel better, but don't say where you will be staying.'

Eve thought about protesting again but she could see that Kincaid was deadly serious. 'All right,' she said, 'if it's okay with Lisa.'

'She'll be delighted,' said Kincaid, and got up to make the telephone call. He was back within moments to confirm it.

Tolkien had been going through the past twelve months' patient records in an attempt to come up with more questionable deaths, ones that he might have missed at the time. He had found another two, both old people. One had been admitted to College Hospital for an operation to remove cataracts from her eyes which had rendered her virtually blind. She died four days after the operation. The stated cause had been cardiac arrest. The other, a seventy-three-year-old man, had been admitted for a hip replacement. The operation had not been carried out because the patient was suffering from a cold at the time of admission and was deemed to have a slight chest infection. Ampicillin was prescribed. The patient died of pneumonia five days later. These patients fitted the pattern. Tolkien looked at his watch and saw that it was ten-thirty. He would continue the search in the morning; he wanted to check on Feenan's girlfriend before he went home.

Locking up the surgery, Tolkien paused to look up at the stars before going to his car. Although he couldn't see it from where he stood, there was a moon tonight which silhouetted the chimneys of the building across the way. He wished that he had more time to enjoy it. He got into his car and started the engine. Just before he moved off he looked in his rear-view mirror and saw the sidelights of a car some two hundred yards behind him come on. There was no reason to read anything sinister into this, but Tolkien felt himself go cold. He sat with his eyes glued on the mirror, waiting for the other car to move. It didn't. Tolkien swallowed. The car was waiting for him to move and then it would follow. He was convinced of it.

Tolkien moved off, his eyes reluctant to leave the mirror. He saw the car behind drive away from the curb. It was a BMW in an area where BMWs seldom strayed. The car was now maintaining station about a hundred metres behind. On impulse Tolkien accelerated to the end of the road and turned right, his tyres squealing in protest. He drove hard up to traffic lights which changed to red before he could reach them. He swore and sat with his eyes glued to the mirror again, his heart thumping. There was no sign of the BMW.

He had almost allowed himself to relax when the BMW appeared in the mirror and he held his breath. It moved sedately up behind him and slowed to a halt. Tolkien could see that there were two men in the front seats, although their features were largely obscured by reflections of the traffic lights on the windscreen. They sat there, silent and impassive. He swallowed and moved off as the lights changed. He took a right at the next junction; the BMW followed. He turned left; the BMW stayed with him. He turned left again and the BMW . . . went straight on. Tolkien could hardly believe it. Could it all have been his imagination? Was that what fear did to you? He let out his breath in a long sigh and continued his journey to the Feenan's. He kept checking the mirror with a regularity that a learner driver would have envied. There was another car behind him now but it was a small Ford.

Kincaid drove back to the motel, glad that Eve was safely installed in his sister's spare room. He knew Lisa would take care of her and make her feel welcome. If only he could have felt as secure about Kerry. He and Tolkien had agreed that there was no immediate danger to her or any of the other kids in the home, but just knowing that the Schiller mob were in control of the system and what they were doing was enough to fuel the dullest of imaginations. How would they start on the handicapped kids, he wondered. In pretty much the same way as the other groups, he reckoned. Why change a winning formula? There would be dramatic improvements to the service, engineered by Wellington Endowment money, followed by a reduced life expectancy for the kids, and the figures would be obscured through computer manipulation. 'Bastards,' he muttered under his breath.

Kincaid had a shower and then turned on the television to catch the late night news while he made himself some coffee. The main story was on African famine and how difficult it was for relief workers to reach the stricken area because of civil war in the region. Obligatory camera shots of painfully thin people, barely able to walk, were interspersed with close-ups of babies with flies on their faces. Kincaid reflected on how often he had seen such pictures in the past. The names of the countries changed but only on a regular rota basis. He felt sure that he would see much the same pictures from the same country in about four years' time. He wasn't sure who to blame so he didn't blame anyone. He lifted the telephone and made a credit card donation to the number that appeared on the screen. It was better to light a candle than curse the darkness.

The programme returned to the London studio and a serious-looking presenter announced that news was coming in of an explosion in London. Kincaid poured boiling water on to the instant coffee in his cup and thought that this story also had an all too familiar ring to it. He looked at the pictures coming in from the outside broadcast unit and stopped pouring. He was wrong. This story was quite different. The police cars and fire appliances were lined up outside a building that he recognised. As the camera panned upwards he could see that the black smoke was pouring from his own flat.

SIXTEEN

Kincaid sat in front of the television with reflections of the screen flickering in his unblinking eyes. He felt as if he was watching his own funeral. It was not yet known how many people had been in the building, said the report. The IRA was mentioned, but a policeman with braid round his cap said in a painfully roundabout way that it was too soon to say who was responsible. A politician who had been dining nearby appeared briefly to express his concern and say what an outrage it all was. Two eye-witnesses were put in front of the camera to say little more than that they had heard a loud bang and saw glass flying everywhere. No motive was suggested, but the seat of the explosion seemed to have been in the flat of a journalist on a national newspaper. It was not known if the journalist, James Kincaid, had been in the building at the time. Back to the studio. 'We'll bring you more on that story as soon as we have it,' said the presenter, gathering papers in front of him with an air of finality. 'And now a look at the weather.'

Kincaid turned down the sound, reluctant to take his eyes from the screen in case the scene should come back. He dialled Fletcher's home number. It was engaged. It was engaged for fifteen minutes. When he finally did get through, an angry-voiced Fletcher snapped, 'Yes?'

'It's me.'

'Christ, James, you saw it? The phone's been red hot.'

'I was watching.'

'When you decide to make enemies you don't fuck around, do you?' said Fletcher.

'I know what they are doing up here,' said Kincaid. 'They are killing people, ordinary patients, everyday people. They're doing it systematically and cold-bloodedly.'

'But that's incredible!' exclaimed Fletcher. 'Why?'

'Our magnificent new health scheme is a cover for a "clean-up" of the population,' said Kincaid bitterly. 'They're getting rid of the imbalance. You know, too many old people living for too long, taking up far too much of the country's resources? And while they're at it they're pruning the handicapped and the addicted. Then, of course, there's Aids; these patients get a special helping hand because they're responsible for an imbalance creeping in at the other end of the age spectrum.'

'You're serious?'

'I wish I wasn't.'

'No wonder the researchers were beginning to think they had leprosy. Mention the name "Schiller" around Westminster and you turn into the invisible man. People look through you; suddenly you're not there anymore.'

'What about Opposition members?' asked Kincaid.

'They came out with a lot of rude words, but nothing useful. I don't think they know anything.'

'So we don't know how deep it goes?'

'No, but we must have stood on somebody's corns. Our proprietor has been summoned to the Home Office. I had to brief him on what we knew before he went.'

'What did you tell him?' asked Kincaid.

'That we had reason to believe that the Schiller group, despite having been officially disbanded some years ago, was still active within the Party, with or without government approval.'

'That's all?'

'Yes.'

'Good. Right now we can't trust anybody. The less we say, the better,' said Kincaid.

'Agreed,' said Fletcher. 'Now for the big question. Can you prove it all?'

'Not yet, but I'm close. I may get what I need tomorrow. I'm working with Neil Tolkien.'

'The doctor who called the office?'

'That's right. He's worked out how the bastards are doing it and we think we have a way of proving it,' said Kincaid.

'You'll have to hurry,' said Fletcher. 'All the questions we've been asking about the Schiller group must have started alarm bells ringing by now.'

'They don't know how much we know,' said Kincaid, 'and with a bit of luck, they might think I was in the flat tonight. Don't disillusion them, will you?'

'Of course not,' said Fletcher, 'I'll even let it be known when you don't turn up for work tomorrow. Do you need any help?'

'I don't think so.'

'James?'

'Yes?'

'I think it would be a good idea if you wrote down everything and posted it to me. Just in case.'

'You're right,' said Kincaid. 'I'll do it.'

'Are you sure there's nothing you need?'

'I'd like you to pull out all the stops on finding out the source of the Wellington Endowment money.'

'Will do. The researchers do have some information for you about Fields and Sutton,' said Fletcher.

'Shoot.'

'Five years ago, Fields worked for a Public Relations firm called Krebs and Segal. At that time he was responsible for some of their best work, including corporate imaging for two of our national banks. We don't know why he left or where he went after that.'

'Corporate imaging?' snorted Kincaid. 'A professional liar.'

'We also dug up something on the good Dr Sutton. He served for a while with army intelligence in Northern Ireland. There's some suggestion that the psychiatric techniques he designed for the interrogation of suspects went a little too far. Amnesty International began to take an interest in him. He wasn't charged with anything, but he resigned under a bit of a cloud.'

'He fits the picture,' said Kincaid. 'There's something I would like you to do for me if anything should go wrong in the next few days.'

'Just say,' replied Fletcher.

'Get Kerry out of here, will you? Just till the paper runs the story and the police clean out this garbage.'

'I promise.'

'A rather special lady called Eve Laing will help. I'll put her number in the letter.'

'Call me tomorrow, and be careful.'

Kincaid put down the telephone.

Kincaid decided that there were several other people who had better know about the explosion at his London flat. He called his sister and warned her not to assure anyone in the morning that he was still alive. He would explain everything soon, but in the meantime she should say nothing.

'What have you got yourself into?' whispered Lisa urgently.

'I can't tell you just yet,' said Kincaid softly. 'Trust me?'

'I don't have any option,' said Lisa, but her comment was tinged with affection.

'Let me speak to Eve.'

The sleepiness disappeared from Eve's voice when she heard why he was calling. 'Oh God, Jim, I'm afraid.'

Kincaid tried to assure her that the situation could work to their advantage if the opposition thought he might be dead, or at least, still in London. 'Just lie low and I'll call you tomorrow.'

'Please take care.'

Kincaid found the paper with Tolkien's home number on it and was surprised when Tolkien answered so quickly. 'I thought you'd be asleep,' he said.

'I've just got in,' said Tolkien.

Kincaid told him about the bomb attack.

'Good God,' murmured Tolkien. 'I wish I could wake up from all this.'

'You and me both.'

Tolkien told Kincaid that he had gone through his files and come up with two more possible cases of suspicious death.

'Good, we need all we can get. Is that the reason you were out so late?'

Tolkien told him about Karen Feenan. 'How is she now?'

'She's responding to the drug I gave her,' said Tolkien, 'I think she'll pull through.'

Kincaid hung up and stood for a moment, staring into the middle distance. The rain had started again and it was pattering on the windows. He was considering what Tolkien had told him about the Feenans. Up till now he had been assuming that the doctor's earlier nervousness had been because of what he had discovered. He hadn't realised that Tolkien had actually had an argument with a computer manager at the hospital over treatment for Karen Feenan. Tolkien had good reason to be afraid; his own fear had just doubled.

Sleep was out of the question. Kincaid tried to watch television but found he couldn't concentrate. Thoughts of the Schiller group would not leave him alone for more than a few minutes. In the end he stopped trying to avoid them and brought out all the notes he had made in the past three weeks. He spread them on the table in front of him and positioned the small reading lamp to give an even pool of light. In the past he had found it impossible to keep every snippet of information he picked up in his head, so he had developed the habit of making brief notes at the time. At a later date he would look at them all together. Sometimes new facts emerged, and things that had seemed totally unimportant when first unearthed sometimes took on new meaning.

He started with information about Carlisle as presumed leader of the group. Successful, charming, well-liked but with a background of academic mediocrity which seemed at odds with his later achievements. Charles French and Paul Schreiber, on the other hand, had been academic high-fliers of outstanding ability. He put the notes about these two under Carlisle's file. French in particular was impressive and he had had political ambitions before he blotted his copy-book. If it had been French's career record instead of Carlisle's it would have made more sense . . . .

Ye gods! That's it, thought Kincaid. He thumped the heel of

269

his hand against his forehead. Carlisle's brilliant parliamentary career wasn't his own at all! He was just a figurehead, a charming, charismatic lightweight who was the front for the brains of the Schiller group. No wonder Carlisle had done so well at all his parliamentary jobs. It had been a team effort. With brains like French and Schreiber behind him, plus all the facilities that these two had at their beck and call, he could hardly go wrong.

Kincaid found the little note he had made about Carlisle being nicknamed Trojan. Now it made more sense. It wasn't a reflection on Carlisle's wooden intellect as Fletcher had suggested. The analogy was much more apt. Carlisle was the acceptable entry vehicle for the policies of French and his colleagues! He was the man who was going to get the Schiller group into Number Ten!

Kincaid was filled with excitement and fear. They were perilously close to doing just that, and the stakes were big enough for them to stop at nothing. There was only one crumb of comfort to be had. If the Schiller group was working to get into government, that must mean that they weren't already there. The corruption did not extend that far. He opened the letter he had prepared for Fletcher and added this new information before sealing it in a new envelope and addressing it. It was two-thirty in the morning. He went out to find a postbox.

Tolkien was in his surgery before eight o'clock to prepare his request for antibiotics for his two fictitious cases before the morning patients started arriving. That way he could slip them in with the real prescriptions over the course of the morning. He selected two likely names from his list: James Livermore, aged seventy-four, chronic invalid, advanced rheumatoid arthritis, also with a heart condition. For this man he invented an infected cut on the left arm for which he was prescribing Benzyl penicillin. For the second patient Tolkien chose a twenty-seven-year-old engineer with no medical history to speak of. His only visit to the surgery had been for inoculations prior to a holiday in North Africa. For this man an outbreak of boils on the neck was to be treated with the same antibiotic, Benzyl penicillin.

In both cases the drugs were to be delivered to the surgery. Tolkien wrote down the details on two separate record cards and placed them beside the computer console. By nine-thirty the requests had gone in. By a quarter to eleven he had the two vials in front of him. One was labelled Livermore, the other Kenyon, the name of the engineer. Tolkien opened both vials; the capsules looked identical. He put the caps back on and locked them in his desk drawer. As he set off for morning rounds a doubt was nagging at him and he confided in Kincaid, whom he spoke to on his return.

'It won't be enough,' said Tolkien.

'Why not?'

'Even if the lab shows what we suspect, the hospital could explain away the whole thing as one isolated incident, an unfortunate one-off mix-up in the pharmacy department.'

Kincaid agreed that Tolkien might be right. 'So we need more samples? More drugs prescribed for vulnerable people?'

'Yes, that's one way,' said Tolkien slowly, 'but what we really need is the programme.'

'The computer programme?' exclaimed Kincaid. 'How do we get that?'

'Good question,' agreed Tolkien.

'We have to meet,' said Kincaid.

'Do you want to come here?'

Kincaid did not. He had to consider the possibility that Tolkien might be under surveillance after his run-in with the hospital. 'Do you remember where we first met?' he asked.

'Your father's house?' said Tolkien.

'Yes, I'll meet you there at two o'clock. See that you aren't followed and bring everything you have with you.'

It had been raining for twelve hours without a break and the roads were awash as Kincaid turned the Honda into the street where his father had lived. He parked opposite the house and noticed that the faulty gutter was just as he had left it. Rainwater was cascading on to the cobble stones outside the door and running out in a wide shallow river across the pavement. It was five minutes to two and he felt like a cat on a hot tin roof. What if Tolkien was followed? Two birds with one stone for the Schillers. His life could end here in the street where he had been born.

Kincaid heard the sound of tyres on wet road and looked in his rear-view mirror. A car pulled up behind him and after what seemed a terribly long time Tolkien got out and hurried to join him.

'You weren't followed?'

'I kept looking. I saw no one.'

'You've got the antibiotics?' asked Kincaid.

Tolkien brought out a padded envelope containing two vials from the case he was carrying. 'I thought you might want to post them,' he said.

Kincaid accepted the packet and asked, 'Do you have any papers for me?'

Tolkien brought out a cardboard file from the case. 'These are the details of the patients I told you about.'

'It's best that we send them off somewhere safe just in case.'

Tolkien did not need to ask in case of what.

Both men stopped talking as a car turned into the street and came slowly towards them. It stopped thirty yards away on the other side of the road. Kincaid sensed Tolkien becoming tense. 'I think it's okay,' he said, as he saw the car's door open. A woman carrying a shopping bag got out and waved goodbye to the driver. She put her key into the lock of the door of the house opposite the car and turned again to wave. The car took off with a toot of its horn. Kincaid and Tolkien breathed out simultaneously. 'Let's not prolong this,' said Kincaid. 'I'll go and find a post office.'

'Have you thought any more about getting the programme?' asked Tolkien.

'I need more time,' said Kincaid.

Kincaid watched Tolkien's car turn right at the end of the street and disappear from sight. He started his own engine and took comfort from the sound. A moving target was harder to hit.

As he himself waited to turn at the end of the street a white BMW crossed his path. It was moving in the same direction as Tolkien. There were raindrops on the driver's window and visibility through his own windscreen was not perfect where the wiper had smeared the glass, but Kincaid felt his stomach tense. The driver of the BMW looked very much like one of the male nurses from Fingleton Grange.

Kincaid turned left and started to travel quickly in the opposite direction. He felt vulnerable in the Honda because it was his own car and registered in his name. A simple check and the opposition would know not only that he wasn't dead, but that he was back in the area.

Kincaid felt better when he had put the envelope containing the two vials of penicillin capsules in the post to Fletcher with instructions that they were to be analysed urgently and by a top independent lab. He did not enclose Tolkien's papers because he wanted to look at them first; that meant waiting until he had found a new place to stay. But before he did that he had business to do with Cinemed.

'Hello, this is Anthony Miles, surgical registrar at College Hospital,' lied Kincaid.

'Yes, Doctor, what can we do for you?'

'I've just done the stupidest thing,' said Kincaid, 'I've ruined one of the surgical teaching tapes. I don't suppose you keep back-up tapes, do you?'

'Not as a rule, Doctor, what date was it?'

'March twenty-fourth,' said Kincaid.

There was a pause during which Kincaid could hear the pages of a book being turned over. At length the man said, 'Oh, that one.'

Kincaid remained silent; he bit his bottom lip in anticipation.

'The thing is, Doctor, we don't make back-up tapes as a rule. It's something we'd do only if there was some doubt about the quality of the original. In that case we might make a copy and try to clean it up a bit.'

'And that wasn't the case on the twenty-fourth?'

'No.'

Kincaid was disappointed. He said, 'Well, it was just a thought.'

'Sorry about that,' said the man.

'Thanks for trying, anyway,' said Kincaid, sounding disappointed but grateful. For some reason he felt that the man on the other end was holding something back. It was the kind of nuance he had become sensitive to over the years, and he was reluctant to break off the call in the hope that the man might say more. He was right.

'Doc,' said the man uncertainly, 'is this very important to you?'

Kincaid felt his excitement grow. It was time to play the sympathy card. He said with resignation, 'It was, but if there's no copy then there's no copy. I'll just have to face the music . . .'

'Actually, Doc . . .'

'Yes?' Kincaid bit his lip again and mentally tried to push his man over the top.

'To be quite honest, there is another copy of the tape.'

'There is?' said Kincaid, trying to sound calm when his nerve ends were screaming.

'It was the Martin Freeman tape, wasn't it?'

'Yes.'

'I caught one of the technicians making a copy of it because of all the high drama with Freeman dying and all. I bawled him out; we have strict rules in the company about confidentiality and that sort of thing, but the fact remains that I didn't destroy the tape. If you need it, you can have it.'

'I'll be right over,' said Kincaid.

'Oh, Doc?' said the man.

'Yes?'

'You do realise that I didn't have to tell you what I just did, don't you?'

Kincaid assured him that there would be no more said about the unauthorised copy. By five o'clock he had collected the tape and was on his way back to Newcastle.

* * *

Kincaid called Fletcher at home to let him know what was happening, telling him that the suspect penicillin was on its way. 'Am I still dead?' he asked.

'They are still sifting through the rubble,' said Fletcher, 'mainly because you didn't turn up for work today.'

'Good. Did you get the envelope I sent?

'No.'

'Time enough yet, I suppose,' said Kincaid on reflection. 'I didn't post it until the early hours of this morning.' He told Fletcher about his theory regarding Carlisle.

After a long pause Fletcher said, 'That makes a lot of sense. Any idea who the puppet master might be?'

'Charles French must be favourite. He has the brains and the background, but there may be others we know nothing about.'

'What a can of worms,' sighed Fletcher.

'What did the Home Office have to say to our esteemed proprietor?' asked Kincaid.

'Her Majesty's Government are not "unaware" of the problem of extremist groups working within the Party,' said Fletcher.

'Did they say what they were doing about it?' asked Kincaid.

'Alas, no. He did point out, however, that this problem was not confined to his own party.'

'He would,' said Kincaid.

'They would, of course, like to be kept informed of any developments and, as our leader was reminded, any criminal activity uncovered must be reported to the police immediately.'

'Pompous twerp,' muttered Kincaid.

'Par for the course,' said Fletcher.

Kincaid said that he would be in touch and rang off.

Kincaid suddenly had an idea about how to view the video tape he had obtained. He called his sister.

'Yes, we have one. Why do you ask?' said Lisa.

'I'd like to use it later on this evening. Is that a problem?'

'No, of course not,' said Lisa uncertainly. 'What time can we expect you?'

'Not until it gets dark. About ten?'

'Jim, I'm worried about Eve.'

'What's wrong?' asked Kincaid, feeling his throat tighten.

'She insists that she's just got a touch of the flu, but I think it's something more than that.'

'Can I speak to her?'

'I persuaded her to go to bed about half an hour ago and I think she's just dropped off,' said Lisa.

'I'll see her later, then,' said Kincaid.

Kincaid put down the telephone and rubbed his temple. Maybe he should ask Tolkien to take a look at Eve? Or maybe he should wait until he had seen and spoken to her? He decided on the latter. In the meantime he opened the file Tolkien had given him and started to read through the information.

Tolkien had already told him about these cases, but reading through them in black and white seemed to add an even more sinister aura to them. He found himself staring at the lab reports on his father, on Madeline Bell and Linda Holland. When seen altogether, they looked absolutely identical. Perhaps this was their best piece of evidence? When combined with the analyst's report on the penicillin, surely that would be enough to convince the Home Office? But it wouldn't, Kincaid reminded himself. Outbreaks of infection in hospitals were not uncommon, even fatal ones.

Kincaid conceded that he was at a loss when it came to considering how to get a copy of the computer programme that was running the nightmare scheme. He feared that in the end it would mean him breaking into the control centre at the hospital and stealing it. That was bad enough, but there was an even bigger problem lurking. Once inside, how would he know what he was looking for? He knew very little about computers. His entire knowledge revolved around being able to use a word processor with two fingers. What he needed was the assistance of an expert . . . someone like the man he had spoken to at the open day at the hospital. What was his name again? Holland, Dave Holland. Kincaid looked down at the papers in front of him. One of the dead girls had been called Holland. Was that just a coincidence, or could they be related?

*   *   *

Kincaid sat with the telephone directory on his knee and started dialling. 'Is that Mr Holland who works at College Hospital?'

'No, it isn't.'

'Sorry to have bothered you.'

He dialled again.

'Have I got the right number for Mr Holland who works at College Hospital?'

'I'm afraid not; this is 7768.'

'Sorry to have bothered you.'

He dialled again with the same outcome, but at his fifth attempt a woman's voice replied, 'Yes, that's right, but Dave's not here at the moment, I'm afraid.'

'Can you tell me when he'll be back?'

'Not till tomorrow morning, he's on night shift at the hospital. Who shall I say called?'

'Smith, Harry Smith,' Kincaid lied, 'I was in the area and thought I'd look old Dave up. It must be six or seven years since I last saw him. I think I met you at the time, too?'

'I'm sorry, I don't seem to remember . . .'

'Well, as I say, it was a long time ago. You had a baby as I recall, a little girl. Was it Linda?'

There was a pause before the woman said, as if it pained her, 'That's right. I'm afraid Linda passed away earlier this year.'

Kincaid felt guilt tie his insides in knots. He said, 'I am so sorry. I don't know what to say.'

'I'll tell Dave you called, Mr Smith,' said the woman, and brought the conversation to an end.

Kincaid felt disgusted with himself but he couldn't afford to dwell on it. He would do worse before the night was out. He called the hospital and asked for the computer centre. Could he speak to Dave Holland?

'Holland here.'

'Dave, this is Jim Kincaid. You may not remember, but . . .'

'I remember,' said Holland. 'You're the journalist who asked the questions at the open day.'

'That's right. I need your help.'

'I don't think I understand. What kind of help?'

'We can't speak over the phone. Can we meet?'

'I'm on duty all night.'

'Do you get a meal break?'

Holland sounded bemused. He said, 'I get off at two. What's all this about?'

'Meet me at two and I'll tell you. Believe me, it's important.'

'Where?'

'I'll be waiting outside the gates and please, don't say a word to anyone.'

'Surely you can give me some idea of what all this is about?'

'Two o'clock,' said Kincaid, and put down the telephone. His pulse rate had been over a hundred for the past few minutes. He breathed deeply and evenly, calming his mind but knowing that he was riding a roller-coaster. There would be no going back. When he met Holland he would have to tell him that his daughter had been murdered, and then start trying to convince the man that he should help him obtain the evidence. He got up from the bed and walked over to the window to look out at the view from his latest hotel. The rain had stopped for the moment and the streetlights had started to come on. Up on the main road car headlights sent moving pencil beams into the gathering dusk. Two cats were lurking near the rubbish bins at the kitchen door, cautiously getting nearer as if they knew what would happen if they were caught but were determined to try nevertheless. Kincaid sympathised.

It was a little before ten o'clock when Kincaid knocked on Lisa's door. He had parked the car in a nearby cul-de-sac so that it would be out of sight of the main road.

'Come in,' said Kevin Hardesty.

Kincaid could tell that Kevin was not pleased. He could sense the tension. Lisa came up and kissed him on the cheek. 'Can I get you anything?' she asked. 'Something to eat?'

Kincaid shook his head and said, 'No thanks, really.'

'Eve is awake,' said Lisa. 'Go on up and see her.'

Kincaid could hear whispered angry words coming from below as he climbed the stairs. He put his head round the first bedroom door he came to and smiled. 'I hear you're not feeling so good.'

Eve smiled but did not sit up. She held out her arm limply and said, 'I'm sure it's nothing, but I feel so weak it's ridiculous.'

Kincaid took her hand and rubbed the back of it gently. He could see a film of perspiration on her brow. 'You've got a fever,' he said.

'Just a bit of a temperature,' said Eve, 'I'll be right as rain in the morning. I hate being such a nuisance to Lisa and Kevin.'

'You mustn't worry about that,' said Kincaid. 'I told you, my sister is the nicest person in the world, the complete opposite of me.'

Eve managed a smile, 'I think you take her too much for granted,' she said. 'How's the investigation going?'

Kincaid told her that he had managed to obtain a copy of the video of Freeman's last operation. He also said that he had sent off the suspect penicillin for analysis. He did not say anything about Holland or what he planned to do later. He would leave that for a bit.

Eve sat up with difficulty and said, 'I want to see the film.'

Kincaid gave her a hand to get out of bed but could sense that she was too weak to stand unsupported. 'I think you'd better lie down again,' he said. Eve agreed without protest. Kincaid brought up the covers and tucked her in.

'This is crazy,' she said. 'I just don't seem to have any energy.'

'Just take it easy. I'll be back when I've had a look at the video,' said Kincaid.

Eve nodded. Kincaid came downstairs into a strained atmosphere. Lisa and Kevin had been arguing.

'I'd like a word,' said Kevin. He turned and walked into the kitchen. Kincaid looked at Lisa and she gave a little smile and shrugged. He followed Kevin into the kitchen and the door was closed behind him.

'I'm not happy about all this,' said Kevin.

Kincaid could see that this was an understatement. Kevin's hands were shaking. 'I'm sorry, Kevin,' he said, 'I understand how you must feel.'

'This is my home,' said Kevin. 'I will not have it turned into a refuge for waifs and strays while you play James Bond.'

'Eve is neither a waif nor a stray, Kevin. By association with me, she may be in danger. I turned to Lisa for help.'

'Did it ever occur to you that you might be putting us in danger too?' demanded Kevin.

'I did consider it,' replied Kincaid evenly. 'I reached the conclusion that this was not the case. There's no reason for the people I'm up against to make any connection with this house.'

'And what if you were followed?'

'I wasn't.'

'How do you know?' demanded Kevin.

'Because I'm good at that kind of thing,' replied Kincaid.

'I don't want to see pictures of my house with smoke billowing out of the windows after a bomb has gone off,' said Kevin. 'I want you both to go.'

Kincaid looked down at his feet for a moment, then said, 'I understand. We'll be gone in a little while.' Kincaid was already making mental plans about taking Eve back to the hotel. 'I'd like to look at this video tape in your machine before I go. Okay?'

Kevin nodded and opened the kitchen door. Lisa looked embarrassed. Kincaid smiled reassurance.

'Do you want to be on your own?' asked Lisa, as she took the tape from Kincaid and loaded it into the machine under the television set.

'It might be best,' replied Kincaid.

Kevin was first to leave the room. When he was outside Lisa turned and mouthed to Kincaid, 'I'm sorry.'

Kincaid nodded and blew her a kiss. He dimmed the lights and settled down to watch the tape. He felt a little queasy as he watched the preliminary incisions at normal speed. He used the fast-forward facility to bring the film to the point where Freeman became ill. He watched as the surgeon suddenly went rigid and swung his hand round to catch Claire Affric across the face with his scalpel. He re-wound the action and played the scene again and yet a third time.

The first two times his eyes went to Claire Affric as the blade caught her on the face, but on the third occasion he kept his eyes on Martin Freeman. Freeman's eyes were fixed on Claire and they were filled with pain . . . or could it be something else? He played the film a fourth time and this time he was convinced it was something else. It was hatred!

Why, Kincaid asked himself, but all he was left with was another question. If Freeman had been so full of hate for Claire Affric at that moment, was the swing of the scalpel really a reflex action as everyone had been assuming? Or had it been a deliberate attempt to cut Claire?

Kincaid took the film back a bit more. He wanted to study it in detail, particularly what had gone on just before Freeman freaked out. He steeled himself to watch just one character in turn throughout two-minute segments of the film. When it came to Claire Affric's turn he immediately saw something he had missed before.

When all eyes naturally went to Freeman, who was having his glove changed by the theatre sister, Claire was doing something else. Kincaid saw her hand go under the folds of her gown and bring out something. He couldn't see what it was, but he saw her hand make a sharp jabbing movement towards Freeman's hip as she leaned forward, ostensibly to check on the patient. A few seconds later Freeman went rigid.

Kincaid was breathing rapidly. This was dynamite. Freeman had been murdered during the course of the operation. Claire Affric had done it. Freeman had realised what she had done and tried to take her with him. Claire Affric was with the opposition! She had duped him into believing that she was just a poor victim of circumstance.

Kincaid tapped the knuckles of his right hand rapidly against his teeth as he tried to work out what difference this would make to his calculations. He had been assuming that Fields had mounted the cover-up over Greta Marsh in order to keep the press away from College Hospital, and that he had conned Claire into believing it was being done to save her career. This wasn't true at all. Claire Affric was in it up to her neck, and what was more, she had given Eve an injection a couple of days ago after cutting her in theatre. He had to get Eve to Tolkien.

SEVENTEEN

Kincaid rushed out into the hall and picked up the telephone. Lisa looked on anxiously.

'Can you get Eve ready to leave?' he asked.

'Of course,' replied Lisa, unsure of what was happening but sensing that something was desperately wrong. She couldn't bring herself to ask; Kevin's attitude had temporarily distanced her from her brother.

Tolkien wasn't at the surgery. Kincaid dialled his home number and waited impatiently. The possibility that Tolkien might be out tortured him until the telephone was answered sleepily after the fifth ring.

'Neil? It's me. I need your help.'

Kincaid explained quickly what he thought Claire Affric had done to Eve.

'Give me your address and I'll come,' said Tolkien.

'No, it's best if we come to you,' replied Kincaid.

'In that case, come to the surgery. I'll leave as soon as I'm dressed,' said Tolkien. 'Get there as quickly as you can.'

Kincaid removed the videotape which had been rewinding and sprinted upstairs to see how Lisa was getting on with Eve. He met them coming out of the bedroom. Eve was leaning on Lisa's arm but she smiled at him.

'Can I help?' he asked.

Lisa said no; he should go and bring the car round.

Kincaid hesitated, uncertain that Eve would manage to walk downstairs, but she looked at him and said, 'Go on.'

With the car parked outside the door, its engine running,

Kincaid supported Eve on one side with Lisa on the other as they walked her slowly down the path and helped her into the back.

'Thanks, Lisa,' murmured Kincaid as he shut the door.

'I'm sorry about Kevin,' said Lisa.

Kincaid smiled as he opened the driver's door and got in. 'Nothing to be sorry for,' he said softly. 'We have to go.'

There was no time to consider the dangers of being spotted near Tolkien's surgery; Eve needed help urgently. He would have to hope that any surveillance on Tolkien might be suspended when he went to bed at night.

Tolkien's car was already outside the surgery when they arrived. Kincaid parked in front of it and helped Eve inside. She was weak, but still conscious enough to be embarrassed by what she saw as 'being a nuisance'. Tolkien appeared when he heard the car doors close and ushered them inside. Kincaid, who was last to enter, stopped on the doorstep and looked up and down the street. There was no obvious watch being kept on Tolkien's surgery but he felt uneasy; the street was full of shadows. He went inside and closed the heavy door behind him, taking comfort from the metallic thud of the bolt as it slid home.

'We'll put you down here,' said Tolkien, gently guiding Eve to the faded red leather couch that stood against the back wall of his consulting room. He saw to it that she was comfortable before starting to question her about her symptoms and finally examining her.

'Would you like me to wait outside?' Kincaid asked nervously.

It was Eve who answered. 'Don't go,' she said.

Kincaid looked on anxiously, frustrated at Tolkien's silence and his own impotence at not being able to do anything practical.

'I'm sure it's only flu,' said Eve weakly, but the difficulty she had in saying it told a lie.

'You have a fever,' said Tolkien.

'Can you say what's wrong?' asked Kincaid, when Tolkien finally stood up and took the stethoscope from his ears.

'From what you've told me and what I can see, it's blood poisoning.' Tolkien said to Eve, 'You're suffering from septicaemia, Miss Laing.'

'But . . . how?' asked Eve dopily. 'I don't understand. The cut was cleaned so well and I had treatment immediately.'

Kincaid said, 'We think it was the injection that Claire Affric gave you.'

'Oh God,' said Eve. She was breathing the words rather than speaking them, as if she couldn't afford to waste breath on speech.

'Will she be all right?' Kincaid whispered anxiously to Tolkien.

Tolkien looked unwilling to commit himself. He said, 'It depends on what was injected into her to cause the infection. Ideally we need a blood culture report, but there's no time. I'll take a blood sample but I'll have to start her on antibiotics right away and hope for the best. I'm going to assume that the bug they've given her is the same one they used on your father and the girls.'

There was no need for Tolkien to tell Kincaid that Eve should be in a hospital, but under the circumstances they both knew that it was not an option. Kincaid looked on while Tolkien applied a tourniquet round her upper arm to make the lower veins stand out. He cleaned the smooth, white skin of Eve's inner forearm with alcohol and then inserted the needle of a large syringe into one of the veins. Deep red venous blood slowly welled up into the barrel as Tolkien withdrew the plunger.

Tolkien injected the contents of the syringe into a blood culture bottle and cleaned the site on Eve's arm with a fresh swab. 'This is for the lab,' he said, labelling the culture bottle. 'And now for some antibiotics.' He injected the contents of a vial he took from his drugs cupboard.

Eve moved her head restlessly on the pillow; she seemed increasingly detached from what was going on around her. Kincaid smoothed her hair away from her forehead and whispered words of encouragement; he felt her squeeze his hand in response and it made him feel better. Kincaid turned to Tolkien and whispered, 'Couldn't we get her to a hospital outside the region?'

'It's best that she isn't moved again tonight,' said Tolkien. 'We'll keep her comfortable here and hope that the infection responds to the antibiotics. Frankly, this is all a hospital could do until a lab has analysed her blood and performed an antibiogram. That will take two days.'

Kincaid accepted this reluctantly. He told Tolkien about his contact with Dave Holland, but didn't let go of Eve's hand.

'But this is a chance we cannot afford to miss,' whispered Tolkien. 'It may be our only chance to get the proof we need.'

'I'm not going to leave Eve,' said Kincaid.

'I know how you feel,' said Tolkien gently, 'but there's really nothing you can do here except wait. We need that computer programme. I'll stay here with Eve, I'm more use; you keep the appointment.'

Kincaid wrestled with his conscience. He wished with all his heart that Eve was in a large London teaching hospital instead of lying here in a decaying northern villa. The initial cold and damp of the surgery was beginning to respond to the heat of the gas fire, but there was something he hated about the room they were in. Perhaps it was the unkindness of the lighting which cast so many shadows, or the faint smell of mouldiness that permeated the whole building, or the darkness of the walls, but it all felt very depressing, a long way from the paraphernalia he associated with modern medicine. 'I'm supposed to meet Holland at two,' he said. It was just after midnight.

By one o'clock Eve seemed more comfortable. Tolkien said that this was a good sign. 'I think the antibiotics are starting to work,' he said. At one-thirty Kincaid bent down and kissed Eve gently on the forehead.

'Good luck,' said Tolkien.

'Look after her,' said Kincaid.

Kincaid had allowed himself plenty of time to reach the hospital because he wanted to make sure that he wasn't being followed. At that time in the morning he thought that he should be able to spot anyone tailing him without difficulty. He started out on a circuitous route and kept watch in his mirror. After a short time he noticed headlights behind him and his pulse rate rose. He slowed down but the following vehicle showed no desire to overtake. Taking no chances, he took a left turn and accelerated hard as soon as he was out of sight. He weaved in and out of back streets for a few minutes before resuming his journey. The road behind him was clear.

It was just on two o'clock when he pulled up outside the hospital. All was quiet and nothing moved. A few moments later, however, an ambulance swung out through the gates of the hospital, its blue light flashing but the siren eerily mute. Shortly after that Kincaid saw Holland walking smartly towards him; he flashed his lights. Holland opened the passenger door and got in. Kincaid started the engine immediately. 'Where do you usually eat?' he asked.

'In the hospital,' replied Holland.

'Is there anywhere else?'

'There's an all-night café up on the ring road.'

'Give me directions.'

Kincaid followed Holland's instructions and they ended up in the car park of a motorway service station. There were only half a dozen other cars there. One was on the back of an RAC rescue vehicle. The eating area had a vaguely antiseptic smell when they entered and Mantovani was playing on the sound system. Kincaid put the smell down to the floor-cleaning operation going on in a roped-off section of the restaurant.

Holland chose a hot meal from under the infra-red lamps of the heated counter; Kincaid settled for black coffee alone. He chose a table well away from the counter and at least ten tables away from the nearest customers, a subdued family of three sitting with a man wearing an RAC uniform.

'Are you going to tell me what all this is about?' asked Holland.

Kincaid was unsure of where to begin. How did you tell a man that his daughter had been murdered when he was eating lasagne at two in the morning and Mantovani was playing 'Charmaine'?

'It concerns Linda,' he said.

Holland put down his knife and fork. 'My daughter Linda? What about her?' he asked guardedly.

'Not just Linda,' said Kincaid, 'Other people too.'

'Go on,' said Holland, whose eyes were now fixed on Kincaid.

'These people, they were all patients at College Hospital, and they all died sooner than they should have.'

Holland screwed up his face in puzzlement. 'What the hell does that mean?' he asked.

'Certain patients have not been receiving the appropriate treatment for their condition. Your daughter was one of them. My father was another.'

Holland shook his head as if unwilling to accept what Kincaid said. 'I'm sorry,' he said, 'you're not making sense. What exactly do you mean? Are you saying that some kind of mistake was made?'

'No,' said Kincaid, looking directly at him. 'I mean that they were murdered.'

Half a dozen different emotions registered on Holland's face and his mouth fell open before he recovered and said angrily, 'Just what the hell is this? What kind of nonsense are you talking, mister?'

Kincaid put a restraining hand on Holland's arm as he made to rise. 'If you never believe anything else in your life, believe this. I know what I'm talking about. The people in this region have been subjected to a political experiment. The old, the chronically sick, the handicapped, Aids patients, drug addicts, they have been subjected to a programme of systematic culling.'

'Culling?' repeated Holland as if the word was an obscenity.

Kincaid told him everything, about the Schiller group, what they had been doing and how they were manipulating the health figures in order to disguise the facts. Holland looked as if he was locked up in a bad dream. Kincaid knew that soon he would start to dwell on his daughter and what might have been. He had to get through to him before it was too late. 'So you see we have to get the programme

that controls the pharmacy service,' he said. 'Do you understand?'

Holland nodded absently, as if he were miles away.

'Will you help?'

Holland did not reply.

Kincaid repeated the question. Holland looked at him and
said, 'I'll help. What do you want me to do?'

'Can you guess at how they are doing it?'

Holland thought for a moment, then said, 'It would have to
be done through secondary reference.'

'What does that mean?'

'When a request comes in for treatment, the computer is
programmed to check the data bank for further details of the
patient. Ostensibly this is a safeguard. A doctor might mistak-
enly prescribe penicillin for a patient who is hypersensitive
to the drug. The computer will have this information in the
database. It will warn the doctor and change the prescription.'

'So it would be possible for someone to add instructions at
this stage?'

'In theory, yes,' said Holland. 'It could be done through
sub-routines.'

'But in practice?' asked Kincaid, hearing doubt in Holland's
voice.

'I would know about these sub-routines and so would the
other programmers, unless . . .'

'Unless?'

'Unless the sub-routines are on the back-up database.'

Unable to contribute anything, Kincaid stayed silent to let
Holland think about the problem.

'I think that must be it,' said Holland. 'I don't usually have
access to the second database.'

'I'm lost,' said Kincaid.

'There is a second copy of the patient database,' said Holland.
'It's supposed to be there in case anything goes wrong with
the main one. Mr French has control of it. If sub-routines had
been added to that database, neither I nor any of the other
programmers would know about them.'

Kincaid began to understand. He said, 'So if a request is

diverted to the second database, then new instructions might be added without anyone knowing?'

'Except Mr French, of course,' said Holland. 'And if that's true . . . I'll have the bastard's eyes.'

There was such conviction in Holland's voice that Kincaid felt a slight chill on his neck. He said, 'The best thing we can do is get hold of that other database. With that we can put the whole lot of them away.'

Holland blinked for seemingly the first time in the last five minutes; he rubbed his hand over his face. 'You're right,' he said, regaining his composure.

'Can you get it?'

'I'm the senior programmer. I have a key to French's room.'

'Is the database something we can just steal?' asked Kincaid.

Holland shook his head. 'It would take four of us to lift the disc. We'll try for the back-up tape. I'll also ask the computer to compare the two databases and list the differences.'

'Maybe we could fake a couple of requests?'

'What did you have in mind?'

Kincaid told him what he and Tolkien had done in order to get two samples of penicillin to send away for analysis. 'Perhaps we could see what actually happens?'

'That's a good idea,' agreed Holland.

'Can you get me in there?' asked Kincaid.

'There are two of us on duty. Frank will go for his meal when I return. I could let you in then. That gives us forty minutes.'

'Let's go,' said Kincaid.

Tolkien looked at his watch and wondered how Kincaid was getting on. At two-thirty in the morning a mixture of tiredness, fear and pain from his back was making him uncomfortable in his vigil beside Eve. She was sleeping comfortably and he was confident now that the antibiotics were working. He stood up and stretched his shoulders with his hands on his hips; he would make himself some tea. He smiled to himself at the thought of the generations of English people who had made tea in times of crisis. He went through to the kitchen at the back of the villa, rubbing his arms against the cold in the hall.

As he turned on the light he thought he heard something and stopped in his tracks. There was nothing but the sound of the wind rattling the windows. He lit the gas ring and took the kettle to the sink to fill it.

The room was reflected in the window in front of him which moved to and fro in the wind, distorting the image. Tolkien watched the reflection as the kettle filled, thinking how good it would be to move out of this dilapidated place. A face suddenly appeared in front of him and he dropped the kettle. The face was hidden behind a dark balaclava mask. Tolkien stumbled back in fright and the window exploded as a sledge-hammer hit it, shattering the frame as well as the glass. The remaining glass was removed with further short blows.

Tolkien was showered with the broken pieces and felt his face start to bleed. He tried to turn and make a run for it, but the athletic figure who leapt in through the window-space had him firmly in his grip before he had reached the door. 'You're not going anywhere,' he hissed. Another figure came in through the window-space.

Tolkien found himself pinned to the floor with both arms twisted painfully up against his back.

'We lost the smart-arse journalist. Where was he going?' rasped a voice in his ear.

'I don't know who you . . .' Tolkien let out a yell as his fingers were pressed back against the joints.

'Don't play silly buggers with me,' rasped the voice. 'Where did Kincaid go when he left here?'

'Home.'

This time the man separated Tolkien's right index finger from its neighbour with a sideways jerk. The joint broke and Tolkien almost lost consciousness with the agonising pain. Sweat flowed down his face in rivulets and he found it hard to breathe as his lungs went into spasms induced by shock.

The other man, who had been checking the house, came back and said, 'The nurse is out for the count.'

'Hold him,' said Tolkien's torturer, getting to his feet. He had seen an instrument tray that Tolkien had used earlier for lancing boils on one of his patients. He selected a scalpel handle and examined it before removing the foil wrapping from a new blade and inserting it into the handle. He seemed pleased with the slight snapping sound it made. He turned to look down at Tolkien with a smile which was not reflected in his eyes. 'Now,' he said, 'I asked you a question.'

Tolkien was sitting on the floor with his arms pinned behind him and his legs apart. He shook his head. 'He went back to his hotel. I can't tell you any more,' he gasped.

The expression on the man's face did not change. He knelt down and slid the scalpel under Tolkien's scrotum, pausing to savour the look of terror on Tolkien's face. He increased pressure on the blade until the stitching of Tolkien's trousers parted and the seam opened round his crotch. 'Last chance.'

'I told you,' protested Tolkien.

Tolkien's scream reverberated round the whole building as the scalpel returned for a second, deeper cut, slicing deep into his scrotum and separating his testicles. When he came round he felt the warm wetness of blood between his legs; he told his tormentor everything.

'Call Schreiber and get up there,' said the man to his accomplice. 'I'll finish him off and deal with the bitch.'

Tolkien was only half-conscious when he saw the syringe come towards him and felt his arm being bared. He tried to struggle but was too weak. 'Wh . . . what are you . . .'

'Bleach,' said the man without emotion, and pushed the plunger.

Tolkien died with agony etched on his face. The man left the syringe stuck in Tolkien's arm and stood up. He turned as he got to the door and looked back at the scene. He said quietly, 'Now you look like one of the junkie bastards you loved so much.'

Eve woke up when she heard Tolkien cry out. She was disoriented and had no idea of what had happened, but she did realise that she too must be in great danger. She was painfully weak but perfectly lucid. She looked about her for something to use as a weapon if the worst came to the worst; her gaze settled on the discard bin where Tolkien had put the syringe after taking her blood sample. The bin was nearly full; the plunger of the syringe was sticking out of the top.

With great difficulty she got off the couch and managed to crawl over to it. She hauled herself up and pulled the syringe clear, but she let it go as her legs gave way and it fell to the floor. She had to pause on her knees for a moment before picking it up.

Tolkien's scream rent the air and terror gave her the energy to get back to the couch. She pulled up the blanket and lay there with the fingers of her right hand wrapped tightly round the syringe. She waited for her visitors to arrive. She closed her eyes and listened, but the house was silent.

After what seemed an age Eve heard the door being pushed open and felt the presence of a man in the room. As he came nearer she could smell him, a mixture of aftershave and sweat with perhaps just a suggestion of . . . bleach?

'What a pity,' she heard the man say. 'Good-looking woman and all.'

Eve felt his hand go under the blanket and slide up her left leg. She steeled herself not to move. As his fingers continued to probe she moved involuntarily and the man stopped. 'Maybe we're not so unconscious after all?' he whispered. Eve moved her head and groaned as if she were having a bad dream.

'No matter,' whispered the man. He freed Eve's left arm from the blanket and bared it.

As soon as Eve felt the needle touch her skin she suddenly opened her eyes and said, 'Hey, you!'

The man turned his head sharply in surprise. As he did so Eve swung the syringe up into his face. The needle entered the inner aspect of his left eye and went on upwards to the hilt.

Eve looked on in horror as the man went rigid. He made a wheezing noise as though he were having an asthmatic attack and staggered back to fall to the floor, his whole body jerking as if being subjected to electric shocks. This went on for nearly a minute with Eve becoming more and more distressed. A spreading wet patch on his trousers said that he had lost control of his sphincter muscles.

'Please God, make it stop! Make it stop!' she murmured, fearing that she would lose her mind.

At last the body was still. Eve got off the couch and sank to her knees. She gave the corpse a wide berth and crawled out of the room to go in search of Tolkien. The sight that met her eyes pushed her beyond the limit. She passed out.

Kincaid parked his car well away from the hospital and returned on foot. He followed the instructions he had been given and waited until he had seen Holland's colleague leave for his meal-break before approaching the door to the computer centre. Holland let him in and locked the door behind him. He checked his watch.

Holland was clearly on edge. It showed in his eyes.

'Take it easy,' said Kincaid, who did not feel much better himself.

Holland led Kincaid to a seat in front of a computer console and said, 'When I tell you, I want you to type in the following details.' Although they were alone in the centre Holland spoke in an urgent whisper. He put a sheet of paper beside the keyboard and Kincaid saw that it was a request for treatment. Holland disappeared next door. A few moments later Kincaid heard him say, 'Now!'

Kincaid typed in the details with two fingers, taking care not to make mistakes. Painkillers were being requested for a thirty-year-old man with shingles on his face. Holland came back and said, 'Good, now type in this.' He handed Kincaid a second sheet of paper and Kincaid again typed in the details, this time a request for sedatives for a seventy-eight-year-old woman with polyneuritis.

Holland came back into the room; his eyes were shining with success. He said, 'I was right. The first request went straight on line to the pharmacy but the second was referred to the back-up database. I've asked the computer to compare the programme routines on both databases and print out any differences.'

'How long?' asked Kincaid.

'A few minutes.'

Kincaid checked the time.

While they waited for the result Kincaid said, 'I'd like to know how Claire Affric fixed Eve's treatment.' He told Holland what had happened.

'Maybe I can call up the request,' said Holland. His fingers moved lightly over the keyboard as if engaging the computer in a game, waiting then responding, waiting then responding, until he had what he wanted on the screen. 'There you are. Dr Affric requested antibiotic cover for a possible infected cut. The patient was Eve Laing, aged . . . eighty-seven?'

'Eve is twenty-seven,' said Kincaid.

'You have your answer,' said Holland. 'There was a mistake in the age.'

Kincaid smiled bitterly at the word 'mistake'.

The sound of the printer reached them from next door. Holland collected the print-out and examined it anxiously while Kincaid looked on.

'Shit,' whispered Holland.

'What is it?'

'I can't make out all the codes, but requests can be referred to the back-up database for a number of reasons. We know that advanced age is one of them and we can guess at a few of the others. The second database alters the instructions to the pharmacy computer and dictates that the patients be given a series of substitute preparations. The term "Lander" seems to be used a lot.'

'Lander,' repeated Kincaid.

'Yes, Lander 1, Lander 2, etc. The request that you put through for the seventy-eight-year-old was prescribed Lander 5.'

Kincaid suddenly saw the light. 'Lander!' he exclaimed. 'That was the pharmaceutical company that Schreiber worked for! These must be concoctions prepared by Lander!'

'So it fits,' said Holland.

'Can we get into the pharmacy?' asked Kincaid. 'Can we get our hands on these preps?'

'The pharmacy is closed at night.'

'Locked?'

'Very securely,' replied Holland.

Kincaid conceded silently that it had been a stupid question.

'What happens if a request comes through at night for drugs?' he asked.

'Routine drugs are supplied automatically from feeders in the pharmacy store to a conveyor belt system. There's a pick-up point outside the Path Lab.'

'So that's where the drugs you asked for earlier will be?' asked Kincaid.

'I'd forgotten about them, but yes.'

'We'd better pick them up,' said Kincaid.

Holland looked at the clock on the wall and said, 'You'll have to go. Frank will be back in seven minutes.' As he said it, there came a knock at the door.

'Shit,' said Holland. 'He's early!'

Kincaid looked about him. 'Where does he sit?' he whispered.

Holland pointed to a swivel chair.

Kincaid responded by pointing to an area of the room where the wall cut back at ninety degrees forming an alcove. 'I'll hide there until he's seated. Distract him while I let myself out.'

Holland nodded but Kincaid could see that his nerves were strung to breaking point. The knock on the door was repeated.

'Coming,' said Holland, but it sounded like a croak. He picked up the computer print-out and handed it to Kincaid. 'You'd better have this,' he said, then he remembered something. 'Christ! The back-up tape,' he exclaimed, and flew off to get it. He was back within moments and thrust a metal canister into Kincaid's hands. 'All the proof you need.'

As soon as he heard Holland open the door Kincaid knew that things had gone wrong. Instead of the expected exchange of greetings between Holland and Frank, he heard the sound of somebody being bundled into the room. 'Get over there with him!' a voice barked.

Kincaid flattened himself against the wall in the alcove and held his breath. He heard a man, whom he took to be Frank, say, 'Christ, Dave! What the hell is this all about?'

'Where is he?' asked a cultured voice.

'Who, Mr Schreiber?' asked Holland's voice.

'Don't play silly buggers,' said the other voice. 'Answer the question. Where's Kincaid?'

'Who is Kincaid?'

The question was followed by the sound of a vicious blow and a yell of pain escaped from Holland. Kincaid looked down in time to see three teeth rattle across the floor. One stopped just a metre from his feet; it was attached to a small piece of bloody tissue. He screwed up his face.

'Christ, Dave! Tell him what he wants to know,' urged Holland's colleague. His advice was punctuated by the metallic slap of a silenced gun. The man fell silent.

'You've killed him!' exclaimed Holland. 'You rotten, stinking . . .'

Holland's tirade was ended with another fierce blow.

Kincaid could visualise a gun muzzle being whipped across Holland's face. Suddenly he could see him. Holland slid across the floor under the impact of the blow and now lay less than two metres from him. He was looking directly up into his eyes, his face a bloody mess.

The right shoulder of the man who had hit him appeared slowly as he followed his man.

'Where is Kincaid?' he hissed, levelling the gun at Holland's chest.

Holland's eyes showed all the terror he felt. He was looking past the man at Kincaid.

The man suddenly realised the significance of Holland looking past him and spun on his heel as Kincaid was preparing to deliver a blow to the back of his neck. As it was, the blow caught him on the cheek. It was enough to knock him off balance but not hard enough to do any real damage. He still had hold of the gun. Kincaid could see that the man was the male nurse who had been driving the BMW, one of the two who had thrown him down the embankment. He kicked out at the gun hand and made contact, but not before the weapon had gone off. He felt a searing pain in his right calf but had the satisfaction of seeing the gun spin away across the floor.

'Jim!' came the warning from Holland.

Kincaid looked to his left and saw Schreiber take aim at him. He dropped to the floor and rolled over as the bullet ripped into the wall. The computer tape canister was within reach. Kincaid grasped it and threw it at Schreiber. It caught him in the midriff and he fell, doubled-up, to the floor. Behind him Kincaid could see that the male nurse was just about to retrieve his gun. Holland tried to obstruct him but was too weak to make any impact. The man turned the gun on the hapless Holland and fired two bullets into his body. In horror Kincaid saw Holland's body jerk twice like a rag doll. On the verge of blind panic he charged headlong towards the door, pausing only to grab the computer tape canister as he passed. He heard Schreiber say, 'Get after him, you cretin!' as he started to half-run, half-limp down the corridor.

The fear of a bullet crashing into his back at any second helped Kincaid ignore the pain from his wounded leg until he reached the safety of the first corner. He rounded it and anxiously looked for a way out. The corridor stretching out in front of him was at least a hundred metres to the other end; he wouldn't have a chance if he continued along it. There were several turnings off. The first led off to the left and had a green sign above it. It said, PATHOLOGY. Kincaid took it but it was a dead end.

There were two double doors at the end. The first was locked, the second, a glass-panelled one, opened. Kincaid slipped inside and closed it behind him. There was a Yale lock on the inside; he snibbed it. He was breathing heavily as he looked about him. He rested his back against the door, trying to get his bearings in the dim light and listening for the sound of approaching footsteps. He did not have to wait long. He heard Schreiber's voice say, 'Look! The blood goes this way!'

Kincaid looked down and saw that he had been leaving a trail of blood from his leg.

Kincaid could see by the light coming through the frosted glass door that the room was some kind of outer office. It was so sparsely furnished that he could see why it had been left unlocked, then he saw the real reason. A tray in front of an opening in the wall held two drug bottles. This was the night pick-up point for pharmaceuticals. The two bottles in the tray were those requested earlier by Dave Holland.

Kincaid picked them up and slipped them into his pocket. As he did so the shadows of his pursuers moved slowly across the glass door. There was a blue door at the end of the room; Kincaid tried it and found it open. He passed through and closed it before fumbling for a light switch. Praying that the seal round the door was good, he pressed it and found himself at the head of a flight of stone steps.

The walls on either side were of whitewashed brick but the cobwebs said that no one had been down here recently. There was no going back; he descended as quickly as he could, hoping that he might find a way out through the basement. At the foot of the steps he had to duck his head to avoid several pipes which traced the route of the ceiling. Steam was seeping slowly from a valve in one of them. He could feel the heat against his cheek as he passed. Kincaid stopped in his tracks. Ahead, the tunnel was closed off by a brick wall; he was trapped!

There were still two doors between him and the wall. He tried the first one. At first he thought that the room was an old operating theatre, but then he decided it was more like a post-mortem examination room. This would also fit with it being in the basement of the pathology lab. The table was so old that he could imagine frock coats and top hats being worn by those who had used it, silver dissecting knives in their hands. The white tiling round the walls had crazed with age, giving the room the air of an ancient public toilet, the kind guarded by Victorian railings in public parks.

Kincaid came out and tried the next door. He clicked on the light and recoiled at the sight of a malformed foetus floating in front of him. When he recovered his composure he could see that he was standing in a very old pathology museum.

This was a much larger room than the last one, long and narrow with an island bench in the middle, so that visitors could walk round the room in a circle viewing the exhibits. Rows of pathological specimens, given immortality by the fixative solutions they floated in, were lined along dark wooden shelving in sealed glass tanks. Kincaid had to choke back the urge to vomit. He had no stomach for this sort of thing. It was all right when he couldn't make out what was in the tanks, but when he could . . .

Kincaid heard the distant sound of breaking glass and knew that Schreiber and his accomplice were breaking into the outer office upstairs. He ran back to the foot of the staircase and switched out the light before returning to the museum and closing the door. He made an urgent search of the cupboards beneath the benches, looking for anything heavy or sharp. Glass specimen tanks and bottles of fixative solution were all that came to hand.

There was a twenty-litre drum of industrial alcohol on a metal stand in the corner; it was secured by chains to stop it falling off. Kincaid tried to free one of the chains for possible use as a weapon but had to give up. When his frustration subsided he had to admit that it probably wouldn't have made much difference anyway. He couldn't hope to take on two armed men with a length of chain.

If he had a chance at all it would depend on outwitting them. He made a plan. He would hide at the back of the island bench at one end of the room so that he would not be visible when they came in. The natural thing for them to do would be to circle the room in opposite directions in order to trap him. If he could convince them that he was at the opposite end of the room to where he really was, they might both go in that direction, giving him a chance of making it to the door. The lights, which had been making intermittent buzzing noises, suddenly failed completely, plunging Kincaid into darkness before he was ready.

Kincaid felt panic well up inside him. He fought it and remembered that he had seen a box of matches beside an old Bunsen burner in the cupboard to his left. He felt and fumbled his way towards it and moved his palms along the shelves until he found the matches. The first one he struck was so old that it disintegrated without as much as a spark. The second did the same but the third did light, guiding Kincaid to where he wanted to be. He picked up an empty glass bottle on the way and squatted down behind his chosen corner of the island bench before blowing out the match. Timing would be everything.

Kincaid saw a light appear under the door. The basement light had been switched on. He heard footsteps on the stairs, then he heard Schreiber say, 'For God's sake, he isn't armed. Get on with it!'

'Don't rush me!' came the short reply. 'He isn't stupid.'

Oh yes he is, thought Kincaid. He's boxed himself in against two men with guns. He heard the post-mortem room door being opened and then closed again. It was now or never.

The door opened slowly and Schreiber's voice said, 'It's all over, Mr Kincaid. Let's stop playing silly games.' The light switch clicked once and then again.

'Doesn't work,' said Schreiber's accomplice. He opened the door wider to allow light from the basement to come in. 'He's not here!'

'Of course he is,' said Schreiber. 'There's nowhere else. He must be behind the bench.'

This was the moment Kincaid had been waiting for. He lobbed the empty glass bottle up to the far corner of the room, keeping the trajectory low so that it's path would be obscured by the bench. It fell with a crash and the male nurse opened fire at the sound. The slap of the silenced gun was followed by a crash of glass and the splatter of fluid on the floor as two specimen tanks shattered and let out their contents.

Kincaid could see that his plan had worked. Both men were working their way slowly up to the other end of the room. He got ready to make his run.

'He's not here!' exclaimed the male nurse.

Schreiber spun round on his heel just a bit too quickly for Kincaid, who was caught in the open.

'Freeze!' ordered Schreiber.

Kincaid stopped moving. The plan had failed.

'Jesus fucking Christ!' exclaimed the male nurse, reeling backwards from something he had seen on the floor. Schreiber diverted his eyes briefly to look and said, 'Get a grip. It's dead. It's only a specimen. It can't harm you.'

The man still recoiled in horror at the pink and white mess on his shoes and stepped back again to bump into Schreiber as he did so. For a moment Kincaid thought that he might have a chance of making a run for it, but Schreiber recovered too quickly for him and held the gun on him again.

It seemed to Kincaid that his last chance had gone. His life was running out as surely as the fluid from the broken specimen tanks which ran on to the floor at Schreiber's feet. There seemed to be an awful lot of it, though. Kincaid suddenly realised that the sound of spilling liquid was not the fixative at all. It was raw alcohol, from the drum which had been punctured in the shooting. Hope was reborn. He still had the box of matches.

As Schreiber had to reassure his accomplice yet again that there was nothing to fear from the specimen on the floor, Kincaid held the matchbox behind his back and drew out a small bunch with his fingertips. He struck them together against the side of the box and heard them ignite. He pushed them back inside and hurled the box, which burst into flame in mid-air, towards Schreiber. Schreiber fired at him but missed because he was startled by the object racing towards him.

The flames made contact with the alcohol and the floor round the two men erupted in a holocaust of blue flame. Their screams rent the air as they were engulfed. The heat was so intense that neither had any chance of survival. Their screams faded and their bodies sank to the floor, with flesh already melting off their faces.

Kincaid collected the computer tape canister and made off up the stairs. There was a good chance that the fire would be contained by the brick-built room but, as a precaution, he hit the first fire alarm he passed.

Kincaid realised that he was not out of the woods yet. He had no idea what the rest of the opposition was up to. Maybe all the exits from the hospital had been sealed off.

The fire alarm had sent people running in all directions. This could only work to his advantage. As he crossed the bridge connecting the computer centre to the main hospital he saw the duty ambulance waiting on its stance below. It gave him an idea and he found a way down.

Kincaid familiarised himself with the controls of the vehicle and turned the key; the engine sprang to life. He looked about him anxiously for signs of people coming to stop him but the fire alarm seemed to have occupied everyone. He moved the ambulance off its stance and gathered speed. He swung out through the gates with the blue lamp flashing but siren off, just as he had seen earlier. Three blocks away from the hospital he turned the siren on. A swift passage back to Eve and Tolkien was assured.

When there was no answer to his third knock on the surgery door, Kincaid's imagination knew no bounds. Only one of the male nurses had turned up at the hospital. What had the other one been doing? Had they all come here to Tolkien's surgery first? Was that how they discovered he was at the hospital?

Kincaid went round to the back of the house and found it in darkness. He had difficulty in climbing over the wall because of his injured leg, but thoughts of Eve took precedence over everything else. He saw the dark gap where the window had been and approached cautiously. A cat suddenly leapt out through the window space, its fur brushing against his face, making him recoil. He leaned inside the window-space but could not see anything; it was too dark.

Gritting his teeth, Kincaid climbed inside and felt his way along the wall to the light switch. He clicked it on and found Tolkien. The sight made him retch. He was filled with anger, but there was no time to dwell on it because the possibility that Eve had met the same fate had arisen to torture him. He caught sight of Eve lying face down in the doorway and froze in his tracks. Fearing the worst, he sank slowly to his knees and lifted her head gently to cradle it in his arms. He was filled with such feelings of sadness that his limbs were powerless.

Eve groaned as he moved her then opened her eyes. She looked up at Kincaid and then closed her eyes again in relief. 'Oh thank God, you're safe,' she sighed. 'Is it over?'

Kincaid now felt weak with relief. 'Just about,' he replied. He held her in his arms for a long moment, then picked her up and started to take her back to the couch in Tolkien's consulting room.

'Not in there,' she said.

Kincaid stopped.

'I'll tell you later,' said Eve.

'I have to call Fletcher,' said Kincaid.

'Then put me down.'

'James? Thank God you're all right. Did you get the proof you were after?' asked Fletcher.

'I got it,' replied Kincaid, close to exhaustion. 'But all hell's broken loose. They've murdered Neil Tolkien. Schreiber and one of his henchmen are dead and a nice guy called Dave Holland is also dead. Eve is suffering from septicaemia and I need help, too. On top of that I've no idea what the rest of the Schiller mob are up to. They could turn up here at any moment.'

'No they won't,' said Fletcher.

'Why not?'

'Because they are in custody,' said Fletcher.

'What do you mean?'

'When I got your package I decided that enough was enough. The proprietor and I went to the Home Office and told all. Scotland Yard was asked to provide a special police unit. They were sent up there this morning and told to stand by. When the antibiotic analysis came in early this evening saying that one set of capsules contained penicillin while the other actually contained bacteria, the unit was given the go ahead to start picking up the Schiller crowd. They are awaiting further instructions if you need them.'

Kincaid gave Fletcher details of what had happened at the hospital. 'I've got a copy of the computer programme that runs the whole operation and a video of Martin Freeman's death, which shows that he was murdered. If they haven't picked up Claire Affric they should do so now. She murdered Freeman.'

'I'll pass that on. Where are you?'

Kincaid told him.

'I'll get help to you. Do you have the tape and the video with you?'

'Yes.'

'Help is on the way.'

Kincaid put down the telephone and paused as he felt the knot in his stomach subside. It was finally over. All that remained now was to write the story, and God, what a story!

'Is everything all right?' asked Eve.

'Yes,' replied Kincaid. He knelt down beside her and smoothed the hair from her face. 'It's over. Help is coming. How are you feeling?'

'I'll live,' smiled Eve.

'Did I tell you how much I love you?' said Kincaid.

'I don't believe you did,' said Eve.

'Well I do.'

'I'm glad,' smiled Eve.

'Will you marry me?'

'On one condition,' said Eve.

'Yes?'

'That we take Kerry out of the home and have her live with us.'

'But . . .'

'I know how much she means to you. Forget the reassessment. I'll get through to her. I promise.'

Kincaid kissed Eve lightly on the forehead and held her close.

Back in London one of the two men with guns said, 'I think you said all that very well, Mr Fletcher.'

Both guns fired, and the editor slumped to the floor.